O, The Brave Music

&

Dorothy Evelyn Smith

Publisher's Note

This British Library Women Writers series brings back and contextualises works by female writers who were successful in their day. These authors have been selected, not just for the strength of their writing and the power of their storytelling, but for highlighting the realities of life for women and society's changing attitudes toward female behaviour through the decades.

The books in the series are historical texts and, on a small number of occasions, the originals use dated and unacceptable racist and pejorative terms and phrases which have been changed or deleted in this modern edition

First published in 1943

This edition published in 2020 by
The British Library
96 Euston Road
London NW1 2DB

Copyright © 2020 The Estate of Dorothy Evelyn Smith
Preface copyright © 2020 Lucy Evans
Afterword copyright © 2020 Simon Thomas

Cataloguing in Publication Data
A catalogue record for this publication is available from the British Library

ISBN 9780712353380
e-ISBN 9780712367912

Text design and typesetting by JCS Publishing Services Ltd
Printed in England by CPI Group (UK), Croydon, CR0 4YY

Contents

&

℘ ℘ ℘

The 1940s

℘

During the Second World War, about 3.75 million people are evacuated (mainly children, but also teachers, mothers with under 5s, people with disabilities, and pregnant women), with waves of evacuations in 1939, 1940 and 1944.

℘ **1940 (January):** Food rationing begins, starting with bacon, butter and sugar. Throughout the period, food equality was aimed at subsidising the food of poorer citizens.

℘ **1940 (February):** Paper rationing begins, with publishers having their paper supply cut by 40 per cent. Like thousands of other books, *O, The Brave Music* was published with a 'Book production war economy standard' stamp.

℘ **1940–41:** The Blitz sees mass air attacks by German forces across the UK, starting in September 1940 and ending in May 1941. At least 40,000 civilians are killed.

℘ **1941 (June):** Clothes rationing is introduced, initially 66 coupons per adult per year – 11 coupons plus cash were needed for a dress. The allocation decreased throughout the war.

℘ **1942:** Agatha Christie's *The Moving Finger* is published, which, like *O, The Brave Music*, takes its title from Edward Fitzgerald's translation of *Rubáiyát of Omar Khayyám*.

℘ **1943:** *O, The Brave Music* is published.

℘ **1949 (March):** Clothes rationing ends in the UK.

ℰ ℰ ℰ

Dorothy Evelyn Smith
(1893–1969)

ℰ

Dorothy Evelyn Smith was born Dorothy Evelyn Jones in Derby, in 1893, the daughter of a Methodist minister. After going to school in Yorkshire she moved with her family to London, where she later attended art school. She married James (Jamie) Norman Smith in 1914: after her marriage, she was known by friends and family as 'Miffy', presumably a form of 'Smith'. Jamie worked in banking in London but went to fight in the First World War. Dorothy worked as a clerk for the War Office during that time, and started writing stories, poems and articles for periodicals, which she continued doing after Jamie returned from fighting at the end of the War. She would write in the mornings and read the day's work to Jamie later in the day.

Smith had two children, Julia in 1920 and Michael in 1927, by which time the family had moved to Essex. At the beginning of the Second World War they were living at Thorpe Bay close to Southend, and from there moved to the neighbouring district of Thundersley. By this time Dorothy had turned her hand to writing novels: *O, The Brave Music* was published in 1943, and she described herself as writing 'on the end of the kitchen table with bombs falling around the house'. The Luftwaffe had a tendency to drop unused bombs on the coast as they returned from a raid, and this is most likely what she was referring to. *O, The Brave Music* would be the first of 11 books published over the next two decades or so, many of which were translated into various languages including French, Dutch and Danish.

Like Ruan in this novel, Smith had a passion for the moors, but she also loved the coast, which features prominently in a later novel, *Proud Citadel* (1947), and was proud of being the last person out of the sea when Thorpe Bay was closed by the army at the beginning of the Second World War. Other interests included playing the piano, listening to Gilbert and Sullivan records, and (according to a quote on the back of an American edition of one of her novels) helping care for the family's 'prodigious number of pets'.

Smith's husband died in 1952 and her final novel, *Brief Flower*, was published in 1966, three years before her own death.

Preface

§

O, The Brave Music is a novel about love told as a classic coming-of-age story. The protagonist is Ruan, the daughter of a Nonconformist minister. She is considered a misfit with an overactive imagination in the tightly controlled world of the vicarage. The novel follows her through her crucial years from child to young adult as she finds freedom and a place in the world through books, the outside world and the new and complex relationships that will change her life.

The author, Dorothy Evelyn Smith, like Ruan, was the daughter of a Methodist minister. She also shared her passion for the moors. Smith published *O, The Brave Music* during the Second World War and the novel itself looks back from the perspective of the 1940s. The story takes place in a world before the defining moments of the twentieth century, an innocent time before the impact of the two World Wars. Although the novel explores the restrictions on a young girl's life at the turn of the century, it also exists in a time before the devastating losses of the First World War. This is something a contemporary reader would surely have appreciated.

As the novel follows Ruan, Smith allows the reader to fully experience her feelings, her enthusiasms and her joy, and sometimes confusion, with the relationships that influence her young life. Love in all its forms is explored throughout the novel, from the difficult but unconditional love Ruan has for her parents, to the affection and respect she develops for the people in her life who encourage and facilitate her love of reading and the natural world. Above all this is the

ℰ ℰ ℰ

importance of her relationship with David. This relationship will colour not only her childhood but, the reader is led to believe, her adult life. Rare is the novel which allows the reader to experience so directly the impact that love and loss has on a character as fully drawn as Ruan.

Lucy Evans,
Curator, Printed Heritage Collections

Book One

&

The Manse

"O, the brave music of a distant drum!"
The Rubáiyát of Omar Khayyám

Chapter One

❦

"And thirdly, and lastly, brethren," said Father's voice. And I came to with a start.

Lastly. That meant that in about ten minutes the sermon would be over and Mr Wister would be playing the organ for *Onward, Christian Soldiers*. Bother! I had just got the lovely pink-silk bow out of Rosie Day's hat. It was all spread out, shimmering in the hot, noonday sunlight that filled the chapel, all ready to cut out into a new suit for my Little Man. Bother! Bother and *Bust*! There wouldn't be time, now, to make a proper job of it, unless I did it during the hymn, and I didn't want to miss the hymn. It was one of my favourites. I had asked for it specially; and because it was my birthday Father had said yes, with his far-away smile.

I had promised my Little Man the pink silk last Sunday, but it had rained, and Rosie Day had come in her old black velvet. And the week before I had promised it, too, but there hadn't been time, because I'd made him one from the brown satin off Mrs Bowers' hat first. He would be terribly disappointed and a bit offended, and it really was all my fault. Because I knew in my heart that I didn't really want to cut into the pink silk. It was such lovely ribbon; so thick and soft and yet crisp; so bright and glowing. My fingers itched to cut and snip and stitch; to fashion the stuff into a darling little suit, and trim it with some of the fascinating narrow lace that frilled the edge of Elsie Beedles' leghorn. My Little Man would look sweet in it. I hugged the thought of how sweet he would look.

But I didn't really want to cut the silk. If I cut it, it would be finished. Done with. If I didn't, it would always be there; the beautiful little suit that I could make any time I liked. ...

All the people were rustling, easing strained backs, clearing their throats for the hymn. So it was too late now, anyway.

"Never mind," I whispered to my Little Man, "I'll make you one next Sunday. An extra special lovely one." I took him off my lap and put him carefully on the yellow varnished ledge in front of me. He looked very hurt.

"Never mind!" I said again.

"Ssh!" said Mother, putting on her chapel face.

I saw Sylvia peering round her, smiling the maddeningly superior little smile that I was always going to smack off her face, and never did.

The organ began to play and the choir rose behind Father. Rosie Day's pink bow flamed in the full light from the window; and now I was definitely glad I had not cut it. Some day I would cut it; feel the bright scissors go sheer through the lovely stuff and have my will of it. But not yet. I felt, confusedly, that while I never possessed it, it was most truly mine. Afterwards, it would be lost to me.

"Onward, Christian soldiers …"

The choir began to sing, and we all fell in behind them; faltering at first, but gradually falling into step and becoming one united whole. The sun streamed on the coloured banners, the stones rang beneath our feet. And away in front shone the Cross, miraculously turned to gold.

I let myself go, and Satan's legions fled, Hell's foundations quivered. Onward, onward, Christian soldiers …

"Don't shout so, Ruan," said Mother in my ear.

I stopped singing at once. Several people were staring at me in an amused sort of way, and I realised I had been Making Myself Conspicuous again. I felt myself going very hot and knew I was looking hideous. … The banners faded, the Cross went on before and left me alone. There was no mighty army. Only Rosie Day and Miss Gault and Mr Binns and the Galloways stuck up each side of Mr Wister, bellowing away for dear life, and a lot of dull grown-ups wanting their dinners as soon as possible.

I looked across at Sylvia. She was piping away demurely, not making herself conspicuous at all; behaving, as she always behaved, in exactly the correct way. She infuriated me. I stared until I caught her eye.

– 4 –

"Mister Wister!" I mouthed, and had the satisfaction of seeing her falter.

Poor Alfred Wister was a never-failing joke. He was choirmaster as well as organist, and he conducted with his head jerking and bobbing, playing wrong notes while he turned to glare at offenders, in a way we thought irresistibly funny. His very name was enough to send us into convulsions in chapel, though it never seemed half so funny at home.

"Mister-Wister, Mister-Wister," we would whisper to each other, and our insides would tie themselves into knots. Once, when the poor man was absent because he had boils and couldn't sit down, and Father prayed for "Our suffering brother," I was inspired to hiss at Sylvia: "Mister Wister had a blister!" It was no sooner out of my mouth than the rare beauty of my wit utterly overcame me, and I was led from the chapel choking and disgraced.

This morning, however, the joke misfired, and Sylvia returned to her singing and I to my glooming until the hymn was over and Father pronounced the Benediction.

"The peace of God, that passeth all understanding, fill your hearts and minds with the knowledge and love of God …"

I have never heard these words said more beautifully than my father said them. If I had nothing more to thank him for than that, it would be enough. He had an exceptionally sweet voice, deep and pure. And for one fleeting moment of each week, at least, the peace of God passing all understanding really did fill my small troubled heart and mind. But only, alas, for a moment.

It always incensed me that right on top of my exaltation, hot, slow bodies should press against mine in an aimless meander down the aisle; that hateful, kid-gloved hands should paw me and even kisses be forced upon my cheeks.

"Well, luv?" hearty voices would exclaim, and Mr Wister would play bright, twiddly tunes to encourage us. Polite laughter would cackle above my head, and I would shuffle and push and fidget until I was free of them all and out in the blessed air at last. But by that time the peace of God was gone for another week. …

The chapel was quite two miles from home, but, unless circumstances were unusual, we had to walk it. Weather was not taken into account. We were well shod, and provided with waterproof capes and goloshes, and stupid little umbrellas that got in everybody's way and served every purpose but that for which they were designed, and we were told we should take no harm. I am bound to say we never did. But it was far from an inspiring walk. The chapel lay in the oldest quarter of the town down by the canal, and was crowded by hideous factories and endless streets of mean little houses, whose open doors gave us glimpses of sordid and sometimes frightening existences beyond the ken of our nicely brought-up minds. Slatternly women stood at the doors of the houses and watched us walk by. Both Sylvia and I were terrified of these women and of their loutish children, who often leered or jeered at us, or made sudden movements to make us jump. We walked close together, hand in hand, and glad of it for once, and looked straight ahead as we had been told. Mother walked in front with Mrs Bowers and Mrs Galloway.

How well I remember those streets on that hot June morning of my seventh birthday. The crowded little houses of dark grey stone; the littered pavements, along which Mother picked her dainty way, maroon cashmere skirts held high; the smell of cooking cabbage and other, less agreeable smells; the noise of the Salvation Army at the corner; and a man's laugh, coarse, indescribably brutal, growling:

"Here come the holies!"

"Does he mean us?" I asked Sylvia.

"Yes."

"Are we holy?"

"I expect so," she replied complacently.

The thought disturbed me. Somehow I felt it wrong that we should parade our holiness before these people who were so obviously and inevitably damned. They would be well within their rights, I felt, if they tripped us up, or threw out their cabbage water over our new, cream alpaca coats.

And then another, more terrible thought assailed me: my Little Man! I had left him sitting on the hymn-book ledge in our pew!

I stopped and gasped: "I've got to go back. I've got to. Come with me!"

"Go back? You can't go back. Don't be silly. You haven't left anything."

"I have. I've got to go back."

"Well, I'm not coming. You'll get into an awful row!"

"Can't help it, I'm going."

I pulled my hand away and ran. I heard Sylvia calling me, but I wouldn't stop. I had never been in the street alone before, and I was frightened to death, quite unnecessarily. One loutish fellow called out 'Whoa, Emma!' but nobody touched me.

Nearly all the people had gone, and I was afraid the chapel doors would be locked, but they were still open. I tiptoed into the porch and pushed open the inner door. It cracked like a gunshot. The chapel was dreadfully empty. I crept silently down the aisle and into our pew. Oh, my poor Little Man, sitting on the narrow ledge in his brown satin suit, crying, with his tiny knuckles screwed into his eyes! I picked him up and kissed him and put him into the pocket of my alpaca coat.

Then I turned to go, and as I stood for a moment in the aisle I saw with a shock that I was not alone in the chapel, for Father was there, praying.

I stood in the aisle awkwardly shuffling my shoes and wondering what to do. The sight of Father praying as a preacher was familiar enough; but Father praying as a man embarrassed me. I knew I ought to go away, and yet I couldn't. Something made me tiptoe down the aisle and stand beside him. He knelt in the front pew, facing the ugly varnished pulpit where he stood week by week, high above us all, and his face was sunk in his long, thin hands. There was something terribly pathetic about him; and for the first time I realised that Father was just an ordinary man, like Mr Day and Mr Wister and Dodds, who came to the back door with greengroceries twice a week.

It was a shock, but rather a comforting one; and I came nearer to loving Father in that moment than ever before—or after.

Presently he lifted his head. And, child though I was, my heart dissolved in pity for the sheer misery written on his face.

"Oh, Father," I whispered, "what is the matter?"

He got up quickly, and his face was at once the stern, aloof mask I knew.

"What are you doing here, Ruan?" he asked.

I gasped and breathed heavily. With anyone else I would have edged round the truth or lied outright; but not with Father. Such a thing never occurred to me.

"I came back for my Little Man," I whispered.

"Dolls in chapel, Ruan?"

"No, Father."

"What, then?"

I did not hesitate. Father might be angry, but he would neither fuss like Mother nor laugh like Sylvia. There was even the faint hope that he might understand.

"It's a—a pretend Little Man. He's my friend. I take him everywhere with me and we talk about all sorts of things. I left him in our pew, so I had to come back, you see."

"All alone?"

"Yes, Father."

For a long moment he regarded me thoughtfully.

"But if he is a 'pretend' Little Man, you could surely have pretended you hadn't left him."

I shook my head. The faint hope that he might understand died its inevitable death.

"Well, we had better get home as soon as possible. Your mother will be very worried."

We went out into the hot, odorous sunlight once more. Father walked quickly and I had to run by his side to keep up. I wore too many clothes for either comfort or hygiene. When I see the youngsters of to-day, in their brief, sensible garments, I sigh for that sturdy little figure in its petticoats and frills, its buttoned boots and woollen stockings and tight cotton gloves, its alpaca coat well and truly buttoned to the chin and its hard straw hat with the tight elastic.

But it didn't occur to me to grumble. In those days, in our family, at least, if grown-ups walked fast, you ran to keep up with them, and that was that.

"Ruan," Father said suddenly, "imagination is a wonderful gift from

God and it should be used wisely. Control it, and it will be your friend. Give it rein and it will destroy you. Like fire, it is a good servant and a bad master. I think you must get rid of your Little Man."

"Oh, Father—no!" I whimpered.

"Before next Sunday," he went on implacably. "Will you give me your promise?"

"Yes, Father."

"And for running away from Mother, and causing her distress, you must learn the hundred and twenty-first psalm, and repeat it to me to-night."

"That isn't a punishment," I said promptly. "I know it already." And I began to repeat the green, sweeping cadences:

"I will lift up mine eyes unto the hills, from whence cometh my help.

"My help cometh from the Lord, which made heaven and earth. ..."

Words. They have always been the very stuff of my life. Lovely, shining words, in whose fire the tongue may burn and yet be unscarred; at whose trumpets the heart lifts to ecstasy or falls to hell; in whose colour, shape, and texture the mind sinks, drowned in beauty. ...

"The sun shall not smite thee by day, nor the moon by night.

"The Lord shall preserve thee from all evil: he shall preserve thy soul.

"The Lord shall preserve thy going out and thy coming in from this time forth, and even for ever more."

Father's long, jerky stride slackened. He began to repeat the words with me. When we had finished the psalm we went on to another:

"The Lord is my shepherd; I shall not want."

And after that, the fierce clarion of:

"Make a joyful noise unto the Lord, all ye lands."

So we went through the noisome streets together, saying our lovely words; and an odd couple we looked, I dare say: the tall, black parson with the emaciated, saint's face and the prematurely white hair, and the square little girl plodding in her buttoned boots. But if any laughed or sneered at us we were unaware of it—so what matter?

"Where did you learn all these psalms?" Father asked.

"You say them in chapel, Father. And I can read," I told him proudly.

"H'm. How old are you, Ruan?"

- 9 -

"Seven. I'm seven to-day."

"Ah, yes. Well, beware of the sin of pride, my child," he remarked austerely.

We had Boston pudding for dinner, because of my birthday. Tanner made it beautifully, with plenty of red jam sliding down its golden sides, and the whole weltering in a thick white sauce tasting of butter. It came to table on a lovely old willow-pattern dish that would have made even the menace of macaroni less disgusting. Tanner may have been a cranky old thing, and a thorn in my flesh many and many a time, but she certainly could cook.

Sunday dinner was an event in any case, because of Clem.

On weekdays Clem took his dinner with Tanner in the kitchen. Tanner adored him. But on Sundays his high chair was placed by Mother, and Sylvia and I took it in turns to tie on his bib and cut up his food. He was nearly two, and without question the best-tempered baby I have ever known. Everybody loved Clem. Everybody, I sometimes think, except Mother. Perhaps that is not true. I hope not. But there is truth in it. There was a sharply sliding scale in Mother's affection for us children. Sylvia, born at the height of her infatuation for Father, was the apple of her eye. I came eighteen months later, more or less of an intruder into the happy trinity. While Clem, poor darling, attempted to reawaken an ecstasy already five years dead.

My mother was a raving beauty. There is no other way of describing her. More beautiful, I used to think, than that Helen whose face once launched a thousand ships. And indeed, that is very likely. I have always had grave doubts about a face that could cause disaster on so gigantic a scale. Beauty is a thing to live for, not die for.

Mother's hair was the longest I have ever seen on any woman. Sheerest gold, it hung in thick, springing waves far below her knees, and shone like silk. I was not often allowed to see it; in those days it was considered rather indelicate to appear before one's children scantily attired; but sometimes, waking at night with some terror or pain, I would see that marvellous curtain of living gold between me and the night-light, and its loveliness always shocked away my breath. Mother's eyes were brown, with dark, curling lashes, and her little mouth curved always, whether in joy or sadness. She was tall and slender and walked with an air. Her clothes must have been shabby, for there was little above Father's salary to live on, yet I remember her always as an elegant, well-dressed woman, who made poor Rosie Day and Mrs Bowers and the other women at the chapel look more homely and awkward and ordinary than they could possibly have been. They admired and resented and utterly failed to understand her, those good women. They copied her clothes, while ridiculing her soft, refined accent. They said she was too lah-di-dah, but they were proud to be seen with her in public. Poor Mother, she tried so hard to be a good minister's wife; but she was fighting her own instincts and inclinations all the time.

She was the only daughter of a landowner in the Shires; a ranting, roaring yeoman squire of a type now long extinct, who hunted his own pack, spending his days in the saddle and his nights under the dining-room table, very much the worse for vintage port.

It is difficult to understand how she and Father met, and I never came to know the way of it; but meet they did, and fall in love they did: he with her beautiful body and she with his young saint's face and deep, unforgettable voice. They opened to each other completely strange worlds, and they tried to live in them both: tried, and failed.

Poor Father; poor, lovely Mother. They learned too late what a bitter thing compromise can be. For three years they knew an ecstasy and a torment beyond the telling. And after that, there was only the torment. ...

We children knew nothing of all this. Mother was not without courage, and bravely she tried to make the best of it, doting on Sylvia's beauty, proud of my cleverness, doing her duty as the wife of a Nonconformist minister with cold determination. Father went his appointed way, conscientious, tireless, aloof. And no one could have known that his soul was in perpetual torment because, for a brief space, he had loved a woman's body better than his God.

Grandfather had made the traditional gesture, completely disowning his daughter on her marriage. He had no patience with saints or with Nonconformity, and no illusions about romantic love. No illusions about anything, indeed, except horses and old port. He died of the latter shortly after Mother's marriage. And his son reigned in his stead.

So Mother came to Father with nothing but fifty pounds a year. And with her came Tanner, some bits of real lace, the willow-pattern plates, and a portrait in oils of a horse she had loved. Its name was Starlight. She never talked about the horse to us, and when she took us out walking and we clamoured to go past the Riding School she always refused.

"You'd get yourselves kicked," she used to say, in a voice that held contempt and, perhaps, pity.

But when Tanner took us out we often went past the Riding School; and if she were in a good mood, as she occasionally was, she would tell us about Mother and the lovely home she came from, and the horses and hounds, and the Hunt balls, and all the rest of it. She would hold Clem up in her arms as the pupils clattered past on the great creatures, sorry enough hacks some of them, but none without nobility.

"Look, gee-gees!" she would cry. And Clem would leap up and down in her arms and echo: "Gee-gee-gee!"

"Lovely hands on a horse your mother had," Tanner would say, settling Clem in his pram again. "The best in the Shires. Rode straight as a die. Dance half the night she would, an' up again before dawn, thunderin' over the countryside with half the men in the county after 'er."

And off she would go, pushing the pram at a great rate and sniffing in an angry way she had. "An' look at 'er now! Nothin' but prayers an' foreign missions, an' ever-lasting cutting out pink-flannel bloomers to make the angels weep!"

And she would work herself up into a fine rage, as likely as not giving Sylvia a sharp slap, for no reason except that she was Mother's best beloved.

A strange creature, Tanner. She must have been about forty at this time, but she always seemed an old woman to me, and I never discovered her Christian name. She loved Mother devotedly and was terribly jealous of her. Whom Mother loved, Tanner hated in proportion to that love. Thus it was that she disliked me less than she disliked Sylvia; while for little Clem she had a fierce, unbounded adoration that was rather frightening in its manifestations.

I don't know what was the matter with Tanner. In those days nobody talked about fixations or repressions or complexes, and I doubt if much satisfaction is gained by the present-day glib use of those terms. Tanner was simply part of our lives; a cranky old thing, but a faithful servant and an excellent cook. I don't know what any of us would have done without her.

⅁

After dinner I had my birthday presents: a string of blue beads from Sylvia, handkerchiefs from Mother, and from Father, to my surprise and delight, a book called *Ballads, Ancient and Modern*.

"It's rather too old for you yet," he said, smiling a little at my eagerness, "but you'll like it later on."

Later on, indeed! Why should I wait for later on, when one peep inside the book set all my senses tingling with:

> "Oh, it's Keith of Eastholm rides so fast, Sister Helen,
> For I know the white mane on the blast.
> The hour has come, has come at last, Little brother!"

And:

> "Then shook the hills with thunder riven,
> Then rushed the steed to battle driven,
> And, louder than the bolts of heaven,
> Far flashed the red artillery."

Oh, lovely, lovely book! What hours of happiness it gave me. How I wept for the Lady Rosabelle and laughed at stout John Gilpin. How my horse strained beneath me as I galloped with Dirk and Joris through the night to bring the good news from Ghent to Aix. How my heart broke on the dowie dens of Yarrow! Oh, lovely book. I have it still, and I still read it. ...

After I had looked at my presents I had to put them away until the morning, for it was Sunday; and on Sundays we played no games, nor read any books except the Bible or *Pilgrim's Progress*, which I hated and feared because of the pictures, and so missed the beauty of the text. In the afternoons we generally went for a walk with Tanner, and at night Mother stayed at home and read aloud to us from a book of Bible stories, or played and sang to us at the piano with the red-silk fluting and the candlesticks that were polished so brightly but never used. She wasn't much of a musician, but those Sunday evening hours were considered to have an uplifting influence on children, and we listened week by week to: "Out of the church the people came"—*pom pom*—and: "Eye hath not seen it, my gentle boy. Ear hath not heard its sweet songs of joy," and all the rest of the sentimental clap-trap in which people wallowed in those days, and which earned me many a sleepless hour of miserable gloating. Sylvia would stand and sing with Mother, one hand resting on her shoulder, ready to turn over the music at a nod. She had a sweet, high voice, and they made a sort of duet of it.

"Mother, if thou in heaven canst hear," Sylvia would pipe, "the burden of thine orphan's prayer, Oh, take thy child, Oh, take thy child. ..."

And so beautiful they looked, the two of them together in the gaslight, that I would half expect them to be snatched up through the ceiling then and there.

I was supposed to have no ear for music, so I used to curl up on the hearthrug and leave them to it. I hated Sunday evenings. For some reason, I always felt wicked; beginning with an unreasoning feeling of guilt as the solemn bells of St Mark's Church sounded far down the road, and steadily mounting as the evening wore on, through the tragic beauty of Ruth and Naomi or the horrors of Daniel, through the wailing misery of *Ora Pro Nobis*, until I choked over my bread-and-milk with the firm conviction of damnation and ultimate torture.

Sylvia was very like Mother, though she was never to be quite so beautiful. Her hair was a cloud of pale curls that neither rain, wind, nor fog could disturb. Her eyes were brown, too, and her face was round and pink, with deep dimples in either cheek and one in her chin. Very satisfied with herself and with life in general was Sylvia. Sometimes, when she was brushing her hair, she would look at me with actual tears of compassion in her eyes.

"Poor Ruan," she would say softly. "Never mind, you're much, *much* cleverer than me!" Frankness could hardly go further.

Strangely enough, her superior attractions gave me no heartache. I was just as pleased with my cleverness as Sylvia was with her looks, and if it had not been for my hair I should have been completely satisfied.

Fifteen years later my hair would have been considered the last word in *chic*; but in those days the Eton crop was unknown and hair cut short to the head thought ridiculous. My hair was very dark, straight, and thick. It was so wiry, nobody could do anything with it, and any sort of parting seemed impossible. So Mother cut it all off and brushed it flat like a boy's. And then she laughed rather ruefully.

"My poor Ruan! … But anyway, your head is a lovely shape. Nobody would have guessed it, under that mop."

The first time I went to chapel in my shorn state old Mrs Galloway eyed me sharply and clicked her tongue at Mother in commiseration.

"Nits?" she inquired briskly.

§

After dinner on my birthday I was sent out with Tanner and Clem. Sylvia had a slight cold—or a most determined sniff—and stayed in. The afternoon was hot and airless, the streets dead beneath their weight of Sunday. I wanted to go to the park and feed the ducks, but Tanner was in one of her worst moods. I think she was angry because Mother had taken more notice of Clem than usual, laughing at his solemn, endearing antics, and even dropping a rare kiss on his square, tufty head before we set off. So round the streets we trailed, getting hotter and hotter, and crosser every minute, and tea-time seemed an eternity away.

Suddenly I stopped dead and gasped. I clutched wildly at Tanner. I began to tremble all over, my legs weak as daisy stalks.

"Look—elephants!"

Elephants they were, three of them; two gigantic adults, their harsh grey sides sagging over massive muscles, hoary heads swinging to some dimly remembered forest rhythm, and a baby, minute by comparison; a spoilt child in a little coat of scarlet and gold, bordered with bells, who minced along behind them, showing off mightily.

After the elephants came a string of caravans, gay in the sun with their green and scarlet paint, bright brasswork, and snowy curtains. I had seen pictures like them in books, and I knew that wicked people lived in them; people who would nip you up and steal you away from your good home as soon as look at you. People who beat you and made you sell brooms from door to door. I could see some of them now, leaning from the windows of the caravans, smiling and waving. Their white teeth flashed and their coloured handkerchiefs were gay to see. But I drew closer to Tanner, filled with misgivings and making rapid plans for being a better girl, in case God had to be called upon to get me out of their fearsome clutches.

After the caravans came the ponies, a dozen darlings cream in colour, manes plaited with blue and red, long tails sweeping the dust, tiny hoofs agleam. And after the ponies more caravans. Then the horses: great, sleek, polished creatures, trained to the last eyelash. Some more caravans followed, from which issued muffled roars and screeches, mysterious, exciting.

And then, at the very last, came the clown.

I saw a costume of striped cotton, a pink, bald head, a white face gashed into an immense crimson grin like a bloody wound, and brows painted in exaggerated black arches. He was running alongside the caravans, tumbling and squealing, and every little while he would turn a dozen cartwheels and shout: "Here we are again!"

My blood froze in my marrow. Never in all my life had I seen or imagined anything so utterly revolting and terrifying.

It was no use clinging to Tanner. Tanner could save only one of us—and that one would be Clem. If I hung on to her I should probably spoil his chances of survival. …

He was coming nearer. He was looking straight at me with that awful face. I had not the slightest doubt my hour had come.

"Oh, God," my poor little soul squeaked. "Oh, God, Lord God! …"

I ran out into the road. Like a little fool I ran, blind with panic, right across the path of the tumbling clown. And he tumbled over me, so that we fell together in the dust of the road.

I was up again almost before I was down. I had not picked myself up. The clown had picked me up. I felt his strong hands about me. His breath, horrid, yet queerly exciting, was in my face.

"Oops-a-daisy!" said the clown; and his voice was kinder than the angels. "Hast 'a hurt theesen, luv?"

"N-no!" I shuddered.

"That's a gurl!"

I felt something warm on my cheek. When I put my hand up it came away damp and smeared with red.

The clown had kissed me. …

Then he was off again, leaping and turning his cart-wheels and shouting: "Here we are again!" to the torpid trickle of onlookers.

All the way up St Mark's Road Tanner was in a fine flurry; rating and scolding and threatening dire penalties if she "told" of me. But I hardly listened. I knew that I, myself, was going to "tell." I wanted to tell everyone that I wasn't afraid of circus people any more; that they were not wicked at all, but kind and clever and gentle and gay, and that please I would like to go and see them in their big white tents on the fair-ground. That was what I fully intended to say.

As soon as we got home Sylvia came rushing out into the hall, full of importance. She had on her best pinafore, with the goffered frills, and her hair was tied with a blue bow.

"There's a Boy come to tea with Mr Day and Rosie!" she hissed at me. "Specially for your birthday. A big boy. He's lovely! He can tie knots like sailors and he made a rabbit out of his hanky. His name's David, and he's going to stay with us to-night, instead of Mother, and he's going to Do Tricks!"

At this point she broke off to stare at me, as well she might.

"Ruan! Whatever's happened to you? You do look a sight!"

I did look a sight. My face was dirty. My hat was on the back of my head. The knees of my stockings were cut and there was a great black streak down the front of my new cream coat. And on my cheek the red mark of the kiss.

"A clown kissed me!" I said, bursting into tears: incomprehensibly, for I was very happy.

"Ruan, you're fibbing! How could a clown kiss you?"

"I'm not!"

"Well, you'd better not let Mother catch you looking like that!"

"I want to see David."

"Let Tanner clean you up first, for goodness sake!"

"I want to see David," I repeated stubbornly, making for the drawing-room door.

"Ruan, come back! You're not fit to be seen!"

She grabbed hold of me, but I kicked her expertly and pulled her silly blue bow undone.

"I don't care what I look like. I'm going to see David, I tell you!"

Sylvia rushed upstairs and left me to it.

And so, in sackcloth and ashes, in tears and a certain glory, I went to meet my love. ...

Chapter Two

§

There was a terrible fuss, of course. Tears and explanations from Tanner. Tears and explanations from me. I was scrubbed with carbolic soap. I gargled with Condy's Fluid. The small-tooth comb was brought into vigorous play. Father lectured me on the sin of forwardness, Mother searched my clothing for fleas. And at length, disinfected and prayed over and bitterly clean, I was put to bed with a good book and a dose of opening medicine. And all because a clown had kissed me. ...

When, three days later, Sylvia went down with measles the whole thing was blamed on to me—which was manifestly ridiculous and unfair. ...

I lay in bed listening to the Sunday sounds downstairs. The polite hum of conversation. The scrape of a chair. The bang of the kitchen door as Tanner cleared the table in a temper. Tinkle of china. Sylvia playing *"Abide with Me*, with Variations," for the benefit of the guests. The blessed sound of laughter: laughter of Rosie, loud and rich; laughter of the boy David: jolly, infectious, with promise of a comradeship that warmed the heart: essentially male. ...

There was not much laughter in our home. Sylvia and I giggled a good deal. Tanner had a sour chuckle with which she relieved her system from time to time. Mother sometimes laughed, but her laughter was too sudden, too sharp, and often rather cruel. I suppose Father must have laughed occasionally, but I don't remember it. So David's laughter was very pleasant to my ears, and I lay there waiting for the sound of it. Every time he laughed I laughed too; experimentally at first, but with an increasing genuineness that surprised and delighted me. They were all down there enjoying themselves, eating my birthday cake and sharing jokes, and they thought I was brooding over my sins in my carbolic-smelling bedroom. But I was doing nothing of the sort; I was laughing with David.

There had not been much time before the storm fell on me, but I had glimpsed a square, freckled face with very white teeth and brown hair and blue-grey eyes set wide apart above an undistinguished nose. I thought he looked a lovely boy. We met very few children, and those mostly girls whose parents were members of the chapel. Without exception, we loathed them. We were terrible little snobs, Sylvia and I, and we thought all the chapel children common. Uneducated they certainly were, and for the most part poor. The chapel had once stood in a good middle-class district. Its collection plates had been piled with silver, and even gold, each Sunday. But the factories had sprung up around it, and the mean little houses had sprung up around the factories, and the "best" people had moved farther out. Only a few of the faithful made the long journey into the black heart of the town each week, and of these were Joshua Day and his daughter Rosie.

They did the thing in style, spanking up to the chapel door in a smart gig with a blood mare between the shafts, and Rosie Day's great hats blowing upwards and backwards, with the long pins dragging at her flaming and fashionably padded hair, and her rich laugh ringing out. The mare was stabled near by, and Rosie and her father took their Sunday meals with various chapel acquaintances, who were certainly no losers by the transaction.

A generous man was Joshua Day. He liked to give. But he liked to make a display of it. Nothing pleased him better than for some supplicant with a collecting-box to approach him and murmur a deferential request. In high feather he would thrust a stubby hand into his pocket, jingle his money loudly and cry that they would ruin him between them. And then he would bring out a fat, chamois-leather bag, tip its gleaming contents into his palm, and shout—there, that was all he'd got left between him and the poorhouse! Then, as likely as not, he would give the dazzled supplicant five pounds—when five shillings would have been ample—and send him on his way rejoicing, yet somehow resentful. If it had not been for old Joshua and his daughter, Rosie, Cheddar Street chapel would have closed its doors long before it did.

Rosie stuck her head round my bedroom door and gave me a large and luscious wink.

"I can't think what you've got to laugh at, luv," she said. "But I'm right pleased to hear you at it."

"Are you going to chapel, Rosie?"

"I am that, luv. It's the special service for t'missions, and I'm singing t'solo. Doh-mi-soh-doh!" sang Rosie, pulling a funny face and hitting herself a resounding thump in the chest.

"Are they all going, Rosie?"

"All but David. He's staying, and we'll pick him up on t'road home. It's a right pity you got into this botheration to-day. You'd have liked our David. Never heed. See, I've got summat for thee in my pocket, without I've sat on it and squashed it flat; nay, it's all right. Eat it up and say nowt. God bless you. Think of me when you undress you!"

And Rosie placed on my pillow a generous slice of my birthday cake; rather the worse for wear about the icing, but none the less welcome. Good old Rosie! I was always fond of her, and I came to love and admire her increasingly as the years passed over our heads, with their burdens of tragedy and laughter, of aching emptiness and overflowing riches.

The front door slammed. The gate squeaked. The drawing-room door shut with an air of finality. After a short silence I heard Sylvia playing the piano; the *Carnival of Venice*, of all things on a Sunday! I knew it was because she wanted to show off in the twiddly bits. I knew just how she was looking; very earnest and pretty and grown-up, tossing back her curls and arching her fingers, and being Mother's little lady. ... After the *Carnival of Venice* she went on to *Bluebells of Scotland*, but crashed rather badly towards the end. Then I heard two hands that could only be David's thumping out *Chopsticks*, with a great flourish and many mistakes.

After that there was silence. But I lay still, waiting. Something was going to happen. I had no idea what—but *something*. I was quite certain about it.

And, sure enough, the drawing-room door opened, and I heard David and Sylvia in the hall.

"Which room?" said David's voice.

"The first on the right at the top of the stairs. But I'm sure we ought not to, David."

"Rot!"

My heart began to jerk about oddly. I heard his feet on the stairs; coming along the landing. The door opened, and he came into my bedroom and stood at the foot of the bed, looking down at me with a friendly grin.

"Hullo, Tinribs!"

"Hullo."

"Why don't you come downstairs?"

I gazed at him in blank astonishment.

"I was PUT TO BED," I said solemnly.

"I know. It's a rotten shame. My golly! You stink like a hospital. Rather a nice smell, though. I'm going to be a doctor when I grow up. Look here, would you like me to give you an examination?—see if there really is anything wrong with you? Not that it could possibly show yet, I should think. Or I'll take your temperature if you like."

I retired firmly under the bedclothes.

"No, thank you."

"Well, come on downstairs, then. That other kid's no fun."

What a revolutionary boy! ... But the notion intrigued me. I *had* been punished unfairly and I knew it.

"I couldn't *possibly*," I wavered, sitting up.

"Come on," he said impatiently. "I'm going to do some tricks. I can make a watch disappear, or pull a hanky out of your head."

Hesitating no longer, I jumped out of bed and put on my blue dressing-gown, and the blue slippers with pom-poms, and crept downstairs behind David. Sylvia was seated in Mother's chair, pretending to read a book. She threw me a bleak glance.

"I should have thought you'd had enough for one day," she said primly. "I don't want you near *me*! You may be infectious."

"Don't be an ass," said David. "Go on, Tinribs, sit over there. Now I'll do some of my famous tricks." He began to roll back his cuffs, assuming a professional air. "Ladies and gentlemen," he squeaked in a dashing falsetto, "I will now proceed to entertain you with my Magic Mysteries, as performed before His Majesty King Edward the Seventh, and all the Crowned Heads of Europe. May I request the loan of a watch? Any sort of watch. Has anyone a watch, ladies and gentlemen?"

Nobody had a watch.

"All right, I shall have to use my own, then," he grumbled. "It's a blooming nuisance because they're always getting smashed."

He produced his watch, held it up for us to see, and bowed graciously.

"Nothing up my sleeves, ladies and gentlemen. No deception whatever. I will now place the watch in my mouth, swallow it, and bring it out of that blue vase over there on the piano. As performed before the King of Siam, to His Majesty's unbounded amazement."

With some difficulty he placed the watch in his mouth, made a few passes in the air, and said "Z-Z-Z-Z!" in a choked voice.

Immediately there was a thud and an ominous crash. David leapt across the room.

"Blast!" he yelled. "I told you so! That's the second watch this month!"

"The vase is broken!" Sylvia wailed. We looked at one another in dumb dismay. Mother's beautiful vase!

"Pooh, what's a beastly ornament!" David said scornfully. "I'll make Uncle Josh buy your mother a new one." But he didn't look too happy. He suggested pulling a hanky out of somebody's head, but little enthusiasm was shown.

"I don't know *what* Mother will say," Sylvia whimpered. "I do think you're a rough boy."

However much Sylvia might exasperate me, I hated to see her cry. I threw my arms round her and hugged her tight.

"You won't get the blame," I promised her. "It was my fault for coming downstairs."

"Then you'd better go back before anything else happens," she sobbed.

The door opened and Tanner came in.

"Now then, more trouble!" she grumbled. "What are you doing out of bed, catching your death, Miss Ruan? And who broke that vase?"

"I did," said David and I simultaneously.

Tanner pursed up her mouth at me.

"Born to trouble as the sparks fly upwards!" was her acid comment. She went out of the room, but came back in a few minutes carrying a vase that was the twin of the other. She placed it on the piano and swept up the broken pieces from the floor. "There's been bother enough in this house to-day," was her only remark as she left us alone again.

We stared at each other, stunned, but vastly relieved.

Months afterwards, I discovered that the vases were sixpenny rubbish from a stall in the market, and that the second one had actually belonged to Tanner herself. As for the reason I was not immediately ordered up to bed again, I can only suppose it was her queer way of getting even with Mother for punishing me. Whom Mother loved, Tanner chastened. But the reverse held good, too.

Poor Tanner, with her warped mind and twisted loyalties; none of us ever loved her, and all she did for us we took for granted. A small, dark woman, like a witch she was, without a grey hair to the day of her death, and a long, pointed nose that she had a habit of pulling as she sat rocking before the fire, until it had attained a high polish. There was a hymn she liked—*Shall We Gather at the River?*—and she sometimes sang it by the hour, marking time with the clacking of the rockers.

> "Shall we *ga*-ther at the *ree*-ver?
> The beautiful, the beautiful, the *ree*-ver?"

And her face would be the face of one seeing visions. Perhaps she really did see the river; the dark green water swirling and rushing between the rocks, and the long arms of spray flinging up, beckoning. Who knew what Tanner saw, rocking away before the kitchen fire? Certainly not we children, nor did we care—poor, lonely Tanner.

When she had gone we sat on the hearthrug and looked at one another soberly.

"What shall we do now?" David asked. We had not the slightest idea. One just didn't do things on Sundays. "Have you got any cards? I know a good card trick."

But there were no cards in our house.

We sat and shuffled, and David whistled the *Carnival of Venice*—out of tune, as Sylvia pointed out. Then Sylvia suggested telling stories.

"Ruan can make lovely stories up."

David looked at me.

"Ruan. Is that your real name?"

"Yes, of course."

"Why? I mean, who thought of it?"

"I don't know."

"Ruan. ... I rather like it. Yes, it's a good name."

I was immensely gratified, having always loved my own name.

"How old are you?"

"Seven. How old are you?"

"I'm twelve. I'm going to Lowton soon. And then I'm going to be a doctor."

"What are you going to Lowton for?"

"What *for*? Why, Lowton's a school. Didn't you know that?"

"Isn't she silly?" giggled Sylvia—who hadn't known either. "When I'm grown up," she announced smugly, following up this success, "I'm going to marry a very rich man and go to London and have ten beautiful children. Their names will be Alexandra and Launcelot and Rupert and Dorothea and Maud and Edward—"

With great presence of mind, David staunched this maternal recitation with a sofa cushion; and we began to scuffle and wrestle and push each other about. We grew wild and hilarious. David pretended to faint when we managed to hit him, and made us shriek with excitement by his tumbling antics on the polished linoleum.

Presently, exhausted, we flopped down, and Tanner sprang her second surprise on us by bringing home-made rock cakes and glasses of lemonade—for which I was truly thankful, not having had any food since dinner, except Rosie's squashed piece of cake.

"Are you going to write books when you grow up?" David asked me.

I said yes, though it was the first time such an idea had occurred to me. I stored it away at the back of my mind, as a lovely thing to think about later on.

"I'm not keen on books myself. I like real things. Still, there have to be books," David conceded handsomely. "I suppose you're always making up stories, and so on?"

"She's awfully silly," Sylvia said, in her elder-sister voice. "She pretends things all the time. She's got a pretend Little Man, and she takes him to chapel and everywhere. I do think she's silly!"

I went sick and cold. Not because Sylvia was telling my secrets to David, for somehow I felt he would understand, even if he did not approve; but because I had suddenly remembered my promise to Father.

"You should just see how silly she looks," Sylvia went on, giggling, "sitting in chapel, whispering away to Nothing. She makes herself conspicuous, and people stare. She pretends to make him clothes out of the stuff off people's hats and dresses. It's awful, really."

"I think I'll go back to bed now," I said in a small voice.

"Cry-baby!" triumphed Sylvia.

"Stop it, you!" David commanded.

He came up the stairs with me.

"What's up, Tinribs?" he asked kindly.

"I promised Father I'd get rid of my Little Man, and I—I love him awfully."

David looked uncomfortable.

"I shall put him on my window-sill to-night and—and tell him to go and find another little girl to—look after him and make his suits and—and put the special bits he likes on the side of her plate—"

The thought was too much for me and I burst into tears of real anguish. David put his arm round me and gave me an awkward hug.

"Hop into bed, Tinribs. I'll tuck you up."

I hopped in. And very thoroughly and efficiently he tucked the bedclothes round my sobbing form.

"Better stop crying," he recommended, and walked to the door. Then he paused, and suddenly came back, his shoulders hunched and his voice gruff with embarrassment.

"Will you give me your Little Man, Tinribs? I'd like to have him awfully. I'll take care of him, and any time you want to see him, you can."

I gasped with joy and relief. I flung my arms round him and pressed my wet face to his stomach.

"Oh, David—will you *really*? Oh, *thank* you, David! You are lovely! I don't know how to thank you! I'll get him now, this minute."

He was asleep in my glove-box. I lifted him tenderly and kissed him, and put him into David's hand. David closed his fingers round him, as if he saw him as clearly as I did. He put him in his pocket.

I got back into bed, and he tucked me up again.

"Good night," he said. "You're not a bad little kid. It's a pity you're not pretty, like the other one."

He gave my hair a tug, and grinned. And I loved him.

Chapter Three

&

Three days later Sylvia went down with measles, and the whole house was in a ferment.

We were not used to illness. Mother was as strong as a horse, and Father, though he looked delicate, must have had an iron constitution, or an iron will, or both. We children were brought up sensibly, with very few sweets or luxuries and no late hours; and we mixed with few other children, so that the doctor and his black bag were unfamiliar and very disturbing phenomena in our house.

Sylvia and I shared the same room, one blue-and-white bed on either side of the dressing-table. But that night I was put to sleep in a tiny room at the top of the house, next to Tanner, and immediately under the hot-water cistern, that gurgled alarmingly in the dark hours. Clem was put in Tanner's room, to her great joy, and Mother hung up a carbolic sheet at Sylvia's door, and went inside and stopped inside, nursing her day and night.

A strange time for me, those days alone with Father and Clem and Tanner. I tried to take Mother's place at table, but Father didn't seem to notice me, and when I made bright conversation told me to get on with my food. I tried to put Tanner in her place; but she very quickly put me in mine, with no uncertain hand. I tried to be a mother to Clem; and here, indeed, I had more success, for Clem was obligingly ready to be mothered by anyone, and Tanner was only too glad of my help, with all the extra work she had.

At the back of our house was a long, narrow strip of garden, very much overgrown with weeds, because Father did not care for gardening and had no money for professional help. But it was a garden, at least, and, the weather turning very hot and dry, I was allowed to wheel Clem up and down the weedy path, or sit on the rank lawn and play with him. I had always loved my baby brother dearly, and in those long, quiet June days my love became more articulate and, alas, more sharp of vision. I began to watch Clem more closely; to think and worry and make comparisons; but it was Annie Briggs who finally tore the scales from my eyes, and gave me my first, salt knowledge of the sorrowful thing love can be. ...

The Briggs had lately moved into the house next door. They were noisy and common, and not over-clean, and we had nothing to do with any of them, by Mother's orders. Besides Annie, a girl of about my own age, there were three older boys, who terrified us, and a baby of about a year. They all had mean, rats' faces and bright, cheap clothes, while the number of their visitors was astonishing.

One lovely morning, as I sat making a daisy chain for Clem, Annie Briggs pushed her furtive little face through a gap in the fence and stuck out her tongue at me. I immediately stuck mine out, and made a better job of it, too. I had to be polite to the chapel people whether I liked them or not, but I felt under no obligation to the Briggses.

She watched me for a while in silence. Then she said: "Shall I come over and play with you?"

"No," I returned flatly.

"I got some toffee," she said cunningly.

"I don't care."

"I got a dolls' house, an' a musical box, an' a book with coloured pitchers 'at stands up."

She *would* have, I thought bitterly. All the things I most longed for, and was never likely to get.

I took refuge in silence; and perhaps Annie mistook this for encouragement, for she began to squeeze through the gap. A sort of loathing seized me, as at the approach of a noisome reptile.

"Go away!" I cried sharply. "We've got measles here."

"I've had 'em," Annie panted, grinning and showing the gaps in her teeth.

There was no stopping her. She came towards us steadily, inevitably, inexorable as death.

She stood and watched us; me making my daisy chain, and Clem rolling on his fat back, laughing and grabbing at the darting flies.

"What's your baby's name?"

I did not answer.

"Glah! Pah!" Clem gurgled.

"Can't he talk?" Annie asked.

"He doesn't want to talk," I said shortly.

She looked at me with her narrow eyes.

"Our baby can say lots of things, and she walks all over the place. And she's only one year old, too!"

I went on with my daisy chain. Suddenly I was dreadfully aware that Clem should have been walking and talking long ago. Other babies did. Why not Clem? My hands went hot and sticky and the chain of flowers broke. I threw it away and got up.

"We've got to go in now."

Annie bent over Clem and tickled him. He laughed up into her rat's face, the darling, his great blue eyes smiling and his downy hair ruffled.

"Ga—glah—ga!" he rejoiced.

"Let him alone. Don't touch him!" I said fiercely. I lifted him in my arms. He was a great heavy boy, and I staggered under his weight.

"I know what's the matter with *him*," Annie said softly. "I heard someone who goes to your chapel telling Ma. She said he was only elevenpence-ha'penny in the shilling."

I had never heard the phrase before, but my heart turn to ice in my breast.

"Shut up!" I gasped.

"And what's more," she went on, squinting with malice, "I know *why*! … It's because your mother didn't want—"

A red mist blurred my sight.

I plumped Clem in his pram and I rushed at Annie Briggs and tore at her mean, spotty face with my finger-nails. I pulled her rat's-tail hair and kicked her bony shins until she fled, screaming, through the gap into her lair. Then I rushed Clem into the house and took him to the empty dining-room and shut the door. I put him on the hearthrug and knelt before him. I hugged and kissed him and pressed his round head against my cheek, rocking him in an agony of doubt and fear.

"Say 'Mother,' Clem. 'Mum-Mum.' Say 'Mum' ... Say 'Ruan.' ... Clem ducksy, say 'Ruan.' 'Ru, Ru.'"

"Glah! Ga!" he laughed.

I sobbed helplessly. I picked him up and tried to make him stand alone. He fell down at once and lay on the rug, blinking and smiling at me.

"Oh, Clem! ... Darling, darling little Clem! Baby!"

That night, when I was alone with Father for a few minutes, I plucked up my courage and said:

"Father ... Is Clem all right? I mean—will he walk and talk soon, like other babies?"

He stared at me searchingly.

"Who has been talking to you?"

"Annie Briggs, Father. She came through the fence and I couldn't stop her. She—she said—"

"Well?" he demanded harshly.

"She said Clem was—was only elevenpence-ha'penny in the shilling, Father. ..."

For a long time Father stood still, looking, not at me but right through me. Then he said in a queer, strangled voice that was humble, yet angry:

"'Thy will be done,' Ruan. Always."

I was frightened and crept out of the room. An hour later on my way to bed, I peeped round the door to whisper "Good night." And Father was still standing there, quite still, his face hidden in his hands.

Rosie came to bring a book and some big black grapes for Sylvia, and she brought David with her.

I was so happy to see him again. David was so thoroughly normal, and our house was anything but normal in those days. He was like a breath of clean air blowing across the dark waters of the Manse, and I stood as near to him as I could get, filling my lungs with his wholesomeness.

They had brought some sweets for me, too—a rare treat. But what gave me more pleasure was David sending me a secret smile and patting his coat-pocket to show that my Little Man was there, quite safe and happy. He lifted the flap of the pocket, so that I could wave and smile if I wanted to. But my Little Man did not appear; and I couldn't blame him, either, for I couldn't imagine anyone not being happier with David than he was with me.

Father was out when they arrived, and Mother, of course, was behind the carbolic sheet, so I had to do the honours. Rosie lifted me on to her ample lap and looked me over frankly.

"Now then! You're looking none too grand, my lass!"

David whipped out an imaginary stethoscope and prodded me in the back.

"Say ninety-nine!"

"Ninety-nine!" I squeaked joyfully.

"Double pneumonia, with complications and bright green spots!" he moaned; and I folded up with laughter. Rosie smacked his head.

"Give over!" she ordered. "When did you last go out, luv?"

I couldn't remember. Rosie clicked her tongue and frowned.

"Well, you're coming out with us, luv, and that's flat. Measles or no measles. Our David's had 'em, anyhow."

"Tell you what, Aunt Rosie, let's take her to the circus," David suggested. I felt quite giddy at the bare notion. But Rosie shook her head to that.

"Nay, that wouldn't be jannocks, not with all t'crowds of other children. She may have got 'em, for all we know."

"Incubation period, three weeks," he informed us with a professional air.

"But I tell you what, luv. We'll take you in t'trap and give you a run round town, and you'll see t'fair-ground, and all t'swing-boats, and the brass band, and what not. And then you shall come up to the House and get your dinner with us, and happen your tea too. And that'll be better than a poke in the eye with a stick, won't it?"

It would, indeed! I was speechless at the beauty of the day spread out before me. If only Father would let me go!

He came in at that moment and, to my great joy, agreed to let Rosie take me for the day.

My new cream coat, newly cleaned by Tanner, was fetched out, with my hard hat and a clean handkerchief. I was hissed at privately by Tanner, and I hissed back reassuringly. And thus, clad in all the paraphernalia of respectability, I went out into the June sunlight with Rosie and David. And there stood the gleaming gig, with Sally, the blood mare, pawing the ground with impatience. David jumped in and hauled me up. Rosie took the reins. I waved to Father and we were off, spanking and jingling down St Mark's Road at a grand pace; and I so happy I could have cried, and so scared that I must laugh very loudly and brightly, to show how much I enjoyed it.

"That's right, luv," said Rosie comfortably.

But David, after one quick glance, quietly took my hand, unclenched my rigid fingers and wrapped them round his own. And so he held me until my laughter grew genuine and I was accustomed to this novel feeling of flying through space. Dear, dear David.

We drove right through the town, down Heathgate, where all the best shops were, and where we ate cakes such as I had never seen before, much less tasted, with coffee for Rosie and lemonade for David and me. Then round by the teeming market-place, with Rosie showing off a little in her driving, greeting acquaintances with a wave of the whip and a cheerful "Now then!" Under the roaring railway arch and up the Doncaster Road—and the fair-ground lay before us; a bewildering medley of jolly sound and queer, exciting smells and rocking, swirling, screaming colour.

I sat quite still, drinking it all in, staring until my eyes felt like popping out of my head. I remembered the darling little cream ponies, the grey, swinging, mountainous elephants, the tumbling clown that no longer frightened me, the people. They were all in there, somewhere among the white, pointed tents and the crowded booths; all living their strange, exciting, incomprehensible lives behind a door to which I should never have the key.

The brass band suddenly struck up and Sally reared, her ears wickedly flat.

"Now then!" Rosie said sharply.

I knew what Sally felt like. I wanted to rear up, too; to flatten my ears and dance impatiently on the cobbles; to break out of the shafts and go tearing away over the distant blue hills, unburdened, unfettered.

I am supposed to have no ear for music, and perhaps I have none. But I have an ear for sound. Sound of words, silver and sonorous; sound of water, deep green, rushing between dark rocks, or breaking in shallow kisses on flat, yellow sands; sound of birds' wings in sudden, upward flight; of marsh grasses rustling secretly; of rooks' voices harsh against an evening sky; of the clash of steel on steel from the black, thundering factories. Sound of a ship's siren from the fog-bound river; of the creaking of row-locks as a dinghy pulls inshore; of rain on winter windows. ... All these are my music; the music of life and living.

From a musical point of view the circus band was probably shocking, but I cared nothing for that. For me it held the rhythmical stamping of elephants and the spicy smells of the jungle earth they trampled. It held the twang of guitars, the jewelled flash of dark eyes beneath gay kerchiefs. It held the tears and laughter, the vanities and bravery of the show people; the tiny folk, the shivering giants, the flashing, leaping elegance of the riders, and the kiss of the clown. ... All the colour and clash and gaiety, the dark secrecy and the bright courage of the circus were thumped and blown and piped and beaten into one glorious essence of sound and flung at my feet. Here you are! Here's life. Here's living. Here's everything you'll never know, parson's brat that you are!

A long sigh escaped me.

"Never heed, luv, you shall go next year," Rosie comforted me. "D.V.," she added prudently.

I thanked her politely; but I knew now that I didn't want to go to the circus. To go, would spoil the splendour that I now possessed. Like the pink ribbon out of Rosie's hat, if I never had it I could never lose it. O, the brave music of a *distant* drum!

But I didn't attempt to explain that to Rosie.

Bolton House stood high up on the moor, a great sprawling barracks of a house, built in grey stone, up which creepers were for ever being encouraged to climb, and for ever failing. It had fifteen echoing rooms, furnished "regardless of cost" by a London firm, and four servants, who had to be paid colossal wages to stay. It had been built by Joshua Day for his wife, Mary Ellen, who had promptly died of it, poor woman, and left him lonely in his magnificence.

Joshua had been a steel-worker. He had actually first seen the light of day in one of those same small houses that crowded about the chapel, and in it he had lived for many years, working and saving, pushing his way up in a dogged fashion that nothing could stay. Whatever he touched turned to money. He bought a small factory and it flourished exceedingly and became a large factory. He moved into a better house and went on working; and his wife, Mary Ellen, worked too, and never a servant would she have, nor even a woman to whiten the doorstep on a Saturday. She washed and baked and cleaned and brewed did Mary Ellen—and so, all unwitting, helped to hasten her own end.

Joshua grew rich. He took a partner, one George Shane; not for financial reasons, but because Shane was "county," and Joshua was dreaming dreams. Mary Ellen was to be the mistress of a great mansion. Their Rosie was to be a lady. There were to be grand doings at Bolton House, with lines of waiting carriages in the drive, and music and champagne within, and all the flower of the countryside gathered under its roof.

All these things he kept to himself, his precious secrets: which was a thousand pities, for Mary Ellen would have knocked them flying from his head with one great laugh, and they would all have been the happier for it. But while Mary Ellen scrubbed her doorstep and baked her lovely crusty bread, Joshua built his house, and the very first thing she knew about it was when he drove her up there and, bursting with pride, handed her the key. Too late, then, to do anything but smile bravely and kiss Joshua; open the great door and go in. But a bare year later they carried her out, and laid her quietly to rest in the little churchyard of Staving, down in the valley. And the light of Joshua's life went out.

After a while he remembered Rosie, then a great tomboy of fourteen and the spitten image of her mother.

Looking at Rosie as I knew her, it was hard to believe that she had ever been to an expensive school in Eastbourne, and afterwards for a whole year to Switzerland, to be "finished." But so it was.

At this time she must have been about twenty-four or -five; a great strapping woman with blazing red hair, enormous vitality, and the biggest heart in the north country—which is saying something. Her fine schools had taught her nothing; neither to speak well, dress well, nor even to walk across a room without giving something a hearty kick. Her only accomplishment was driving, which she did magnificently—and that she learned from Luke Abbey up at the Farm, and cost her father nothing!

"Money thrown down t'drain," Joshua used to growl, shooting her a sardonic glance. But Rosie never minded. She would fetch him a hearty smack and tell him not to talk so daft, or happen she'd pack her bags and go, and how'd he like that?

And he wouldn't have liked it, either; for he had the sense to know she was the salt of the earth.

On Rosie's twenty-first birthday Joshua gave her a string of magnificent pearls and the shock of her life.

The partner, Shane, had not been all they thought him. He had monkeyed about with the firm's money, helped himself to somebody else's wife, and got half-way to America before he changed his mind and blew his brains out instead. He had left a young son in the inefficient care of an aged and grudging aunt, for the mother had died at his birth. Joshua proposed to adopt the boy, and Rosie was to have the job of bringing him up.

The boy was David.

§

I had never been to Bolton House before. The four-mile uphill walk was deemed too much for our childish legs—which it probably was, hung about with clothing as we were—and there was no sort of public conveyance in those days. The House (the Days always referred to it like that) stood completely isolated, on the edge of the moor, the nearest village being Staving, two miles distant, to which David rode daily on a grey pony for lessons with the Vicar. On Sundays he usually stayed at the Vicarage all day. For Shane had been "Church," and Joshua had the sense to know that Cheddar Street Chapel was the wrong setting for Shane's son.

When I first realised that David was "Church" I was filled with horror. Mother, of course, had been "Church" before her marriage, but Father was not only Nonconformist, but violently so. As for the Roman Catholic Church, it was never alluded to in our home, though the phrases "the Scarlet Woman" and "the Whore of Babylon" were not unknown to me. Everything that was not "Chapel" I lumped together as sinister and dangerous, and I never walked past St Mark's Church without the secret fear that some rampaging female in a red dress would leap out and seize me in her venomous clutches. It was a sincere surprise to me that anyone so essentially kind and normal as David could possibly be "Church."

I was not in the least intimidated by Rosie's big house, nor by the stiff parlourmaid who whisked the dishes about under our noses and tossed her starched streamers. I had always been used to having Tanner wait on me; and if I had never lived in a large house, at least I had never lived in a small, mean one, as Rosie had. I was the Minister's daughter, wasn't I? And my mother was a lady, which Rosie's mother most certainly was not. In God's eyes I might be no better than the poorest of the chapel folk, but I was perfectly aware that in the eyes of Rosie's parlourmaid I was infinitely better than Rosie, and I acted accordingly.

The House left me quite cold. It was filled with stiff, grand furniture that looked unfriendly. Rosie never plumped herself down in a chair without a certain air of bravado, and I have seen her walk right round a room on the polished boards rather than sully the carpet's pale, thick pile.

The Manse was shabby and inconvenient. Its carpets were threadbare and its furniture plain and mostly ugly. The sideboard had been kicked by countless ministers' children with highly unecclesiastical consciences, and the mattresses were lumpy and lean. But everything in our house had been used, and either loved or hated. Rosie's house was just a house filled with furniture, and I liked it only because it was her home.

But the Farm was another matter.

It was little more than a good-sized cottage, standing in about thirty acres of land that was mostly reclaimed moorland. It was an old cottage, with sloping floors and dim, twisting stairs, and tiny square windows at which ivy tapped with friendly fingers. There was a porch with clematis growing over it, and a little bench to sit on each side of the green door, that was blistered by sun and scratched by dogs' impatient feet. Geraniums bloomed at all the windows; such geraniums as I have never seen since; their queer, musty scent filled the whole house. The kitchen was the largest room; square, with polished red flags and an immense cooking range; the friendliest room I ever was in. There was a small, prim parlour, with an aspidistra behind lace curtains, and framed funeral cards on all the walls, and there were three bedrooms above, violently papered in climbing roses, and almost completely filled by the big beds, so high you had to take a flying leap to get on them.

As soon as I clapped eyes on the Farm I loved it, and, to this day, whenever I say the word "home" I think first of that small and lowly dwelling in the heart of the moor.

Joshua had bought the place derelict, soon after Mary Ellen's death, because he wanted something fresh to distract his mind, something new to plan for. But all he could think of was how much better his Mary Ellen would have liked it than the grand House he had built for her, and he soon lost interest in it. But he had got the place cheap, and a bargain was a bargain, even when weighed down by sorrow, and not lightly to be parted with. So Joshua installed a capable, hard-working man called Luke Abbey, gave him a lot of conflicting orders, and left him to "make a do of it."

Luke had worked on the land all his life, and knew just how much and how little he could get out of that stubborn soil. He was a slow, dark man, with the bluest eyes I ever saw and a smile of rare sweetness. His mother, a tiny faded woman with a merry laugh, kept house for him.

Wisely ignoring Joshua's orders, Luke set himself to a task he loved.

Bit by bit he built up the stone fences, repaired the barns and outhouses, whitewashed the cottage, mended the roof and the sagging window-frames and broken gates. Six Jersey cows were put to graze in the meadows, and some of the land was ploughed and planted with roots for the winter feeding. The pond was cleaned out and white ducks made it their home. A good-laying strain of fowls made a cheerful noise in the yard with their fussy domesticity. Luke cleared the orchard ground of weeds, whitened the tree trunks, and pruned back the locked branches. The vegetable garden was dug over, manured and restocked, and the little patch of earth around the cottage made to bloom with gay flowers. Luke had "made a do of it."

Joshua liked to stroll down the hill from the House, wearing breeches and leggings, and walk over the place with Luke, chewing a straw, rapping out what he hoped were knowledgeable questions and disagreeing every now and then, just for the look of the thing. He liked to run his hands down the cows' sleek flanks, weigh the warm brown eggs in a horny palm, bite into a sound red apple. He liked to drink a cup of tea with Luke's mother in the warm friendliness of the kitchen, and chink his gold, and order this or that to be bought. "The best's good enough for me, eh, missus?" he would say. And she would laugh her merry laugh and call him a caution; and Luke would smile slowly and promise to get whatever was necessary—which was seldom what Joshua had ordered.

It was a rest from the bleak grandeur of the House. But Joshua never loved the Farm as Rosie loved it. To him, it was just another of his achievements. To her, it was sanctuary.

$\mathcal{G}$

We went to the Farm as soon as we had finished dinner. We all went without hats or coats, which I thought a most odd and exciting thing to do, and the wind blew my short hair straight up on end.

"Doesn't she look a funny little Tinribs?" David laughed; and Rosie laughed, and I laughed too, knowing I must look funny, and not caring.

I was completely happy.

Accustomed as I was to streets and houses and smoke, the beauty of the moor took me unaware. Miles upon miles of it, pricking away into eternity with a sweeping grandeur that took my breath away. A world without end.

The road rushed steeply down into Staving, and up again; and down and up, far as the eye could follow, to where the blue hills beat up into the sky and melted there in tender lines of mist. I could hear the smith's hammer on his anvil down in the valley, and a lark hung suspended above us, stabbing the silence with his silver arrows.

A lane turning sharply off the road led to the Farm. At the gate stood a cream-coloured knobbly calf, thrusting its pale moist nose against the bars and watching us with velvet eyes. I had never seen a calf before.

"Put your fingers out, luv," Rosie said. "He'll none hurt you."

I put them out timidly and the calf took them into his mouth and sucked at them strongly. My heart melted in tenderness. I could have gone on my knees to the lovely gawky little creature.

"You won't do that in six months' time!" David laughed.

We went first to the cottage, where I was clucked over and laughed over by Mrs Abbey. Then Rosie told David to show me everything, and she made me take off my thick stockings and roll up my sleeves, so that for the first time my limbs made the acquaintance of the sun.

I was happier than I had ever been in my life.

We collected brown eggs, warm from the nests, and chucked handfuls of golden grain to the greedy fowls, who pecked at it with jerky little movements like clockwork birds. We ate gooseberries in the vegetable garden and swung from the big apple-tree in the orchard, and raced about meadows brazen with buttercups. We flung ourselves down in the long grass, sown with daisies and pink clover and tiny blue speedwell, and gazed up into the vast, aching arch of the sky, and then rolled over, blinded, to bury our hot faces in perfumed earth.

I was happier than I had ever been in my life.

I had not dreamed it possible to be so happy. My cramped and lady-like little soul felt near to bursting with a heavenly humility and a passion of praise. The peace of God, that passeth all understanding. … Father's voice had brought me fleeting glimpses of it. But here, high up in the hot, sweet silence of the moor, with David beside me, the peace of God came to me without words, and with a singing fullness no church could have contained.

We went back quietly to the Farm for tea. There were hot scones and home-made jam and crusty bread spread thickly with golden butter. There were brown eggs for David and me in eggcups shaped like swans, and each egg wore a comical little knitted woollen cap, to keep it hot.

Rosie had baked the scones. Her cheeks were flushed with heat and there was flour on her chin and she looked contented. She was not allowed in the kitchen at the House, and she loved cooking, so Mrs Abbey let her cook whenever she went to the Farm. Luke ate three of the scones, keeping his eyes on his plate.

"How are they, Luke?" she asked.

"Ah niver tasted better, missus."

Rosie looked pleased, but she said quickly:

"Nay, they're not a patch on your mother's."

Toiling back up the hill, I was suddenly very tired. The day had stretched out before me, seemingly without end—and here was the end already. Soon I should be back home, with Mother invisible behind the carbolic sheet and Father shut in his study and Tanner hurrying me to bed. And all the dark, slow tides of the Manse, vaguely sensed, and not at all comprehended, closing round me again, and all this loveliness behind.

"I don't want to go home," I said flatly.

"Nay now, luv!" Rosie exclaimed, and she signed to David to take my other hand. "Your father and mother will be wanting you."

But they didn't want me. Oh, most blessedly they didn't want me!

A telegram had been brought to the House asking Rosie to keep me for a while; for Clem had measles too, and Tanner's hands were full.

"Oh, hurray! Hurray! Hurray!" I shouted, jumping up and down and forgetting my tiredness.

It was not until I was half asleep in the strange, too-grand bedroom that I remembered to be frightened for Clem.

Chapter Four

S

I stayed with Rosie all that lovely summer.

The days flowed imperceptibly through the green, jewelled hours of June into the white-hot stillness of July; on through the smouldering purple noons and thunder-haunted nights of August into the quiet harbour of September's gold.

But for me, time stood still.

I was allowed to do exactly as I liked. I, who had never been used to more than a decorous walk once a day, was out on the moor from morning to night. I learned the blessedness of being alone, and my own company delighted me.

Clothing was a problem at first. My frocks were too long and full, too "fancy" for freedom, and they were reinforced by petticoats, starched and frilled. Rosie, wise beyond her generation, put me into a pair of grey shorts that David had grown out of, and bought me some blouses with short sleeves. My legs went bare. I wore sandals and no hat. The villagers clicked their tongues and said "Ee, well, I don't know!"—but that didn't worry me. Father would have been disgusted had he seen me; but he did not see me, so no harm was done.

As soon as breakfast was over I was out and away down the hill into Staving with David. We took it in turns to ride the grey pony as far as the Vicarage gates. There I would leave him and toil back up the hill as far as the Farm. I spent most of my time there. Luke gave me a garden of my own; a tiny patch of earth that I dug and planted and weeded, joyed in and mourned over. I was given a yellow duckling that I called Milly, and it soon came to know my voice and follow me about everywhere, voicing its opinions at my heels. I fed the chickens and fetched the three gentle little

Jerseys home for the milking, and picked fruit for Mrs Abbey in the hot, sweet-scented orchard. And when it rained I helped with the baking, or rubbed away at the brasses till they shone, or lay up in the apple-smelling loft with a book—any book I could get hold of. Mrs Abbey's taste in literature was single-minded. All she demanded in any story was High Life. She possessed a pile of twopenny paper-backed novelettes to which she made regular additions, and I read these avidly, storing my mind with an astonishing jumble of wicked earls and heroic younger sons and maidens whose virtue was only exceeded by their stupidity and their aptitude for falling into the most elementary traps. They did me no harm, these books. What I did not understand I ignored and what I did understand I soon forgot.

Mrs Abbey thought me a prodigy of learning.

"Books like them—and her nobbut seven!" she would exclaim to Rosie. Sometimes, when she was extra tired, she would get me to recite the psalms to her, while she put her feet up on the red-covered settle. With my face pressed to the hot, geranium-smelling window-panes I would gaze out over the moor to the distant hills, and my heart would thrill with beauty.

"I will lift up mine eyes unto the hills, from whence cometh my help. ..."

I received no sort of schooling during those months. From the age of five, Sylvia and I had been tutored rather spasmodically by a gushing spinster called Joycey, with prominent teeth and eyes, and absolutely no aptitude for her job. I suppose she taught me to read, and for that I should be grateful; but she certainly taught me nothing else. The fact that at the age of seven I knew more than most children of ten was due largely to my excellent memory, and to the fact that I had the run of Father's study. There was a shelf of children's books—relics of his own childhood—in the study. But there was also a complete set of Dickens, another of Scott, and a lovely edition of Shakespeare, sonnets and all. There were also histories, geographies plentifully supplied with maps, and a very second-hand *Encyclopaedia Britannica*. Could any child with an inquiring mind ask for more?

I often had dinner at the Farm, and afterwards I would either go to my secret hiding-place on the moor, or walk down into Staving again to wait for David.

One day I arrived far too early, and as the sun was very hot on my bare head I wandered into the shade of the old church. I walked about the churchyard for a little while, looking at the half-obliterated names on the weather-beaten headstones. It was here that Mary Ellen lay at peace, and I searched until I found her grave. Not that it was difficult to find, for Joshua had done his Mary Ellen proud, with iron railings gilded at the spikes, and a marble angel, life-size, holding a book flat against her tummy so that all might read the recorded virtues written thereon. I took a dislike to this angel, who had a silly simper and a piece knocked off the end of her nose, and I felt that Mary Ellen would far rather have had an ordinary grass mound with maybe a simple cross at its head.

I decided that Isaac Smiley, aged seventy-four, would have been happier if they had put him farther out into the sun. Wandering farther, I almost trod upon the tiniest grave I had ever seen: a grave without a headstone and without any flowers but the daisies that starred the waving grass; and my heart was wrung with a sudden anguish. Somehow it made me think of Clem. And for a moment the dark waters of the Manse swirled about my feet.

I stayed a moment by the grave of an old lady of ninety-five, whose incredible name was Karenhapuk Foljambe, by whose stone her sorrowing relatives had placed a jam-jar, but had forgotten to put anything in it, despite the announcement that she was "gone but not forgotten." I had an idea that Karenhapuk would have seen the funny side of that.

I passed the open door of the church; and my old fear of the rampaging woman in red stirred within me. I forced myself to conquer that fear, and went slowly through the door into the cool, quiet place. Standing by the ancient font I gazed fearfully around.

Though I didn't know it, Staving Church was a beautiful example of Gothic architecture, with delicate pointed arches and a rose-window of rare workmanship. All that meant nothing to me. It was the sense of age and dignity, of hallowedness, that caught at my heart and drew my feet slowly down the aisle to the altar rail.

It was all so different from Cheddar Street Chapel. The beautiful carvings on the pews; the remote dignity of the altar with its gleaming brasses and simple flowers; the queer, attractive scent that hung on the still air, and the rainbow shaft of sunlight slanting from the window high above.

Scarcely knowing what I did, my knees bent and I knelt before the altar.

I don't think I prayed. My heart seemed to open, and beauty and peace flowed in until it was quite full. Perhaps that is prayer.

I must have stayed there a long time, for when I rose to my feet the sunlight was gone from the high window. Turning, I saw a man in a black frock down to his heels, and I knew it was Mr Lord, the Vicar. He was watching me, and his face was kind and wise. He came near and put his hand on my head, tilting it back.

"Who are you, my boy?" he asked.

"I'm a girl," I said shyly.

"Dear me. So you're a girl? And very sensibly you wear clothes that won't tear or get in the way. What is your name?"

"Ruan Ashley."

"Ah, you must be David's little Tinribs, I think." His eyes twinkled. "I'm afraid you've missed David to-day. He went home half an hour ago."

He ruffled my hair and, remembering, I blushed uncomfortably.

"I forgot I hadn't got a hat on. I'm sorry."

He smiled and gave my rough locks a gentle tug.

"I don't think we'll worry about it."

"Do you think God really minds?" I asked diffidently.

"I doubt it. I doubt it very much. Saint Paul was apt to be a little fussy about things like that. But then, we all have our failings. Mine is unpunctuality. I meant to be up with Mrs Abbey by now. If you are going home, perhaps we might walk together, eh?"

We walked out into the hot sunshine again and up the road through the village. He took my hand in a comradely fashion, and we talked together of many things, as if we had been friends for years.

"So you are Helena's daughter," he mused. I started, staring up at him through my thatch of hair.

"Do you know Mother?"

"I knew her years ago when she was a young girl. She was very beautiful." He was talking more to himself than to me. "Much too beautiful for a stodgy old parson, of course. Much too young and beautiful. … And yet she married a parson after all, didn't she?"

I don't know why I felt on the defensive.

"My father is the Reverend Everard Ashley," I said, with some pomp. "And we go to chapel," I added severely, trying to stifle a sudden sense of dismay at the memory of pitchpine pews and ugly windows and Mr Wister's head jerking.

"Indeed!" he returned courteously. "You are a staunch little Nonconformist. That is a good thing to be. But you like my beautiful church, don't you, Ruan Ashley?"

"Yes."

Loyalty to Father made me blurt out:

"I didn't go to say my prayers there. I just wanted to—to think."

He inclined his silvery head.

"Please use my church to think in whenever you wish to, my dear."

At the lane to the Farm we parted. I ran home and found David in his bedroom, making up a bottle of rich red fluid. He had made a sort of surgery in one corner with a shelf of bottles and paper packets, and he spent many happy hours there, inventing panaceas for all ills.

He shook the concoction and held it critically to the light.

"It's for Cook. She's got spasms."

"Suppose you poison her?" I suggested ghoulishly.

He grinned, and corked the bottle and wrapped it in white paper with a certain deftness.

"It's nothing but soda bicarb. and water, and a dash of cochineal. Well, I shoved a few drops of peppermint in, just for luck, and a spot of rhubarb. Oh, and a couple of aspirins to deaden the pain. I should think it's almost bound to do her good. I shall be jolly well surprised if it upsets her."

"I expect it will kill her," I assured him. "Have an aniseed ball?"

He took one and sucked it appreciatively. Rosie gave me sixpence a week to spend. I always saved threepence of it towards buying Clem a getting-well present, but the other threepence bought me more sweets than I had ever been allowed before.

"I wish I'd thought of aniseed," David said. "It's good for something or other. I've a good mind to shove one in."

I gave him one, but it was too big for the mouth of the bottle.

"Use the one you've sucked."

"Jolly good idea."

He produced it, washed it carefully in his toothglass, and added it to the mixture. He began to shake the bottle methodically.

"Of course, this sort of thing's just child's play," he said loftily. "Surgery's what I shall go in for. David Shane, F.R.C.S. Golly! ... I say, you might give us another aniseed ball, you little beast. And take your sticky paws off that photograph."

I gave him the sweet.

"Who are they, David?"

"My mother and father. Golly, this sweet isn't getting much smaller."

I looked at the two pictured faces; the plain, fragile woman with the trusting eyes and the exceedingly handsome man who was so like, and yet so unlike, David.

"They both died, didn't they?"

He nodded.

"I never knew my mother at all, but I can just remember Father. He was a splendid chap, Uncle Josh says. He died at sea you know. Somewhere between here and America. Do you think this *is* getting any smaller?"

"I don't think so. ... Do you go on loving people after—after they are dead, David?"

"I don't know. How can you? They're not there."

"They must be *somewhere*," I argued.

"Well, I expect so. But they're not *here*, anyway, and it was all so long ago. I like to think about them, and how jolly it would have been all together. I hope I'll be like my father when I'm a man. I think he looks a grand chap, don't you?"

I did.

"Come on," said David, "let's take this to Cook."

I very seldom ventured into the kitchens, but David was always welcome there. The servants adored him. He was "gentry," and they reacted automatically to his easy ways and speech. If he had sworn at them they would have resented it less than Rosie's timid: "Now then!"

Cook was doubled up in a chair, hugging a stone hot-water bottle and groaning loudly.

"Here you are, Cook," David said, in his best bedside manner. "Better take a dose now and another in—er—about an hour. Pour a dose out for her, Rawlings," he told the starched parlourmaid.

"Oh, Master David," she said, in a scared voice, "you're sure it's all right, sir? I mean, of course, I know it is if you say so, but—"

"I should jolly well think so, Rawlings!" David replied coldly. "Give her a tablespoonful in water, please."

"Gimme here!" Cook screeched. "I don't care if it kills me, I couldn't feel worse!"

To my utmost horror, she pulled the cork and drank the entire contents from the bottle. The aniseed ball must have stuck in her throat, for she began to choke, purple in the face and very terrifying; and suddenly she made a dash for the sink, and the awful sound of Cook being sick filled the air.

"There you are!" David said jauntily, though he looked rather white about the gills. "That's what she needed. She'll be as right as rain now." And he walked rather quickly out of the kitchen.

And, astonishingly, she *was* as right as rain, to David's unfeigned relief, and she promised us some of her extra-special cheese-cakes for a picnic next day, by way gratitude.

"Of course, it's all faith really," David told me airily, "That's why I can't be bothered with it. Now in surgery you do a good solid job of work." And he made sinister sawing movements with his hands upon an imaginary leg.

$\mathcal{S}$

We went through the village to buy sweets and then we climbed up the steep face of the moor to Walker's Ridge.

It was a lovely day. A mist clung about the valleys, warm and exciting, heavy with the weight of the sun pressing upon it. The grassy verges of the roads were wet with dew, and every scent was stronger, more pungent, than usual.

Mrs Shufflebotham was frying bacon in the little room behind the shop. She came out smiling and wiping her hands on a coarse apron. We bought toffee and peardrops and a large slice of a terrible substance called pink-pudding, which was pink only on the outside and a violent yellow within, and was compounded of heaven knows what rubbish. David and I were very partial to it.

"Going a picnic?" she asked pleasantly. "That's right! Nice to be bairns. That'll be fourpence the lot, thank you, luv."

The shop bell shattered the silence of the street, and our feet clattered more loudly on the cobbles than usual. The village was empty, save for Cracked Willy, who sat outside his mother's cottage, endlessly rocking himself to and fro. David gave him a smile and two peardrops, and his poor, silly face lit up with joy.

We left the village behind us, and began to climb. There were sheep up on the moor, and their voices were like the voices of lost souls behind the mist. The short turf was strong and wiry. Our feet slipped on it and we had to cling to the heather as we climbed. The heather buds were pinkish purple. Everywhere arose a strong, heady smell of heather and hot earth and sheep-droppings.

And suddenly we were above the mist and the sun was beating down on our heads in fierce welcome. The voices of the sheep became real. They huddled in little groups, staring at us with blank, snobbish expressions, then turned and bundled away to a safe distance, jostling each other in their stupid fashion.

"Phew!" David exclaimed, flinging himself down to rest. I followed suit, and we lay there for a long time. We had all the day before us.

"The bilberries will be ready soon."

I thought of bilberry-pie. Brown short crust stained with rich purple juice, arched over the luscious, heaped berries with their indescribable taste. And a tide of yellow cream mingling in marvellous pattern with the juice. Tanner had a masterly way with bilberry-pie. But would Tanner make them for me this year? ... Hastily I thrust the thought behind me. I loved my home. But that summer I was caught in a dream of beauty; and who would wish to wake from a lovely dream?

After a while we pushed on. We passed a decrepit farm-house, where an old woman squatted at the door shelling peas. We gave her "good day" but she looked right through us without answering. David told me she was mad. Her husband had quarrelled with their only son; and one day he had taken his gun down from the wall and shot him through the heart before her eyes. He had been hanged for it, and the old woman had gone mad. But they had let her alone, for she was harmless enough.

Up, up through the sweeping purple, the grey-green and the sudden, blazing gold. Up through the enchanted silence and the strong, sweet smells of the moor, until the breeze met us on top of the Ridge.

I don't know who Walker was, but he gave his name to one of the grandest viewpoints I know. On either side the land fell away in purple waves, losing themselves in the valley mists and sweeping up again in coloured curves into a white-hot sky. For mile upon endless mile these great waves curved and rolled about us, with here and there a grey village riding that enchanted sea like a little ship.

The silence was stupendous, broken only by the harshness of a peewit's cry as it flashed overhead with the sun on its wings. We were so used to the voices of the sheep that they were fused into the quietness, making it even more complete.

We found a tiny hollow half filled by a grey rock and shaded by a twisted rowan-tree.

David lay on his face and went to sleep, and I slept, too, for a time, though I struggled to keep awake; I didn't want to lose one moment of this marvel.

Sometimes I think that was the happiest day of my life, those hours of heat and silence and colour, alone with David high up on the moor. But then I remember that I have said that of many other days, so I cannot be sure. This I know—that it was almost perfect. Not quite, for perfection is dull: it took the serpent to make Adam and Eve appreciate their garden.

And into our Eden—David's and mine—there came the serpent also.

He was a big, loutish boy from Buckham, the next village beyond Staving, and what he was doing alone on the moor I do not know; perhaps even the serpent liked his own company on occasions. Anyway, there he suddenly was, slouching past our little hollow with a bulging sack over his shoulder and an unpleasant grin on his red face.

The rock hid David from his view, and I suppose he thought I was alone. He stopped and let the sack slip from his shoulders. He stared at me and his grin widened.

"Wow-wow!" he said softly. And I find it impossible to convey the disgust and fear those sounds aroused in me.

He made one step towards me. Only one. Then I yelled, and David woke and sprang up, startled.

"What's up! Did he touch you?" he stammered.

"No—no!" I muttered, ashamed.

"Wow!" the boy jeered on a different note. He picked up the sack and heaved it on to his shoulder again.

"Clear out, you!" David said in his lordly fashion.

"Moor's free," the boy retorted.

"Then go to another part of it, before I smash you to smithereens!"

He leapt out of our hollow and advanced upon the boy, with his square chin thrust out. The boy retreated, bawling obscenities.

"Shut up, you filthy tyke!" David roared.

"Yah! Swindler's kid!" That was the boy's parting shot as he dropped over the brow of the hill.

"Loathsome pig! ... Remind me to kick his bottom next time we're in Buckham," David commented, returning to our hollow. "'Swindler's kid!' I suppose it was all his futile brain could think of! ... What about those cheese-cakes, Tinribs?"

The shadow passed quickly; but it had been there between us and the sun. The shadow of Annie Briggs, with her pointed, evil tongue and her dark, unspoken knowledge. ...

Besides the cheese-cakes there were ham sandwiches, tomatoes, and great dark-red plums, dropping with juice. There was also a bottle of bitter, home-brewed beer; and if you think that strange refreshment for children of seven and twelve, I can only say that we liked it, and that it was a great deal better for us than the acid, highly coloured drinks in Mrs Shufflebotham's shop.

I held a dusky plum against my lips, savouring its bloomy sweetness, half reluctant to bite into the firm, golden flesh.

"This is exactly the colour of my name," I murmured. "Ruan. A dusky, purply red. Lovely!"

David stared and grinned at me.

"Aren't you a daft little Tinribs!"

"David is dark brown, with a kind of goldy shine in it. And Sylvia is the very palest yellow, like sunlight on water. And Joshua is a hard, shining grey."

"What's George?" David wanted to know.

"Sand colour."

"And Mary?"

"Red, but not so dark as mine. Michael is red, too; flaming red; and so is John. Maud and Arthur are pinkish and Phyllis is pale green."

David was interested.

"I can do it, too. Ada's red, isn't it? And Evelyn's silvery green and Edward is light brown."

"Yes. And Walter's a darker brown, and Luke's blue, and so is Dorothy. Daniel is black."

"It's orange."

"I tell you it's black. As black as coal. It's my game, so I ought to know."

"And I, who am twelve, tell you, who are only a measly seven, that Daniel is orange. O.R.A.N.G.E."

I shut my eyes tight and yelled "Bla-a-a-ack!" at the top of my voice, with my mouth as wide as it would go. The next minute it was completely filled with a clod of earth. I sat up, spitting and fuming, and David writhed about the heather in his mirth.

"If you could have—*seen* yourself!" he gasped. He pushed the beer-bottle towards me. "Here, rinse it out with beer, you little chump."

Which I did, very thoroughly. And the last mouthful I shot out at David with admirable accuracy, which quite restored my good humour and did nothing to impair his.

It was getting a little cooler now.

"Let's play at something," I suggested.

"Righto. We'll have a hospital and I'll do some operations on you."

"No, we won't." I had been cut up by David before. "We'll be explorers. Oh, yes, David! We'll find the North Pole and plant the Flag of England on it!"

"All right. Only look here, I'm going to find a convenient bush first, and so must you. It's quite time." There was no false modesty about David and he took care that I had none, which was a very good thing for me.

We played explorers and David's hanky was duly affixed to the North Pole, discovered, after many hardships and trials, in an outcrop of stone some half a mile distant.

Afterwards I good-naturedly allowed David to remove my tonsils, to put my arm in a splint with the aid of a stick and a very grubby piece of string, and to resuscitate me after drowning. In return, he kindly allowed me to tell him a story, in the middle of which he fell asleep again. I waked him with a small boulder and the rest of the beer.

We ran races, which David took care to lose sometimes. We acted a play, with me being very tragic and thorough, and David being sheepish. We ate the last of the plums, and I wondered if I were going to be sick, and David was disappointed when I wasn't, because he wanted to try out a new cure on me.

A lovely day, that seemed endless—and then suddenly it was ended, and we were tobogganing down the steep slope of the Ridge, hungry and dog-tired.

We trailed in through the back door, conscious of our stained and weary state.

Cook and Rawlings stared at me in a curious way. I went in search of Rosie, but she wasn't to be found. Then I heard her voice and Joshua's talking in the little smoking-room, off the hall.

"Best tell her, and be done wi' it," said Joshua.

"Nay," was Rosie's reply. "She'll be done up to-night. To-morrow's soon enow, poor lamb."

I was too tired to speculate. I wanted only to be washed and tucked up in bed. And Rosie saw to it, in the shortest possible time.

Chapter Five

§

The next day was Sunday. David was sent off to church. Joshua went to chapel in the gig, with Luke driving him. Rosie stayed at home with me. They never now took me with them, although all fear of infection was long past, but Rosie rarely missed a service.

"We'll go for a walk, shall we, luv?" she suggested.

We went out through the stiff gardens, ablaze with geranium, calceolaria, and lobelia. It was a hot morning, but dull and heavy with promise of rain. Rosie was quieter than usual, so I was quiet too. But it wasn't the right sort of quietness. Something was vaguely wrong. I was not happy.

Presently Rosie took my hand.

"Ruan, luv, I've got summat to tell you. Summat as will make you unhappy, just for a bit. … But you mustn't let it upset you too much, luv, because … maybe … I expect it's all for the best."

She was floundering badly, as unhappy as I was.

"It's about Clem, luv."

An ice-cold finger touched my heart, and it stopped beating just for a minute.

"Is Clem worse, Rosie?"

She nodded.

We walked on, the white, glaring road crunching beneath our feet. The bell of Staving Church began to ring for morning service, and across the valley another bell sounded faintly, half a tone higher.

"Rosie," I said suddenly, "Clem's dead. Isn't he? Isn't he, Rosie? Clem's dead!"

"That's it, luv."

I went a few steps farther and then I stopped. My legs were very weak. My throat felt hard and stiff and my eyes like pebbles. I leaned against the stone wall and watched a cloud, shaped like a bear, moving slowly across the sky.

"Well, there's a brave girl!" Rosie said, watching me apprehensively.

I knew I was expected to cry. But I couldn't cry. I felt dry and hard all over and there was a buzzing sound in my ears.

"Rosie—do you suppose Clem will be able to walk, now, and talk like other people?"

"I'm sure of it, luv," she replied simply.

"Nobody will call him elevenpence-ha'penny in the shilling in heaven, will they?"

She pulled me round and looked at me searchingly.

"Who said that to you?"

"Annie Briggs," I said dully.

"Oh, she did, did she! ... The little rat!" ...

Rosie swallowed violently and blew her nose.

"Look here, Ruan," she went on, in a gentler tone, "you don't want to take any notice what that Annie Briggs says. People like her never catch hold of the right end of the stick. ... This is how I see it. God never meant Clem to stay with us very long, so it wasn't worth while learning him to walk and talk. ... Everybody loved Clem, didn't they, luv?"

"Oh, they did, Rosie!"

"Well, you see, God loved him too. He'd made something very extra special when He made Clem, and He wanted him back as quick as possible. He only lent him to you for a little while, just to show what He *could* do, when He'd a mind."

Simple, wise, loving Rosie. What learned divine could have thought of an argument better able to ease my misery?

I laid my head in her lap, and the tears came gently, gently, with a healing flow that cleansed as well as healed. And Rosie cried with me, and felt the better for it. So that when the skies wept too, fat, heavy drops of thunder rain, we could scurry back to the House and even make a little joke about it.

Everybody was very kind to me. Cook made some of my favourite hot scones, and Rawlings gave me a brooch with MIZPAH on it, out of a cracker, and which I had often admired. Joshua rattled his money and asked if I knew a penny when I saw one; and eventually gave me two enormous five-shilling pieces, declaring loudly that I should be the ruin of him, I should an' all! I was considerably embarrassed by the heavy silver. I gave one of them to David, who bought with it a very second-hand book on anatomy, the pictures in which kept me awake for several nights.

But it was David who thought of the one thing that could bring me real comfort.

That Sunday evening we went down to the Farm. David went into one of the barns, telling me to wait outside. I heard his voice speaking soothingly, and an answering whine and a rustling of straw. Then David came out with Nell, the farm dog, tied to a rope and obviously reluctant to leave.

"Don't touch her!" he warned me.

"Don't be silly! She's very fond of me. I can do anything I like with her—you ask Luke!"

"Not now you can't," he grinned. "She'd have the nose off your face as soon as look at you. Wouldn't you, old girl?" He tied her to the wheel of a cart and patted her agitated head. "All right, old girl. All right, then! Now you come and look in here, Tinribs."

I followed him into the dark, warm barn and we bent over a bed of straw from which arose a funny, exciting smell that somehow caught at my heart. In the straw lay five squirming, snuffling little bodies, dark gold in colour and rather damp to the touch. They huddled together, making feeble sucking noises and squeaking at the loss of Nell's warmth.

"Oh!" I cried, enraptured. "The little darling puppies, David!"

David picked one up and laid it against my neck.

"Hold it carefully. Not too tight, fathead! That's better. Like it?"

Did I like it! I was speechless.

"I'll ask Luke to give you one when they're old enough to be taken away from their mother. Which do you like best?"

"Oh, this one—this one! Oh, David, do you think he will?"

"I expect so. They're mongrels, of course, but Nell's not a bad sort of dog."

"What's a mongrel?"

"Oh … it's when your father and mother are frightfully different."

"Oh." I wondered if I were a mongrel. It seemed more than likely.

"Put it down now. Nell will go barmy if we keep her away much longer. And mind, now, you're not to look at them unless I'm there, or Luke or somebody."

I laid the golden baby back in the straw and departed to a prudent distance while David untied Nell. She was back in that barn like a streak of lightning, and all I could see was two golden eyes glaring over the edge of the bed, as she snarled her maternal defiance.

David locked the barn door.

"Mind what I say, now. She'd have the nose off you face if you touched one of them. Not that it'd be much loss," he added frankly.

I thought of nothing but the warm, golden feel of the puppy against my neck. When I went to bed, I held it between me and the memory of Clem's death; a memory already blessedly fading. For once having established the fact that Clem was safe in heaven, walking and talking like all the other children, it was difficult to visualise him as the baby who had once lived in our house and banged his spoon on the table, and laughed at the sunbeams. Only one thing worried me, and one evening, as Rosie was helping me to bath, I questioned her about it.

"What do you think it was that Mother didn't want about Clem?"

Rosie blinked at me through the steam.

"Is this some more of that Annie Briggs?"

"Yes. She said she knew why he wasn't like other babies, and it was because Mother didn't want—something or other … only just then I flew at her and scratched her face till she ran away."

"An' the best day's work you ever did!" Rosie cried vigorously. "Something'll have to be done about them Briggses. A nasty, fast, lying lot!"

And something must have been done about them; for when I got back to the Manse their house was empty, and a "To Let" notice swung crazily in the garden. I did not know then that most of the houses in St Mark's Road belonged to Joshua Day.

It never occurred to me that Rosie hadn't answered my question; and gradually it faded from my mind.

But there were still five more weeks before I went home. Father and Mother and Sylvia went away for a holiday to Aberystwyth, and Tanner to some relations in Shropshire. The Manse was empty. They were putting new papers on all the walls and painting the woodwork green instead of its old drab brown. Rosie told me this, and I knew it was her own kind heart that had suggested it.

I did not see any of my people before they went. Father came up to the House unexpectedly but I was out for the whole day with David, and so missed him.

"Am I going to Aberystwyth too?" I asked.

"Nay, luv. Your father did say summat about it, but I told him you was right enough here."

And vastly relieved I was to be left with David on the moor. It never occurred to me that David might have missed his annual holiday by the sea, and that he gave this up voluntarily on my account.

But, as it fell out, both David and I were to have a seaside holiday that year.

All that August the weather had been exceptionally hot, and the last few days were almost phenomenal. The moor burned with a sullen, purple flame beneath a molten sky. Grass was parched and brown and flowers drooped in cottage gardens. The village lay in a drugged torpor. Children quarrelled sluggishly over their play in the trees' meagre shade. Women sat on their doorsteps with idle hands, staring vacantly. Only Cracked Willy continued to sit in the full glare of the sun, grinning and rocking himself to and fro, endlessly. Horses stood in shade, muzzle to haunch, lashing their tails at the swollen blue flies and the merciless midges. The church bell cracked the silence like a stone shivering a glass vase. Thunder rolled round the hills incessantly and lightning danced on them, but the storm held off and no rain fell. Tempers were brittle and rows at the Red Lion were of nightly occurrence: the air was so still you could hear the brawling right up at the House.

The House and the Farm were both affected by the heat. Rosie spent hours lying on her bed with her corset undone. The maids were unapproachable. I was afflicted with a heat rash, and David was being up-stage because I refused to be anointed with a sticky yellow paste he had concocted in his surgery, and which I knew for a fact contained onions.

I trailed down alone to the Farm, but it wasn't much better there. Mrs Abbey's feet hurt and made her snap, and even the gentle Luke had no smile for me. I was not allowed near the puppies. Even Milly, my white duck, refused my blandishments, and remained under the willow's shade, motionless on the tepid, scummy water.

David went off alone on his pony. I stood in the scant shade of the dusty laurels and watched him, scratching my burning arms and legs, near to tears with rage and irritation.

"I'm coming, too!"

David only laughed disagreeably. I picked up a clod of earth and chucked it at him, but it missed him by yards, and he laughed again and clattered away down the white, glaring road.

I went to the Farm again. Mrs Abbey was in the kitchen, baking. The heat was unbearable. She was making bread and fruit-cake and apple-pie; there was a ham boiling in a great iron pot and a dumpling steaming beside it: exactly the same sort of food as she cooked all the year round. The garden was full of vegetables, lettuce, and fruit, but it never occurred to her to make a salad.

"Hot enough for you?" she said absently.

I said it was. She gave me a cake, and I wandered out again, looking for something to do.

Rosie and Luke were in the orchard. I could hear their voices long before I got there. They were quarrelling about something. Rosie said Luke had got no more sense than a rabbit, and what did he think she was made of? And Luke told Rosie to give over nagging at a chap, and wasn't he made of the same stuff as she was? And if it wasn't for the blasted money, he'd show her! ... And Rosie said, what did money matter! And Luke said, damn and blast everything, how long was she going to stand there talking like a fool! And anyway, he was off to get a drink.

I heard Rosie say: "Luke!" in a queer sort of way. And after that there was silence. ...

I thought Luke must have gone, so I went forward. But at the edge of the orchard my feet became rooted to the ground with sheer, overwhelming surprise.

Luke had got Rosie in his arms. His face was pressed down on hers, forcing it back. Her hair was coming down. Its thick, red coils streamed over her shoulders and over his brown, hairy forearms. Their eyes were closed, as if they were asleep, but Luke's right hand was moving about Rosie's body, up and down her thick white throat, pressing against her silk blouse, pulling at the great ropes of hair. ...

I was astonished and I was frightened. I wanted to run away and I wanted to stay and watch them. I felt as if a spell had fallen upon the orchard, rooting us all to the spot. ...

The church clock struck the hour; the spell was broken and I could stumble away, thankful not to be seen.

As I passed the cottage Mrs Abbey stuck her head out of the door.

"Seen our Luke, Miss Ruan?"

I turned scarlet and mumbled that he was in the orchard. She looked at me sharply.

"With 'er?"

I nodded. Her lips went thin and she pushed at her wispy hair.

"Nay!" she muttered. "Drive a man to drink, she would!" She went in and shut the door.

I didn't feel very well. The heat was like an iron weight pressing down on my head, and I thought I might be going to be sick. I trailed down through the dormant village, past Cracked Willy, who grinned and jerked his thumb at me, and into the churchyard. I had not been inside the church since the day I had talked with Mr Lord, but now I remembered its dim coolness with a sense of gratitude. I pushed open the door and went inside.

I sat in a tall pew and gazed at the rose-window.

Luke and Rosie. ...

I still felt stunned by what I had seen; stunned and rather frightened. But I was not shocked, except—God forgive me—by the fact that Luke was Rosie's servant. He often smelt strongly of manure. He ate noisily, and blew his nose, very cleverly, without a handkerchief. I knew that ladies and gentlemen kissed each other. On the rare occasions when Father went away he always kissed Mother on the cheek, just as he kissed Sylvia and me. But he never pulled her hair down, or messed up her clean silk blouse; and certainly he never shouted "damn and blast" at her. ... Why kiss anyone, if you were so cross with them?

And a servant too—there was the rub!

I tried to imagine Father kissing Tanner, but imagination boggled. The whole thing was incomprehensible.

I sat very still. From the half-open door came a continuous murmur of bees. The sky was darkening. Even in the comparative coolness of the church the air was heavy with a sense of waiting for the storm; waiting for it, longing for it, dreading it.

In one of the windows was a picture of Jesus carrying a lamb on His shoulders. I remembered suddenly that Jesus had been more than just Someone we sang about in chapel: He had been a man, a carpenter's son. He had come from a very poor home, and probably His table manners weren't any better than other poor people's. And a carpenter was a sort of servant, wasn't he? ... I knew it was probably very wicked of me to think things like that—and yet I couldn't feel wicked. If it was true, how *could* it be wicked!

I remembered the kindness of Luke's eyes; the sweetness of his smile; the little boat he had carved for me with his penknife; the gentle way he had with animals.

The sky grew darker still. I felt very sleepy. I lay full length on the seat and pulled a hassock up for a pillow. The smoky smell of incense that always hung about the church grew stronger. A wave of it caught me and held me suspended in a mist of coloured light and sullen buzzing of bees. ...

I woke with a start. There had been a terrible noise, as if the House were crashing down. I screamed for Rosie and made a blind movement to get to her. I fell on to a hard floor and hurt my head. And then I recalled that I was not in bed at the House, but in Staving Church, alone. Alone in the dark church, with the lightning turning the windows into sheets of flame, and thunder rattling and crashing overhead. ... It must be midnight! ... I was too terrified for tears, but the breath tore out of my body in long, choking gasps. I remembered the Scarlet Woman, and all my old fear of her returned sevenfold. In one vivid flash I distinctly saw her standing by the organ, looking at me. Another flash—and she had come nearer! I stumbled down the dim aisle, fell over the base of the old font, and reached the door of the church.

I couldn't open it! ...

For one instant I stood silent, paralysed, too appalled for effort. Alone in the locked church at midnight. ... There were dead people under the floor of the church, waiting to push up the stones and grin, or beckon. The Scarlet Woman was slipping noiselessly down the aisle, in pursuit of me.

I hammered at the iron-studded door, pushing with all my might, pushing and kicking and screaming, on a high, hysterical note.

The door did not budge an inch.

"Rosie! Rosie! ... Da-a-a-vid! ... Let me out! Open the door! Let me out. David! David! ..."

I was answered by an appalling crash of thunder, right overhead, and a rushing sound of mighty rain.

Perhaps it's the end of the world, I thought. And the magnitude of the idea silenced my screaming. Of what use to scream and kick and call to David, when in a few moments the dead would be rising up out of their graves, and the awful sound of the trumpet would fill the four corners of the earth? Too late, too late, you cannot enter now. ... I tried to remember my sins, but everything was a blur.

And suddenly, like a miracle, the door stood open and Luke came in and picked me up and held me against his great shoulder that was soaked with rain. He smelt of manure and horses and sweat and beer, and it was the loveliest smell on earth. I clung to him, drenching his neck with my tears.

"Nay, luv, door warn't locked! See, it opens this road—pull, not push, sitha!" He demonstrated, and I was quietened a little. He laughed kindly and took me out in the porch and sat on a bench, and I sat on his knee. He pulled from his pocket a bag of bulls'-eyes and we each had one. Luke sucked his loudly and I didn't mind a bit. I sucked mine loudly, too, so that I shouldn't be any better than he was. I clung to him in a passion of gratitude, still sobbing in long-drawn, quivering spasms.

"I reckon it were a right good job I were passin'," Luke said comfortably. "You mighta squaked while Monday week, and none the wiser."

"Is it midnight yet, Luke?"

"Midnight? Not it, luv. It's nobbut around seven. Storm'll be ovver soon, I reckon, but there's more rain to come. I'm thinkin' I'd best get thee home, or Missus'll be worrited out'n her life. You'll not be frit o' thunder, shall ye, luv, if I carry thee?"

"I can walk," I said.

But I could not walk, for terror had robbed my limbs of all strength. So Luke took off his stained and odorous coat and wrapped me in it and laid me over his shoulder. And thus, in his shirt-sleeves, and singing a jolly song which—perhaps fortunately—I did not comprehend, he carried me all the way from Staving to the House and put me into Rosie's arms.

And if his steps were not perfectly steady, or his language when he stumbled of the most polite, no lost lamb could have had a tenderer shepherd than I had in Luke Abbey.

Rosie kissed and scolded me, bathed me and put me to bed. Then she sat beside me and stared out of the window. She was a bit worried about David, too, for though he had only ridden as far as Buckham, he had not yet returned.

"I do love Luke," I said sleepily.

"Do you, luv?" Rosie's voice was rich and soft. "So do I. He's a grand chap, yon."

"Don't drive him to drink, will you, Rosie?"

She started, and her face flamed scarlet.

"Nay!—wherever did you get that from, Ruan!"

"Mrs Abbey said it."

Rosie's fingers drummed a tune on the window-pane. She kept her face turned away from me. After a time she said quietly:

"You don't want to repeat all you hear, luv. There's things you don't understand, and things Mrs Abbey don't understand, neither—aye, and even Luke! … Get you off to sleep now, luv."

And she went out of the room.

Chapter Six

S

I woke up to find David standing in the doorway. He was in pyjamas, and his hair was ruffled. His eyes looked queer, as if he had been crying—but I could not imagine David crying. His lip was swollen and there was a big black bruise on his forehead.

"Hullo," he said. He sat down on my bed and hugged his knees. The room was full of grey dawn-light and the sound of rain.

"Hullo," I said sleepily.

"It's teeming cats and dogs!"

"What happened to your lip, David?"

"Nothing. I had a fight."

"David! Who with?"

"Nobody much. ... Golly, hark at that rain! It'll flatten the crops like pancakes." He shivered. "Let me come in, Ruan, it's jolly cold all of a sudden."

He wriggled in beside me and we lay listening to the water racing along the gutters.

"Who with, David?"

"You remember that great lump of a tyke on the moor—the one who frightened you that day?"

"Yes."

"Well, him. ... He called after me again to-day. There was a whole crowd of them, and they all called out things. So I went back and hit him. ... Are you asleep, Ruan?"

"No, David."

"Don't go to sleep. I want to ask you something. Ruan ... do you think there could possibly be … any truth in it? … What they were shouting, I mean?"

"What were they shouting?"

"Swindler's kid," David said slowly, "like that lout did before. And there were other things, too. … It seems awful to—to have a moment's doubt. Only … oh, Ruan, you don't think it could possibly be the tiniest bit true, do you? … *Do you?*"

"No," I said faintly.

And suddenly—I can never explain how, even to myself—I knew that it *was* true. The shadow of Annie Briggs was in the room, pointing her pale tongue through broken teeth, leering unspeakably.

"It doesn't matter! It doesn't matter, David!" I cried miserably. And David turned and looked at me, and then rolled over on to his face and lay there motionless. I knew he was crying, and that I must not do anything about it.

I lay still beside David, thinking what a lot had happened to me since I was seven. Before that, life seemed a dream; an ordered dream of waking and sleeping and eating and going to chapel and going for walks with Tanner. But since my birthday, life had spun dizzily. The clown had kissed me. David had come. Sylvia had been ill and Clem had died. I had found the freedom of the moor and had lived with laughter. Laughter and sorrow and fear and courage and joy had crowded my days: a pattern of lovely colour. And now there was this new business of David's father.

I thought David was funny to mind so much. I didn't know what a swindler was, except that it was something unpleasant. But his father was dead, long ago, and David remembered only nice things about him; why should it matter so much all these years after?

I put my arm round David, and presently I must have slept. When I woke it was full daylight and I was alone in the bed.

§

For three days and nights the rain never ceased. It hung like a thick grey curtain between the House and the moor. The white road was a river. The gutters sang. The flowers were beaten flat on the black, steamy earth.

Rosie kept me in bed for a whole day; wisely, for the shock I had suffered had been severe. On the second day I got up and wandered about the House looking for David. There were fires in all the rooms, and we were glad of them.

"Don't go in there, luv!" Rosie said, quite sharply. "David's talking to his Uncle Josh."

I hung about outside the room. Presently David came out and pushed past me. His face was different. I didn't dare to speak to him. He went into his own room and shut the door against me. I heard the key click in the lock.

"Come and hold this wool while I wind it, luv," Rosie said kindly.

I stood before her, my arms stiffly extended, and she rapidly rolled the wool into large balls. It kept slipping off my hands and getting into an awful muddle, but Rosie never got impatient over things like that.

"What's it for, Rosie?"

"I'm going to knit a jersey for you to wear this winter. It's same colour as t'moor, see, luv? I reckoned you'd like that."

I did like it. It would be lovely to have the moor wrapped round me warm and tight. I thanked Rosie and cheered up a little.

"Aye, I thought you'd be right set up with that!"

She began to knit. Clack clack clack. But I soon got bored with that and crept upstairs to David's room again. I tried the door, and it opened.

"Hullo," I ventured.

David was sitting in his surgery. He was reading the anatomy book and pretended not to hear me.

"Come and play pirates, David?"

"Huh."

"Well, ludo, then."

Silence.

"David."

"Huh."

"Would you like to operate on me? I don't mind. You can cut my leg off again if you like."

"Go away. I'm not going to be a doctor. Never."

He laid his head down on the book and burst into tears. Real, scalding, noisy tears, such as I had shed many a time, but never dreamed that David was capable of shedding.

After a while he mopped his face with a grubby handkerchief and began drawing on some blotting-paper.

"Ruan ... it was true, what that boy said. All of it was true. Every beastly part of it. ... I've been having it out with Uncle Josh and I made him tell me the whole thing. I *am* a swindler's kid. And everything else."

"What else, David?"

"Lots of things. You wouldn't understand. I don't know that I do altogether, but I understand enough. ... My father was a rotter. He stole a lot of money from Uncle Josh and ran away, and—and—" He jabbed at the blotting-paper, and the point of the pencil snapped. "And after all that, Uncle Josh fetched me away from the aunt I was left with, and adopted me; and he's always been as decent as pie. I can't understand that, either. ... But you see now why I can't be a doctor."

I didn't see at all.

"Because he wants me to go into the factory. He hasn't got anybody else to carry on after him, you see. So I've got to. It's the least I can do. ... I'll have to go down to the works every day and go through all the departments, learning it all. I shall hate it like poison, but there's simply nothing else to be done. ... And I don't want to talk about it ever again. I want to forget the whole beastly business until the time comes, see? So don't keep on jabbering about it."

Which, seeing that I had barely uttered a sound, seemed an unreasonable remark, I thought.

We mouched about the House all day; woebegone figures staring out at the pouring rain, playing half-hearted games, reading listlessly; until Rosie suddenly swept up to her room and began plucking clothes from her wardrobe and throwing them into a travelling trunk.

"We're off to t'sea," she declared loudly. "We've all got pip, and a change is t'best thing for that. David, get out what you want packed. Help him, Ruan—men's right soft at packing. That's the ticket. Heave ho, and in they go! …"

ℰ

We went to Blackpool.

All the way there it rained unceasingly. We slept, that first night, half deafened by the clatter of rain on a corrugated roof of a shed somewhere outside. But the next day September came, and she opened her arms and poured gold upon us; gold that danced and shimmered on the blue water, on the white towers and coloured flags of the pleasure beach, on the bright brass instruments of the band, on the thrusting pier and the hot, teeming curve of the promenade and the gay shop-windows.

For a whole week Rosie rushed us off our feet. We pushed amongst the loud, good-natured crowds, listened to the band, ate ices and whelks and immense sticks of pink rock, splashed and screamed in the sea, wearing the most astounding garments hired from the old man with the bathing machines, and rode races on grey, scabby old donkeys with patient faces. We swooped dizzily in swing-boats painted scarlet and gold, yelled murder as we swirled down the spiral course on little mats, and showed off on the roundabouts. We went on the *Skylark* and were sick. We drove to Morecambe on a coach pulled by four horses, and everybody sang, "*Daisy, Daisy, give me your answer, do!*" We laughed ourselves silly over the pierrots, and I fell in love with one of them; a thin, brown-faced fellow with sad, monkey's eyes and a soulful tenor voice, and I hung about after the show and followed him, adoring, until suddenly he spat on the pavement and turned in to the Rising Sun, which horrified and disgusted me, and completely cured my passion.

Rosie thought Blackpool the next best place to heaven. And if that was not quite my impression, nor David's, we had no complaints to make. That week did us all good, and was certainly the best possible thing that could have happened to David and me at that time.

When we got back to the moor no ghosts but gentle ones awaited us.

Luke gave me the puppy. It had turned lighter in colour and had one black ear and a black tip to its tail. It was quite small and was like no other dog I had ever seen. I asked Luke what breed he would call it, and he advised me to ask him another. He said it was the ugliest little devil he'd ever clapped eyes on, and Nell ought to be right down ashamed of herself. But to me, the puppy was perfect. I called him John.

He slept in a basket by my bed for the first hour of each night. After that, he yelped until I picked him up and cuddled him under the bedclothes. He made sleepy little noises that melted my heart, nuzzling my neck in the vain hope that I might turn out to be Nell, after all. As soon as I put him down in the morning he made little puddles all over the carpet, and chewed the pom-poms off my slippers, and made dashes at my bare feet, growling in a ridiculous soprano. I tied a blue ribbon round his neck, and he ate it, and David had to assist in its subsequent evacuation, with the pincers.

Rawlings grumbled about the carpet, and Joshua was always treading on him, and being startled into curses by his screams. And he had worms, and was sick on a blue-silk cushion. But Luke assured me that all these things would pass, and they did pass; and always, and whatever he did or did not do, John was perfect for me.

That last fortnight flew, and before I realised it I was waking up for the last time in my now familiar bedroom; walking for the last time to the Farm; looking for the last time at the church, at Mrs Shufflebotham's shop, the forge, Cracked Willy, and the sunlit top of Walker's Ridge.

Good-bye to Bolton House. To Cook and Rawlings and Joshua and the grey pony. Good-bye to the moor, its purple fading now to dun-brown, its distant hills raising dim hands in a last, solemn salutation. Good-bye to the Farm, to Luke and Mrs Abbey and Milly, the white duck, diligently treading water upside down; to Nell, who no longer cared what happened to her puppies, and the sweet, gentle Jerseys, knee-deep in grass.

Good-bye to David.

We stood together awkwardly, not looking at each other. David whistled shrilly. I tugged at my hot, unfamiliar stockings. Then he shoved out his hand and said: "Good-bye, Ruan"; and I stared at it in astonishment. And by the time I had tumbled to the idea of shaking it he had dropped it shyly, and mine was thrust out, stiff and unwanted. We both giggled self-consciously, and David fiddled with the mare's bit. Then Rosie bustled out, pulling on driving gloves. I was lifted into the gig, my trunk was pushed in, and the door slammed.

The mare danced disdainfully on the gravel and my heart suddenly felt as if it must break and break again.

"Good-bye, David! David, good-bye, good-bye! …"

"Bye, Tinribs."

He grinned at me miserably. Then he lifted the flap of his pocket, and I remembered that he still had my Little Man.

David—dear David. … Surely the world must end here and now; crack and split into a thousand thundering atoms, and the ultimate darkness fall.

§

We drove down into the town, making bright, jerky conversation. The long, smoky streets came up to meet me and twined their grimy fingers round my sun-steeped body. Then we were in St Mark's Road, and then we were outside the Manse, and I was jumping out unaided, and rushing in to greet a mother and father grown suddenly, inexpressibly dear; so dear that I wondered how I could possibly have stayed away from them so long. And Tanner came, smiling stiffly. And there was Sylvia, so tall that she seemed practically grown-up, and very much the elder sister. And John made a puddle on the dining-room carpet, and Mother—actually, Mother!—mopped it up herself, and only laughed and called him an ugly little pet.

So I came home; and the moor was nothing but a lovely dream, already half forgotten.

And that night Sylvia broke the news to me that our education was to begin in earnest; for next week we were to attend Dover Street Board School.

Chapter Seven

§

Dover Street School.

How shall I describe it?

The building was kept clean. The world was by now thoroughly awake to the importance of education for the masses; cleanliness was acknowledged to be not only the neighbour of godliness, but within nodding acquaintance of scholarship also.

So the school was kept clean. But it was that deadly species of cleanliness that smells so strongly of the fight with filth as to be almost indistinguishable from the filth itself. When I remember that first morning Sylvia and I walked into the school my nose still wrinkles in the same horrified disgust I felt then.

The rooms were large, the walls distempered in pale green. The windows were ornamented by bright pictures of flowers and birds, done by the teachers in soap, and then coloured. The desks were battered and very uncomfortable, and each accommodated six children, boys and girls together. There was a large central hall, where the Headmaster's desk stood, and where we gathered each morning for prayers, and off this hall the glass-partitioned classrooms opened, so that Mr Sturges could keep an eye on all that happened. There were four women teachers and two men, besides Mr Sturges, who taught Standard Seven himself.

Father took us that first day.

Sylvia wanted Mother to come, too, but she wouldn't. She gave us each a red apple and kissed us rather quickly and shut the front door. Dover Street was yet another rock on which my parents' marriage was splitting. Mother argued that no education at all was better than Dover Street. Father maintained that any education was better than none.

I suppose Father was right. But, right or wrong, the poor man had no option but to send us there. Education was compulsory, and a Nonconformist minister's salary—in those days, at least—did not cater for expensive schooling. Indeed, looking back, I often wonder at the way we lived in those days. Certainly the house was provided free, as was most of the furniture; but there was Tanner to keep, and we always had an abundance of good food, and our clothes, if few, were nice, and we had a fortnight's holiday each summer. Yet Mother must have had the poorest possible training for such a life, coming as she did from a home where the catering was left to a pack of servants and the bills paid, or left unpaid, by a master whose sole idea of hospitality was to fill the house with men and get them all drunk in the shortest possible time.

Father talked for a while with Mr Sturges, and then he patted our heads and went away, and Mr Sturges gave us over to Miss Patten, who was young and rather pretty in a fair, fluffy sort of way; and she, in turn, gave us over to a tall girl called Ada Morris, who wore steel-rimmed spectacles and a clean, patched frock, and whose hair was dragged back from her face and tied with a black bootlace.

Ada Morris was the cleverest girl in the school by a long chalk. She told us so herself, without delay, adding that she was going in for the Scholarship next year, and expected to get it, too, and that her aim in life was to become a teacher. She showed us where to hang our hats and coats, asked us our names and ages, and looked us over severely, as if she thought us very poor specimens indeed, and not at all likely to win the Scholarship.

"Always hang your things here, next to mine," she said. "Keep to this corner, and you'll be right enough. Some of the girls have got Things in their heads. I hope *you* haven't," she added sharply, with reference to my short hair.

"I haven't!" I gasped.

"What's your hair like that for, then?"

"Mother likes it this way."

Ada sniffed incredulously.

"Well, keep away from Vera West and Kitty Curtis. They've both got 'em. *And* fleas," she added severely.

We were lined up and marched into the hall, to the tune of *Weel may the Keel row*, played by Miss Patten on a bright yellow piano. We sang: *We plough the Fields and scatter*, and we gabbled the Lord's Prayer, and somebody pinched me from behind, so that I yelped "Amen—Oh!" And Mr Sturges banged on his desk with a ruler and said "Silence!" in a weary voice.

After that all the others went into the classrooms. Sylvia and I stood awkwardly in the empty hall, holding hands and wondering fearfully what was going to happen to us next.

Presently, a grey-haired teacher, whose name was Miss Arne, took Sylvia away to Standard Three, because she was nine now; and after another interval Miss Patten came out of Standard One for me.

I was put in the front row, between a fat little boy who snored when he breathed and a thin little girl who picked her nose with great deliberation, using a clean pocket-handkerchief only when this process was complete. I watched her with great interest. Then a sudden memory shook me.

"Are you Kitty Curtis?" I whispered.

"Naw."

"Are you Vera West?"

"Naw."

I heaved a sigh of relief.

The little girl continued to pick her nose.

"An' I'm not Queen Alexandra, neether," she volunteered. "Shall yer know me next time yer see me?"

I turned my gaze away from her, rebuked.

We had sums. We wove coloured raffia in and out of the holes in squares of canvas. We stood in our places and sang: "Doh, ray, me, fah, soh, lah, te, doh"; and then we bawled at each other the inquiry as to whether John Peel were an acquaintance or not, and implored Polly to Put the Kettle On, and we'd All Have Tea. We went out into the asphalt playground, and Sylvia came running to me and said wasn't it *awful?*—and she was going to ask Father to take us away immediately. And for once in our lives we were in complete agreement.

We went home at dinner-time fully expecting never to set eyes on

Dover Street school again. But we were doomed to disappointment. Father was adamant. Mother was silent, her lips pressed together in a hard line. So back we went for afternoon school; and I remember it was not quite so bad as the morning had been, because we had poetry, and the poem the class was learning was one well known to me: "I wandered lonely as a cloud that floats on high o'er vale and hill." I stood up and said it right through without a mistake, and Miss Patten praised me. But then we had sewing—and my pride suffered a sharp set-back.

All my life I have been an utter fool with a needle. At the age of seven I was guaranteed to turn any teacher of needlework into a raving lunatic in half an hour. Miss Patten taught us every subject except sewing, and for that we had Miss Foley, a fat, bad-tempered woman with a pointed red nose and bad feet.

Of my sewing lessons with Miss Foley I remember very little, save that both she and I were wrecks at the end of them, and that never, in the whole time I stayed at Dover Street, did I achieve any article that could possibly have been given a name.

At the end of the day the thin little girl addressed me voluntarily for the first time.

"Are yer likin'?" she inquired.

I replied passionately that I was not. The admission left her quite unmoved.

Next day Sylvia was put down and I was put up into Standard Two.

It happened that in Standard Two classroom there was a small bench only large enough for two. Sylvia and I were put in it together, and we had cause to be thankful.

I don't know how it happened that all the dirtiest children in the school were in Standard Two, but so it was. Vera West and Kitty Curtis were both in it. Nowadays, I understand, doctors and nurses are in constant attendance at all Council schools; scholars are weighed and measured regularly, eyes and teeth are overhauled, and heads examined. But in those days such amenities were unknown—and a fair proportion of the children at Dover Street came from the most deplorable homes. The teachers did what they could, but there was not much they could do, beyond separating, as far as possible, the sheep from the goats. And Mr Sturges, poor man, was altogether the wrong person for his job; the squarest of pegs in the roundest of holes. He had no authority whatever. The school was virtually run by Mr Gough, his second-in-command, grey-haired Miss Arne, and Ada Morris, who could quell insurrection in the Junior School with one glance from those formidable spectacles and a twitch of the bootlace that held her hair clamped in place. Had there been another free school within reasonable distance of the Manse we should certainly have been sent there.

St Mark's Road was a long, straggling thoroughfare, beginning in the heart of the town and finally petering out amongst the scrubby fields and scattered houses that constituted our "country walk." There were doctors and parsons living in St Mark's Road, and a few wealthy business men who still clung to their old-fashioned, smoke-grimed houses; but there were also foul little cottages, furtive alleys, and mean shops plying dubious trades. Dover Street cut at right angles through St Mark's Road, and was only ten minutes' walk from the Manse, so that we were allowed to make the journey alone—though never with Mother's consent. She would have sent Tanner with us, but Father put his foot down again; and again I have to record that he was right. Amongst that crowd of lusty young hooligans our peace was, at the best, precarious. To have been provided with a constant escort would have been fatal.

Even the fact that we were, to some extent, segregated from the rest of the class, in our two-seater desk, was the cause of much comment and a certain amount of wit at our expense. And this, in the beginning, was Sylvia's fault more than mine. Three months in David's company had done something to squash my snobbishness. Without either of us being aware of it, David had taught me that people were not either Ladies and Gentlemen or Common Folks, but just men and women. But Sylvia was very much Mother's daughter, and to be obliged to share a book, or play a game, or even sit in the same room with a child who scratched its head unceasingly and whose nose looked after itself was, to her, torture almost past bearing.

It was easier for me. I had grown used to the Staving children, many of whom were uncommonly dirty. My shorn head protected me, to some extent, from Things. I was far cleverer than Sylvia, and so enjoyed the day's work, with its problems and triumphs. Above all, I had my own secret world, into which I could shut myself when Dover Street became too ubiquitous. I could play with David on the moor, or sit again in Staving Church and let its peace fill my heart. I could run at Luke's heels, help Mrs Abbey with the jam, or drive with Rosie behind Sally's gleaming quarters. I might have lost my Little Man, but nobody could take away my memories.

One weapon she had that I had not—her beauty. And it was not long before she came to understand this, and to know how to use it to her advantage. Children love beauty and will respond to it when they will respond to nothing else. The two most popular girls in the school were the prettiest ones, Kitty Curtis and Phyllis Sharman; and very shortly there was a third—Sylvia.

Kitty Curtis was big and dark, heavily built for her age, with red cheeks and slow-moving, insolent eyes. She came from one of the mean shops in St Mark's Road; a newsagent's amongst other, less savoury things. She was not poor. She always had money to spend, sweets to give away, and her clothes were more expensive than ours; but she was terribly dirty. Her head was alive, and always there hung about her a peculiar smell, half fascinating, half repellent, that I have never been able to categorise. Sylvia loathed her. I loathed her, too, and yet she fascinated me. When she looked at me with her lazy dark eyes, and showed her white, even teeth in the queer way she had, with the tip of her tongue like a scarlet bud between them, my bones turned to water and my heart thumped. And well she knew it, too!

Phyllis Sharman was one of the few children who came from nice homes. She was a quiet, studious girl, with brown curls and very large grey eyes, and great strength of character. Her mother was a widow in very reduced circumstances and Phyllis was her only hope in life, and her only joy. Sylvia and Phyllis gravitated together inevitably, and they made a strong team. At first there was a certain amount of animosity in the playground, and cat-calls and horse-play in the streets, but Phyllis taught Sylvia the right way of dealing with this, and very soon it all died down, and the two were always in demand for "He," or whatever game was in fashion at the moment.

Not so myself. I hated all their games like poison. The great, heavy skipping rope, slapping the broken asphalt, catching me round the neck or by the heels as I leapt for my life in a jumbled crowd. Rounders, with my side screaming vengeance if I didn't try, and the ball hitting me a merciless whack if I did, and my lungs bursting. Hopscotch, at which I was never the slightest good. Whip-top, which usually ended by my legs being heartily slashed both by my own whip and others'.

But there was one game—I think they called it "French He," but I cannot be sure—which filled me with such real terror that I would do anything to escape it, even to lurking for the whole of playtime in the smelly lavatories at the bottom of the yard. One girl was chosen as "He"; the rest ran about screaming until one of them was caught, and then the two joined hands and ran together until a third had to join them, and so on—until everybody was running linked up, with the one set purpose of catching the last player left. There was something cruel in that game; something—probably accounted for by mass psychology—that made it less of a game than of an organised man-hunt. To see that long string of girls, with flying hair and legs, and wide, yelling mouths, bearing down upon me; to know that, dodge and leap and run as I might, they would get me, sooner or later, and I should be swung at the end of the cruel chain, was like a little death to me. They were fond of that game, at Dover Street.

So there we were, Sylvia and I: she, hating and despising nearly all the children, yet, because of her golden hair and neat, small features, accepted by them at her own valuation; and I, quite willing to be friendly, yet scorned and teased and often roughly treated. I know now that Dover Street was merely the world in little; but at the time I felt the injustice to be monstrous, and more and more I retreated into my own secret world.

I don't want to give the impression that I was unhappy all the time—or even most of the time—for that was not the case.

I loved learning for its own sake, and none of the lessons, except sewing, presented any real difficulties to me.

I had the world of books, which Father had opened when he gave me the run of his study. I read everything: fiction, history, travel, biography, even science. I did not understand one-tenth of it, but I read it. I lay on my stomach, poring over coloured maps. I devoured poetry. I laughed and cried over Dickens, and galloped about the Border with Scott. Once, seeking for pastures new, I dipped into a volume of sermons by some learned dean whose name I have forgotten. I forced myself to read them, became interested, and read right through the whole book in a week. For some time after this I made Sylvia's life a burden to her at nights by undertaking to explain the Trinity, and other mysteries. And she was so stupid, and I so exasperated, that I broke a china shepherdess over her head, for which she repaid me by biting my arm so deeply that I have the marks of her teeth to-day. After that, Mother decided that we were old enough now to sleep apart—and I was moved up to the tiny room next to Tanner's.

And I had John. Each day when I got back from school he was waiting for me at the window, a wriggling mass of joy, with ears going up and down, and tail wildly waving. Although he was naturally a one-man dog, a great deal of his faithfulness to me was Mother's doing. Nobody but I was allowed to feed him. He slept in a basket by my bed, and I was responsible for putting him out last thing at night. I had to wipe his paws when he came in, with a special cloth that hung on the scullery door. I had to exercise him regularly, and this added greatly to the joy of walking. He was a very obedient little dog, and good-natured to the point of imbecility, and he never had a day's real illness in his life.

And then there were my friends; for I did find friends, even at Dover Street. And a queer lot they were. Ada Morris, Vera West, and Moses Hallelujah Johnson.

This last-named was a boy of about eight, a full-blooded black kid of whose home life I never learned more than that he lived in the basement of a block of offices, of which his father was caretaker, that his mother went out washing, and that he had the incredible sum of half-a-crown a week for spending money. He was very clean, very strong, and very quick at his lessons. He arrived at the school about a month after my own entry, and in three days he had fought and won some dozen fights, had been caned twice, and had made me a proposal of marriage. And I am glad to remember that I accepted him without a moment's hesitation. We all called him Hally, and for his sake I have loved black people all my life.

Ada Morris was not so much a friend as a guardian and preceptor; one of the very few to whom my brains made more appeal than Sylvia's looks. She was to sit for the Scholarship examination the following spring and, having no doubts of the outcome, was by way of letting her mantle fall upon me. I had no objections whatever to becoming "the cleverest girl in the school." What I did object to was being made into "a good influence," and Ada had a hard struggle with me before she finally gave up this darling project.

Ada's father kept a greengrocery shop. Her mother was dead, and in the intervals of school, homework, and helping in the shop, Ada ran the house and catered for her father and three lumping grown-up brothers, who brought their money home from the factory each week and meekly handed it over to Ada. How she accomplished everything will always be a mystery to me. "Our Ada's a right champion!" her father was fond of saying. And certainly he and his sons looked fat and well-cared-for—and why Ada had to wear a bootlace for a hair-ribbon I shall never know.

Vera West was one of those girls with Things in their heads against whom Ada had warned us on our first day. And Things she certainly had; nevertheless, I no sooner spoke to Vera than I loved her. She was the kindest creature, packed full of common sense and as clever as a monkey. She came from a very poor home, packed with children. Her mother drank and her father had run away with "another lady" some months before I knew her. She was a brown little scrap, like a gipsy, with an impudent nose that wrinkled when she laughed—and she was always laughing—and bright, dark, squirrel's eyes.

I learned a lot from Vera. Some of it, no doubt, would have been better left unlearned, but a great deal was helpful. I learned the rudiments of tap-dancing, three swear words, how to make coconut-toffee, paper-boats, and tiny furniture with acorns and pins. I learned the gentle art of self-defence by kicking, and how to make a ha'penny into a penny by laying it on the tramlines. I learned to manage my laughter in class so that somebody else got the blame. I learned a choice song which began: "Can your mother ride a bike, in the park, in the dark, with her feet upon the handlebars?" And I learned the best method of catching and killing fleas.

This last was a lively and interesting lecture, during which she demonstrated her method, and actually caught one, and drowned it in the inkwell with suitable rites. And very useful information I found it; for, though I seemed to have no appeal for insects of any sort, Sylvia suffered terribly from them. If there was a flea in the vicinity, Sylvia got it. I used to search her clothing every night, so that Mother should be spared the ignominy of knowing it. I think we both realised that, while it was we who actually had to put up with Dover Street, Mother was the one who suffered most from our attendance there.

Mother never took any interest in our schooling. She asked no questions, made few comments. Bitterly she had fought against Dover Street, and she had lost, so there was no more to be said. But she was far less strict with us now; more tender and indulgent, as if she were trying to make up for it. She spent hours contriving new clothes for us. She often bought us sweets, and gave us pennies she could ill afford to spend on our way to school. She went for more walks with us, and even began to tell us stories of her own girlhood; of the horse Starlight, and the long, happy days in the saddle, with hounds streaming across the winter fields and a straggle of pink coats behind; of her dogs, Peg and Searcher; of the clothes she wore at the Hunt balls and the partners she danced with and the drives home through the cold dawnlight. We loved these tales of Mother's girlhood, and not until long afterwards did we know there had been another, less inviting aspect of the picture. She said nothing of her father's ungovernable tempers; of disgusting, even terrifying, episodes with his drunken friends. And she never told us how she came to meet Father.

What a strange meeting that must have been! Many and many a time I have tried to picture it. Sometimes I see Mother in hunting kit, mounted on Starlight. She gallops recklessly round a curve in a lane. Starlight swerves, nearly throwing her. Father appears from nowhere, a tall, handsome saint with quick, strong arms and a smile of surpassing sweetness. He stands calming the nervous beast, and they look into each other's eyes, and are lost. … And again, I see Father in the pulpit, arms outstretched above a sea of bowed heads; all bowed save one, who stares as if heart and soul were already gone from her lovely body. "The peace of God, which passeth all understanding, fill your hearts and minds. …" Their eyes meet across the bowed heads; and there is no peace for them now; never any more in this world. … More rarely, I see them meet in a crowded drawing-room. "Miss Mallinson, may I introduce the Reverend Everard Ashley?" "How do you do?" "How do you do?" This time their hands meet as well. The drawing-room fades, and they are alone together in a no-man's-land between their two worlds. He sees heaven in her face. She sees in his, peace and safety. …

But however I picture that first meeting, I see always their love flame up between them sudden and terrible and not to be denied. And I hope and believe that those first, lovely years they knew together were worth everything that came after.

Chapter Eight

§

"Let's go past the Riding School for a change, Mother."

Thus I, greatly daring.

"No," said Mother automatically.

"Oh, Mother, *please*! For John's sake. Then I can let him off the lead, and he does love it so."

"Well …"

So John accomplished what even Sylvia had never done, and round by the Riding School we went.

It was a raw, February day, with leafless branches stark against a leaden sky and the grass soggy with water. We walked quickly to keep warm. John rushed backwards and forwards, blowing violently down holes at imaginary rats, and racing up to tell me how nearly he had caught *that* one!

Mother looked lovely. She was dressed quietly in dark brown with some sort of fur round her neck and a little fur toque on her bright hair. The cold never made her nose red, as it did other people's. She glowed with health and her eyes were like stars beneath their ridiculous lashes.

Sylvia and I were dressed alike in blue coats and tam-o'-shanters, and woolly gloves and long brown leggings. We had a bag of chocolate drops, and we were very happy. It was Saturday, and there was no more school till Monday morning.

We walked past the last of the houses, up a steep and muddy lane, and across a field path. Behind us lay the town in its black hollow. The factory chimneys thrust up through the smoky mist like the masts of half-drowned ships.

We went through a gate into another lane, and before us stretched the paddock, where the learners trotted carefully round and round, and more advanced pupils jumped over hurdles and showed off generally for the benefit of proud parents, or anyone who happened to be passing.

We stopped to watch them. I put John on the lead, as a precautionary measure.

The Riding Master was sitting astride a huge chestnut, a lovely beast with a skin groomed to satin. He sat erect, yet easily, as if he and the horse were one.

"Keep the hands *down!*" he shouted. And I saw Mother glance up quickly, with a startled look on her face.

She stared at the Riding Master's back, half-turned towards us. It was a broad, heavy back, clad in a checked coat of black and white, and his cap was checked, too, set rakishly aslant black, smooth hair.

"Hands down, *please!*"

A giggling, frightened novice cantered past him.

"Don't saw at his mouth! Easy, now, easy! And for God's sake, *keep* your hands down!"

"It's too cold to stand," Mother said hurriedly. "Come along, Sylvia, Ruan."

But it was too late. The Riding Master had pulled his horse round to watch the hurdling. He looked across at Mother and came cantering up to the fence, and jumped off his horse with a pleased sort of laugh.

"Nell Mallinson!—by all that's holy!" he exclaimed.

"Captain Dalton!" Mother said primly. "This is a surprise! What are you doing in these parts?"

"Running this blasted show, for my sins," he said, pulling a wry face. "I dropped a packet at Sandown. Got this cheap, and I'm trying to make a go of it, but I don't know how long I can stick it. And you—how's the world using you, Nell? Why, how long is it—ten years? Didn't I hear you'd married some Bible-thumper or other?"

"I married the Reverend Everard Ashley, Captain Dalton," Mother said coldly. "And these are my daughters, Sylvia and Ruan. Say how do you do to the Captain, children."

"D'jerdo," I mumbled. But Sylvia held out her hand and showed her dimples and did the thing properly.

"Your daughters, eh? Funny to think of you with daughters, Nell. Sons, I'd have said, every time."

I wanted to tell him about Clem, but one glance at Mother's face forbade that.

"By Jove!" he said, grinning down at Sylvia, "you've got a grand little filly there, anyway! Can you sit a horse as well as your mother, young 'un?" He swung her up to the chestnut's back, and she sat up straight and laughed, as though she liked it, though I was pretty certain she was scared to death. Me, Captain Dalton ignored, to my great content. I had taken a violent dislike to him; to his hard blue eyes and shiny white teeth and black, black hair; to the strange inflexion of his voice and the way he looked at Mother.

"Do any huntin' now, Nell? I've got a grand bay I'd be proud to lend you any time."

"Don't be ridiculous, Fergus," Mother said, laughing a little, yet with a curious, eager voice. "I've just told you I'm a Nonconformist parson's wife. I go to sewing meetings and cut out red-flannel garments to be sent to darkest Africa. Hunt, indeed! ..." She stroked the soft, quivering nose of the chestnut. "I must get along home now, if you'll give me back my daughter." But she made no move to go. "Do you ever see Alaric, Fergus?"

"Very rarely, since the old man went. It's not the same, now, at Cobbetts. Frankly, your brother's got none of his father's vices—and none of his virtues, either. A pity he never married."

Mother made a soft little sound.

"Theo gave him up?"

He nodded, switching his gleaming leggings with the riding crop.

"There was some row or other. ... Have you lost touch altogether, Nell?"

"Altogether!" she answered in a hard voice.

"Pity, don't you think? Cobbetts would have made a good hide-out any time you got too sick of red flannel. Though I can't say it's done you much harm, if looks go for anything. You don't look a day over twenty, and that's a fact!"

"Ridiculous!" Mother said firmly. She put on her chapel face again. "Say good-bye, children. It's been so nice seeing you again, Captain Dalton. Good luck to your new venture and—good-bye."

"Au 'voir, Nelly." His cap was off. His hard blue eyes were laughing down into hers. "Good luck to the red flannel!"

We walked home rather quietly. Mother showed no inclination to talk about the Riding Master, except to say vaguely: "Oh, he's just someone I used to know before I married Father." But as we approached the Manse she said, in a funny voice: "Don't say anything about Captain Dalton to— to Tanner." And she added quickly: "Let's make toast for tea, shall we? And I'll read you a story afterwards, before you go to bed."

I don't know how I understood that it was not Tanner, but Father, whom Mother meant. But I did understand, and so did Sylvia, I think. Anyway, we never did mention him to either of them. Until we had to. …

It was lovely to lie on the rug before the fire, tired after the walk and stuffed with buttered toast, listening to Mother's voice. The story didn't matter much; it was the pattern the words made, weaving in and out of the flickering flames, and dropping like jewels, and rising like coloured bubbles, and darting like silver swords about the quiet room. The gas sang and popped in its little white incandescent towers. The Venetian blinds were down, fold upon fold against the dark February night. John snored and twitched in his dreams. The clock ticked contentedly. The head of the little mandarin on the mantelpiece nodded as some great dray-horse thundered down St Mark's Road. It was all safe and warm and happy. There was no Dover Street, no hard-faced Captain; nothing there that could hurt us, snugly together in the warm room, with Mother's voice going on and on.

$\mathcal{G}$

I had not forgotten little Clem. None of us ever spoke his name, but I often thought about him in bed at night, or on our walks. I don't think I grieved for him or ever consciously wanted him back. Thanks to Rosie, I saw him only as a happy baby, walking and talking, just like all the other babies; rolling about on the flowery floors of heaven and grabbing at the celestial sunbeams; a great favourite with God and all His angels. It seemed not so much that he had gone away, as that he had never really been here.

There was nothing to remind us of him. His toys were gone, and his high chair and his cot. The pram no longer blocked up the hall. And all the rooms were a different colour and the furniture had been moved about. Annie Briggs had gone, too; and now the house next door was occupied by an old lady and gentleman who smiled at us over the fence and gave us apples and sweets.

One night I woke in my little room at the top of the house. I lay wondering what could have waked me. There had been a noise of some sort; but it had been more than a noise; a feeling of something like fear coming in through my open door, making my heart hammer and my throat go dry.

The noise came again; quiet, yet harsh and desolate. I woke completely and sat upright, listening. The noise came from Tanner's room. The noise *was* Tanner—crying! But surely that was incredible; Tanner *couldn't* cry! Tanner, lying in her small, stuffy bedroom, crying her eyes out! …

My first impulse was to hide under the bedclothes. Then I knew that I could not do that. I slipped out of bed and padded across the cold, oilclothed landing to Tanner's door. A streak of light showed underneath. I turned the handle and pushed the door wide open. She did not hear me. She was kneeling on the floor with her black hair straggling about her shoulders, bony beneath the flannelette nightgown. Her face was hidden in the patchwork quilt. Her feet, long and thin, with glazed brown soles, stuck out behind her. One hand was flung outward over the bed. The other was holding a white woollen rabbit she herself had made for Clem.

I did not love Tanner, but I was used to her. She was part of the Manse, and I couldn't imagine life without her. She could not be left alone to cry, in the middle of the night, without anyone knowing or caring.

I went and knelt down beside her and stroked her arm rather awkwardly. "Don't cry. Please, Tanner, don't cry!"

"Miss Ruan! … What are you doing here, catching your death!"

Her voice reassured me. She was Tanner; old and cross and stupid, but *real*—real and familiar.

"Don't cry!" I repeated angrily. "Don't cry!"

"I've got the toothache. Something awful I've got it," she mumbled, trying to hide the rabbit.

I knew she was lying, and she knew that I knew.

"It'll be better in the morning." She stood up and lifted me as if I had been a baby, and carried me back to bed. I clung to her. She smelt funny. Not dirty, exactly, but funny and stuffy; what Sylvia called "poor person's smell." I hated the smell, yet I clung to her, glad to have her cross and real and familiar again.

Next day we avoided each other's eyes.

Sylvia and I were supposed to walk together going to and from school. At first we did so, but after a time it became the accepted thing to part as soon as we were out of sight of the Manse. Phyllis Sharman would be waiting for Sylvia at the end of the road, and they would link arms and put on exasperatingly grown-up voices and tell me to run along. I used to drag behind them, getting what comfort I could from kicking small stones or showers of puddle water after them. I wished very much that Hallelujah Johnson or Vera West went my way, but alas, they both lived in the opposite direction.

One day Kitty Curtis stepped out of the door of the newsagent's shop just as I passed, and she smiled at me and asked if I would like some sweets: if I went into the shop, her mother would give me some—anything I fancied.

I said no, thank you, quite politely. And Kitty laughed, with her red tongue showing between her teeth, and my heart went *thump-thump*, in the way it always did when Kitty laughed at me. She terrified and she fascinated me. She was dirty and elegant, coarse and beautiful, stupid and cunning and alluring. She was two years older than any child in her class, and she looked far more than that.

She fell in beside me and took my hand.

"It's a shame, the way they treat you, Ruan." Her voice was different from the other children's; not flat and slow, but soft, full of music, with a rising inflexion at the end of each sentence. She was not north country, but came from somewhere down south and had not been brought up in the town.

"They won't let you walk with them, will they?"

"I don't mind," I said gruffly, trying to wriggle my hand away. But Kitty held it fast.

"You *do* mind, Ruan. You mind awfully. You're very lonely without a friend, aren't you? I tell you what—I'll be your friend, shall I? We'll walk together and go to the Park on Saturdays and have lots of sweets. I can take what I want out of the shop. Won't that be lovely?" Her face came close to mine. Her hand gripped my fingers till I whimpered with pain and fright.

"No!" I gasped.

"Yes, it will. It'll be lovely. I think you're nice, Ruan. I think you're a dear little thing. Do you like me?"

"No!"

"Yes, you do! You like me ever so. You know you do."

"I don't! Let go my hand, please. *Please!*"

She laughed again, quite close to my face.

"I'll wait for you after school."

"No—no!"

"Yes—yes! … You can come home to tea at our house if you want. I've got some lovely things to show you. I've got a real silver bracelet a gentleman friend of my mother's gave me. P'raps I'll give it to you. Would you like a silver bracelet, Ruan?"

"No," I cried desperately.

Would we never reach the school?

"I've got some books with funny pictures of ladies and gentlemen in them. Awfully funny they are—you know!" She nudged me and giggled—I couldn't imagine why. "Look, I'll give you a penny all for yourself. Here—" She let go my hand for an instant—and I was off! Away across the road, under the feet of a dray-horse; down Dover Street, into the school yard. I heard her running after me, laughing.

I ran into school, threw my things on the peg, and crept to my desk. This was a forbidden thing to do before the bell rang, but I didn't care.

Hallelujah Johnson was filling the inkwells. He was monitor that week, and full of importance.

"Better git out afore there's trouble," he warned.

"I don't care. I don't care if they *kill* me, Hally. I'm frightened of Kitty Curtis."

Hally rolled his round eyes.

"What's that gurl been adoin' to yer?"

"Nothing." How could I explain to Hally my unreasonable dislike, my shrinking fear of Kitty and the horrible fascination she had for me?

"Nothin'—huh?"

"No. Nothing."

"What you cryin' for, then?"

"I'm not crying."

"What you frightened of, huh?"

"I don't know. ... She's going to wait for me after school, Hally. What shall I do? Oh, Hally, whatever shall I do?"

He stared at me in surprise.

"Go home with yer sister."

I shook my head. Sylvia and Phyllis might put up with me for that once, but there would be to-morrow and to-morrow and to-morrow. ...

Hally's black face split suddenly in a white, shining smile.

"I'll go home with yer—see?"

"Oh, Hally—would you? ... But you can't. You live so far away."

"I can, too. I can go down St Mark's Road and then go on the tram."

"But what about dinner-time, Hally? There wouldn't be time then."

"Yes, if I run fast. I go home with yer, an' I wait for yer, see? That Kitty Curtis, she can't do nothin' to yer while I'm around!"

Miss Davis came into the room.

"Haven't you finished those inkwells yet, Johnson? Ruan, what are you doing here?"

"A—a girl frightened me, Miss Davis."

"Which girl?"

But I knew better than that, and so did she.

She looked at me kindly, a little perplexed. Miss Davis was always kind to me. She did what she could to make things easier, but there was so little she could do. She called me up to her desk and took my hand.

"You mustn't take any notice if the others tease you, Ruan. They don't mean to be cruel really. Try not to mind, and they'll soon give it up. Crying's no good, you know. Or hiding. They won't help. You've got to face up to things in this life, Ruan. As soon as you face up to things, they stop frightening you. Remember that." She smoothed my hair back and looked searchingly into my face.

"I wonder if I ought to speak to your mother about you. Would you like me to come and see her? Perhaps something might be arranged. ..."

"Oh, no! No, thank you, Miss Davis," I cried. I couldn't bear the idea of Mother being made more unhappy. "I'm all right. Truly I am! I was silly to be frightened. Please don't speak to Mother about me. Please don't!"

"Very well," Miss Davis said, with a little sigh. "Go back to your place now, Ruan. And I think, perhaps, next week you might be monitor; then you can come in here as soon as you reach school."

Hally waited for me outside the gates. Kitty Curtis waited, too; but when she saw me going off with Hally she only laughed and showed her tongue, and went home with somebody else.

For a whole fortnight, four times a day, I was escorted by Hallelujah; and a very gentle knight he proved himself. It cost him twopence a day in tram fares, but he never mentioned the fact. It was a good thing he had such a colossal allowance. I have often wondered how his parents could afford to give him so much. To Sylvia and me half-a-crown was a fortune, but Hally thought nothing of it. He spent quite a lot of it on me. He was fond of buying me jelly babies and bars of chocolate cream, and those flat, round sweets with leading questions printed on them, such as: "Do you love me?" "When will you be mine?" "How's your father?" And once he brought me a little bunch of cold, wet violets in a circle of glossy leaves.

Hally was a gentleman, from his woolly head to his well-blacked boots; and I can only hope he felt himself repaid by the rather patronising affection I gave him.

One evening—a sweet April evening it was—we were walking homewards down St Mark's Road together, when I heard the cuckoo for the first time that year. I stood still to make sure. Yes—there it was again! The unreal quality of its cry made time stand still, and St Mark's Road was nothing but a noisy dream.

"Hally! Did you hear it? The cuckoo!"

He grinned and listened.

"I never heard nothin'."

"Yes, yes! *Listen*! There—did you hear it that time? Oh, you are stupid, Hally! There it is again. Spring's coming. Spring's coming." I threw my arms round his neck and made him dance, half choking him in the process. But he responded nobly, and we danced and staggered about the pavement, shouting: "Spring's coming! Spring's coming!" at the top of our voices.

Suddenly we were wrenched apart. A large, gloved hand grasped Hally by the back of his collar. Another held me by the arm. I looked up, breathless and annoyed, into the face of Captain Dalton.

"Good lord!" said the Captain, in half-amused disgust. "Aren't you one of the Ashley kids? Yes, I thought so. What the devil d'you think you're doing with your arms round this black boy? 'Pon me soul, I don't know what your mother will say! Here, you—cut along. And don't interfere with this young lady again, d'you hear me?"

"Yessir," said Hally stoically.

His dark eyes looked mournfully into mine; but there was nothing either of us could do. With more dignity than you can imagine, he turned on his heel and walked away, never looking back.

"He is my friend!" I fumed.

The Captain laughed disagreeably.

"Your friend, eh? Well, you can't be friends with him, my good kid."

"Why not?"

"Well—can't you see why? ... They're different from us. It simply is not done, I assure you. I'll come along home with you. I was on my way to call on your mother. Good job I happened to recognise that hair of yours! Where's the other one—the one with curls?"

"I don't know."

He walked beside me, whistling softly between his teeth.

"I suppose your father's out most evenings, isn't he? Meetings and so forth?" he said presently.

"Yes."

"Which evenings is he in?"

"I don't know."

"Oh, come on," he coaxed. "You tell me, and I'll say nothing about your pal. Is that a deal?"

"No."

"H'm. Pleasant little party, aren't you? Well, please yourself. Oh, this is the house, is it? Lead on, Macduff!"

Tanner's eyes nearly popped out of her head when she saw Captain Dalton; and when he actually remembered her name her pleasure was pathetic.

"Oh, Captain Dalton, sir! What a surprise! Oh, the Mistress *will* be pleased. Come in, sir, do!"

I had never heard Tanner so enthusiastic.

The Captain came in, grinning; gave his cap and gloves to Tanner and stalked into the dining-room. He bowed over Mother's hand in a fashion strange to me.

"Fergus! Why—why have you come here?" Mother's face was pink and her voice sounded cross; but her eyes shone.

"Need you ask?" he replied confidently. "And if any excuse were needed, there's this young shaver here, that I've just rescued from the grip of a black boy." He grinned maliciously at me. "A chance for some of your red flannel, Nell!"

Mother glanced at me in dawning horror. "You're joking, Fergus!"

"Not I!" he laughed. "They'd got their arms round each other's necks, and they were capering all over St Mark's Road, I do assure you, Nell. A fast piece, this daughter of yours!"

"Ruan, is this true? I can't believe it."

"He's my friend," I said in a small voice. I knew it wasn't going to be any good. "He's a nice boy, Mother. He looks after me."

"Ruan! He's black!" If she had said "leper" her voice could not have been more shocked. "And with your arms round him. Oh, I can't believe it!"

"It was the spring," I explained miserably.

The Captain shouted with laughter, and even Mother bit her lip and turned away. They didn't understand. They wouldn't ever understand.

"It's that wretched school," Mother said, in a low, troubled voice.

"What school?" asked the Captain.

"Dover Street Board School!" Mother said clearly and very bitterly. "Everard cannot afford anything better. And in any case he considers it is good for their souls!"

"My poor Nelly!" he said quietly.

Mother sent me into the kitchen to have my tea. Sylvia came downstairs, looking clean and fresh. She always washed and changed her school frock when she got home. Her hair shone like the sun in the dim hall.

"*Now* what have you been doing?" she whispered.

"Mind your own business!" I returned.

Her smug expression outraged me. I stuck out my foot with a quick movement Vera had taught me, and had the satisfaction of seeing her make a headlong entrance into the room.

"Born for trouble!" Tanner commented, eyeing me gloomily. But she gave me a good tea, and allowed me to iron my dolls' clothes afterwards.

It would be all right when Father came in, I thought. Only last Sunday Father had preached a sermon all about black people and missionaries and the universal love of God. He had stated, quite clearly and distinctly, that everyone was equal in God's eyes, no matter what colour the skin happened to be. Perhaps Mother had forgotten that. Or perhaps, I thought virtuously, she hadn't been listening like I had. ...

I heard Father come in at last. The dining-room door opened and voices became loud and unnaturally polite. I heard Sylvia's attractive giggle and the Captain's loud, deep laugh.

Soon afterwards the Captain departed and Tanner went in to clear away.

"You're wanted," she told me bleakly, dumping the loaded tray on the kitchen table. "Now be'ave, and don't give no back answers."

"What is this I hear, Ruan?" Father said sternly. Sylvia was crying in an armchair. Mother was fidgeting with the music-stand. I looked at Father boldly.

"It's about a black boy, Father. His name's Moses Hallelujah Johnson. He looks after me, because a big girl frightened me one day. He's a very nice boy, and quite clean and polite. I think you'd like him."

"You and Sylvia," Father went on coldly, "were told to walk together, always. I understand you have both disobeyed me in that."

I looked at Sylvia, but she went on crying into a lace-edged hanky. Her hair fell over the arm of the chair in a gold shower. I looked back at Father silently.

"What did this big girl do to you, Ruan?"

"Nothing," I said dully.

"Nothing? ... But you have just told me she frightened you!"

"She did. She—she wanted to be my friend, and she asked me to tea and—and she tried to give me a penny and some sweets."

Father looked at me gravely.

"It would appear, Ruan, that you are not telling me the truth. This girl, apparently, was trying to be kind, to be friendly. Why should that frighten you? You must tell the truth, Ruan. I will not tolerate these lies."

"It is the truth!" I cried desperately. But I had no hope that he would understand. How could I explain my loathing, my certain fear of Kitty's offer of friendship, when I did not understand it myself? I made one last effort, aiming a barb at Mother.

"She's dirty!"

"So you chose a black boy, instead!" Mother flashed back furiously. "And you made yourself conspicuous dancing with him in the road. ... It's no use, Everard, they must be taken away from that school!"

"And sent where?" Father said wearily.

Mother shrugged and went upstairs to turn on the bath for me. I was to be thoroughly disinfected once again. Sylvia bolted after her.

"Father," I said, as the door closed after them, "you said black people were just as good as white ones, didn't you? Last Sunday—you remember."

He passed his hand across his forehead in a gesture of discouragement.

"In the eyes of God they are equal, child. In the eyes of men they are—different."

"But it doesn't matter what anybody thinks, so long as God's satisfied, does it?" I said eagerly.

"No," said Father's eyes. But his mouth said: "Yes, it does. It's difficult to explain. You are too young. Some day you will understand, and in the meantime you must trust my judgment and obey me. This friendship with the boy must stop. You must always walk with Sylvia. Not necessarily alone together; no doubt you each have your friends; but certainly together. Is that quite understood?"

"Yes, Father."

I turned away, bitterly disappointed. Father had failed me. He had failed the black people he pretended to love. In a way, he had failed God. I never completely trusted him again.

Chapter Nine

One Saturday morning in May I was helping Tanner in the kitchen. Mother and Sylvia were out shopping. The bell rang, and Tanner looked at her floury hands and told me to answer it for once.

I opened the door—and there stood David!

"Hullo, Tinribs!" he said.

"Hullo!"

"I've come to take you out. I met your mother on my way up, and she said it was all right. So go and get your funny face washed—it needs it!—and hurry up. I'll count two hundred and then I shall go without you."

In a great flurry I was washed and dressed and threatened and encouraged by Tanner, and presently David and I walked down St Mark's Road to the tram, rather shy with each other but very happy. Lilac bloomed in front gardens. Its scent was strong in the sunshine; the very smell of happiness. I hopped first on one foot, then on the other.

David had grown much taller. He was nearly fourteen, and was going to Lowton next term.

We rode right into the town and got out by the clock tower. I showed David the big Central School where I should go if I were clever enough to win a scholarship. I wished David were going there, too, instead of Lowton, but David said: "God forbid!" which surprised me very much.

He took me into the cake shop we had visited with Rosie. He behaved just like a grown-up, frowning at the menu card, giving orders to the waitress, and stooping a little when he spoke to me—as if I were extremely small and rather deaf and not very bright. He ordered black coffee for himself and a glass of milk for me, but I kicked his shins sharply under the table, and soon put a stop to that nonsense. I hated the coffee when it came, but had it been hemlock I would have drunk every drop rather than admit it. David didn't like his very much, either. We both ate quantities of cakes to take away the taste.

"There's half an hour to spare," he said, as we came out into the street again. "What shall we do?"

"Let's look at the shops."

"Right. Come on, I'll buy you something," he threw out grandly. "What would you like?"

"A book, please."

"Good lord, would you really!"

We gazed in all the bookshops, and eventually I chose a volume of Tennyson's poems. I was dismayed at the price, but David forked out three-and-sixpence quite cheerfully. Money meant very little to David; it was just something to get rid of as pleasantly as possible.

I hugged the book to my chest. It smelt new and exciting. I kept peeping inside, and each time I caught a glimpse of some new beauty.

> "Borne on a black horse, like a thunder-cloud
> Whose skirts are loosened by the breaking storm. ..."

And again:

> "Lo! In the middle of the wood,
> The folded leaf is wooed from out the bud
> With winds upon the branch. ..."

And crossing Market Square, with David tugging at my arm, and drivers shouting at me, and horses dodging to right and left, I read "The Eagle" right through.

> "He clasps the crag with crooked hands;
> Close to the sun in lonely lands,
> Ring'd with the azure world he stands.
> The wrinkled sea beneath him crawls;

He watches from his mountain walls,
And like a thunderbolt he falls."

"Oh, David!" I breathed.

"Oh lord!" David groaned, as he dragged me on to the pavement. "I'll never buy you a book again! What you want is a strait-jacket!"

"Are we going home now?" I asked.

"No. We're meeting Uncle Josh at the factory, and you're sleeping at the House to-night. Rosie'll take you down with her to-morrow. It's all right. I fixed it up with your mother."

Oh, joy! Oh, unbelievable, exquisite pain of joy! David and the moor and my lovely book—all together!

We went down some black streets to the factory. And there was the gig, with Sally jingling an impatient head, and Luke standing by with his slow, sweet smile, to lift me in. And there was Uncle Josh coming out of the big gates with his rolling, swaggering walk (I'm a self-made man, and proud of it!), and a workman touching his greasy cap, and the clatter of the machinery coming out after him like greedy tentacles that grudged his going.

Joshua struck an attitude of tremendous surprise.

"Nay, if it isn't our Ruan agen! Seems to me, tha's nivver off t'doorstep, lass! Nay, hitch up, and let a chap get a seat in 'is own trap, will t'a?"

I knew this was his way of saying he was pleased to see me, and I responded warmly.

We went clattering out of the town and up the moor road. And Rosie was waiting by the gate with her red hair blowing, and there were all the things I liked best for dinner.

And outside the windows the moor was waiting for me.

$\mathcal{S}$

I told David about Hallelujah Johnson and Kitty Curtis and he agreed that it was a fearful shame. He said there were black fellows at some of the public schools and nobody thought anything of it; and what difference did it make whether they were princes or caretakers' sons? They were black, just the same. Which comforted me a little, though it presented no solution to my problem.

I think I must have realised, in fact, that David understood nothing at all of the life I led at Dover Street. How could he, indeed? Those few months had taught me more about life and the world than he had any idea of, even though he was five years my senior. Still, it was immensely comforting to tell him everything; to be called "Poor little Tinribs," and to hear his disgusted "Good *lord!*" when I described "French He," the smelly lavatories, the Things in the head.

The moor put us right with each other. Our stiff shyness dropped away. David stopped treating me like a weak-minded two-year-old, and I shed my gruff defences. We rushed about in the bright May sunshine, yelling our pleasure at being together again.

Mrs Abbey was glad to see me, but she looked ill and tired, and she laughed hardly at all. Milly pretended she had forgotten me and hurried away towards the pond; but after a while she consented to be fed and stroked, and she chuntered with her flat, yellow beak, as if saying thoughtfully: "Don't tell me! Don't tell me! It will come back to me in a minute. ..."

Nell remembered me. I told her all about John, and promised to bring him up to see her one day. David said she was going to have some more puppies, and I said how did he know? And he showed me her swollen belly, and explained, briefly and sensibly, how she would rid herself of her burden when the time came. I was glad to have reliable information on this subject, which had greatly occupied my mind. I had asked several people about it, but they had only told me to hush, or babbled unconvincing stories about storks, or doctors' black-bags. Even Mother had put on her chapel face; though by all accounts nobody had been over-squeamish in her own home when she was a girl. Poor Mother. She wanted to be a good Nonconformist minister's wife, but the harder she tried the more she failed. But I could not have loved her more had she been perfect. ...

We had tea with Luke and Mrs Abbey.

Rosie walked down from the House with our coats, for the evening had turned cold. As soon as she came into the kitchen, Luke got up, muttering something about the cows, and went quickly out. I saw Mrs Abbey glance at Rosie; but Rosie was looking down at her hands with a funny stiff sort of smile.

David and I went to get eggs for Mother.

"What's the matter with Rosie and Luke?" I asked him.

"I don't know," he said, wrinkling his forehead. "Perhaps they're sweet on each other, or something daft like that."

I remembered a hot August noon, an enchanted orchard, and Rosie's hair flaming over Luke's brown arm.

"Perhaps they've quarrelled."

"Um. Here's a big brown one. Do for your breakfast. Catch!"

I caught.

"I wish they hadn't quarrelled, David."

"What? ... Oh, well, they'll get over it, I expect. Anyway, it's no use worrying about what other people do. You can't stop them, and you only make yourself miserable into the bargain."

The day was over all too quickly.

We had boiled chicken and mashed potatoes and spinach for supper, with little red jellies topped with whipped cream afterwards.

Joshua rattled his money and gave me two shillings "to put in t'plate to-morrer"—this with a wink that plainly told me to do nothing of the sort—and I went to bed under the pink eiderdown, and cried a little because Dover Street had come a day nearer.

Then I suddenly remembered the book David had given me. I scrambled out of bed and found it; and, by the feeble flicker of the night-light Rosie always gave me, I read and read and read. ... And there was no Dover Street, no Manse, no House or Farm; nothing in all the world but me and my lovely words.

And David, of course. Whatever happened, and though the whole world were lost, there would always be David. ... David.

*

It was queer to drive up to chapel in the gig. I felt important and rather superior, especially as our arrival synchronised with Mother's and Sylvia's. Sylvia was inclined to sulk because she hadn't been asked too. Rosie seemed conscious of this, for she smiled kindly at Sylvia, and said next time she must come with me, and we'd all make a right do of it.

Sylvia smiled and thanked her prettily, making us all feel selfish brutes. But all the time Father was praying I was praying, too.

"Oh, Lord, don't let Sylvia come, too! Oh, Lord, my God, I'll do anything if only you'll stop Sylvia coming up to my moor. I'll give her anything she wants of mine—well, almost anything (remembering my book)—and I'll walk home with Kitty Curtis and take all the blame for it. And I'll do her sums for her. And she can sit next to the wall. And I'll give her my Saturday penny. Only don't let her come to the moor, Lord, please. Not ever, please! For Christ's sake, amen."

Crimson with self-consciousness, I put my two shillings in the plate, as an added inducement to the Almighty. I saw Mother look at it sharply, and Sylvia's eyes popped, and I felt vaguely noble and self-sacrificing.

I do not know if my poor little jitterings were heard by Almighty God or not. Who knows anything about prayer? But perhaps He did hear. Perhaps that small and rather dingy little offering that floated up from the ugly chapel through the bright May sky was taken by Him and cleansed of its imperfections, so that He could see what it was really all about. ... I like to think so.

Anyway, Sylvia never did go to the moor with me. Once or twice Rosie remembered to ask her, but something always happened to prevent her going.

And if I did not keep all my fervent promises, at least I never forgot to thank Him, kneeling beside the pink eiderdown, with one eye on the moor stretching beyond the window, and one ear listening for David's whistle, signifying that he had beaten me into bed.

The moor and David were mine.

$\mathscr{S}$

So, all that summer, Dover Street was made endurable by week-ends on the moor. I was there when the calf was born that cost Jenny, the prettiest of the Jerseys, her life. I was there to help with the hay. I was there when Luke collected the swarm of bees that hung in a dim, shapeless mass from the may-tree. I was there at Whitsuntide and August Bank holiday. I was there for harvest. I was there when David went off to Lowton, unfamiliar in long trousers, and cap, and with more luggage than I should have thought necessary for twenty boys.

And this time it was he who climbed into the gig, and I who stood forlornly kicking the gravel, and pretending, with no success whatever, that the whole business left me cold.

He lifted the flap of his pocket, and I knew that my Little Man was going to Lowton too.

Uncle Josh was taking David as far as London, handing him over to a master there.

Rosie and I wandered indoors; and Rosie said she must get on with some needlework; and I got a book and sat with it open on my knee.

"I'm glad he's got a nice day," Rosie said presently. And I said "Yes."

"I hope he'll not change into his thin vests too soon. … And he's that careless about wet socks. Still, I should think they'd keep an eye on him, wouldn't you, luv?"

"Yes."

A long silence.

"It'll be no time before he's back, luv."

"Yes—no!"

And at last Rosie said: "Nay!"—and threw down her sewing and put her arms round me; and we cried together very long and comfortably; and afterwards we laughed and sniffed and ate buttered toast and went down to the Farm for cream.

Soon after that Sylvia began her riding lessons.

Mother had a tough job persuading Father to let Sylvia ride. He argued, reasonably enough, that he could not afford it; that it was an accomplishment little likely to be of use to her in after life, and that if she were to pass the examination for the Central School she had her work cut out without other distractions.

To all these arguments Mother had answers.

Captain Dalton was willing to teach Sylvia for nothing. Some of the horses needed more exercise, and a charming little girl like Sylvia was good advertisement for him. As for the scholarship—surely she would be more likely to pass if she were healthy and fit: hadn't he noticed she had been looking pale lately? And for the rest, did he honestly think it fair that Ruan should ride and not Sylvia?

I was considerably astonished by this last argument. It had never occurred to me that tumbling on and off the grey pony could possibly be referred to as riding!

But apparently it had weight with Father, for he gave a reluctant consent; and somehow Mother contrived a charming little outfit of breeches, coat, and jockey cap in which Sylvia looked positively ravishing.

I was not in the least envious. I was more than content to stand with John by the fence and watch her trotting round and round. I was glad it was not me! There was no love lost between the Captain and me. He always laughed a good deal when he saw me, and never ceased a cruel, stupid teasing that I tried, but failed, to ignore. "How's the little black boy?" he would roar. Or: "Heard the cuckoo lately, eh? Felt the call of the spring again?" And he would give me a playful swipe across the bottom with his crop—a trifle harder than mere joviality allowed.

There was nothing in it, I suppose. I am not suggesting that Captain Fergus Dalton was a brute. No doubt he thought me a silly and tiresome little girl, which I probably was quite often. We simply disliked each other and made no bones about it; and Mother learned to laugh and say: "Now, you two!"

Mother was very happy in those days. At least, she laughed a great deal and took even more pains over her appearance, and I often heard her singing as she went about the house. *Annie Laurie*, she would sing, and *On the Banks of Allan Water*. And another song I loved dearly: *Over the Sea to Skye*.

Sylvia went up to the Riding School every Saturday afternoon, and

Mother went with her. I generally went, too, but sometimes I was left with Tanner; and it was on one of these occasions that I once again came up against Kitty Curtis.

Since Hally had taken me under his protection she had left me alone. And here let me explain that his protection had never been withdrawn from me. In the fatalistic way of all black people, he had taken his buffeting from the Captain, and had kept the letter of the law in that he never again walked home *with* me. But for a whole year he was my faithful shadow, whether six yards in front or a dozen yards behind—and Kitty never managed to get within whispering distance of me. In time, she tired of the whole thing, and attached herself to a tall, pale girl with weak eyes, who was vastly flattered by her attentions.

Tanner gave me tuppence and told me to run up the road for some sewing cotton.

It was a brown-and-gold, spicy day in October. I had not run many steps before a sense of adventure gripped me. This was the kind of day I loved. A tang in the air: soot and horses and chrysanthemums. A nip in the breeze that dispelled the last of summer's languor. The sort of day that would be quite perfect up on the moor, and which, even in St Mark's Road, was lovely and exciting. The sort of day when anything might happen.

The first thing that happened was Kitty Curtis.

She was standing outside her shop door, idly swinging a skipping rope and looking very bored. When she saw me her eyes brightened and she smiled, but she made no effort to molest me. She looked extraordinarily attractive, and the old spell stirred in my blood.

"Hullo," I mumbled; and against my will I halted.

"Hullo, Ruan!"

She had such a pretty voice.

Hadn't I been awfully silly and babyish over Kitty? Hadn't I, in fact, behaved quite abominably to her? Father had thought so, hadn't he?

"Where are you off to?"

"To buy some sewing cotton."

"Can I come?"

"If you like."

We walked up to the shop and bought the cotton. I did not want to go straight home again. Tanner wasn't in a good mood, and the day was enticing. At any corner, at any moment, something might happen! …

"You are pretty, Ruan," Kitty said.

I knew I wasn't, but I had no objection to being told I was, especially as Kitty kept at a respectful distance, and didn't put her tongue between her teeth. I decided that I had been a complete fool over Kitty. She was a very nice girl indeed, and much maligned.

We walked along in complete amity for some time, gazing in shop-windows bright with chrysanthemums, bronze and gold and pink; with coloured wools, toys, and sweets, luscious cakes and tarts, billowing rolls of flowered dress materials and exciting-looking books. From the chemist's door issued the sharp, clean odours of iodine and scented soap. The bakery made our mouths water. All colours and smells were heightened and intensified in the clear air. Kitty walked demurely by my side, swinging her skipping rope and humming under her breath.

A gay little wind ran at us round street corners and horses' hoofs gleamed in the sunshine.

"Would you like to see a dead man?" Kitty said softly.

It had come. The thing I had been waiting for. Now I had got to deal with it. …

The sun was still shining, but now it had a different quality; it was hard and terrible; a bright sheet pulled tautly over a world where dead men lay in stiff silence, waiting for me. …

"Yes," I said.

I heard myself saying it. I knew that really I meant "no." That I ought to say "no." But that I was quite incapable of saying anything but "yes."

"I know where there is one."

I gulped. This was awful. Exciting and alluring and utterly horrible.

"I'll take you if you like."

I nodded. My throat ached and a little hammer was beating in my head.

"Come on."

Kitty turned out of St Mark's Road into a narrow street called

Newbold Street. I had never been down it before. The houses were all stuck together in a long, grey, dreary line with no gaps in between; only dark little passages, every fourth house, leading to back premises. The pavements were littered with torn paper and bits of straw. There were women standing at most of the doors, their arms wrapped in coarse aprons and their hair in steel curlers. They shouted and laughed to each other, or bawled at children playing in the roadway.

Outside one of the houses black stuff had been spread over the road. I knew what that was for. It was to deaden the sound of traffic, because of someone who was ill. I had often seen it before, but now it had a terrible, personal significance.

Kitty looked at me and said: "Come on!"

She slipped into one of the dark entries. I followed, but with leaden feet. The little hammer was beating on my brain. It was beating out a tune. *Dai*-sy, *Dai*-sy, *give* me your *an*swer, *do. Pom*-pom, *pom*-pom, *pom*-pom-pom *pom*, pom-*pom*. ... We had sung it on the coach, going to Morecambe with Rosie. *Ro*-sie, *Ro*-sie ... no, it was *Dai*-sy. ...

"*Come* on!" Kitty whispered.

We were in a back-yard full of dustbins and rubbish. There was a very dirty lavatory, in the open door of which a little girl stood, struggling with a pair of dingy pink flannelette drawers. Her nose was running.

"Hullo, Cissy," Kitty said kindly. "It's her father," she hissed at me. She helped the child with her drawers and plumped her on the seat of the lavatory. "Poor little thing!" she said.

Kitty opened a door and went in, and I felt myself going in after her. The door led straight into a room. It was poorly furnished but fairly clean. The remains of a meal cluttered the table and there was a strong smell of vinegar. A woman sat by the fire, sewing something black. She looked up and smiled vaguely at us, and I saw that her eyes were reddened and her nose shiny. She did not seem in the least surprised at our intrusion.

In an angle of the room, and at the top of two wooden steps, another door stood slightly open. It led into an inner room, from which issued a subdued murmur of voices and the horrid, snuffling sound of somebody crying.

"Don't take on, missus," one of the voices said. "'E's out of it all now, reight enough."

"Aye, that's reight, poor chap!" another voice agreed.

Snuffle, snuffle. ...

The smell of vinegar was overpowering.

The woman stitched away at the black stuff and coughed hollowly.

"Come on!" Kitty commanded.

She went on tiptoe up the two steps.

Dai-sy, *Dai*-sy, *pom*-pom-pom, *pom*, pom-*pom*. ...

Stitch. Stitch. Stitch. Snuffle. Snuffle. ...

"Aye, poor soul, 'e's reight enough where 'e is! You don't want to call 'im back."

Snuffle. Stitch. Smell of vinegar.

"*Come on!*"

I took two steps forward. Another. Another.

Kitty pushed at the door. It was opening. It was opening. ... I saw the brass rail of a bed, the edge of a sheet, taut and white. I felt deathly sick.

Three enormous women stood by the brass rail. They were all staring at something. Kitty stood by them and stared too.

I put one foot on the bottom step.

And suddenly a coal fell in the grate behind me, with a loud, sharp crash.

The hammer crashed on my head, so that it hurt, and the tune went out of it. The shackles fell from my feet.

I turned and rushed across the room and out of the door into the yard. Oh, the blessed air! I stumbled through the dark entry into the street, and I ran and ran, dodging round corners, charging through the traffic of busy roads, until my legs had no more strength and my lungs laboured for breath.

Leaning against some railings, I closed my eyes until I felt better. When I opened them I knew I was lost. This was a part of the town that was strange to me. I trailed along, too relieved to be rid of Kitty and her dead man to care where I went.

Melton Street. Morland Street. Ladyship Lane. ... I had heard of that before, surely! Kingsley Road. Pennistone Street.

Rows of shops, some of them already lighting up, though the sun was scarcely gone. A grocer's. A tailor's, whose waxen dummies made me shudder and quicken my steps. A toy-shop. A greengrocer's, bright with chrysanthemums and polished piles of fruit.

And suddenly I knew where I had heard of Ladyship Lane before. Ada Morris lived there. Ada, and her greengrocer's shop and her fat brothers and her bootlace. ... I turned and ran back to Ladyship Lane. A little boy directed me to Morris's.

Ada was serving in the shop. She shot me a sharp glance, but she didn't speak until she had finished with her customer. I stood drinking in the sight of Ada as if she had been a celestial vision. She was cleaner and tighter and more earnest than ever. She had passed the Scholarship with flying colours and had been attending the Central School for a year. The bootlace had given place to a narrow black ribbon, but the steel-rimmed spectacles and the severe voice were there, and the rough, capable hands. I knew I should be safe with Ada.

The very smell of Ada's shop was reassuring. Damp wood and cabbage and apples and earthy potatoes; real, alive things. I stood and sniffed it all up gratefully. A yellow canary darted about in its cage, sharpening its beak and giving vent to sudden shrill cascades of song.

Presently Ada could attend to me.

"Ruan Ashley! What on earth are you doing so far off your home! Does your ma know?"

I poured the whole tale into Ada's ears, and she listened in grim silence. When I had finished she pushed open the glass-panelled door behind the counter, and shouted for Walter to come and mind the shop, she was going out. There ensued a short altercation, in which the invisible Walter informed the world that he was mending his bike; but Ada dealt quickly and competently with that argument, and emerged from the back premises in a round, navy-blue hat bearing the Central School badge, and followed by a stout, peevish brother who repeatedly implored heaven to inform him *when* he was going to get his bike mended, if their Ada was always going gadding off. A piece of rhetoric which Ada very properly ignored.

She gave me a huge, glossy apple and a William pear in a paper bag.

"I'd give you your tea, only that your ma'll be off her head worriting about you. Eat them up now, and never mind Mister Manners. Folks 'ave seen a kid chewing a pear before now, I reckon."

We boarded a tram that took us to the bottom of St Mark's Road, and then we got off and walked up the road together, Ada holding my hand, to my great indignation. At the gate there fell an awkward pause. I didn't want Ada to come in and tell Mother all about it. There would be such a frightful fuss, and nobody would understand. Nobody. I decided to take a high hand.

"Well, thank you very much, Ada, for coming along with me," I remarked, with an attempt at cheerful nonchalance. "It's been such company. And the pear was *delicious*. Good-bye."

I was through the gate and it was shut between us. Her bleak look smote at my heart; but it couldn't be helped. I knew Ada would have loved to come inside; to see my home and my people, and be grown-up about me with Mother; but I had enough troubles before me without worrying about Ada's.

I rang the bell and then rattled the letter-box, as I always did. John whined joyfully and blew under the door, but nobody came. I rang again. I rattled. I called through the letter-box and John set up a shrill accompaniment.

At last I heard Tanner come hurrying from the kitchen. She opened the door blinking and yawning. And with a rush of relief I knew that she had been asleep.

"Well, you've taken your time, I must say!" she grumbled.

"How do you know?" I challenged. "You've been having forty winks."

"That's one thing I never do," said Tanner. "Wipe your feet. Your Mother's not in yet. I can't think what's keeping her. Did you get fifty cotton? That's right."

So nobody ever knew about that day's doings, except Ada; though I nearly gave myself away a few days later, when Father said casually:

"There are several cases of typhoid about—two in Newbold Street, I believe. I hope we're not going to have an epidemic. The children had better gargle night and morning."

Nobody obeyed him more heartily than I!

David wrote me three letters in his first fortnight at Lowton.

The first stated that Lowton was a very fine old school. That the weather was fine for the time of year. And that he was quite happy (and then a squiggle, part of a private code, meaning that the foregoing statement was a thumping lie).

The second told me that Lowton was a fine old school. That the weather was rotten. And that there was a boy called Stebbing who could play footer like an angel. An ill-advised simile, I felt.

The next was an enthusiastic account of a football match in which, one might have deduced, nobody had taken part except Stebbing.

After that, there was a gap of some weeks. Then an inky epistle informed me that Thomson's had whacked Beale's into a cocked hat (which conveyed nothing whatever to me; the public school House system being as yet a mystery). That Stebbing and he had celebrated and been gated for a week in consequence. That Stebbing's people were probably going to India. That Stebbing had a punch like an elephant. That Stebbing was exactly three months older than David and a good half-inch taller. And that he had told Stebbing about me, and Stebbing had said I sounded all right.

I never recall an item of news that left me more unmoved.

I wrote to David, too, but not often. It was difficult—almost impossible—to make David understand about Dover Street, and there was little beyond Dover Street in my life. Nothing that I could explain in a letter, anyway. Nothing that I could explain to myself.

But there was *Something*.

Something that reached out to Father, shut in his study; to Tanner, shut in her kitchen; to Mother, in spite of all her laughing and her *Annie Laurie* and *Over the Sea to Skye*. And it reached out to Sylvia and me, too, when we came home from school; a dark, intangible presence; inimical. ... I felt it even in chapel.

I see a little picture, sharply clear, of Mother and Sylvia and me going home after the morning service. It is very cold. The streets have a bleached, drawn look. Very few people stand at the doors, but the smell of cabbage is as strong as ever. Mother walks quickly, humming a tune under her breath, and Sylvia and I run to keep up with her.

"Why don't we walk home with Mrs Galloway and Mrs Bowers now, Mother?"

"Must I always walk with them?"

"You always did before."

"Before what?" sharply.

I do not know before what. I just look silly, and Mother gives an impatient little laugh and walks faster than ever.

Before *Something*. That's all I know. But I do not remark on it again.

That picture fades, and another takes its place. A picture so astonishing that even now, after all these years, my pulse quickens to look on it.

I am driving in the gig with Rosie. It is a cold, brilliant day, a week before Christmas, and we have been for a jaunt in the town. I am full of toasted scones and tinned apricots and cream and cakes, and I hold on my knee an immense box of chocolates and a book about Russia, in which country I am deeply interested at the moment; it has lovely coloured plates and it is my Christmas present from Rosie, who would much rather have given me a doll. I am very happy. Christmas is near. David is coming home. I have my book and the chocolates and a satisfactory fullness in my stomach. I am moved to suggest that we drive round by the Riding School and give Mother and Sylvia a lift home.

Rosie agrees, and takes the opportunity of reminding me that half the chocolates are for Sylvia, as well as the doll in the blue box.

We tie Sally to the railings and walk up the lane on the far side of the paddock. Sylvia is jumping her pony over a low hurdle. She waves her crop to us and begins to show off, and I don't blame her; if

I looked like Sylvia looks on a horse I know very well I should show off, too.

"Ee!" Rosie exclaims, "she's a right little champion, isn't she!" And I feel proud of Sylvia—and hug my book still closer.

"That's Captain Dalton, up there at the top of the paddock," I inform Rosie. "The one talking to the man on the brown horse."

"Is it, luv? ... Ee, I believe yon's a woman, not a man!"

"Not with *breeches* on!" I object, scandalised.

"Aye, she has, the hussy! I've seen one or two going about lately, brazen as brass."

We are both properly shocked. Riding breeches on children are daring enough, but on grown-up women they are an outrage.

The bold creature turns her horse and gallops down the field. She rides superbly. She puts her horse at the highest fence. They rise in the air, strong and full of grace; a perfect picture, etched for a lovely instant on the clear December sky.

They come to earth and gallop round the field. In another moment they will be passing us. But suddenly the rider has seen us. She pulls at the rein, and Rosie gives a little gasp of dismay, and I gasp, too, for I know now that the rider is Mother. ...

She wears fawn breeches and coat and shining top-boots, and a high, white stock, and her hair is hidden under a soft, green felt hat. She looks strange, but very, very beautiful; and if Mother does it, it cannot be shocking. I feel suddenly angry with Rosie, who is still gasping and muttering "Ee—well, I never!" in a silly, helpless sort of way.

Mother dismounts and comes towards us, smiling. Her colour is high, but she holds her head gallantly.

"What a good thing I didn't see you before I took that fence!" she cries lightly. "It's years since I did this sort of thing, and I'm terribly rusty. Have you come to fetch us? How kind ! If you can wait just five minutes while I get out of these borrowed things. ... Come, Sylvia, we are going home with Rosie and Ruan. Hurry up, now!"

Not a word of explanation or apology. No hint of embarrassment.

I am so proud of Mother, and so fearful for her, I could cry. ...

And down the years I still salute her courage.

For she *was* brave. Nobody who has not lived in that dour, Nonconformist, north-country town, and in those times, has any idea how brave she was.

Father stayed in that night, and we all sat together in the warm, lighted room. I was absorbed in my Russian book. Sylvia undressed and dressed her doll. Mother fiddled with some embroidery and Father read.

"I gave Rosie Day the shock of her life this afternoon," Mother said suddenly.

I didn't look up, but I stopped reading, because of the quiver in her voice.

"How was that?" Father asked.

"Well, you see, Captain Dalton wanted me to try out a new mare he's just bought. And Rosie came on the scene while I was doing it. Her eyes popped out like organ-stops."

"But you had no riding-habit?"

"Oh, I borrowed some things. There are always plenty lying about."

There was a short silence. Then Father said quietly:

"I'd rather you didn't ride, Helena. We can't afford such luxuries."

"Fergus doesn't want payment. I was doing him a favour, as it happens."

"I don't care to be under any further obligation to Captain Dalton."

"Obligation! I tell you I was doing him a favour. And we're old friends, anyway!"

"That may be. In any case, it's hardly suitable."

Mother laid down her embroidery. Her mouth was thin.

"What is wrong about riding a horse, Everard?"

"I did not say wrong. I said unsuitable. I am glad it was only Rosie who saw you, and not Mrs Galloway, or any of the others."

"Do you imagine I care tuppence what an old gossip like Mrs Galloway thinks?" Mother said scornfully.

"She'd have had a fit!" Sylvia giggled.

"Go to your room," Father told her sternly.

Sylvia went out with an aggrieved expression. I sat tight. Nobody had told me to go, and I wanted to see this out.

Father leaned back wearily in his chair and passed his hand over his thick, white hair.

"Whether you care what Mrs Galloway thinks or not, Helena, is beside the point. You are the wife of a Nonconformist minister. We cannot always please ourselves what we do. We must avoid even the appearance of evil."

"Evil! ... Really, Everard!"

"To Mrs Galloway, for instance, it would probably appear evil."

"That old witch!" Mother cried angrily. "She has always hated me. They all hate me. Do you think I don't know it? ... And I hate them! Yes, I do! It's no use keeping up appearances any longer, Everard. I'm a rotten wife for a parson. I shall never, never get used to their niggling ways and their narrow outlook. Never in this world!"

"Be quiet, Helena. You don't know what you are saying."

"I do know. I do know. I'm saying I'm a rotten parson's wife; the wrong wife for you, Everard. We ought never to have married. I've tried and tried, and I'm sick to death of trying. I tell you I'm sick of it all! I can't go on. I never have any fun, any life. ... I hate your chapel and your religion. It's mean and narrow. It's ugly—ugly! ..."

I slipped out of the room, unnoticed. I was shaking from head to foot. Up in my dark little room I tore off my clothes and crawled, unwashed, into bed, and lay there, shivering and terrified.

That Father and Mother should speak like that to each other! ... I had not believed it possible. The solid foundations of my world were shaken. Mother had not looked like Mother at all, but like some rather frightening stranger. Father's voice had been like ice.

The Something I had sensed for so long had us all in its deadly grip. And now I became aware that it was connected in some vague way with Captain Dalton.

In the morning there was a letter from David.

Stebbing's people were definitely going to India, and Stebbing was coming to the House for Christmas. And wasn't it jolly?

Very jolly.

So jolly that I cried for three days, until Mother said I was reading too much, and took my Russian book away.

I had been looking forward so much to this Christmas. The last one had been quiet and rather dreary, still over-shadowed by Clem's death. The thought of presents and gay shop-windows and voices singing carols in the dark streets; of being away from Dover Street for a whole fortnight, and of seeing David again, had seemed almost too lovely to be borne.

And now it was spoilt. Utterly spoilt!

Everywhere was darkness and misery.

Three days before Christmas, Rosie came in the gig and asked if she could take me to the station to meet David, and up to the House to stay until Christmas Eve.

Mother agreed listlessly. I was listless, too. I didn't care to share David with Stebbing. But everybody took it for granted I was delighted, and I had to go. I didn't even want to see David; he would be certain to have changed.

The weather had turned warm and muggy. Roads were greasy. The pavements were thronged with shoppers sweating under their bright burdens. It didn't feel a bit like Christmas. The station was a black sea of people and rattling trucks and mail vans, unloading gigantic piles of parcels and bags of letters. We sat in the gig, because Sally was too nervous to be left. We heard the train come in, and presently a spate of passengers poured out of the exits.

"There he is!" Rosie shouted, and waved her whip.

David waved back, grinning widely. He turned to the boy beside him, pointing us out. A porter followed them with their trunks on a trolly. Fancy being able to travel alone and command porters, I thought enviously; and when I saw David nonchalantly tip him I was filled with awe.

"Hullo, Aunt Rosie. Hullo, Tinribs. This is Stebbing. Get in, old man. Good lord, it's grand to be back. How's everything, Aunt Rosie?" He

- 116 -

pulled my hair. "Still the same scrubby old nut! ... Go on, old man, you sit in front. I'll squash in with Tinribs at the back."

He grinned happily at me, and lifted the flap of his pocket.

And suddenly it was all right. Stebbing or no Stebbing, it was all right. David was the same as ever, and would be the same, world without end. I felt Christmassy and excited and very happy.

We sat close together, not saying much. David whistled between his teeth. Rosie laughed loudly and asked a lot of questions, which Stebbing answered with great politeness in a grown-up manner. I looked at this paragon out of the corner of my eye.

He was tall and red-faced and heavily built. His hair was very dark—as dark as mine—and very smoothly brushed. His clothes were tidy, too, and he wore them with more of an air than David. His voice was beginning to break. It rumbled in the bass and then shot up in a silly squeak. He wore thick brown kid gloves, which he ostentatiously removed before shaking hands, and then replaced with much smoothing and tugging. The process took him about ten minutes. Altogether, he was much too grown-up for my liking. When we got to the House he handed me out of the gig with the same courtesy he accorded to Rosie, and very uncomfortable it made me. David had always given me a sharp push in the back and yelled: "Go on, fathead, jump!" I much preferred David's way.

But Stebbing was a very polite boy, no doubt of that.

We had all the things David liked best for dinner: beef-steak pudding and mashed potatoes and brussel sprouts, and apple-pie drowned in cream. And then David took Stebbing upstairs to unpack, and I followed them and sat on Stebbing's bed, which embarrassed him so much that he could do nothing but stand about, smoothing his hair and clearing his throat. So David unpacked for him, by the simple method of tipping his trunk upside down and putting the contents into the drawers armful by armful. There seemed to be an awful lot of clothes.

"Come on," I urged. "Let's get out before it's dark."

"Yes, come on!" said David cheerfully.

"Ur—um ..." Stebbing was muttering.

"Don't you *want* to come out?" I asked him.

"Oh, yes, rather! Yes, it'll be awfully jolly!" he said hastily. His face was redder than ever. "Er—er—" He was making faces at David and trying not to let me see.

Light dawned suddenly.

"He wants to go to the lavatory," I said impatiently.

"Oh, sorry, old man. Why on earth couldn't you say so!" David went out, whistling, and Stebbing plunged after him, scarlet to the ears.

What a silly boy, I thought disdainfully. I hoped to goodness we weren't going to have much of *that* nonsense, or we should never get far from the House.

There was none of the town's mugginess up on the moor. It was clear and cold, all that a December day should be. We went to the Farm and showed everything to Stebbing. He took off his gloves to Mrs Abbey, and again to Mr Lord, whom we met in the lane. "Why not stuff 'em in your pocket?" David said impatiently. Neither he nor I wore any gloves. Our hands were red and cold, but at least they were free. But Stebbing stuck to his gloves with ferocity.

I suggested playing Arctic explorers, and after a rather sheepish glance at Stebbing, David agreed. We let Stebbing be the Leader, because of being a guest. He wasn't much good at it, though he tried hard, even to the point of removing his precious gloves and hauling a sledge with appropriate cries. But when David suddenly shouted: "My god! Polar bears! Every man for himself!"—and I screamed shrilly, visualising vast numbers of white, shuffling shapes advancing with outstretched paws, he only grinned and started an argument with David as to whether polar bears hugged you to death or not. It was disappointing, and David felt it as much as I did. Suddenly there didn't seem much point in fooling about on the moor. Our feet were very wet. We wondered if it were tea-time, and began to make for the House. And then Stebbing discovered he had lost his gloves, and we all had to go back and scratch about among the sodden heather until we found them. He put them on with an air of relief, as if they had been armour.

"You mustn't judge him by to-day," David told me privately. "He's quite different at school, honestly. He's really an awfully good chap. Got a punch like an elephant, and plays right wing for Thomson's already. Which," he added solemnly, "is pretty good, you must admit!"

I was ready to believe that Stebbing could kick and punch, but these were not traits that endeared him to me. I had to go home on Christmas Eve, and I might not see David again before Easter. I wished it were not wicked to pray that Stebbing might be smitten with some disease; nothing dangerous, of course; just something that would keep him safely out of my way for the next few hours.

I put it to God in a shuffling, apologetic way, as I knelt with my head in the pink eiderdown that night.

It was not a little startling, therefore, to be waked by David next morning with the news that Stebbing felt funny and had spots.

"Where?" I demanded, instantly alert.

"On his chest. You come and look."

Stebbing eyed my advance with extreme hostility, and hoarsely invited me to hop it, which I ignored. His face was redder than ever. He flatly refused to show me his spots, and also to drink anything David might make up for him in his surgery.

"I shall be all right," he kept saying. "Go away, I shall be all right."

But he had to let Rosie look at his spots. And Rosie had the doctor there in no time, and he said the spots were German measles. We were quite sorry for Stebbing—until it was revealed that I should have to spend at least a fortnight at the House, in case I had it too.

David and I both had it, but very lightly. In no time, it seemed, we were out on the moor again, tearing about on the grey pony, strong and lusty as ever. Not so poor Stebbing, who developed minor complications which kept him in bed for a full fortnight, and in his room for a further week.

I was so glad to be rid of Stebbing that I got quite fond of him, and spent many of the hours I might have spent with David, curled up on the foot of his bed, reading aloud. To my great astonishment I found he liked poetry.

The enterprising firm that had undertaken the complete furnishing of

Joshua's home had not forgotten the claims of culture, and behind locked glass doors stood rows of richly bound books, their pages often still uncut, and so little loved that they shrieked when you opened them. I wormed the key out of Rosie, and searched until I found a magnificent green-and-gold Tennyson.

I tried Stebbing with the "Idylls of the King"—and he simply ate them. He liked "Maud" too (which surprised and gratified me), and most of the short poems. He liked, as I did, the lines written to "rare, pale Margaret," to "faintly smiling Adeline," and "airy, fairy Lilian, flitting fairy Lilian." And he adored "The Eagle."

David sometimes came in and sat by the fire, whittling a stick, listening. He didn't care for poetry, but he admitted it wasn't quite so putrid when you heard it read aloud; it was having to plough through it alone that got you down. Darling David.

One day—I had just finished reading "Madeline"—Stebbing said gruffly:

"There ought to be a poem about 'Ruan.'"

"Do you think it's a nice name?"

"It's all right," he conceded grudgingly, face aflame.

"Why don't you write one, then?" I suggested idly.

After a pregnant pause he blurted out:

"I have."

"Oh! … Oh, Stebbing, let me see it. Do let me see it!"

"I tore it up," he growled. "But I can remember it," he added, as my face fell.

"Go on. Go on!"

There was an awful silence. The bedclothes heaved as Stebbing laboured with his reluctance and his pride. Then finally he brought forth in a shrill soprano, with baritone *obbligato*:

> "Ruan! Thy name is like the purple night,
> Aglow with stars that shine both pale and bright."

At this point David came in and demanded to know what we were gabbing about; and before Stebbing could prevent me I had told him, repeating with passionate pride the two lines that seemed to me, in all honesty, the equal of anything Tennyson ever wrote.

"Good lord!" David ejaculated, staring at Stebbing in deep disgust.

"Cheese it!" Stebbing glowered.

"I'll make a poem up about you," David promised me in a sinister voice. He began:

"There was a young lady named Ruan," and there stuck, muttering under his breath, "buan, cuan, duan. ..."

"Whose heart was of gold, and a true 'un," Stebbing offered. I followed with: "Who wanted a beard, so she grew 'un," which was very well received. "Who took codliver oil in a spoo-an!" David shouted.

Nobody could think of anything else, and Stebbing flatly refused to divulge the rest of his poem, so we left him to his measles and went out together.

It was a bright and blowy day. White clouds raced over Walker's Ridge, and cottage smoke was scattered in all directions. The dun heather bent before the wind with a sound like the sea. I wanted to shout and run, but David was in an awkward mood. He showed off, chucking stones incredible distances, vaulting a five-barred gate, and pretending he didn't hear when I spoke.

"Good lord!—*Stebbing!*" he burst out at last. "Ruan, thy name is like the purple night!' ... Good *lord!*"

I said warmly that it was a very good poem, so far as it went. But David just kept on muttering "Good *lord*," and "*Stebbing*, of all people!"

"D'you know what I think?" he pronounced at length. "I think Stebbing's sweet on you!"

"How d'you mean, *sweet?*" I wanted to know.

"Well—you know—sweet on you," he explained.

"Oh!"

"Are you sweet on him?" he asked suspiciously.

"I don't know."

"Dash it!" he exploded. "You must know if you're sweet on him or not. Don't be such an utter ass!"

"How can I know, if I've never been sweet on anybody?" I wailed.

"Oh, aren't you a daft little Tinribs!" And suddenly David began to laugh. And the sun came out, and we raced about the moor and shouted and sang; the world was a lovely place again, and we forgot Stebbing.

As we were going home we heard the sound of horses' hoofs—cupper-*lup*, cupper-*lup*, cupper-*lup* ... away behind us on the moor road.

"Look!" David cried, swinging round. "Two of them. They're having a race. Stand well back."

Cupper-*lup*, cupper-*lup*, cupper-*lup*. ...

The two horses were going all out, neck and neck, the riders leaning forward, raised in their stirrups.

My heart suddenly leapt with fear and pride and joy. Fawn coat and breeches. Glossy brown boots. Gold hair whipping out from under the small hat. ... Mother. Riding so beautifully, so recklessly.

They flashed by us with creaking leather and laughing breath. They didn't notice us crammed back against the stone wall.

"Golly!" David said admiringly. "I say, wasn't that like your mother?"

"It was Mother," I said, choking with pride.

"Golly! Who was the other one?"

"It was Captain Dalton. He's somebody Mother used to know before she was married."

"Golly!"

We walked along in silence.

(What is wrong about riding a horse, Everard? I said unsuitable. I don't care to be under any further obligation. We must avoid even the appearance of evil. Do you think I care what that old witch thinks! They all hate me. I'm a rotten parson's wife. I can't go on. I can't go on. ...)

Oh, Mother, Mother! Don't go riding away from me, right out of sight! Don't leave me with my ears straining after the sound of your horse's hoofs and my eyes straining over the darkening moor, and my heart beating so strangely, so painfully. ... Cupper-lup, cupper-lup, cupper-lup. ... Come back, darling, beautiful Mother. Mother! ...

"What's up, Tinribs? Cold?"

"I want to go home," I said. "David, I want to go home. To-night!"

I don't know what David told Rosie; I do know that she took me home as soon as tea was over, and asked me no questions.

I said good-bye to Stebbing, and he clutched the bedclothes and went the colour of a beetroot and asked me in a hoarse whisper to call him Harry. Which request I refused with proper indignation.

Chapter Eleven

§

I never told Mother I had seen her riding on the moor. I told nobody.

I was astonished and rather resentful to find the Manse going on, to all appearances, exactly as before. Nobody seemed particularly surprised or gratified to see me again. Nobody, it would seem, had missed me much or needed me now. Tanner tutted over the state of my stockings and Mother ruffled my short hair absentmindedly and said: "Back again, chicken?" Sylvia was so engrossed in a game she was playing with Phyllis Sharman, who had been to tea, that she barely lifted her head at my entrance.

Far, far too soon, Dover Street started again.

And here, indeed, were changes.

I was put up into Standard Four. Sylvia, though eighteen months my senior, remained in Standard Three. Father went to see Mr Sturges about this, for he didn't want the pace forced too much for me.

"It isn't a question of forcing the pace, my dear sir," Mr Sturges assured him, with his weary smile. "We can't hold her back. That's where it is, we can't hold her back."

But there were other changes. Moses Hallelujah Johnson was no longer there. He had gone with his parents back to America, whence they had come, and I saw him no more. I was very sorry about this; not only for the loss of his protection, but because I really missed his honest, friendly grin flashing across the room to me; and also because I had never, I felt, adequately expressed my sorrow at the Captain's treatment of him. I never think of him now without experiencing a sharp wave of shame and indignation at the memory of that incident.

Another change—and this time a most welcome one—was the sudden disappearance of Kitty Curtis. And it was very sudden indeed. One day she was there, smiling her deadly smile at me across the hall, and the next she was gone, and gone for ever. Nobody appeared to know anything definite about Kitty, though I made extensive inquiries. Somebody said she had gone to live with her grandmother in London. Somebody else thought she had merely moved to another part of the town. There were whisperings I was not allowed to hear, and giggling suggestions I did not understand. But what I did understand, most joyfully and with a sense of grateful release, was that Kitty had gone, and gone for good.

There was nobody else I was really afraid of. Dover Street was used to us and our "swanky" ways and speech, and no longer pointed its opinion of us with well-aimed stones, whips, and skipping ropes. Sylvia was revered for her beauty. I was respected for my brains; and also—thanks to Vera's tuition—for a certain hefty kick which I used without hesitation or scruple.

Miss Arne was the teacher of Standard Four, and an excellent teacher she was, too. A strict disciplinarian, but patient and understanding and filled with enthusiasm for her work. Long afterwards, I was told that she and Mr Gould had been engaged for years, and the reason they could not marry was that Mr Gould had two sisters with tuberculosis in a sanitorium, which drained his resources to the last drop. Of this commonplace tragedy, naturally, I was unaware, and I often wondered why Miss Arne's face was so often sad, and why she sometimes went off into a sort of trance, staring out of the window with her eyes blank and her grey head set at a weary angle.

I did not look forward to Standard Five with any enthusiasm. Miss Foley taught that standard, and my deplorable efforts at needlework had thoroughly embittered that poor lady against me.

Just before my tenth birthday, however, up I went—but not, happily for me, into her care. Miss Foley was transferred to a school in the Midlands, nearer to her own home. A new teacher came and was given Standard Four, and Miss Arne went to Standard Five with me; to my great satisfaction, and also, I think, to hers, for we had grown fond of each other.

That dark Something that was hidden in the Manse was still there. Darker, more definite than ever before. So dark that I cried myself to sleep many and many a night, feeling its hateful presence crouched outside my door. So definite, that Sylvia and I began to speak of it furtively, only half comprehending; and Tanner, too, could no longer keep silence.

"Your mother's late," she would mumble, anxiously watching the clock. "I hope nothing's happened."

"What could happen?" Sylvia said scornfully, one evening when we were waiting tea for her. "Mother's a splendid horsewoman. And Diana's as quiet as a lamb, anyway; I could ride her myself."

"You don't need to go telling me what your mother's like on a horse, Miss Sylvia. I saw her riding long before you was born, or even thought of." She pressed her thin lips convulsively. "There's more dangerous beasts than horses in this world."

"What do you mean, Tanner," I asked, frightened.

"I don't mean nothing," she answered sharply.

"Well, don't fuss so," Sylvia snapped. "I know one thing—if Mother doesn't come soon, I'm going to have my tea. I'm absolutely famished."

"You'll do no such thing!"

"I shall! I'm going to start now."

"Put that bread-and-butter down, miss! I'll let your father know how you go on, see if I don't!"

And then Father was standing in the doorway, wanting to know what all this was about, and where was Mother, and why were we starting tea without her?

We had to start without her in the end, because time was getting on, and Father had to go to a meeting.

I remember that tea-time so clearly.

It had been a pale, bright day, very warm for March, and Tanner had only just lit the dining-room fire. The gas was not lit, nor the Venetian blinds down, and the daylight made the flames look weak and uncomforting. There was black-currant jam, which I hated, and ginger-cake, which

Sylvia hated, and there was water-cress, which we both hated, but were obliged to eat because of the iron it contained. No comfort there.

Father was quiet and stern. I looked at his face and noticed how pale he was, and how deep the lines that ran from nose to mouth, and scored his broad forehead. Sylvia wanted to pour out, but he told her to sit in her usual place, and he poured out himself, slowly and very carefully. I don't know why, but it always makes my heart ache a little to see a man pouring out tea.

We spoke scarcely at all. Father asked us a few questions about school and we answered him politely and, on the whole, truthfully, but he wasn't attending, and we knew it. We were all making a pretence of everything while we listened for Mother. We could hear Tanner fiddling about in the hall, every now and then opening the door to peer out into the dusk-filling street, and quietly shutting it again. The dining-room was depressing; the spring sunlight gone and no winter cosiness to take its place.

Suddenly we heard the clatter of horses' hoofs in St Mark's Road. They stopped outside our house. Sylvia and I looked at each other, wide-eyed with apprehension. Surely, *surely* Mother hadn't ridden right up to the door after all Father had said! Suppose Mrs Galloway had seen her! (We must avoid even the appearance of evil.) Oh, dear! *What* was going to happen now! ...

We heard Mother's laugh, and a man's laugh—Captain Dalton's!— loud and hard in reply. Hoofs clattered and grew fainter. The front door opened and shut. Tanner's voice, speaking quickly and quietly. Mother's voice: "Oh, don't *fuss!*"

And then the dining-room door opened and there she stood, breathless and beautiful, and looking less like a Nonconformist parson's wife than you can possibly imagine. Fawn coat and breeches. Polished brown boots. Gold hair springing from under the rakish soft hat. Cheeks flushed and breath uneven. Eyes bright and hard, like lovely stones. There she stood, tapping her riding crop against her boots, glancing with a faint, derisive smile at the thin, stern man who was her husband, and the two solemn, pop-eyed little girls who were her daughters, and the ugly, shabby room that was her prison.

"Well?" said Mother, in a queer voice.

None of us answered her. Sylvia looked down at her plate. I stared at Father.

And Father got up from the table and, without a word, went from the room, and out of the house. The door slammed with an awful finality.

Tanner brought in a pot of fresh tea.

"Oh, Miss Nell!" she murmured, sniffing a little.

"I'm late," Mother said, in a hard, bright voice. "I'm very late, aren't I, chickens? Did you wonder where on earth I had got to?" She poured out some tea and drank feverishly. "Well, why are we all looking so solemn? Is it such a terrible thing to be late for tea? Is that another of the wicked things one must never do? Is it?" She laughed, and her laughter was dreadful to me.

Sylvia began to recover. She joined feebly in Mother's laughter.

"Tanner thought something had happened. Wasn't she an old silly?"

"Yes, wasn't she?"

"Mother, Tanner said there were more dangerous beasts than horses in this world. What did she mean?"

Mother set down her cup with a sharp click. She stood up abruptly and walked over to the fire, pushing at the coals with the toe of her boot, so that the flames shot up brightly.

"How should I know what Tanner meant! You'd better ask her. Or, better still, ask your father!" Her voice was harsh and angry. She stared at Sylvia and me almost as if she hated us. Then she stalked out of the room and ran upstairs. We heard the bath water running, and the opening and shutting of drawers. And we heard Mother singing *Over the Sea to Skye*.

"It's all right," Sylvia whispered, looking at me in a frightened way. "It's all right, Ruan, isn't it?"

"I don't know," I replied miserably.

We helped Tanner to clear away, and I threw John's ball for him in the hall, but there was no fun in it. That dark Something had suddenly become more real; an almost tangible presence whose ugly shadow lay over everything.

Mother came downstairs at last, and both Sylvia and I gasped with relief and delight. Here was no hard-eyed stranger, booted and breeched, but *Mother*, dressed in an old green gown we loved, with soft lace at neck and wrists and little crystal buttons down the front. She smelt of lavender soap, and she had put on her topaz brooch and the bracelet with the tiny silver trinkets. Her hair lay in a smooth gold knot in her neck.

"Come along, darlings," she cried gaily, "let's have a real cosy evening, just like we used to have. Put some more coal on the fire, Ruan. Sylvia, get out the spillikins and the halma. And look, I've brought some chocolates for you."

Oh, the joy—the unutterable rapture of that evening with Mother! She was so sweet, so gay, so tender and loving. We played all the games we knew. We ate chocolates and asked riddles and laughed immoderately. We sang all together, with Mother's long, white fingers flashing over the keys, and Sylvia's voice high and sweet, and mine faint but pursuing—*Annie Laurie, Over the Sea to Skye, The Last Rose of Summer, Caller Herrin', Comin' thro' the Rye*. And the gas popping, and John protesting comically from the hearthrug, and the little mandarin nodding away on the mantelpiece. The smell of lavender. The rising wind rattling at the windows. The fire's warm glow. Tanner smiling as she brought in the hot milk and a plate of delicious little sandwiches on a paper doily. Mother's long, tender kiss and the lingering pressure of her arms as she bade us good-night. And that glimpse of her, standing in the dim hall, as we turned to throw a last kiss at the corner of the stairs; tall and beautiful in her shabby green gown, with the light from the dining-room door turning her hair into a golden halo, and all the little crystal buttons shining like tears running down her breast.

Darling, beautiful Mother, what a wonderful evening that was; lifted sheer out of the black shadow into a shining memory for two little girls. Thank you, Mother, for that evening, sweet and unforgettable; for that memory nothing can ever spoil.

"It's all right, isn't it?" Sylvia said, sighing happily as we divided the last of the chocolates.

"Yes, of course," I replied. "Don't take all the walnuts, pig!"

"I'm not. Pig yourself. There's Father just come home. There's somebody with him. Listen!"

"It's Captain Dalton, I think."

Sylvia crept to the bedroom door.

"Yes, it is. I wonder why."

"Don't know. But it must be all right, mustn't it, Sylvia?"

"Of course." She yawned widely. "Golly, I'm sleepy, aren't you?"

We said good-night and I went up the top stairs to my own little room, and fell asleep immediately, happier than I had been for months.

That night Mother went away with Captain Dalton.

We never saw her again.

§

I was ten in the June of that year. Sylvia was over eleven. She should have sat for the Central School examination, but Father was advised against it. The truth is, she was not advanced enough to take even the entrance examination, let alone the scholarship.

This was a severe blow to Sylvia. Phyllis Sharman was taking the examination that year, with certain result. Dover Street without Phyllis seemed insupportable. She begged Miss Arne to let her try with Phyllis, but Miss Arne was briskly adamant.

"I dislike saying 'I told you so,' Sylvia, but you force me to say it."

"But, Miss Arne! You *know* I'm not clever like Ruan!"

"There is no need to be as clever as Ruan simply to pass the entrance exam," Miss Arne said crisply.

"But, Miss Arne! What am I going to do?"

Miss Arne smiled her thin, patient smile.

"You're going to stop making big eyes at people, and cooing at people. And you're going to put your back into it, and work as you've never worked before. And then, perhaps, next year will spring a surprise on all of us, my dear Sylvia."

I think Miss Arne was rather hard on Sylvia. Indeed, in those sad, empty months after Mother went away, I was more sorry for Sylvia than for anybody; even myself; even Father.

Father had his God. I had David and my secret world and my dog.

Tanner had some mysterious consolation that enabled her to go about her work with dogged vigour, and to sit rocking herself by the hour in the kitchen, pulling at her nose and singing: "Shall we meet beyond the Ree-ver? The beautiful, the beautiful, the Ree-ver?" … There was a queer, almost an exalted look on Tanner's face in those days; a look I did not understand, and did not want to understand. A look which frightened me when my mind groped out to follow it. She took very little notice of Sylvia and me; hardly seemed to realise our existence. Indeed, I do not believe we ever had existed for Tanner, save in relation to Mother's likes and dislikes. She did her duty by us, and we obeyed her, more or less, and we let each other alone. She never spoke to us about Mother, and we asked her no questions.

Nor did we question Father, beyond an occasional "Will Mother come back soon?" in a timid voice; to which he invariably replied with a curt: "I don't know."

I often wonder now about Father's feelings in those days. I don't think he suffered greatly, beyond a sense of outrage, of dignity impaired, and of defeat. Enough, you may think: and, yes, it would have been more than enough for any ordinary man. But Father was no ordinary man. He was a saint. A fanatic, if you like. God's reluctant outlaw, who saw, perhaps, in Mother's going, the possibility of his own return to unswerving service and ultimate pardon.

And thus, although I might have hated Father then, had I known all, now, I can and do pity him with all my heart.

But Sylvia had nothing; nothing at all. Not even her riding lessons— which seemed to both of us an unjust whim of Father's and was resented accordingly.

"I was getting on so nicely!" Sylvia wailed. "Captain Dalton said I was his best pupil. He said I should ride as well as Mother in a year or two. And Mother said so, too. It's not fair to stop me doing the one thing I can do well!"

"Look here," I suggested brightly. "Let's go up to the Riding School next Saturday, and ask Captain Dalton about it. Perhaps *he* might be able to persuade Father."

Sylvia gave me an uneasy glance.

"I don't believe the Captain's there any more."

"Not there? D'you mean he's gone away for good? Or just for a holiday?"

"I don't know. I asked Tanner if she thought I should have any more lessons, and she said he'd gone away. And when I said how soon would he be back, she just put on that look—*you* know—and said if I asked no questions I'd get no lies. I do *hate* Tanner when she says that, don't you?"

"I don't suppose she knows anything about it. Let's go up there and find out for ourselves."

So we went up to the Riding School on Saturday morning. I followed Sylvia across the paddock to a square, cobbled yard, down one side of which stood a row of loose-boxes. Friendly heads, chestnut and dark brown and dappled grey, looked over the doors at us, hopefully mumbling our hands with soft, rubbery lips. At the end of the yard was an office, and out of this came a tall, thin woman with a red, wind-bitten face and a shabby riding-habit, who told us sharply to be off. Sylvia drew herself up and said in Mother's voice:

"I am Miss Ashley. I wish to speak to Captain Dalton, please."

The woman gave a sudden grin.

"Oh, you're Miss Ashley, are you? Well, and I am Miss Murray-Field. And you can't speak to Captain Dalton, because he's gone away—and I don't mind telling you that I'd like to have a few words with the gentleman myself, about a number of things. Now then, I'm busy."

She turned away, but suddenly hesitated and swung round on us.

"Here—*what* did you say your name was?"

"Miss Sylvia Ashley. And this is my sister Ruan. You see, Mother's gone away, and nobody seems to know anything about my riding lessons; so I thought I'd ask the Captain if he'd try to persuade Father to let me go on with them. Because I'm very good, you know. Captain Dalton said I was his best pupil, so it does seem rather a shame, doesn't it?"

Miss Murray-Field stared at us between narrowed eye-lids for a moment. Then she muttered: "Poor brats!" and disappeared into the office, only to reappear a moment later with a large tin box.

"Here, have some biscuits," she said gruffly. She stuffed our pockets and filled our hands. They were the sort of biscuits we loved, but were seldom allowed to have; with coloured whirls of hard sugar stuck on them, or flat pictures of stags and dogs, white on chocolate, pink on yellow, very lickable.

"Now you'd better be getting along, hadn't you? And, by the way, I wouldn't say anything about your riding lessons just now—not to anybody, see? I'd wait a bit, and something'll turn up, you see if it doesn't. Never rush your fences. Good-bye, Miss Ashley. And you, kid."

She nodded and grinned at us, kindly enough, and we turned away, somewhat comforted.

"What a funny woman!" Sylvia said, with her mouth full. "I wonder what she wanted to see Captain Dalton about. I wonder where he's gone."

"Wouldn't it be nice," I said thoughtfully, "if he'd gone with Mother? I mean, she liked him, didn't she? And I've got a sort of feeling that Mother must feel lonely all by herself, without any of us."

Sylvia began to cry, and after a short struggle I joined her; and we went home drearily enough, with blotched faces and crumby coats. We had not the faintest notion of the true state of affairs, and would not have understood if we had. Mother had gone away, and we were forlorn without her, that was all. The dark Something that had lived in the Manse had gone, too; but that was little comfort, for its shadow remained, turning Tanner into a mysterious stranger and Father into an unapproachable ghost.

Everything was mysterious and muddled. I, who had hated Captain Dalton, now hoped he was with Mother, helping her to bear the separation from her family. Tanner, who had welcomed his coming, now refused to speak his name. The hard-bitten lady had called us poor brats. Why? Some of the older boys and girls at Dover Street whispered together and giggled when they saw us. Why? Mrs Galloway and Mrs Bowers gave us sweets and sniffed over us, and came to see Father—a thing they had rarely done before—and talked to him for hours in his study. Why, why, why? ...

Once, in the middle of the night, I woke with a sudden notion searing into my brain like a red-hot iron. I leapt out of bed and ran downstairs and woke Sylvia.

"Sylvia," I gasped, trembling, "d'you think Mother's *dead*?"

She sat up, looking lovely and sleepy and cross.

"Of course not, stupid. Go back to bed, for goodness' sake."

"But, Sylvia … everybody seems to be so sorry for us. It might be … it might."

Sylvia fastened the collar of her nightgown, which had come undone. She was always a prude.

"If I tell you something, Ruan," she said, in her elder-sister voice, "will you promise *on your honour* not to *breathe* it to a living soul?"

"Yes."

"Well, I asked Phyllis about it, and she asked her mother, and Mrs Sharman said Mother had done something wicked, and Father had sent her away."

I trembled so much that I had to sink on to the bed.

"You—you don't believe that, do you, Sylvia?"

Sylvia stared at the counterpane.

"*Do* you? … Sylvia, you can't possibly believe that Mother was wicked!"

"Oh, Ruan, I—I hope not! I don't know!"

I stared at her in the utmost horror.

Sylvia, to doubt Mother even for one moment! She, whom Mother had loved above all others; whom she had nursed so devotedly in illness; whose lovely features were a reflection of Mother's own; who had received the last, the longest, the tenderest good-night, that last, lovely evening we spent with her. … Sylvia—even for an instant—to doubt darling Mother!

Suddenly I struck her hard with my clenched fists, once on the right cheek and again on the left. Red patches flamed on her tender skin. I sobbed with rage and sorrow.

"You beast! You *beast*, to say Mother was wicked! You utterly beastly beast!"

I rushed upstairs and flung the bedclothes over my head. Crying myself to sleep, my last memory was of those red patches on the white blur of her face; and of the strange look of sorrow that she had in her eyes; not anger, just bitter, unchildlike sorrow. "Ruan!" she had whispered. "Oh, Ruan!"

Chapter Twelve

S

I wanted David very badly at this time. I longed for him, and for kind, cheerful Rosie and gentle Luke. And I longed for the moor; for the wide, sweeping curves and the soft, grassy hollows, and for the hills beyond. … "I will lift up mine eyes unto the hills, from whence cometh my help." … If only I could get to the moor everything might come right again—must come right, surely! Sorrow was imprisoned in the town, boxed up and driven down the dark streets, sheltered in the Manse and in Cheddar Street Chapel. But what sorrow could live long on the moor?

But that consolation was denied me.

Rosie had been unwell all that winter, and Joshua had taken her away for a long holiday. They had gone to Switzerland. I had received several highly coloured postcards, depicting incredibly pointed white mountains with incredibly small villages clinging to their sides. I tried to imagine Rosie and Joshua toiling up those snowy slopes, swinging over precipices at the end of ropes, leaping from one pointed crag to another, but utterly failed.

David had spent the Easter holidays at the home of a school friend, somewhere in Devon, and from him, too, I had received post-cards; these of snug red roofs half hidden by foliage, and of contented cattle knee-deep in lush green grass, with a twinkle of blue sea in the offing.

How I envied them all! It never seemed to occur to Father that two lonely and bewildered little girls might well have benefited by an occasional jaunt into the country. Father was concerned only with fighting his own battle. He had no time for other problems.

But if Father and Tanner did not think about us, other people did. Mrs

Galloway and Mrs Bowers made us their special concern; and Sunday became a nightmare which we dreaded increasingly week by week.

We walked to chapel with Father now, and so arrived very early. We sat alone in the long pew and took what comfort we could from the back view of Mr Wister playing the voluntary. If Mrs Galloway got to chapel before Mrs Bowers she would beckon us across the aisle and make us sit in her pew. And if Mrs Bowers got there first we had to sit with her. A strong rivalry sprang up between these ladies. On several occasions they arrived together, and then there was the nearest approach to a stand-up fight that I have ever witnessed in a place of worship.

It was all very boring, but there were compensations. With Mrs Galloway it was peppermints, very large and of a surprising strength. With Mrs Bowers it was cokernut candy, home-made, in pink and white layers. There was a further attraction in Mrs Bowers' pew, in the shape of a smelling-bottle which she always placed on the hymn-book ledge, and which we were allowed to sniff, cautiously and with many violent starts, provided we made no actual noise.

After the service was the worst part. We had to wait for Father, and the ladies of the congregation, and quite a number of the gentlemen, made a terrible and sickening fuss of us; almost literally passing us from hand to hand, folding us in smelly Sunday blacks, kissing our reluctant cheeks and murmuring "Poor little things!"—and hushing each other, and talking about us as if we were rare little specimens out of a showcase.

Going home with Father one morning, after a worse bout of this than usual, we plucked up our courage to ask him if we might always stay in our own pew.

To our utmost surprise and consternation, Father replied that henceforth we should certainly remain in our own pew, since Miss Joycey was coming to the Manse to look after us, and we should be entirely in her charge.

Sylvia and I looked at each other, speechless with indignation. Miss Joycey! That old rabbit! We thought we had done with her, years ago!

But we had not done with her. Not by any means. She arrived the very next day, complete with battered brown tin-trunk and two suitcases, a bag of rather faded chocolates, and an apologetic smile. The chocolates were for us. The smile was for Tanner, who ignored it; so Miss Joycey tried being haughty and commanding, and Tanner ignored that, too.

As far as Tanner was concerned, Miss Joycey might not have existed. She said, "Yes, miss," and "No, miss," and carried on exactly as before, whatever Miss Joycey said. And very soon Miss Joycey decided it was too much for her, and reverted to her old scuttling, muddling ways; perpetually on the run looking for lost odds and ends of personal property, eyes popping and teeth protruding; a thoroughly ineffectual, incompetent spinster, but kind and well-meaning withal.

It might be imagined that Father could have found a better companion for us, but I don't suppose that was easy. There were no aunts or cousins to be called into the breach, and competent people are not cheap.

Father had so little money, and the small amount Mother had was lost with her. Miss Joycey was prepared—even eager—to do her very best for practically nothing at all, and Father had to accept that, and be thankful.

After the first few days of strangeness and discomfort we settled down to it all. We learned to keep our eyes away from Miss Joycey at meal-times; the combination of protruding teeth and lightly boiled egg we found exceptionally revolting. We forgot to be surprised and resentful at finding her on the doorstep, awaiting our return from school. We became inured to the smell of moth-ball, to the visible evidences of catarrh, and to the sound of the piano being played with lively inaccuracy and the loud pedal down all the time. We didn't mind sitting in chapel with her; indeed, we preferred it to sitting either with Mrs Galloway or Mrs Bowers, in spite of the peppermints and cokernut candy; for Miss Joycey had the habit of prolonged and devout kneeling after the Benediction, and though this was at first the cause of some embarrassment to us, we soon perceived it to be of incalculable value in warding off would-be fussers.

I don't know if Miss Joycey prayed or not. Perhaps the beauty of Father's Benediction lit some lamp in her feeble heart, so that she was reluctant to leave that pure flame for the everyday sights of Cheddar Street. Perhaps she was merely "feeling her knees again"—to which condition she was prone whenever the weather changed. Perhaps she did it from kindness, knowing that Cheddar Street would regard such a prolonged display of reverence as verging on the indecent, and would go outside for its greetings and its gossipings, and so give us a quick get-away.

This, at any rate, was the gratifying result, whatever her intentions may have been; and for this, at least, we were truly thankful to her.

And so, endured by us, ignored by Tanner, and by Father treated to such a cold, impersonal courtesy that almost any other woman would have regarded it as an insult, Florence Joycey lived her brief span beneath the roof of the Manse—and, most strangely, found happiness there.

I cannot imagine—even now, when life has taught me how strange and varied are the ways of happiness—what made her happy. Can it be possible that she really was devoted to two unappreciative and rather sullen little girls, who were often disobedient and sometimes downright rude to her? Did the grim and shabby rooms of the Manse mean home to her, and Tanner's forbidding presence in the kitchen spell luxury, after her own scrubby housekeeping in a top-back bedsitting-room? Was it Father who made her happy? Did his mere presence in the house, the courteous bend of his head, the cold, sweet tones of his voice, fill her with a trembling ecstasy that she could only regard as wickedness? Was the pink feather that suddenly appeared in her Sunday hat a defiance of wickedness, and the nightly warming of his slippers a challenge to fate, or God?

How should I know, who see Florence Joycey through the mist of years, what went on in that kind, silly, lonely heart of hers! I only know that she was, unquestionably, happy with us, and that I am glad to remember it. When she left us, which she did after five months, most surprisingly to become the wife of the greengrocer, Dodds, who called at the back door for orders, we howled with hidden laughter, presented her with a picture of ladies and gentlemen being extremely gallant and coy with each other in a garden largely composed of stone balustrades, and promptly forgot her.

After Miss Joycey came Mrs Dane, Miss Winter, and Miss Bottomley, in rapid succession and in that order.

But, long before that, Rosie had come home, and life assumed a brighter hue for me.

I was so happy to see Rosie again.

She came to me almost as soon as she set foot in England, and gathered me on to her lap, with her arms most reassuringly around me, and promised me David and the moor, as soon as ever the holidays released me from Dover Street. She had brought me presents. A lovely little Swiss chalet, and some tiny figures carved out of wood, and a cuckoo-clock. She smelt of eau-de-Cologne, and wore a terrible hat covered in violets that shrieked defiance of her blazing hair; and she was my own dear, dependable Rosie, just as she always had been.

No, not quite as she had been. She was a little quieter, a little thinner, and her cheeks were not quite so brightly coloured as of old. The result was becoming, but disturbing, too.

"Are you *quite* better, Rosie?"

"Me, luv?" She laughed hugely. "Nay, I'm as right as a trivet. And I learned to yodel like a mountain climber. I dursen't do it here, but you wait while we get up on't moor, I'll give you a sample fit to split your ear-drums! Happen I'll learn you, an' all!"

Joshua had come with Rosie. He was shut in the study with Father for a long time, but presently they came out together, and Joshua slapped his thigh when he saw me, and said, nay, who was this young lady? And wouldn't somebody introduce us? And when I laughed and said it was Me, he made great play with his spectacles, viewing me doubtfully from all angles, until at last he cried out that I was right an' all, and it *was* Me, and that you could knock him down with a feather! And then he jingled his money and said it was a right good job I wasn't fond of lollipops, as their Rosie had ruined him, rushing him all over them cold mountains. After which he gave me half-a-crown, and another one for Sylvia, who was out with Phyllis.

Miss Joycey came in simpering, and we all had tea in the dining-room. The talk was of Switzerland and of chapel affairs and a little of Joshua's factory. I ate my tea in silence, longing to get Rosie alone, so that I could ask her the truth about Mother. But I only had a moment before they went, and somehow it was the wrong moment. So I could only cling to Rosie and whisper how I was longing for the holidays and David and the moor. And Rosie hugged me and said the time would soon pass—and if yon gormless woman in there made me unhappy, I was to let her know, that was all!

And then Luke was outside with Sally and the gig, and I must run out to greet him. He shook hands and grinned at me kindly, with his blue eyes wrinkled into slits; but when Rosie came out he turned away, and busied himself with the harness.

"Aren't you just glad Rosie's home, Luke?"

"I am an' all, missie," he muttered. And Rosie laughed briefly and told him to give over fiddling with the harness, and to speak up like a man. He straightened up slowly and their eyes met for an instant and dropped again; and Rosie bit her lip and called out to Joshua that the mare wouldn't stand for ever.

When Sylvia came home I showed her my treasures, and gave her the half-crown and a set of beautifully embroidered dolls' clothes Rosie had brought for her. I told her I was going to the House for the summer holiday, and said, reluctantly, that of course she would be coming too. To my secret delight, Sylvia disclosed a plan she had formed for going with Phyllis to Scarborough, to stay with some relatives. She had not cared to mention it before, because of me, but if I were happily disposed of the thing became simple. Mrs Sharman would write to Father and fix everything up.

I wondered how Sylvia could contemplate a happy holiday with anyone who thought Mother wicked. But it was not my business, and it certainly left David and the moor to my own, undivided possession, so I agreed that it was a good plan, and hoped that it would work.

It did work. And in due course Sylvia went off to Scarborough, almost inarticulate with excitement; and Rosie came in the gig for me, and we spanked away down St Mark's Road, *en route* for the station and David.

Father was going away on some mysterious mission of his own; Tanner to Shropshire; Miss Joycey—already, perhaps, the victim of Dodds' charms—had elected to muddle along in lonely grandeur at the Manse.

Everybody said how David had altered, but to me he seemed exactly the same. Certainly he had grown tall, and his voice was doing the same silly tricks that Stebbing's had done eight months before, and he was always looking in the mirror at something he referred to as his beard, and which was completely invisible to the naked eye. But he was David; unchanged, unchangeable. And I loved him.

We lay in the hot, purple heather and let the sun soak into our bodies. I was wearing a pair of his grey shorts and one of his old white cricket shirts with the sleeves cut above the elbows.

I watched a multicoloured beetle negotiate a stalk.

"David," I said, "if you knew why Mother had gone away—would you tell me?"

"Yes, I expect so," he said, after a moment's pause, "but I don't."

"Nobody will tell me anything! I thought at first she was ill—but they'd have told us *that*, surely! I even thought she—might be dead. But Sylvia says she's certain it's not that. Sylvia says Phyllis Sharman told her that Mother had been wicked and Father had sent her away. I hit her for saying it. But lately … I don't know. … Grown-ups *are* wicked sometimes, aren't they, David? I mean, even nice grown-ups."

"My own father was," David said simply. "I used to think I hated my father, when I found out; but now I don't hate him. After all, mothers and fathers are only children grown up, aren't they? And you can't say *you* never do anything you shouldn't. … I had a long jaw about it with Mr Lord. He said people were most likely to do rotten things when they were unhappy, and I've found that's true. And another thing he said: whatever people have done, it's not our business to judge them. You don't know what temptations they had, or what unhappiness, and you can jolly well bet you might easily have come a mucker yourself, if you were in their place. See what I mean?"

I did see, and it comforted me, but only a little.

"I could bear Mother being away—I could even bear it if I never saw her again—so long as I knew she was happy. That's what worries me."

"Was she happy when she lived *with* you?"

"No," I had to admit. And the word stabbed me like a little knife.

"Well, then!" said David.

The beetle fell off the stalk for the twenty-fourth time and finally gave it up.

I was always going to tackle Rosie about it, but somehow I never did. It never seemed the exactly right moment. And, as the hot, slow, happy days went by, the arms of the moor drew me closer and closer to her broad, peaceful bosom, and the anguish went out of my heart, as I had known it would. I loved Mother just as much, but I sorrowed for her less and less. Up there, in the pure, clean moorland air, the pattern of life showed more clearly, on a larger scale. I lifted my eyes to the hills; and I perceived how minute, how unimportant, a portion of that pattern we made, all of us; and we no longer seemed to matter greatly.

§

Stebbing had sent me his love.

"He *is* sweet on you!" David grinned. "Absolutely potty!"

We both thought it a huge joke.

I asked if Stebbing were coming to the House these holidays, but David said, no, his people had come back from India. In any case, said David, Stebbing was a bit disappointing away from Lowton.

I agreed heartily. At the same time, I had never forgotten that Stebbing liked poetry. "So all night long the noise of battle rolled," and "O, rare, pale Margaret." I could not wholly dislike him.

It was colder than usual that August. I remember it mainly as long walks over the moors, head down to a blustering wind, with farm-house tea before we turned for home with the wind to our backs and the clouds racing before us. There were long indoor hours, too, when the windows rattled under the massed attacks of wind and rain, and smoke blew into the rooms in great gusts. The corn lay flattened to the earth, and Luke went about the farm with sacking over his shoulders, and Cracked Willy sat behind his mother's window instead of at the door, jerking and grinning to us, as we ran by with the wet streaming off our mackintoshes, to spend our money at Mrs Shufflebotham's shop.

It was that August that I went for the first time to church with David.

We had tea at the Vicarage with Mr Lord, who received me kindly, and afterwards we went into the garden, which was old and very lovely. There was a very fine herbaceous border in all shades of blue, and a rock-garden with an ancient sundial. Pear and plum, dripping with fruit, were spread like jewelled fans against the mellow old walls of red brick, and lawns like green plush sloped down to a copse of larch and fir and delicate silver birch.

When the bell began for Evensong, Mr Lord went into the church by one door and David and I by another. We sat in a pew alone together; the very same pew where I had crouched on that stormy day—how long ago it seemed!—with the Scarlet Woman standing by the organ looking at me and the thunder crashing overhead.

I sat by David, quiet and rather awestruck, watching the light dropping richly from the windows across the quiet church. The organ played softly. A handful of villagers creaked in and knelt on the old hassocks. The choir came in two by two, singing. Six boys and four men. The boys' voices were high and sweet. They looked angelic in their white surplices. With a shock of surprise I recognised the bullet-headed son of the blacksmith, and the two Bunting boys who had made such rude faces at me only yesterday. (But I had made even ruder ones at them!) There was the glint of the Cross, and Mr Lord's voice saying something in a sort of mumble that yet sounded right and pleasing, and we all dropped on our knees. I stood up when David stood and knelt when he knelt; and when he bowed his head at the name of Jesus, I bowed mine, after an instant's tussle between stubborn Nonconformity and a sense of what was right and fitting. I shared David's hymn-book. During the sermon, which was surprisingly short, he gave me a rather battered humbug, which I sucked dreamily. We sang *Our Blest Redeemer*, one of my favourite hymns, and the voice of the bullet-headed boy rose in a descant of such sweet purity that the tears rolled down my cheeks with aching joy. I slipped my hand into David's, and he held it firmly. And when we knelt for the Benediction he kept it still within his own.

And so we knelt together, David and I, while beauty soared and glowed and fell softly around us. It was the end of my holiday on the moor, and a very sweet ending I felt it to be.

As we came out into the half-light I noticed that Karenhapuk Foljambe still had no flowers; even the jam-jar was gone. So David and I got some roots of heather from the moor and planted them on her grave, and we went home sober and satisfied.

Chapter Thirteen

§

In late September Miss Joycey married her greengrocer, and Mrs Dane came in her stead.

She only stayed a week, because I bit her and Sylvia kicked her shins— and I am glad to remember it. She was a detestable woman, both mean and cruel, who should never have been allowed to handle children at all.

After her came Miss Winter. We liked her well enough, but she was too delicate for the job, and after a few weeks' struggle she had to go back to her parents.

It was Rosie who found Miss Bottomley for us. She was, I believe, some sort of distant cousin of the Days, and there was a faint likeness to Rosie that I found very heartening. Daisy Bottomley was a short, stout little body with a pale frizz of hair, a cheerful laugh, and an anecdote to point every occasion. "That reminds me of when I was in Bristol once," she would cry, when we spilt the salt. Or when John was especially amusing out on a walk, she would remember a dog she had known who performed incredible tricks. Everything that happened, however trivial, reminded her of something else, so that our lives became a perpetual recitation of short stories. This might easily have become tedious, but we did not have time to weary of it; and so my memories of Miss Bottomley are mostly happy ones, filled with kindly laughter and common sense and wholesome advice. She stayed with us until the very end.

Until the end …

Even now, as I write those words, I feel the old, quick sense of dread that fell upon me that November day that we watched the telegraph boy cycling up St Mark's Road. He cycled slowly, wobbling a little as he peered at the numbers of the houses, and whistling the Toreador song out of *Carmen*.

Sylvia and I were sitting in the window counting the people who wore green. A hat scored one, a coat two, and a whole green outfit six. The first one to reach a hundred won the prize, which was a ha'penny we had found in the street.

Miss Bottomley sat by the fire knitting socks for her brother. She had a cold and kept sneezing, and every time she sneezed she laughed and said "Bless you!"

"There's a telegraph boy," said Sylvia.

"I knew a telegraph boy who rode slap into the canal, because his brakes weren't working properly," Miss Bottomley remarked cheerfully.

"Was he drowned?"

"No; they got him out in time, but the bicycle was never recovered, I believe."

"He's coming here," I whispered.

The boy fumbled at the gate and sauntered up the path. "Toreador, now arm thee! Toreador, Toreador. ..."

He crashed the knocker down twice with a deafening noise.

Miss Bottomley did not move. It was Tanner's place to attend to the door. Sylvia did not move, because there were two people in green over the way.

I did not move. I could not.

I don't think I am in the least psychic. But in that moment, as surely as though the letters burned through the envelope in letters of fire, I knew that Mother was dead.

"That makes me nineteen. And the little girl in the green bonnet makes twenty," Sylvia chanted. "Ruan, aren't you playing?"

I heard Tanner at the door.

"Perhaps someone's left us a thousand pounds," said Miss Bottomley. "Wouldn't that be grand? A-tishoo! Bless you!"

I heard Tanner go to the study.

After a long time she went back to the door. The boy went away on his bicycle, riding with a swagger, hands thrust through his leather belt. "Toreador! Toreador! …"

"I once knew a man who got a legacy of five hundred pounds, and he had it all spent in six weeks."

I looked at Miss Bottomley. She ran her knitting-needle through her frizzy hair and pursed her mouth.

"Do you feel sick, Ruan?"

I shook my head.

"Well, you look sick. I'll give you a powder to-night. Come nearer to the fire."

I did not move. I could not.

Tanner opened the door and stared at us. No, not at us—*through* us. Her face was strange. The skin looked luminous and the eyes were blank. She was smiling a little.

"Miss Sylvia and Miss Ruan. Your father wants you in the study."

Sylvia was suddenly frightened. She gripped my hand and whimpered. "Ruan. Is anything the matter, do you think? Ruan, you look awful!"

We went into the study and shut the door.

Father was sitting at his desk with the telegram laid before him. He looked old. The lines on his face were deeply carved. His eyes were shadowed and exhausted.

Quite simply he told us that Mother was dead. She had been riding and her horse had thrown her at a high fence. When he had told us, he sat still with his head on his hands, not attempting to comfort or explain.

Sylvia at once began to cry and ran from the room, sobbing uncontrollably. I stood still, feeling dead all over. I felt as if I should never cry again.

Presently Father looked up and asked me to find the time-table. "I shall have to go immediately," he said, in a thin, dry voice.

I found the time-table and he looked up a train and called Miss Bottomley into the room. She began to cry, too, but she got him a quick meal and brushed his coat and packed a few things into a bag for him.

Father kissed me good-bye. When he got to the door he hesitated and turned back and put his hand on my head.

"You must look after your sister, Ruan. She's not as strong as you."

I felt proud; but I should have been glad if he had kissed me again, or whispered one word of comfort in my ear, for I didn't feel strong at all.

Sylvia cried so much that she made herself ill, and the doctor came and gave her something to drink and talked to her in a quick, firm voice. She stayed in bed for two days, but after that she was better, and sat in the window looking frail and beautiful. We were very sorry for her, and we waited on her hand and foot, and she was always so sweet and grateful.

And still I could not cry.

Rosie came flying to comfort me.

"There's nowt I can say, luv, except she's happier now than she's been a long, long while. Try to think of that."

"She wasn't happy with us, was she, Rosie?"

She shook her head and hugged me.

"I wonder why?"

"Nay, luv, that's more than anyone can say about anyone else. She—she wanted somehow to be free, that's what I've always felt. And now she is free."

"Rosie ... do you think she died at once ... without any pain or any fear?"

"Ay, luv, I reckon she did. That's mostly the way of it with horse-riding accidents. Horse were killed too, you know, so it must have been right quick. I reckon that's the way she'd have wanted to go. Clean through the air, and out at once, and free."

Clean through the air—and free! Yes, I thought Mother would have liked that best. I suddenly remembered that day up at the Riding School when I first saw Mother ride. I saw her figure braced forward, eager, tense, at one with her mount. I saw the gold hair blowing in the wind and heard the thud of hoofs on the turf. Then up, up into the air, and for one instant of beauty etched against the autumn sky in grace and strength and power. Then over the fence and away. ...

She was over the fence, my darling, unhappy Mother, riding towards the unknown land, lovely and free. ...

So I could cry at last; in sorrow for myself, but in happiness for her.

Father was away for a week, and then he came back, older-looking and more silent than ever. He wrote quantities of letters, and sometimes he went up to London on business and stayed for some time.

There were a lot of visitors at the Manse. Mrs Galloway and Mrs Bowers came quite often, and made a great fuss of Sylvia and me and tried to give Miss Bottomley orders. But she was too much for them, for Rosie had warned her this would happen. Joshua Day came and a number of the chapel leaders, and Sylvia and I had an embarrassing amount of sixpences and shillings thrust upon us. There was an air of unrest about the house; of energy let loose; of impending change. But the dark Something had gone, quite gone, and its shadow, too; and the air was easier to breathe.

One day we got home from school to find tea already on the table—a very special tea—and a visitor we had never seen before sitting with Father and Miss Bottomley.

He was a tall, stooping man with a fine, pale face and long, thin hands, and his eyes were brown and thoughtful.

"This is Sylvia, and this is Ruan," Father said, drawing us forward. "Children, this is your Uncle Alaric."

We shook hands politely and Uncle Alaric got on with his tea and his talk with Father. I looked apprehensively at Sylvia, hoping she was not going to start crying; for we knew that this was Mother's only brother, who lived at Cobbetts—that home of which we had heard so many wild and lovely stories.

When tea was over Miss Bottomley went out of the room, and Uncle Alaric talked to us for a little. He asked us the usual questions about school, and what sort of lessons we liked best, and what we wanted to do with our lives. I hadn't the least idea what I wanted to do with mine; but Sylvia had it all cut-and-dried, and she told Uncle Alaric all about the rich man she was going to marry, and about her ten beautiful children. She even recited their names, and I wished David were there to deal with her.

But Uncle Alaric listened gravely and with apparent interest; even taking part in a debate about whether Ronald or Ferdinand were the better name for the youngest but one.

Father sat with his far-away smile, thinking his own secret thoughts.

"And what about you, young lady?"

I shuffled and stammered, and Sylvia burst out patronisingly:

"Oh, Ruan doesn't care what happens, so long as she's got her nose in a book!"

"Indeed." Uncle Alaric looked at me kindly. "I should like to see your books, Ruan, if I may."

I said I would fetch them; but he insisted on coming up to the top of the house himself.

There they all were, my lovely books, standing on their white shelves in coloured rows, waiting for me. The *Jungle Books*, and *Alice*, and my *Tennyson*. The book about Russia. The *Ballads*. A work on astronomy and another on wild flowers. The Dickens books that David had given me at odd times. *The Last of the Mohicans*. A book about Spain and another about Thibet. *Brer Rabbit* and *Lavengro* and *Three Men in a Boat* and *The Arabian Nights*, and my latest love: the poems of Dante Gabriel Rossetti.

Uncle Alaric looked at them all with grave interest. Then he turned and looked at me.

"So you don't care about a rich husband and ten children, Ruan. You just want books to read."

"I'd like to write them, too," I said shyly.

"Ah!" He nodded his head thoughtfully. "Well, you will never need riches, my dear. You'll have all you want inside you; a complete world of your own. I have a library at Cobbetts that I think you would like. A whole room filled with books. If ever you come there, I hope you will regard it as your own."

Then he glanced at a very thin gold watch and said he must go, and he shook hands with me as if I were a grown-up, and went away without any fuss, and without kissing me or pressing money into my hand, for which I was grateful. I felt a great respect and liking for this new Uncle Alaric, and I hoped I might go to Cobbetts some day and see his wonderful library.

I had no idea how soon that hope would be fulfilled.

A week later Father told us he was going to Africa to be a missionary, and that Sylvia and I were going to live with Uncle Alaric.

Sylvia was wild with delight, and I was glad, too. The Manse was no longer Home to me. Tanner was a stranger, and Father scarcely seemed a real person at all. We were both glad to know that Dover Street was done with, though I felt a certain regret at leaving Miss Arne. The nightmare of the scholarship no longer menaced Sylvia. There would be horses for her at Cobbetts, and books for me. Miss Bottomley was kind, but we could not pretend to mind parting from her; she had no deep roots in our lives. On the whole, life seemed brighter than we remembered for a long time.

My only worry was David.

How far away was Cobbetts? Should I be allowed to go to the moor for holidays?

But Rosie came to say good-bye, and she assured me that she would fix everything up all right, and I trusted her to keep her word.

"I'm right glad you're going, luv. I'll miss you in chapel, mind you, but we'll make up for it when you come to stay. Write me a letter sometimes, won't you, and tell me all about it?"

"Give my love to Luke," I said, choking back tears.

"I will that!"

"Good-bye, Rosie."

"Good-bye, luv. God bless you. Think of me when you undress you."

I laughed weakly at the old joke, and Rosie laughed, and we both pretended we weren't minding it a bit; and the gig went spanking away down St Mark's Road for the very last time.

"Do we have to kiss Tanner?" Sylvia grimaced. "I don't think I *can*!"

"I can!" I stoutly affirmed.

But Tanner did not give us the chance.

She went away one night after we were in bed, and we knew nothing of it until the morning. She took her tin-trunk and the woolly rabbit that had belonged to Clem. And she took the picture of Mother's horse, Starlight, that had hung in the hall as long as we could remember. Sylvia was furious, and wanted to speak to Father about it; but I promised that if she did I would, amongst other things, push her head through the banisters and swing on her hair, so she gave up the idea.

We never saw Tanner again. I suppose she went to her relations in Shropshire, for a time at least. But six months later her body was found in the river near to the spot where Mother was killed.

I was not told of this until years afterwards; but then I instantly remembered how she would sit in the dark kitchen and sing:

> "Shall we gather at the Ree-ver?
> The beautiful, the beautiful, the Ree-ver?"

Poor Tanner, with her slavish devotions and her warped loyalties, I think she died for love. And I think the river that received her tortured soul would bear it kindly, gently, through peaceful pastures and quiet ways to that Throne she sang about so often.

Book Two

&

Cobbetts

Chapter One

Cobbetts was a square, solid house, in whose yellowed walls the forgotten suns of four centuries lay sleeping. Twelve windows, green-shuttered, faced an immense cobbled yard that had rung to the hoofs and the hallooings of Elizabeth's outriders. A great gate of very fine wrought-iron gave admittance to the yard, and this was locked every night at sundown, as it had been since the first Mallinson lived there. By the gate hung a lantern and a huge bell on an iron chain, and, if this chanced to ring, old Blossom had to shuffle out and attend to the visitor, whatever the time of night and whatever the weather. He grumbled and growled about it, but Uncle Alaric would have it so, for so it had ever been. The lawns lay to the south, fringed by oak and beech and interspersed with ragged flower-beds; unkempt lawns, but green and beautiful to my town-tired eyes, even in that bleak winter month. The stables were empty, save for a scrubby pony and a general-utility horse, both of which were fat with idleness.

The home farm lay little more than a stone's-throw from the house, but it was the home farm in name only, for it had been sold, years ago, to two brothers, Albert and Edward Shore, who lived alone in it, in pigsty fashion.

There were twenty-seven rooms at Cobbetts, and eighteen of them were shut up. Of the remaining nine, Uncle Alaric used the library, the dining-room, and his bedroom. Sylvia and I were given a small bedroom each, with a sitting-room adjoining. The servants used the rest.

There were only two servants living in: old Blossom, who looked ninety, but was probably about seventy, and his daughter Maggie, a great fat idle woman who was outwardly meek, but who ruled her father with a rod of iron. A village girl, rejoicing in the name of Joy Jolly, came in to help each day, and actually did most of the work. She was a half-wit, with a pretty, vacant face and three illegitimate children, who came to meet her after work. We were told they were her sisters, and they had our clothes to wear when we had done with them. The only other servant was the gardener, Fell, a discouraged-looking man with a long black moustache, who struggled wearily against the tides of stinging nettles, and the thrusting dandelions, and the clutching, climbing ivy. He had a passion for bonfires. I never saw so many bonfires in all my life as I saw at Cobbetts. He would stand poking them by the hour, his eyes watering in the acrid smoke. When I asked why, he merely said gloomily:

"It meks a show. Aye, it meks a show."

Long years ago the house had been called Cold Abbot's Hall, and had been a fine mansion standing in a hundred acres of park-land, with a west wing that had a great dancing hall and a musicians' gallery, and a chapel. In those days there had been a great coming and going at the house, with horses clattering on the cobbles and all the windows ablaze with light; with serving-maids a-bustle, and wine brimming the great silver goblets. Companies of ladies and gentlemen had ridden out at dawn to the chase, hawks alert on gloved wrists and hounds baying. At night there had been music and dancing. Satin skirts had swept the wide, shallow stairs, dark corners had thrilled to whispered love-making, and, more than once, swords had flashed out and blood had stained the floors.

There was a room that was still called the Queen's Bedchamber; but it was dank and empty of furnishing, and great damp patches stained the cracked plaster of the walls. There was another room that was said to be haunted, past which I flew for the first week and dawdled in bravado for the next, and at length forgot its sinister reputation altogether. Certainly I saw no ghosts at Cobbetts but those I called up for myself—and these were my friends, and dear to me. A certain Giles Mallinson, whose portrait was one of the few remaining in the dining-room, was the chief of these; and there were two sisters, Cecilia and Rosemary, golden-haired darlings who had died together in some epidemic two hundred years ago, with whom I played and held long conversations.

But the glory that had been Cold Abbot's Hall was long since departed.

As Giles had succeeded Alaric, and been, in turn, succeeded by Alaric and Giles, the place had gone steadily downhill. As the result of some drunken brawl the west wing had been burned to the ground, and never rebuilt. The noble trees had been felled and the timber sold, and the land disposed of acre by acre, until, in Grandfather's time, only the home farm remained; and this also had gone eventually, to help to meet the debts he had piled up and the enormously increased taxation. Even the beautiful old furniture had been sold, and the rooms we used were mostly filled by ugly Victorian pieces not much better than those we had despised so at the Manse.

Grandfather had ceased to care. His daughter had run off with a ranting Dissenter; his son was a bookworm and a milksop. The Mallinsons were played out—and what the hell did it matter, anyway! ...

After his death, Uncle Alaric had done what he could. Bowing his head to the inevitable, he had sold everything saleable, even to many of the family portraits; had shut up the greater part of the house and cut down the staff. He ate nothing but the very plainest food, and very little of that. He ceased to entertain or to visit his neighbours. He lived like a monk, shutting his eyes to dirt and cobwebs and the forlorn, weed-grown gardens, and finding happiness only in his books, and in a history of the house he was compiling for his own pleasure.

To such a slender purse, even the addition to the household of two little girls must have made a decided difference. But Uncle Alaric, though far from being sentimental, was yet a just and conscientious man, and he considered that Mother had been treated very ill. To some extent he blamed himself; but at the time of her amazing marriage; he had been abroad, and when at last he had made an effort to get in touch with her, she, still smarting under her father's tongue, and very much in love with her husband, had persistently ignored his letters. And time had flowed on and nothing had been done—until at last had come the news of her estrangement from Father, and her death.

"I have brought a Mallinson home to Cobbetts for your mother's sake," he said, his eyes resting on Sylvia, "and an Ashley for your father's sake." (He had turned to me.) "There is nothing more I am able to do."

I am afraid Cobbetts was a sharp shock to Sylvia. I don't know what she had expected, but it was certainly not the utter remoteness and seclusion, the elegant, faded poverty of Cobbetts as we knew it.

Very likely she had seen herself as the charming little châtelaine of the Hall, dispensing soup and jellies to curtsying villagers. Or as the centre of the Hunt; by far the youngest and most beautiful, mounted on a spirited horse who obeyed her lightest touch (to the great admiration of everybody). Possibly she had visualised an ancient, silver-haired butler bursting into tears at the sight of her, and quavering how like Miss Nell she was, God bless her! And I'm afraid she may have hoped for a silver salver piled high with visiting cards inscribed with famous names.

If these were Sylvia's secret hopes she was bitterly disappointed, for none of them came true. Most of the villagers kept a better table than we did. Uncle Alaric had never hunted in his life, and he had no friends, titled or otherwise. While Blossom was less like the old family butler of tradition than can possibly be imagined, and if he shed any tears at our coming they were tears of rage.

But I loved Cobbetts. I was happy within its old yellow walls and proud to think that one half of me, at least, was Mallinson. The garden delighted me and I laboured long hours there, digging and hoeing and planting as Luke had taught me, and climbing the ancient oaks. John loved it, too. His little paws, so used to hard pavements, dug ecstatically into the black earth. His nose quivered to a thousand scents. Rabbits bobbed their white scuts for him to chase. Fantail pigeons strutted tantalisingly and rose in sudden beauty, like a white cloud, to the red-brown, gabled roofs.

I wrote long letters to David and Rosie, full of the glories of Cobbetts. For to me its glories still lived. Hooded falcons rattled their chains, impatient on their high perches. Flowered silks and fine laces still swept the shallow staircase. Laughter and sudden oaths filled the empty, echoing rooms. And Giles and Rosemary and Cecilia smiled and beckoned to me from courtyard and corridor and dark, panelled nook.

Yes, I loved Cobbetts, silent and dignified amid the gentle Midland meadow-land. But I never loved it as I loved the Farm, and the wide, fierce tenderness of the moor, and the strong hills.

Cobbetts was an ancient lady, gracious and kind. She gave me favours and suffered my presence, but she did not love me. Her eyes strained ever into the lovely past and her ears listened only for the sound of footsteps long since dead.

But the moor loved me. She waited for me with her arms wide spread; everlastingly patient with my foolishness. And the bills rested on her hands.

§

For the first few weeks we ran wild and nobody took any notice of our coming and going. The weather was cold but fine. We were out of doors all day, and at night we were asleep almost before we had flung ourselves into bed in our small, bare rooms.

We were given leave to ride the horses, and those reluctant beasts lost a good deal of flesh that winter, and were the better of it. Sylvia rode Tom, the general-utility horse. She groomed him herself until his coat achieved a certain gloss, and in her riding habit, though it was rather tight in places by now, she presented a gallant little figure enough. I had the pony, Bob, and did the best I could. I had never been properly taught to ride, but David's method had been effective, if a little crude. He had dumped me on the grey pony, spanked her flanks and yelled: "Stick on, fathead!" A behest I had not always obeyed by any means. But Bob was a sluggish creature, and even I found it difficult to fall off him. I had no riding-habit, but Sylvia, who was practical enough in such matters, slit an old skirt up the sides and, thus caparisoned, I was content to amble humbly in her wake.

Christmas came and went almost without our knowing it. If I had not received a parcel from Rosie I doubt if I should have given it a thought. Times and seasons meant nothing to Uncle Alaric. We never attended church. And the servants were only too willing to forgo the fuss and extra work entailed by Christmas festivities.

David sent me *Bleak House*, which completed my set of Dickens and gave me rare pleasure. I felt myself to be not unlike Esther—though nothing like as noble!—with Sylvia as the golden-haired Ada and Uncle Alaric as Mr Jarndyce, my dear benefactor. But when I tried to cast David for the part of Richard I failed completely. David was himself and nobody else.

One day, soon after Christmas, Uncle Alaric called us into the library and announced in his quiet way that we were to begin school again.

I thought he meant the village school; but he said no; Mallinsons did not attend Board schools. We were to go to Kettleby.

Sylvia gasped for joy, and an awed feeling ran through me; for even I knew that Kettleby was famous and old; one of the best girls' schools in England.

"Oh, Uncle Alaric! How perfectly, perfectly *divine*!" Sylvia sang.

"I am glad you are pleased," he said, looking at me.

I said nothing, and he dismissed us.

"You might have shown some gratitude!" Sylvia scolded. "You are awful, really, Ruan!"

"Why, when I'm not grateful?" I said stubbornly.

She looked at me incredulously.

"Do you mean you don't *want* to go to Kettleby?"

"Well, I don't."

"But, Ruan, why ever not! We're most frightfully lucky to have the chance!"

"You are. I'm not."

"But, Ruan! *Kettleby*—after *Dover Street*!"

It was no use. Sylvia could never see any point of view but her own.

I wandered off to the shrubbery, to a little temple I had made for myself with old packing-cases, and the lid of an old dustbin for a dome, and a little stool to sit on when I wished to meditate. I was rather Eastern-minded at that period, having recently read of divers mysteries performed by wise men of the Orient. I practised Yoga in my temple, and seriously contemplated attempting to levitate myself into the air at no distant date. My hope was to appear suddenly over the shrubbery through the smoke of Fell's bonfire, and give him the fright of his life; which I certainly should have done, had I accomplished such a feat.

At the moment, however, the Orient concerned me far less than

Kettleby. I knew all about girls' boarding schools from my reading. You wore uniform and walked in long crocodiles, two by two. You had a crush on the games mistress, or on one of the senior girls. You organised midnight feasts in the dormitories, stuffing yourself with sardines and chocolate and cake. You were hit with hard pillows and laughed at if you said your prayers. If you were popular you never had a moment's privacy. If you were unpopular you never knew a moment's happiness.

And for this I was to leave the peace and freedom of Cobbetts! For this reality I was to exchange my dreams, my temple, my friends Rosemary and Cecilia and Giles. For this hearty, crowded existence I must turn my back on John and the pony Bob, the panelled library and the silent, satisfying companionship of Uncle Alaric.

It was not to be borne.

There was an unwritten law at Cobbetts that if we wanted to talk to Uncle Alaric we must do so at meal-times, when he gave us his courteous attention. At all other times we were to go about our business and leave him to his. So far, we had faithfully kept this law; but this, I decided, was one of those exceptional cases when laws must be broken.

Uncle Alaric worked in the library between ten and one each day; and so, the next morning, with a fast-beating heart and dry throat, I knocked at the door and slipped inside.

"I am busy," said Uncle Alaric, not looking up.

"I'm sorry," I replied, tremblingly holding my ground.

He went on writing. I did not budge. Finally he sighed and laid down his pen.

"What is it?"

"It's about Kettleby, Uncle Alaric."

"Tell me at lunch."

"No. I can't talk with Sylvia there."

He had been staring out of the window at the bare trees tossing in the wind. Now his fine grey head turned slowly round at me; his impersonal glance warmed to a little life:

"I know what you wish to say, Ruan. You don't want to go to Kettleby with Sylvia. You love Cobbetts, and she does not. You are happy here, and she is not. You believe you are not the sort of person who thrives at places like Kettleby, as Sylvia will certainly thrive. ... Well, I am inclined to agree with you."

I gasped with surprise and relief.

But he continued:

"Nevertheless, Ruan, you are mortal, and therefore fallible. It is just conceivable that you are wrong; that we are wrong, both of us. You might find something at Kettleby—some happiness—some new angle—which has so far eluded you. You might in years to come turn round on me and ask why I had not given you at least the same chance as your sister."

"I would never say that!" I exclaimed passionately.

He shrugged, and raised his eyebrows.

"And there is another thing to be considered. Education is compulsory. Where are you to receive yours if not at Kettleby?"

"Here—with you, Uncle Alaric," I cried, on an impulse.

"God forbid!" he replied quickly. But I thought the idea was not altogether displeasing to him.

We went at it hammer and tongs: my little hammer beating out arguments, and his long, precise tongs picking them up and throwing them away.

As the gong rang for lunch we came to a compromise.

"You must go to Kettleby for one term, at least," Uncle Alaric decided. "If you like it, well and good. If not, I shall not insist on your staying there. On the understanding, of course, that you give it an honest trial. I think I can rely on you for that, Ruan."

He placed his hand kindly on my shoulder, and we went in to lunch together. My heart was lighter. If I had weathered Dover Street I could weather one term of Kettleby. I never doubted that one term would be the extent of my trial.

Uncle Alaric took us to London to a famous shop, and delivered us into the hands of a terrifying lady in black satin, who fitted us out with the Kettleby green, and with all the impedimenta incidental to the spring term there. After that he put us into a cab, and we drove about London seeing the sights. Buckingham Palace. Rotten Row. Whitehall. Fleet

Street. The Mansion House. The Tower and the Bank of England. Sylvia would rather have seen the shops, and I wanted to poke about the old quarters down by the river, about which Dickens had written so vividly. But we enjoyed the jaunt all the same, and I drew the conclusion that I could be happy living in London. It was so large and impersonal. It would let you alone.

§

Kettleby School, as all the world knows, stands high on the cliffs, exposed to all the winds of heaven. Everything that is not normal and decent and right is blown away from Kettleby, along with everything that is unconventional, and a good deal that is beautiful, too.

Sylvia and I were rather young for admittance, but an exception was made in our case; partly because of our circumstances, and partly because the Headmistress came from a place near Cobbetts, and the name of Mallinson meant something to her.

The school was old, as girls' schools go, but it had every modern amenity. Large, airy classrooms; trim, tidy grounds; a well-fitted gymnasium; a good library; an excellent Staff. It catered for everything on earth—except the necessity of calling your soul your own.

I knew at once that I should be unhappy there.

Sylvia dropped into the life at Kettleby like a bolt into its socket. She was impatient of my tears and home-sickness, my dislike of communal life and my failure to make friends.

"Don't be so *silly*, Ruan! You haven't lived at Cobbetts long enough to miss it!"

And I could not explain that it was not so much Cobbetts that I missed, as *myself*.

But I tried hard, remembering my promise to give it a fair trial.

My memories of Kettleby are not very distinct. The whole life there was so alien to my nature that it passed me by, leaving little impression. But I remember it for three reasons: a conversation with the games mistress, a letter I wrote to Vera West, and my parting from Father.

The games mistress was a jolly girl, little older than many of the older pupils. She had a strong crop of brown curls, a white row of teeth perpetually showing in a laugh, and she was exactly the type I had always read about. I eyed her darkly, avoiding her by every means at my command. It was fairly easy to do this, since she was invariably surrounded by girls in every stage of fulsome adoration; indeed, the difficulty would have been to get near her.

But I remember how I came across her one day in an empty classroom, crying her eyes out, and scrubbing them with a handkerchief as grubby as my own.

"Oh, it's you, Ruan Ashley," she said, in a muffled voice, as I backed too clumsily away. "All right, come in. Yes, I'm yelling. Blubbing. Making an ass of myself. And why?" She rubbed her eyes and gave a hearty sniff. "Well, I wouldn't confess it to everyone, but you're different, somehow. … I'm unhappy here, Ruan. Desperately, heart-breakingly, howlingly unhappy." She thrust her handkerchief away as the great bell gave one of its everlasting summonses, and came to me, tipping up my chin with her firm, capable hand and giving me a watery smile. "I have to stay here, Ruan," she said swiftly. "I'm the Right Type. I'm very popular. I get a decent salary. I'm lucky to be here. But *you* don't have to stay. … Don't stay, if you can get away. Go back to your old house and your books, and forget you ever had to be hearty, tidy, enthusiastic. Be yourself, before they turn you into yet another hygienic, well-behaved, conventional little image. And for God's sake," she added, grimacing at me from the doorway, "don't say I said so!"

The next instant I heard her whistle blow, and her bright voice ringing out above the clamour of girls' voices.

It was in the middle of a drawing lesson that I suddenly thought of Vera West.

It had been a particularly exasperating day. My drawing was rather less like a cube and a bottle lying on its side than the "Stag at bay." I had been given an imposition for talking, and another one for not answering when I was spoken to. The girl next to me scratched her head with a pencil—and malice entered my soul.

I said softly:

"The *last* school I was at, I sat next to a girl who had Things in her head, too!"

She was the daughter of a viscount. And I have to record that she behaved like one.

"Really?" she replied delicately, her fair eyebrows raised the merest trifle.

"Yes. *And* fleas!" I continued, with relish.

"Oh."

"She taught me how to catch 'em," I gloated. "You wet your finger and thumb—like this—and pounce before they have the chance to jump. Then you roll them hard, to stun them, and edge them between your thumbnails, and they crack and bleed. Then you drop them in the inkwell. It's quite easy when you know how."

She looked at me as if I had the plague.

And I was suddenly sorry, because of Sylvia, who had begged me with tears in her eyes to keep Dover Street a dark secret.

Of course, the story went round like wildfire. Sylvia wept; but she had the sense not to deny it. In point of fact she elaborated it, inventing miseries we had never suffered, indignities we had never been subjected to; and because her hair was gold and her eyes brown pansies; and because she was a Mallinson, she was soon the centre of pitying interest; a martyred saint to whom everybody must be especially kind, to make up for all she had endured in the dreadful past. Clever Sylvia.

Having remembered Vera West, I bethought me of all I owed to her. In my red post-office at Cobbetts I had quite a lot of money saved, so I wrote to Uncle Alaric and asked him to break it open and send me a postal order for the amount, which he did. With the help of the games mistress I obtained a large box of chocolates tied with a pink-satin bow, and sent it to Vera with my love.

I think she was probably a good deal astonished, and I hope she was pleased; but she never replied to me, and I made no further effort to get in touch with her. But I think of her always with pleasure, Things and all, and I hope life treated her as well as she deserved.

Father went to Africa in March of that year, not long before the end of the term. He came down to Kettleby and gave us each a New Testament inscribed with our names and the date. We were given leave to go out with him, but such an idea probably never entered his head. So we sat together in the elegant, rose-pink room where visitors were received, and one of the maids brought tea and wafers of bread-and-butter; and Father looked at us kindly, but as if he were already far away and had difficulty in remembering who we were. He talked about the journey that lay before him, long and arduous, and about the Mission Station to which he had been appointed. He told us to be good children, obedient to Uncle Alaric, and asked us to write regularly to him, reporting our progress at school. He would write to us, he promised, whenever he was able. "When I come home on leave," he said, smiling a little, "I shall find two grown-up daughters waiting for me."

He told us to kneel down; and we knelt, rather sheepishly, and heartily hoping that nobody would come in, while Father prayed for us and for himself, beseeching comfort and guidance "for this Thy servant and for these Thy little ones, when the seas shall roll between us and the vast forests divide us one from the other. ..."

Sylvia and I both cried a little when he said that: Africa suddenly seemed a very long way off, and we very small and friendless and alone. But Father's face shone with such a light that our tears were replaced by awe. We felt, I think, that he was no longer Father, but the chosen servant of God, impatient to be about his Master's business; and we kissed him good-bye without any fuss or crying.

We stood at Big Gates and watched him go down the cliff road.

And suddenly I broke away from Sylvia and tore after him as fast as my legs would go.

"Father! Father! Wait, please!"

He turned and waited. I put my hand into his and looked up into his face.

"Father, say the Benediction, please. Say the one you used to say in chapel every Sunday."

He laid one hand on my tousled head and smoothed it. Then his voice—his lovely, unforgettable voice—said over me the words I had always loved: "The peace of God, that passeth all understanding, fill your heart and mind with the knowledge and love of God. Amen."

"Amen," I echoed soberly.

He bent and kissed my forehead, and I walked back up the hill without one backward glance.

§

These are my chief memories of Kettleby. I dare say I had happy moments there. I was not bullied or neglected or overworked. I had plenty to eat, friends if I had troubled to cultivate them. But I could not be myself; and that seemed to me important, as it still does.

Uncle Alaric kept his word and, when Sylvia went back for the summer term, I was allowed to stay at Cobbetts; and, after some preliminary doubts and hesitations, he took over my education himself.

Chapter Two

§

And now began for me a quiet and happy period of my life. Each morning I worked with Uncle Alaric in the library. In the afternoons I was free to do whatever I liked. And in the evenings I prepared my lessons for the next day. A regular, quiet, and orderly life. Discipline without the clanging of bells. Friendship without sentimentality. Recreation without compulsion. And above all—freedom.

Uncle Alaric was an excellent, though unconventional, teacher. If he were rather apt to stray from the subject in hand to some aspect of the history of Cobbetts, it was invariably interesting and instructive, and I lost nothing by it. He discovered in me a flair for languages, and, besides Latin and Greek, he taught me French, German, and what little Spanish he knew. He made history come alive for me, and geography was no longer a rather boring affair of map-drawing and lists of imports and exports, but an exciting and never-ending adventure into strange and coloured lands. English literature, always my favourite lesson, became a pure delight, and even mathematics took on a pattern of grave beauty under his guidance.

I was fortunate indeed in having Uncle Alaric as friend and teacher, and I am glad to remember that the lessons gave pleasure to him as well as me.

In the afternoon hours I played my own games, or went for long rides with John running happily at Bob's heels. Far afield I rode, to Ashalby and Holden's Cross; to Abbots Leigh, where the lovely ruins of the Abbey stand on the hill's crest like delicate lace against the blowing sky; and to the tiny village of Crum, almost hidden by a ring of woods and looking exactly like a village built with a child's bricks.

Uncle Alaric saw me setting off on one such ride. He looked at my slit-up skirt with extreme distaste.

"Have you no proper habit, Ruan?"

"Oh, no, but it doesn't matter," I said cheerfully; for I felt a little guilty about the expensive uniforms he had provided for my use at Kettleby, all to no purpose.

That very night he took my measurements and wrote to London. And after that I rode resplendent in grey cord breeches, leather jerkin, and high boots. I fancied myself greatly, though it was an awful nuisance having to change.

This question of the money Uncle Alaric was spending on Sylvia and me troubled me not a little. One day a car drove up to Cobbetts and there was a visitor for Uncle Alaric; a most unusual event. An hour or so later I saw old Blossom and Fell carrying a large flat parcel out to the car. Later still I noticed that a picture was missing from the upper hall. I remembered it well. It was the portrait of a lady, the sister of that Giles who was my friend. Her name was Margaret, and she had been painted at her tapestry. I had never liked her very much. She looked stout and smug, and I thought Giles probably laughed at her a good deal and pulled her hair when they were children, and that she would certainly run to tell her mother.

But I hadn't wanted her to go. Her home was at Cobbetts; and I had a shrewd idea that Sylvia and I had turned her out.

I bluntly asked Uncle Alaric if this were so, and he at once admitted it. He never made any bones about things like that. He smiled at my troubled face.

"Does it matter so much to you, Ruan?" Then he said musingly: "How strange that you, who are nearly all Ashley, should care so deeply for Cobbetts and understand it; while to Sylvia, who is nearly all Mallinson, it doesn't matter a scrap, except as a setting for her own beauty. ... But you must not care about Madam Margaret, Ruan, or indeed about any possessions. They are a nuisance, a hindrance. I have found that out. The less you care about people and things the less hurt they can do you. Always remember that you, yourself, are the only important thing in your life. People and possessions will come and go, making a pattern around you; but nothing really touches you. You began alone and will end alone. The essential *you* is alone all the time."

I said no more about expense. But when Sylvia came home and announced that she intended asking Uncle Alaric to take us abroad I set myself bitterly against the idea. Sylvia said I was a mean thing; that all the other girls talked about Cannes, and Brittany, and Italian Lakes—and all *she* could talk about was Scarborough and Aberystwyth, and it made her sick. I promised passionately that if she dared to ask Uncle Alaric for another single thing I would bang her head against the spikes in the wrought-iron gate, by which we happened to be standing.

Sylvia said in her Kettleby voice that I was utterly impossible; but she moved away from the gate pretty quickly, just the same, and no more was heard of foreign travel.

The question of holidays was, as a matter of fact, concerning me deeply. Much as I loved Cobbetts and Uncle Alaric, I longed for David and the moor. But I did not—oh, most passionately I did not—want Sylvia to come too. She had no desire to come; but I was afraid that Rosie, in the kindness of her heart, would suggest it, and Uncle Alaric, in relief, would jump at it. And, in fact, Rosie did write and suggest it. But, to my unbounded joy, Sylvia was invited to Scotland, to the home of one of her Kettleby friends, and Uncle Alaric made no objections to either of our plans.

An added joy was the news that David himself was coming to fetch me.

$\mathcal{G}$

It was unutterable happiness to have David at Cobbetts even for an hour.

The old house was looking its best, drowsy in hot July sunlight; while within lay a magic of sun and shadow, of delicate line and noble space and old, strange odours that touched the heart to reverence.

I took David everywhere. To my little bedroom under the west gable. To the dark, book-smelling library, to the Queen's Bedchamber, and the haunted room, and the dim, musty attics, whose cobwebby walls held all the silence in the world. I took him out into the gardens, where Fell was at his everlasting bonfire, through the shrubbery to my temple. He sat down on my little stool, and I told him about the lamas and their mysterious powers of levitation, and how I was trying to copy them. David said "Crikey!" And he tried it too, going red in the face in the process.

"It's no good blowing yourself out!" I said scornfully. "You're not laying an egg. You must first make your mind a complete blank."

He immediately looked like the village idiot.

"Now let the thought of rising up into the air kind of soak in. Let yourself relax. Go on, *relax!*"

David's eyes slowly crossed themselves into a frightful squint.

"I can feel it," he rumbled solemnly. "I can feel it coming on! ... Going up. ... Household Furnishings, Millinery, Ladies' Underwear, Haberdashery, Boots. ..."

He tipped the stool and fell flat on his back, and the temple collapsed on him. Weak with laughter, I dug him out, and in sheer happiness at being together again we began to rush about the gardens, uttering wild war-whoops, leaping Fell's bonfire, and jangling the great bell till old Blossom and Maggie came out to scold and Uncle Alaric appeared at the library window.

"For a person who does not care about the company of other people, Ruan," he said mildly, "you are making a remarkable exhibition of yourself."

"This isn't other people," I explained, panting. "This is David."

"Indeed."

Uncle Alaric shook hands with David, who was grinning sheepishly and dusting the knees of his grey flannels.

"It's all right, sir; I'm taking her off your hands now. There's only half an hour before the train goes."

Uncle Alaric smiled and shut the window.

Sylvia came out on the terrace. She did not go up to Edinburgh until the following day. She was looking cool and beautiful in white muslin, her curls tied at the neck with a broad black bow. She held out her hand to David.

"How do you do, David?"

He shook hands awkwardly and smoothed his hair.

"Long time since we met," he mumbled.

She looked up at him under her lashes.

"You look *quite* grown-up, David."

"Oh, rot!" But he looked pleased and fingered his tie.

"You'll never be ready in time, child," Sylvia said in her Kettleby voice; and I could have murdered her.

David made a ferocious pass at me.

"Yes, go and wash your silly face, will you!"

Sylvia's laugh tinkled out.

"She *does* look a sketch, doesn't she! I can't *think* what she does to herself. ... How's Lowton, David?"

I ran off and made myself ready. I said good-bye to Uncle Alaric and put John on his lead and picked up the suitcase Maggie had packed. When I staggered on to the terrace, David was standing with his hands in his pockets, whistling jauntily. Sylvia was leaning against a pillar, her hands filled with pink roses, and there was a pink rose in her hair. She looked quite startlingly beautiful, far above all earthly thoughts and desires. I gaped at her.

David grabbed the case and told me to hurry.

"Good-bye, Sylvia." For some reason I did not want to kiss her, and she made no movement towards me.

"Good-bye," she murmured, looking at David.

We went out into the road and began to climb the hill to the tiny station.

"Golly!" David said suddenly. "She's a stunner, isn't she!"

I agreed staunchly that she was.

A silence fell between us, broken only by David's whistling. I saw the smoke of the approaching train. Abruptly he seized my hand and began to run, and we just got there in time. He threw my suitcase up on the rack and we fell on the seat panting and laughing.

Presently he came and sat beside me and ruffled my short, wiry locks.

"*You* haven't changed, though. Not a scrap," he said. "Nice little Tinribs."

He left his arm lying across my shoulders. And I loved him.

Always, when I went back to the moor, I was fearful lest it should seem less lovely than before. And always it was even more lovely than I remembered it.

I think it was the sense of freedom that I found so elusive. At the Manse, my horizon bounded by the houses across the road; at Cobbetts, brooding deep in its gentle green slopes and woods and hedges; at Kettleby, perilous on the windy cliffs, it was difficult to believe in the vastness, the fierce, tender, wide-flung solidity of the moor. Changing with each changing season, it was yet immutable. Bounded on the north by hills, on the south by black miles of industry, it still seemed illimitable. High above the world, it was ever my stronghold and my refuge, my dear and lovely home.

Rosie was glad to see me; very relieved, I fancy, to find that Cobbetts had not made me despise the House. Until she was quite sure of this she was a little standoffish, hiding her pleasure behind a dour, north-country banter. It was:

"Same bedroom as before, you see. I was thinking I'd happen better get best room fettled up, now you're so grand!"

And it was:

"Nay, I reckon us folks has to pay extra to speak to you now, *Miss Ashley!*"

But Rosie could never be anything but Rosie for long, and she soon got over it, and was laughing and hugging me and asking innumerable questions, just as before.

She was a little dubious about letting me wear David's clothes now I was beginning to grow up, and I had a hard job to persuade her. But in the end she gave in—and once again I knew the comfort of grey flannels, open-necked cricket shirt, and bare legs.

"Hurray, hurray!
It's my holiday!"

I sang, kicking my legs into the air and sliding down the banisters. Rawlings, passing with a tray of silver, was scandalised.

"If I'd shown myself off like that at your age, my pa would have given me a good smack bottom!"

"Rawlings, *please*—not before the children!" David said primly.

I went into the kitchen to see Cook, who, rather surprisingly, enfolded me in a plump embrace and called me her poor lamb. I didn't want anyone crying over me just then; I was too happy. I escaped as soon as I decently could and we ran through the stiff gardens, out on to the moor road, and away down to the Farm.

As we went through the white gate I remembered that Mrs Abbey was dead. Rosie had told me in a letter, and I had been very sorry at the time, but I had forgotten; so much had happened to me. Now, remembering, I hung back. Mrs Abbey had always been very kind to me. I didn't like the idea of some strange woman bending over the hot range, or calling us home to tea. But David reassured me; there was nobody in her place. A girl came from the village once a week, and for the rest Luke fettled for himself.

We peeped in at the cottage, and all was clean and orderly, the geraniums glowing brightly as ever in the windows and the brasses shining. It was strange, though, to see no fire burning in the grate, to hear no laughing welcome, to smell no lovely smells of cakes and bread and bubbling red jam.

"When Mrs Abbey was alive," I pointed out to David, "Rosie used to spend half her time here, cooking. Now, when Luke really needs help, she doesn't come at all."

"She couldn't very well, now."

"Why ever not?"

"Oh, well," he said vaguely, "people are like that. The best thing Rosie and Luke could do would be to get married."

"But, David—Luke's a servant!"

"Oh, don't be a stinking little snob, Tinribs. And anyway, Luke's as good as Rosie—as good as you or me. Better! He can trace his family back hundreds of years, which is a sight more than I can do. Mr Lord found an old book about this district, and there was a reference to a Luke D'Abbaye, who was no end of a swell in Richard the Third's time."

I was startled and impressed.

"But then—why on earth don't they *get* married, if they want to?"

"Oh, lord, how should I know! People are so frightfully soppy when they grow up. … I expect it's Rosie's money that keeps Luke off. It's the D'Abbaye pride in him. No chap likes everyone to think he's marrying a girl for her money. And don't go quacking to Rosie about it, or I'll knock your silly head off. You're rather too apt to poke your nose into other people's business, you know. Come on, let's go down to the orchard."

Luke greeted me with his usual slow, sweet smile. He was doing something to the apple-trees, which had suffered with blight that year. I watched his strong, gentle hands with a new respect. Luke D'Abbaye, a very gentil knight, wielding a strong sword on Bosworth Field against the upstart Lancastrians. Or further back yet; a Crusader, perhaps, in shining armour, Cross blazoned on his breast. Or a gallant outlaw, robbing the idle rich to feed the poor, so hey for the greenwood, O! … Luke D'Abbaye. Luke Abbey, serving his mistress, loving her, but too proud still for favours. Incomprehensible, but gallant in my eyes.

When we had visited all the farm creatures, and seen the new barn Luke was so proud of, we went to visit Mr Lord, and with him drank a cup of pale, fragrant China tea and nibbled a dry biscuit. He listened with interest to David's account of the term at Lowton, and talked to me about Cobbetts, which he had known well many years ago. He did not mention Mother's death in so many words, but when we were leaving he sent David out of the room on some pretext and, placing his hand on my shoulder, said he had something to give me. He took from his desk a little leather box. It opened with a spring; and inside was a knot of faded blue ribbons, smelling ever so faintly of violets, and a small, water-colour sketch of Mother as a girl in a blue ball-dress, with a fan of white feathers widespread. It was, I suppose, an amateurish affair, but the artist had caught the likeness well enough; and as I gazed at the gleaming gold hair, the brown, laughing eyes, the eager poise of the girlish figure, my heart dissolved in tenderness and love.

"Oh, how can you bear to part from this!" I cried, choking back my tears.

Mr Lord smiled gently.

"You will have longer to wait than I before seeing her again," was all he said.

⁊

Cracked Willy rocked himself to and fro in the hot sunshine. We stopped to have a word with him, as we often did, and David went into Mrs Shufflebotham's shop and bought him some liquorice ladders, which he loved.

"Well, how are you to-day, Willy?"

"Hur—hur—hur."

"Pretty bobbish, eh?"

"Hur. Hur—hur."

"Here's some liquorice, Willy."

"Hur! Hur!"

His mother came hurrying out, wiping soggy, steaming hands on a coarse apron.

"Say thanks, Willy, fer t'spice."

"Hur."

"It's not one of his good days, lovey," she apologised. "Times, he'll be like yon all day, an' nivver get a word out'n him—an' then he'll up an' talk same as you or me. Talk like a Christian when he's a mind, can't you, Our Willy?"

"Hur—hur—hur!"

She looked at him fondly. He was the eldest of her large brood; her first-born; her love-child. His forehead sloped sharply back above a snoutish nose, and below it his chin sloped back into his neck. He had little, cunning eyes, and a wet mouth that wouldn't keep shut. He was good-tempered enough unless he was crossed, and then his huge, ham-like fists would clench and his face would go dark red, and he would scream and scream until he got his own way. Summer and winter alike, unless the weather were actually wet, he sat outside the cottage, jerking himself backwards and forwards endlessly. His mother always declared he could talk like a Christian when he wanted to, but I never heard him say anything but "Hur—hur." The rest of the family were lively youngsters, with bright, cheeky grins and strong limbs and tearing spirits; but their mother loved none of them as she loved Willy.

We went down to the forge and saw the blacksmith and his son at work. The bullet-headed boy lurked in the gloom, pulling hideous faces at me when David wasn't looking. I remembered the sweet, unearthly purity of his voice in church singing *Our Blest Redeemer*—and wondered how it was done.

The blacksmith was a jovial fellow, as all blacksmiths should be, with an immense, curly black beard, and muscles like rope. He called me "l'il Miss" and David "l'il Mester," and each time he did so his son squinted at me and pretended to be sick.

We went to Karenhapuk's grave and tidied it up, and we went to see some calves at Clough's Farm, at the farther end of Staving, and we walked back over the moor, hot and tired and well content.

I put my precious box away safely in my suitcase. I showed it to David, but to no one else.

Joshua came in from the factory, carrying the largest box of chocolates I had ever seen in my life.

"Is Miss Ashley, of Cobbetts, living here?" he inquired of Rosie.

"Get on with you!" said Rosie, laughing.

Whereupon he turned to David and me in turn, with the same question. We played up to him, knowing how he loved his joke. And in the end he gave me the box, declaring that, as Miss Ashley was not present, I might as well have it—and immediately afterwards telling me how much it cost, and warning me not to ask for another thing these holidays, because he was broke!

Chapter Three

§

We did a good deal of riding in those holidays. I had the grey pony, and David saddled Sally, who was glad enough of the exercise. I wore the kit Uncle Alaric had bought for me, and David, not to be outdone, arrayed himself in boots and breeches, too. Rosie had bought him some silk shirts, and he gave two of them to me, so we went arrayed like the lilies of the field, and mightily pleased with ourselves.

We rode to places I had never seen before. Clough's Gill, ten miles from Staving, where the outcrop of limestone forms a natural terrace, and silver birches stand in a row like maidens struck into trees by some enchantress, until their lovers come to kiss them into life again. And Setton Gill, where the moor gives place to grass, very fine and green, and where a stream meanders and widens and falls with a sudden rush of energy down a rocky gorge into a pool, foam-flecked and deep, and then suddenly yawns, as it were, and goes sleepily on its way. We went to the tarn, up at Scartop, lonely and bleak, infinitely desolate; so that after an hour of its strange silence we were glad of the noisy gallop down to Scartop Farm, where John Henry Binns and his fat, jolly wife made us very welcome with pink, succulent ham and buttered tea-cake and great curd tarts and bowls of stewed fruit and cream. We rode through Staving and Buckham to the lost village of Close Caulton, where there are no young people, and no shops and no church; only seven cottages and an inn, all in a like state of dissolution and decay. We got no welcome at Close Caulton; only inimical stares from old, rheumy eyes and the blank stares of shut doors and fastened windows. But the country round about the village was very lovely, and we took our own food and sat high above the sinister, unfriendly place, making up stories about it and enjoying ourselves.

But to my mind no place was so dear as Walker's Ridge, and no days so happy as those spent in our little hollow under the stunted rowan-tree.

§

Towards the end of the month I had an accident which effectively put an end to my riding for many weeks. The grey pony—soberest and safest of animals—suddenly shied at a paper bag lying by the side of the road; and I, unused to such temperamental behaviour, was taken unawares and tossed from his back clean over a wall on to the moor.

David was kneeling beside me when I came to my senses.

"All right, Tinribs?" he asked anxiously. His face was so white that the freckles stood out as if they were apart from the skin.

"I think so."

I moved gingerly, and a red-hot pain shot up my left arm. David's hands were moving about me, making careful investigations. I moved my limbs at his direction. There seemed to be nothing amiss apart from the arm.

"Is it broken, David?"

"I think so."

He began to rummage in the rucksack he always carried. In a short time he had my arm in splints, strapped across my chest, causing me an astonishingly small amount of pain in the process.

"I always carry the stuff," he admitted, rather reluctantly. "You never know what might happen, and doctors don't sit on every gate. All the same, we've got to find one as soon as possible," he added. We were eight miles from home. "We'd better make for Basleydyke. There's a chap there called Ranter who's pretty good, and we can get some sort of a lift home for you."

"I'd rather ride," I said mulishly, for I was terrified of David thinking me a weakling.

"Just the sort of damn silly thing you would want to do," he retorted. "Come on, get up slowly, and I'll hoist you on to Sally with me. Then you can lean back and make yourself comfortable."

I grumbled and protested, but it was no good. Up on Sally I had to go;

and I must confess it was pleasant to lean back on David, for the moor had suddenly acquired a disconcerting habit of swinging slowly round and rising up towards me, and then receding in a faint mist. ...

We went in slow and stately fashion the two miles to Basleydyke, David supporting me with one arm and leading the grey pony with the other, and guiding Sally with his heels.

Dr Ranter was a youngish man, with a scowl and red whiskers, and quick, competent hands.

"Who did the bandaging?" he snapped.

"I did," David said, flushing. "Sorry. It's the best I could manage in the circumstances."

"Ah. Where did you learn it?"

"I've got a book," David stammered.

"Oh, you've got a book? ... Now then, young lady, I'm going to hurt you, but not more than I can help ... that's the way ... easy now. ... Oh, so you've got a book? ... Well, I've got a book on rabbits, but I can't rear the damn things. They die like flies."

When he had finished my arm he gave me something to drink in a little glass and sent David off home with the horses.

"I'll bring the patient back in my trap."

"Smart young feller that," he remarked, as we bowled swiftly along the white moor road. "I've seen arms bandaged worse than yours in a London hospital." And I blazed with pride.

So after that it was shank's mare for me all the rest of the month. My arm gave me very little trouble, and I soon learnt to forget it. It was too hot for long walks, so David and I spent most of our time at the Farm, or lying in our hollow, talking endlessly. As soon as I had gone back to Cobbetts, David was going to stay with Stebbing in Newquay. He was looking forward to fishing and swimming, and sailing the small yacht Stebbing's father had given him for his birthday.

"Does he ever talk about me now?" I asked diffidently.

"Sometimes." He twirled a sprig of heather between his white teeth and then spat it out. "Not so much as he used to, though, since I bashed his head for him."

"Why did you?" I asked curiously.

"Oh—always slopping about you. ... I got sick of your silly name!" he explained amiably.

"I bet you had a job," I grinned. "He's twice your size."

"All the more credit to me—the great fat hairy baboon!"

"I like Stebbing, so shut up!"

"Oh, lord—you're at it, now! I'll give him your love, shall I? And perhaps he'll write another stanza of the famous poem. 'Ruan, thy name is like the purple broccoli!' Very touching." He wiped his eyes elaborately. "Why don't you write an ode to *his* name? 'Stebbing, thy name is like a pink blancmange!' ... Not a dry eye in the house!"

"Oh, do shut up!" I said crossly.

We were both rather on edge that day, as we often were when the inevitable parting once more came in sight. There was an added annoyance this time, for David was to spend one of the precious remaining days down at the factory with Joshua. True, I had been invited, too, but I hated the factory, and refused to go. I was terrified of the noise—so different from the jolly bang-clang-clang of the blacksmith's forge, which heartened, even while it deafened you. The factory noise was like a huge black monster, lashing out with cruel claws in its effort to escape. But it couldn't escape, because of the great gates and the endless, thronging streets that encompassed it. And so it grew ever more savage, and tried to snatch you in its claws and drag you down into the blackness and the noisome vapours and the unspeakable terrors of white-hot, molten metal.

"Why do you have to go?" I said angrily.

"Because the Old Man wants it."

"But it's your holiday!"

"Only one day out of it."

"Well, go when you get back from Newquay."

"There won't be time. I go back to Lowton the next day." He rolled over on to his back, and stretched. "I don't *want* to go, heaven knows, but I simply can't refuse. One day out of each holiday isn't much to ask, when you think of all the Old Man's done for me. Besides, I might as well get used to it; it's going to be my life."

We fell silent. I sat cross-legged on the heather, my arm strapped across my chest, and gazed out over the moor. The day was calm and beautiful, very hot, with a steady hum of insects all about us and the scent of sun-soaked heather rising like incense to a cloudless sky. Very faintly the blacksmith's hammer sounded down in the valley. A white drift of smoke hung on the air above the farm-house where the old madwoman lived, and I could hear the tiny clinking of a pail. The heat quivered above the heather. The distant hills were drained of colour, withdrawn into themselves, grey sleeves flung across sleeping faces. Beauty welled up in me like a thrusting bud and burst into lovely flower. How dear, how dear the moor was to me! Unchanged, unchanging, my stronghold and my refuge; my dear and lovely home.

I looked at David. He was lying still, eyes closed against the sun. I saw the soft, golden down outlining his cheek and lip, the firm, rather prominent line of jaw, the pulse that beat in his bare, brown neck. I saw his big, capable hands, the breadth of his shoulders, the length of him stretched out on the heather; and my heart acknowledged painfully, fearfully, what Sylvia had seen in one glance.

David was growing up.

The day's beauty took on the added, wistful glamour of impermanence.

David was growing up.

Soon he would be seventeen. At seventeen he was to leave Lowton and go straight into the factory. He was to begin at the bottom, as Joshua had, to work his way up through each grade and department, until he was able to take the reins from Joshua's hands. Day after day, and all the days, he would be down there in the town with the black, roaring monster. The moor would be here, and I should be here, but David would have no time for us.

I tried to shy away from the thought, but it pursued me relentlessly. Many a time before I had dodged it, but not this time. David was growing up. Things could not go on for ever as they were.

I tried to imagine David grown up. Collar and tie. Moustache. Hard, shaven cheeks. Walking-stick. Pipe. Fountain-pen and cheque-book. Not to-day, I'm in a hurry. Not to-day, not to-day, not to-day. ...

It was no use, I could not visualise it properly. Oh, time, stand still, stand still! Oh, drum, be silent! ...

"What's up, Tinribs?"

David put out a finger and neatly lifted a tear from my cheek. It shone like a diamond in the sun.

"Nothing."

"Liar!"

"Oh, David—don't grow up!"

"Right." He rolled over lazily. "Let's die here and now, both of us. Come on, die!"

I grinned weakly.

"Don't be an ass, David."

"I like that—from you!" he exploded. "You'd be the first one to shout if you really thought you were going to die."

"Well, of course, I don't really want to die."

"Then you must want to grow up."

"No, I don't. I want to stay just as we are for ever and ever. Just like this; you and me and the moor, and nobody else."

"You're an awful little funk, aren't you, Tinribs?" David said kindly.

I did not reply.

"Do you remember the circus—that time when Sylvia had measles and you couldn't go?"

I nodded.

"And when Rosie offered to take you the next year you still wouldn't go."

"Yes, I know."

"Why wouldn't you, Tinribs?"

I prodded the dry earth with my fingers. I thought of the pink silk in Rosie's hat that I hadn't wanted to cut. I remembered the clown kissing me, and my sudden, intense longing to go to the circus. I lived again the moment when I sat in the gig outside the fairground, and the band hurled its strange, stirring challenge at my feet, and I shrank from taking it up. How could I make David understand?

"If I want a thing tremendously," I said slowly and with difficulty, "something absolutely lovely, I—I sort of don't want to take it. In case I'm disappointed. ... I can't explain really, David. It's—a sort of feeling that what I never have I shall always keep. ... Oh, it does sound rot, I know."

"It does," he agreed. He yawned and sat up, rubbing his tousled head free of heather. "The trouble with you, my child, is that you're an idealist—which is a fancy name for a coward. You live in your imagination, and you're frightened to look life in the face, for fear it's not quite so attractive as your own idea of it. It doesn't seem to occur to you what a hell of a lot you may be missing. Your ideas of life may be a jolly sight *short* of the real thing, and then you'll be done in the eye." He stood up and stretched mightily. "Thank God, I'm no idealist!" he said, with satisfaction. "I don't care much if life's beautiful or not; it's life, and I want every bit of it that I can grab. Lungs full of it, fists full of it. Tons of it on my shoulders and miles of it under my feet, and solid walls of it for me to break down. ... Speech by D. Shane, Esquire. The House rose at him, and an instructive time was had by all!"

He bent down and dealt me a resounding smack on the bottom. "Come on, get up, fathead!"

"I don't want to. I want to stay here for ever and ever."

"And lose your good dinner!" he roared. "That's just what I've been saying, isn't it? You grab at the thingummy and miss the what-you-may-call-it. Up you get, young Ashley! Come on."

He walked off whistling.

I sat still. A sudden weight of loneliness fell on me. David was growing up. He was going away from me, walking away, whistling, unconcerned, eager for life whether good or bad. He was going where I could not follow. He would never, never come back.

"David—come back!"

I tried to shout it, but it was only a whisper. The whistling grew fainter as he dropped down over the edge of the Ridge. The blacksmith's hammer was silent; but the hum of insects was like the roll of drums, dark with foreboding.

"David, come back, come back!" ...

I put my head down on my knees and began to cry in good earnest.

Then suddenly I heard the sound of feet running swiftly in the heather, and in a moment David's arms were round me, and he was laughing and scolding, drying my eyes clumsily with a hanky that had a peardrop stuck in one corner; lifting me gently to my feet.

"I thought you'd gone! I thought you'd gone! …"

He pushed the damp hair out of my eyes and bent and kissed me.

"What an idiotic little Tinribs. And in any case, you know very well I should always come back."

§

The next day he went to the factory with Joshua, and Rosie and I were left alone.

We walked down into Staving to get a new collar for John, and some honey from old Miss Starkey, who lived alone in a two-roomed cottage and talked to her bees. She swore she knew each one of them apart. We bought stamps and liquorice all-sorts at Mrs Shufflebotham's, and began the steep climb back to the House.

When we were near the Farm it came on to rain and we had to run for it. We shook ourselves at the door of the Farm, and I wiped John's paws and laid hold of the door-handle; but Rosie told me, rather sharply, to let be.

"Aren't we going in, Rosie?" I exclaimed, in astonishment. She shook her head impatiently.

"It's none going to rain long. Porch is good enough."

The door opened suddenly behind us and Luke stood there. He looked at Rosie with blue, unsmiling eyes.

"You'll come in, missus?" he pleaded.

Rosie's colour was high, her lips pressed thin; but John and I rushed into the kitchen and she could hardly refuse.

The kitchen was tidy with that forced, cheerless tidiness that is almost worse than disorder. The range was blacked but fireless. The curtains were clean, but they hung crooked—a thing Mrs Abbey could never have borne—and the lace was wearing into holes. The cushions had all been put away and the rug made of many-coloured rags was rolled up in a corner. The geraniums needed water. Luke's dinner lay on the table; bread and cheese and a jug of beer. He was using no plates and the table-cloth was a clean newspaper.

I saw Rosie's glance flick round the room, and her mouth went soft and full.

"Ee, Luke!" she said pitifully.

They stood looking at each other across the table, and I felt awkward and in the way. I went back to the door. The rain was stopping already, so I ran out to the barn and picked John up and hugged him in my arms, and his hot, pink tongue comforted me. After a while I got very hungry. The rain had cleared off and the earth gave out a clean, damp breath. I went back to the porch, still holding John in my arms.

There was no sound in the kitchen, but somehow I didn't like to go in. I peeped through the crack of the door. Rosie was sitting on the settle and Luke knelt before her with his head lying in her lap. Her hands were stroking his hair very slowly and gently; she was staring out through the window with a queer, blind look on her face.

I stole silently away and waited for her down by the white gate. And presently she came, and we went up the hilly road together, back to the House.

Soon after dinner Dr Ranter's trap came bowling up the drive.

"Goodness!" I exclaimed crossly. "He can't want to see my beastly arm *again*! He's been three times this week, already!"

Rosie gave me a strange look and laughed rather noisily. She began to straighten her hair.

"Aye, he does come a bit often. He does an' all!"

Dr Ranter asked me a few questions, and then told me that was all, if I wanted to run away now. So I escaped quickly and took John into the kitchen garden until he had gone; but he was a long time in going. When I found Rosie her face was set in a hard sort of smile, and she was staring out of the window with the same blind look she had worn at the Farm.

"What on earth did *he* want all this time?" I said in some annoyance, for the afternoon was half gone.

"What, luv? ... Oh, *him*! ... I reckon he wants to marry me, that's all."

"Rosie!" I exclaimed, gaping.

She gave that noisy laugh again.

"Aye, yon's a chap who knows what he wants, quick, an' doesn't let grass grow under his feet getting it, neether."

"Rosie, you *couldn't* marry him! He's got red whiskers, and an awful temper, I should think."

"So've I, come to that, luv. ... I reckon I might do worse."

"You might do an awful lot better," I said warmly, with what I felt to be exceptional guile.

"Aye, you're right there, luv. A wonderful lot better. So I might—but I doubt I never shall."

"You should go to London, Rosie, and marry a duke. You'd make a splendid duchess."

Rosie became wildly hilarious.

"Fancy me being presented at Court, with white feathers in me head, like a cockatoo, and a train half a mile long! I should look a right fool, shouldn't I, if I fell flat on me face and kicked me legs up in t'air! ... Nay, come on, lass, we'll go down t'road and meet David."

"I bet he's glad to-day's over," I said, as we dawdled along playing with John. Rosie gave me a sudden sharp glance.

"What makes you say that, Ruan?"

I remembered, too late, that David had promised to tan my behind if I ever breathed a word about his hopes of becoming a doctor.

"Oh, I don't know," I said lamely. "I expect he's enjoyed it ever so much." My ears and cheeks were flaming and I hummed loudly and kept my face turned from her.

"You're a poor hand at lying, aren't you, luv? ... Come on, out with it! Does the lad dread going into t'works?"

"Oh, Rosie, he made me promise *faithfully* to keep it a secret! It—just slipped out, sort of."

"Well, seeing as it *has* slipped out, you'd better tell me the whole thing, else happen I shall get all sorts of ideas in me head." Then, as I still hesitated, she said quite sharply: "Go on, tell me, or I shall have to ask David."

So I told her how David had always wanted to be a famous surgeon, and how he'd bought all sorts of books and studied them, and what Dr Ranter had said about the way he had bandaged my arm. And I told her about the day he had found out about his father and about all Joshua's goodness to him, and how he had sworn to give up his ambition and do what Joshua wanted.

Rosie's face was troubled.

"Nay!" she said at intervals. "Nay!"

"Oh, Rosie—promise you won't tell Uncle Josh. I think David would kill me!"

"I know he used to mess about with a lot of muck in his bedroom, but I never thought owt about it being serious," she muttered.

"Rosie! You won't tell Uncle Josh?"

She sighed deeply, bitterly.

"Nay, I won't tell. What's use? ... Ee, luv, I fair hate yon factory. It killed me mother, and it's spoiling my life—and now it's going to spoil our David's. ... Ee, I wish we'd nivver got money. I wish we'd nivver left t'house in Cheddar Street, I do that!"

The gig came spanking over the brow of the hill. David was driving. Joshua sat beside him, massive and erect. Suddenly I could not see them for tears.

Chapter Four

§

Sylvia and I had a fortnight together at Cobbetts before she went back to Kettleby.

She was very amiable, full of the glories of her holiday, and the splendours of Monica's home in Edinburgh.

"Six servants!" she chanted. "Two men and four women. Real servants, in proper uniforms, not like ours. And Monica's father has a motor-car, a beauty. It can do fifty miles an hour, at a pinch—think of that! My dear, we simply *whizzed* about the place. We hardly ever did less than fifteen! The house is gorgeous. You sink up to your neck in carpets, and you simply disappear in the chairs and sofas. And a six-course dinner every night, with everybody in evening dress, and *menu cards* on the table, just like an hotel—yes, *really*, Ruan!"

"Did you stay up to dinner?" I asked incredulously.

"Only twice. But Monica's going to be allowed to for good next year. And my *dear*—her dresses! Honestly, I nearly turned green with envy! I felt an awful frump beside her. I do think Uncle Alaric ought to buy us more clothes. I simply haven't a *thing* to wear in the holidays."

"He can't afford it," I said stubbornly. "And anyway, you've got as many as I have."

"Yes, I know, but—"

Had she actually said "you don't matter" I could not have understood more clearly. "Your riding-kit is better than mine," she added quickly.

"Well, we're only kids, so it doesn't matter," I remarked, not without a certain relish; for Sylvia had suddenly acquired a number of grown-up tricks and airs which I found peculiarly exasperating.

She smiled her maddening, superior smile.

"Monica's brothers didn't think I was a kid. Especially Harold. He's at Sandhurst." Her voice dropped and she giggled a little. "He fell in love with me! He wants us to get married just as soon as I'm old enough. I shall probably go out to India and have a lot of servants; and there'll be military balls and polo, and card-parties every night at the Club."

"Sylvia!" I gasped. There was no use trying to pretend I was not thoroughly impressed by now. I was, in fact, quite overwhelmed. I gazed on her with awe. *Sylvia*—already talking of getting married!

And, in truth, there was not much of the child left in Sylvia, though she was scarcely thirteen yet. She was very tall for her age, with none of the awkward dumpiness or lanky stoops of adolescence. Her movements were graceful and controlled, her figure slender and very beautifully proportioned. Her colouring was almost perfect. She had picked up from somewhere appealing little tricks of hands and eyes and speech which, while they irritated me, I dimly realised must be attractive enough to men. No, Sylvia was no longer a child.

Uncle Alaric noticed it. I knew by the way he spoke to her. He was invariably kind and courteous to us both, but he began to defer to Sylvia as mistress of the house; and if there were a gleam of irony—even of amusement—in the formality, it was certainly not apparent to Sylvia.

The servants felt it, too. Sylvia had all of Mother's way with servants and, I suspect, a good deal of Grandfather's, too. Maggie grumbled unceasingly, but she bullied the unfortunate Joy into sweeping and dusting more assiduously during Sylvia's holidays than at any other time. And even old Blossom nipped about more nimbly and served our meals less untidily at those times. The gardener, Fell, was her slave. Only for Sylvia would he abandon his bonfires and fill the house with ragged sunflowers and leggy asters. On the day before her arrival from Kettleby he would sharpen his scythe and mow the lawns with long, swishing curves. He would tie back the blowsy roses and clip the sprouting hedges and hack in a dispirited fashion at the weeds in the gravel. As soon as the holidays were over he went back to his bonfires again.

Sylvia thanked none of them for their pains—and they thought the more of her for that.

"I should love to have Monica to stay next hols," she confided to me, "but how can I, with the place in this state! You should just see Monica's home, Ruan. It's like a palace by contrast."

I hit out in defence of Cobbetts.

"You ass! Cobbetts doesn't *need* thick carpets and great vulgar chairs and sofas. It's one of the loveliest old houses in England, and it's an honour to be invited here. Monica indeed! ... Her father made a lot of cheap red soap, and bought a 'gentleman's estate' with the money, and had it furnished by a London firm!"

"Just like your precious Rosie's house," Sylvia reminded me quietly.

"Rosie's different!" I flashed.

"Yes—thank goodness!"

"You let my friends alone. They're a jolly sight better than yours, you beast!"

Sylvia daintily tucked a golden curl behind her ear.

"*Your friends!* I You haven't got any friends, except uneducated people like the Days, and that Luke person, who is a *servant*."

I remembered Luke D'Abbaye, and kept my hands off her.

"I've got David."

"David! ... A nice family *he* comes from, I must say!"

And then I let her have it. I clutched at her lovely, hateful hair and jerked her head from side to side while she screamed for help. I pounded her back and shoulders with my one good fist. I kicked her, I regret to say, in the stomach. "How dare you! How dare you!" I yelled. "You hateful, beastly, stuck-up fool of an ass!"

Her shrieks brought Fell at a canter. He danced up and down, roaring for Blossom, who roared in turn for Maggie, who screamed and brandished her rolling-pin. Joy Jolly finally parted us, by the simple method of pouring a jug of water over our heads, and then smacking them together with a crack that jarred our eyes half out of their sockets.

That was the last time Sylvia and I ever fought, and I am glad to remember that we were both properly ashamed.

Uncle Alaric never alluded to this incident, though I am sure he must have been told of it. But some weeks afterwards, when we were reading history together, and a discussion arose as to the part women had always played in war, he remarked dryly that it was just as well for civilisation that men and not women were usually the warriors of the race. "The female of the species is more deadly than the male," he commented, with the ghost of a twinkle in his eyes.

I looked the quotation up afterwards, and found it was written by Kipling, a writer I had not, so far, explored, apart from the *Jungle Books*. I found a complete edition of him on the library shelves; and that autumn was made even more colourful for me by the tramping rhythm of *Barrack-Room Ballads*, the magic of *Mandalay*, and the solemn beat of the *Recessional Hymn*. I cried myself sick over *The Light that Failed*, and laughed myself well again with *Stalky and Co.*

Autumn came beautifully to Cobbetts, her gold and scarlet skirts sweeping the shallow hills and the tree-filled valleys and the winding lanes with a gentle queenliness. Her laces floated serenely on the quiet air, and hung from bush and gateway frosted with a thousand jewels. The garden blazed and flamed with chrysanthemums; not even Fell could prevent that glorious wave breaking over Cobbetts. Their unforgettable scent was everywhere, along with the smells of bonfires and wet, black earth.

There were heady, glorious mornings, white and nippy, mellowing to an hour or two of sun like a memory of summer, and still, cold evenings, white with mist, lost and enchanted.

There were days when time seemed to stand still; when the world lay with bated breath waiting for something to happen; some miracle, half feared, half hoped for; when the very sound of my feet down the long, dim halls seemed sacrilege, and John's bark an outrage against decency.

There came days when the studious decorum of the library was torn into a thousand coloured tatters by the passing of the Hunt. Then I would throw down my pen and leap out through the french windows, and go rushing across the courtyard, heart hammering and cheeks ablaze. There they went, streaming down the lane; pink coats and dark habits; creak of leather; surge of hounds with waving tails and noses down to earth; white horses and grey ones, chestnuts and bays; laughter and clatter of hoofs, and the stirring summons of the horn making the heart leap with a certain, ecstasy.

When they were gone I would return to my books rather sheepishly, and the silence would come creeping round us again, closer than ever.

"So there *is* some Mallinson in you, after all, Ruan," Uncle Alaric remarked on one such occasion. "The blood calls, does it? You'd like to go with them, wouldn't you? The horn wakes something pagan in that sober, Nonconformist little soul of yours, and you'd give your head to go galloping and jumping and yelling after that thin, gasping, terrified streak of red; to come back with blood plastered on your face, proud of yourself and of one of our good old English customs! ... You'll be telling me soon that the fox likes it; it's the thing to say, and if you say it often enough you begin to believe it's true."

"I don't really want to go," I muttered.

"It's a grand sight," he said bitterly, "so long as you are spared the unpleasant part at the end. That's it—isn't it?"

I nodded, perplexed and ashamed.

Uncle Alaric drew a tiny, geometrical design on his blotting-paper.

"It isn't pretty, the death of a fox," he said slowly. "I saw it once, by accident. It's a bloody, beastly affair. I couldn't sleep after it for nights and nights. I had always refused to hunt, and my father never forgave me for having some imagination. He used to thrash me when I was small. I infinitely preferred that to a fox's blood on my face—and on my soul."

"Mother used to hunt, Uncle Alaric."

He nodded slowly.

"It is a thing I have never understood. ... Old Dr Farrell, the kindest man on earth, and Peter Graham, a saint if ever there was one, both liked nothing better than a 'good kill.' And Theodora, too"—he was talking more to himself than to me—"even little Theo ... she was the keenest of them all. Yet she wept for a week when her spaniel died, and she loved all little, helpless things. ... My father gave me up entirely when Theo and I broke it off. He said she'd have made a man of me."

I remembered Captain Dalton saying: "Pity he never married. There was some row or other. ..."

"Why did you?" I asked boldly.

He looked up, as though suddenly aware of my presence.

"Why did I give her up? How could I do otherwise? She was sweet and gracious—but her hands were covered with blood! ... For a time I tried not to let it matter; but I could never forget it, not for a single moment. She even offered to give up hunting for my sake, but that made no difference. None whatever. Her heart was with the pack."

He seemed suddenly to realise what he was saying. And in a moment the mask was on again, and he had picked up the book from which he had been reading aloud.

$$\mathscr{G}$$

I thought a good deal about what Uncle Alaric had said. It was true I had no desire to hunt in reality. It was equally true that my heart leapt to the sound of the horn, and something in me longed to follow, follow, over streams and hedges, across green, sloping meadows, up hill and down dale; and in my thoughts I followed until the bitter, bloody end—at which I shrank and shuddered, but which yet satisfied that nameless urge within me. I tried to find a reasonable explanation, but utterly failed. And all my life I have been trying, and failing, and feeling ashamed of myself; and all my life, my heart has still leapt to the winding horn.

I encountered a strange and touching little sequel to that conversation with Uncle Alaric.

It was some weeks later, just before Christmas, and I had walked a long way from home; for though my arm was well again I was not yet allowed to ride. I went through the cobbled main street of the little market town of Ringwell, and I noticed a tea-shop with a swinging kettle above a sunken door, and a bow-window with leaded lights, through which firelight beckoned invitingly. It was still early, but I suddenly felt ravenous, and I had a shilling in my pocket. I went down two worn, stone steps, and the door opened with the old-fashioned clang of a bell.

The room was empty, save for a lady sitting in a rocking-chair by the fire, doing some very fine embroidery. Her long white hands moved with a quick and delicate precision. Her face was thin and lined with suffering, but with the faded ghost of beauty still about it. She smiled at John and me but did not move, and the next instant I saw why: she was lame: one of her feet was hideously club-booted and a black stick lay within reach of her hand.

I asked if I might have a cup of tea and some toast, and she rang a bell and gave the order to a fat girl who came grinning to the inner door.

"Come and sit by the fire," she invited me.

I admired her work, and she spread it out to show me.

"I wish I could do lovely work like that!" I said politely. But she smiled and shook her head.

"What do you want with needles and silks at your age! You can walk and run and climb and ride—you do ride? … Yes, I thought so! Lucky little girl! I only learned to embroider when *this* happened to me." She touched her deformed foot impatiently. "It's all I have left to do." She checked a sigh and began asking me questions about my horse, and I chattered away happily enough, asking a good many questions in return.

She told me the tea-shop belonged to an old friend of hers, a woman who had once been her Nanny. She always spent Christmas with her when she was in England, but for the most part she lived in Italy. "But my home was near here when I was a girl. You wouldn't think, to look at me now, that I used to hunt five days a week."

My tea came in and I asked her to share it, which she did with a friendly smile. She gave John a saucer of milk and a biscuit, and he did his tricks for her.

And then a stout, elderly woman came in, laden with parcels and blowing from the cold air.

"Now then, Miss Theo!" she exclaimed, sharply maternal. "Didn't I have a grand fire for you in your own room?"

The lady pulled a gay, impudent face.

"I like the shop best, Nanny. Sometimes such nice people come in." And she smiled at me.

My heart beat excitedly. I could have no doubt that this was Uncle Alaric's Theodora—and wild, romantic notions flashed through my head. I saw these two reunited, misunderstandings explained and loneliness past. I saw Cobbetts with a mistress again, the old walls echoing to laughter and music, and the big gates thrown wide. Heaven knows what else I should have seen, or what I should have blurted out in my excitement, if the stout old Nanny had not fixed me with such a penetrating glare that I was moved to announce my immediate departure, stammering a request for my bill.

"I hope you will allow me to be your hostess," Theodora said. "Our little talk has given me such pleasure. Perhaps you will come again before I go back to Italy?"

I thanked her, and on an impulse I put my arms round her neck and kissed her. For an instant she held me tightly, searching my face with her large, clear eyes, as grey as water.

"You're a very dear little girl," she said abruptly. "You remind me of someone."

The old Nanny followed me out.

"Aren't you the child from Cobbetts? Miss Helena Mallinson's daughter, that was?"

I admitted it.

"Well, you seem to be a sensible young lady. I want you to promise me not to say a word about this—about Miss Theo—to your uncle. *Not a word*—do you understand?"

"Oh, but why?" I said, my dreams vanishing.

"You wouldn't understand why. Or perhaps you would," she added slowly, "if I told you that Miss Theo was once the loveliest young lady in the whole county, and that she'd rather die than have your uncle see her as she is now. It's her one dread—and if you have any regard for your uncle, or for her, you'll say nothing. She'll be gone from here soon, and if she thought he knew she'd never come here again. Never. And she's all I've got left, you see."

"I promise."

"Thank you, my dear."

There were tears in her eyes as she turned away, and perhaps there were tears in mine, too—but for whom I shed them I could not tell.

I kept my promise. I never went back to the little tea-shop, and I never saw either Theodora or her stout old friend again. I have often wondered if I did right. But as I have grown older, more and more I have come to believe that I did. A perfect memory is a lovely thing to have. ...

Chapter Five

§

So autumn drooped into winter, and winter crawled slowly up into a lovely spring; a spring whose splendours were dimmed for me a little by the death of Joshua Day.

When Rosie wrote to tell me about this I could hardly believe it. I had seen Joshua only last August, and he had never looked stronger, more vital. He was not the sort of man I could imagine dying at all. He had always professed the greatest impatience of sickness. "Nay, tha'd squeal if thy finger ached!" he would throw out contemptuously, and "Work it off, lad!" had been his remedy for all pain. For any death other than that of the very old he had shown a quick, almost humorous contempt. "Nay, he were allus a wimbly-wambly sort o' creature!" had been his usual epitaph for any who died untimely. The only exception he had allowed was for death by accident, which, strangely, had seemed to invest the victim with a glamour and importance out of all proportion to his deserts. "A grand chap, yon!" and "Ah, we shall nivver look on his like again!" were phrases I had often heard on his lips. He would walk for miles in the funeral *cortège* of an employee who had been burned or scalded or trapped "at t'factory," and genuine tears would fill his eyes as he spoke of him: tears, let me hasten to add, that were by far the smallest part of his generous sympathy towards the widow and children. But for a man who "turned up his toes i' bed," with medicine bottles on the washstand and nurse and doctor in attendance, he had a pity that was compound more of contempt than kindness.

Therefore, though the death of Joshua shocked me profoundly, I could not but agree with Rosie that he had died as he would have wished to die—"down at t'factory"; a violent end, but a mercifully swift one, the details of which I was never told, but which I have shudderingly imagined for myself many and many a time. The noisome beast had got his tamer at last. ...

My first thought was that now David would be the master down at the factory. Whatever his personal feelings in the matter. ... The king is dead. Long live the king! Whether he likes it or not; whether he be suitable for the job or not—long live the king! ... He would probably have to leave Lowton straight away, and start in to learn how to rule his kingdom. And again I had a vision of David grown-up, and grown away from me.

I told Uncle Alaric about it, but he was not so sympathetic as I had expected.

"Some people would consider your David a lucky young fellow!" he commented dryly.

"To be forced to do something he hates doing for the rest of his life?" I protested.

"We all have to do things we hate doing, my child. Life is not a bed of roses."

"I don't want it to be."

"No. There are thorns even among roses, aren't there, Ruan? And possibly caterpillars. Realities. You merely want to dream of living."

"You, too, Uncle Alaric," I said shrewdly.

He was not offended. He only smiled and sighed and passed a thin, white hand over his grey hair.

"I, too, Ruan. We are fellow-sufferers. Or fellow-delinquents—I hardly know which. ... But your David, the little I know of him, strikes me as being made of sterner stuff. I don't imagine that life will ever get him down."

I felt worried about Rosie. I hated to think of her alone in that great, unhomelike House, without David or me. She had been very fond of her father, and would miss his great booming voice, his everlasting jokes, his dependence on her. Luke would work his fingers to the bone for her, but that was not what she wanted from Luke; I understood that well enough now. Rosie wanted love; and if Luke wouldn't give it to her, Dr Ranter would ... and who could tell what foolish things Rosie might do in her loneliness.

"I think perhaps I ought to go and stay with Rosie for awhile," I told Uncle Alaric. He smiled sardonically.

"I imagine that Miss Day is quite capable of deciding that for herself. You are overmuch given to interfering in other people's business, my good child."

"David said that, too," I exclaimed fretfully. "Only he called it poking my nose in."

"My opinion of David Shane," mused Uncle Alaric, "goes ever higher."

But I had been right about Rosie. She *was* lonely, and she *did* want me. David was with her for a fortnight, but after that he had to go back to school; and the House, which had never been friendly to Rosie, became intolerable now she was alone.

One morning there was a letter for Uncle Alaric, addressed in her big, black handwriting, which he read through twice before looking up with his dry, fleeting smile at my eager face.

"Well, you were right. Yorkshire requires you, so Cobbetts must get along without you as best it may."

"I won't go if you don't want me to," I said quickly.

"I contrived to exist very well before you came," he remarked austerely, "and I have not the slightest doubt I shall continue to exist while you are away. Do not overrate your importance in the universe."

I was not in the least deceived. I knew that Uncle Alaric had grown very fond of me, as I had of him. I was not a true Mallinson, as Sylvia was. I had none of her beauty and grace, and nothing of her grand manner. With my stocky little figure and short, wiry scrub of dark hair I did not, as she did, look "right" at Cobbetts; and I knew that Uncle Alaric, whatever he might profess to the contrary, deeply loved the old house and the old name. But I understood Cobbetts as Sylvia never could; it meant more to me than it ever would to her.

Between Uncle Alaric and me this love of Cobbetts was a bond that would have been strong enough of itself; but we had other things in common. We both loved books, beauty, silence, and solitude. We each lived in a world of our own, and we respected each other's worlds, leaving them inviolate. And we were both afraid of life. ... Uncle Alaric was proud of Sylvia. But me he loved.

He wrote to Rosie himself, without consulting me. And it was not until Rosie was actually standing in the courtyard of Cobbetts that I knew I was to stay with her for the whole of that summer.

§

Rosie had come to fetch me.

She looked hot and rather nervous, but almost beautiful with her hair flaming against the dead-black of her hat and coat. Strangely enough, she did not look "wrong," as I had always imagined she would look at Cobbetts. Certainly she was more in the picture than ever she had been at the House. Her immense vitality reached out, seeming almost to inform the old, sun-soaked walls and the shadowy porches and gables with her own life and vigour.

"Nay!" she admired, "it's better than what I ever imagined!"

I took her on a tour of inspection. She exclaimed over the dusty, unfurnished rooms, and shut her lips in an expressive line at the immense disorder of the kitchens. Maggie was baking, and I could tell by the gleam in Rosie's eye that she was doing it all wrong.

"I'd like to have a right clean-up in there," she remarked, as we went out again into the gardens. "Yon woman's a slut if ever there was one!"

Her eye lighted on Fell, who was idly stirring a dying bonfire.

"Hasn't yon chap got owt better to do than that?" she demanded.

Her voice carried on the quiet air. Fell stared at her with dropped jaw. He backed away from the bonfire and disappeared round a corner in some haste. Later, I saw his head and Maggie's close together at the kitchen window. They were watching Rosie as mice, I suppose, may watch a cat who threatens their security.

"You've upset Fell," I giggled. And Rosie laughed grimly.

"I'd upset the lot of 'em if I was missus here—and not before time!"

I reflected how strange it was that Rosie felt that way, when she dared not lift her voice to her own servants. It was all part of the queer, undoubted fact that Rosie fitted in with old Cobbetts far better than with Bolton House in all its stark new splendour. There was something elemental in Rosie that Cobbetts recognised and understood. However far removed from each other, they were yet akin.

Uncle Alaric seemed to feel it, too. I saw him looking at her during lunch. Her red head blazed against the old, black-panelled walls, and her strong laugh woke echoes. Her hands were big and powerful, but they were nicely shaped and very white: Old Man Day's daughter had never had to work with her hands.

He told me long afterwards that she reminded him of a certain Lady Caroline, mistress of a long-dead Alaric, who had made history by smacking the face of an amorous and drunken prince who had made improper advances to her while visiting at Cobbetts. This Alaric had been devoted to his lady-love, and would willingly have married her, but for a trifling obstacle in the shape of a healthy and most disobliging husband who happened to be a crack shot. But he had caused her portrait to be painted, and had hung it, against all precedent, amongst the collection of sober, beautiful, and virtuous wives and daughters of Cobbetts, in the library. It had been sold, of course, as most of the Mallinson treasures had; but Uncle Alaric remembered seeing it as a boy, and had always thought of Lady Caroline with affection.

He bowed low and gallantly over Rosie's hand, when we bade him good-bye. And for a moment Cobbetts stirred in her sleep; hoofs clattered on the cobbles, dogs barked, silks and satins gleamed in the sunlight, and the delicate tinkling of a spinet came from an open window.

"Nay!" Rosie murmured, as we climbed into the stuffy station cab.

I saw with great surprise that she was blushing.

𝒢

The House did indeed seem empty without Uncle Josh. It even seemed in some mysterious way to have shrunk and become shabbier, as if only the sheer force of his personality had kept it together, and with his death the House had died too.

Rawlings, I learned with astonishment, had left at Christmas, to be married. Rosie had shut up most of the rooms and we lived simply and quietly, served only by Cook and a raw, half-trained girl called Ethel, who snorted dreadfully but was willing and kind. The other servants had gone.

I had my twelfth birthday that June. Rosie and I celebrated it quietly at home, all by ourselves. We ate strawberries-and-cream in the garden, and Cook's famous cheese-cakes appeared on the table in my honour. David sent me a box of chocolate walnuts. Rosie gave me a writing-desk, fitted with every variety of pen, pencil, and paper. It was a good, solid piece of furniture, and was intended for my bedroom at Cobbetts.

"You can write your books on it," she said fondly. Rosie cherished an unshakable conviction that I should be an author some day. But, though that conviction has proved true, I suppose, I cannot recall ever having written a line at that desk. I keep in it a number of important-looking reference books to which I seldom refer; stockings awaiting darning; a cracked goldfish-bowl; bulbs in a paper bag; stacks of old letters; a china boot that I won at a coconut-shy, and two pieces of embroidery, begun in moments of enthusiasm and almost immediately abandoned.

Uncle Alaric most surprisingly remembered my birthday. He sent me a small volume of Elizabethan poetry, which pleased me, but not so much as the accompanying note, in which he owned to missing me.

There was a letter from Father, too. It was a long letter, filled with detailed accounts of his work, and descriptions of people and scenery. It ended with the hope that I was well, industrious, and obedient. "To-morrow I start at daybreak on a three-months' tour up-country, visiting the isolated villages," he added in a postscript.

I smelt the hot, damp smell of the jungle, and the smell of black, sweating bodies. I felt the swampy earth giving beneath my feet and the trailing liana ropes impeding my progress. I heard the sullen mutter of drums; the squawk and rumble and chatter of jungle-folk. I saw the camp-fires and the hard, white sunlight, and the black-green forest gloom.

Father would be hearing and seeing and smelling all these things. Living them. Being part of them. His tall thin figure, white-clad, would go tirelessly on, crashing through the dense undergrowth to his journey's end. His pale, saint's face would gaze calmly on the scenes. His lovely voice would sound through the hot, still silence and his hands would bring healing.

"Father's going on a long journey," I told Rosie. "Right into the heart of the jungle. He will be the only white man in the party."

"Did he remember your birthday?" Rosie asked.

"No. … You couldn't expect him to, when he has so much to think about. Could you, Rosie?"

She sniffed impatiently.

"I reckon he's got a rare lot to think about, one way and another. … Here, have some more strawberries, luv."

So Father went on that long journey which was to be his last. Fever got him, and he died and was buried in the jungle. I did not grieve for him as I had grieved for Mother. I did not miss him as I had missed Tanner and Mrs Abbey. I was not shocked by his death, as the death of Joshua Day had shocked me. I had never really loved him; never understood him. But I had admired him very much.

And I hope that he has found at last that which he sought for all his life, and sought vainly: the peace of God that passeth all understanding. …

Chapter Six

We lay flat on our backs up on Walker's Ridge, tired after the climb. I thought Rosie was asleep, but suddenly I heard her say:

"What would you do, luv, if you'd got summat you didn't want?"

"Give it away," I answered sleepily.

I lay quite still, dreamily watching the white clouds swim in single file across the blue lake of sky. I had some pinks stuck in my belt; their clean, sweet scent was making me drunk. I could hear the blacksmith's hammer down in the valley. The bullet-headed boy would be there. ... "Our blest Redeemer, ere He breathed His tender, last farewell. ..." A bird flapped across my vision with strong, slow wings.

"I mean summat valuable."

I flicked a fly out of my hair.

"It wouldn't be valuable to me if I didn't want it," I said reasonably, "but it might be very valuable to the person I gave it to."

I went into a half-doze. In three weeks David would be home from Lowton. The three of us were going for a fortnight to the Lakes, and even then there would still be six heavenly weeks together on the moor. It seemed to me a perfect programme. Even the possibility that Stebbing might share a week of it did nothing to obscure my joy; if anything, it enhanced it. I suppose there was never anyone less of a coquette than I; and yet the thought of David and Stebbing punching each other's heads on my account was not unpleasant.

It never occurred to me that I, too, might be growing up.

Rosie sat up suddenly and shook the hair out of her eyes.

"It's coming down at the back," I told her. "There are bits of heather stuck in it."

With a swift gesture she pulled the pins out of the unwieldy roll, and the heavy, flaming stuff fell in a wild shout of colour over her shoulders and down her strong back on to the moor. She tossed her head like a freed animal. She laughed on a low, excited note. She leapt to her feet and flung out her arms, and her hair streamed in the wind like a cloud of fire. She stretched mightily.

"Ee, luv," said Rosie loudly, "you'll never know what you've done for me this day!"

"Me? I haven't done anything."

She laughed again. The sun glinted on her strong white teeth. Her hair streamed and flamed. The rich lines of her body thrust up sturdily from the heather to the blowing sky. I gazed at her, awestruck. She was magnificent.

She began to bundle her hair together again.

"Come on, luv, I'm going home."

"Rosie! We've brought our dinner!"

"I couldn't swally a mouthful! Are you coming, or do you want to stop by yourself? Do as you've a mind, luv. There's some work I've got to do."

"I'll stay," I said lazily.

I watched her until she dropped down over the Ridge; then I rolled on my stomach and laid my head on my arms. I did not mind being alone in the least. The moor put her strong, kind arms about me and held me to her breast, and I let myself sink into her, and was content. John slept beside me.

It was five o'clock before I reached home. Rosie was out. She had gone down into the town, Ethel told me. I was not to wait tea for her.

I had my tea and went to the Farm. Luke was milking. I leaned against the door of the barn and watched him. The barn was clean and fragrant, dark after the sunlight. Luke's blue eyes smiled at me. His hands moved rhythmically in strong, gentle gestures. The Jerseys chewed their cud contentedly, swishing lazy tails at the flies. The sound of the squirting milk was thin against the bright pail. A bee blundered solemnly about the doorway, and the smell of pinks was strong on the quiet air.

I felt as if I should burst with happiness.

It was seven o'clock when Rosie came home. She stamped into the House, pulling off her driving gloves and humming under her breath. Her face was hot and red and her eyes bright with excitement. She had brought a huge, greasy newspaper parcel of fish and chips. She rang for Ethel and handed them to her with a regal gesture.

"Hot these up for supper."

The girl goggled.

"Please'm, Cook's got cold lamb and salad."

"You heard what I said."

Ethel scuttled away and Rosie winked at me and went upstairs. I felt excited and curious. What could have happened to give Rosie such courage!

After supper she opened the little-used piano, and played and sang. Her voice was untrained but strong and rich, capable of great feeling. If she made mistakes she ignored them, and they didn't matter.

Dr Ranter came in while she was singing. He sat down a long way from the piano and stared at Rosie. She took no notice of him, but went on singing. Song after song she sang, fetching out piles of music from the rosewood cabinet and throwing them on to the floor when she had finished with them. She sang everything she knew, from *Daisy, Daisy*, to *Oh, for the Wings of a Dove*.

After a long time I picked John up and went to bed; and Rosie was still singing.

§

Next day a man called Mr March drove up to the House and was shut into the little breakfast-room with Rosie for a long time. The boom of their voices rose and fell. Mr March sounded angry. Sometimes Rosie sounded angry too, and sometimes she laughed deeply.

At dinner-time Rosie stuck her head out of the door and told Ethel to bring something for them on a tray. She winked at me and gave me five shillings.

"Luke's got to go to town. Should you like to go with him, luv?"

I climbed up beside Luke, and we went bowling down into the town. It was the first time I had been back since our home was broken up.

"Could we go round by St Mark's Road, Luke?"

He looked at me consideringly.

"We could. Happen we'd better not, though. No good," said Luke kindly, "in raking things up."

But I knew better. I wanted to see the Manse again. I wanted to be sure that the dark Something which had frightened me was really gone for ever. It was a thought that had been on my mind for a long time, and I knew that, sooner or later, I had to face up to it.

So we turned into St Mark's Road at the top end. I caught a glimpse of the Riding School on the green slope above the sooty chimneys. We passed the end of Dover Street. The children were going back for afternoon school. They looked hot and incredibly dirty. I looked eagerly for Vera West—but in vain. We passed the little shop where Kitty Curtis used to live. It was no longer a newsagent's. The windows were hung with yellow butter muslin and a few plates of fly-blown cakes reposed in the foreground. A sign over the door announced that it was the "Welcome Café." We passed the end of Newbold Street; and for one instant the smell of vinegar came strongly on the dusty air, and my heart thumped. And then we were passing the very spot where Hallelujah Johnson and I had danced to the call of spring.

Luke pulled Sally into a walk.

There was the Manse. I scarcely recognised it. The iron railings had been painted a resplendent green, and the paint on the door and windows was green, too. The garden was bright with flowers, and a child's toy-cart made a scarlet splash on the closely cut lawn. All the windows stood open and cretonne curtains flapped in the breeze. There was the sound of whistling, and a stout, bald parson in his shirt-sleeves came out and began to clip the hedge. I knew he must be the minister who had taken Father's place, but he was so different from Father. He looked happy and ordinary. Two little boys ran out, shouting. They picked up the cuttings and began to throw them out into the street.

"Stop that!" said their father. "Stop it at once!"

They went on throwing the cuttings, shouting with laughter. The parson aimed a whack at them, and missed, and they ran about, shouting all the louder.

A plain, pleasant-looking woman came into the garden. Over her shoulder she carried a bald, fat baby, and another child clung to her skirt.

"Dinner," she said.

"About time, too," grunted the parson, throwing down the shears. They smiled at each other, and the whole family went indoors.

I stared at the house where so much had happened to me.

From those gay, wide-flung windows did there steal one whisper of *Over the Sea to Skye*? Was that a small, tufty head pressing against the pane? Could that shadow by the porch be waiting, waiting for the sound of horses' hoofs coming down the road; waiting with an angry, black stare and a jealous heart? ... Could I—oh, *could* I hear, very far off, the sound that she waited for ... cupper-*lup*, cupper-*lup*, cupper-*lup* ...? No, no! There was nothing. No one. No whisper, no shadow, no cruel hoofs. There was nothing. No one. ...

I felt happy and at peace. No dark tides flowed about the Manse now. It was filled with happy, ordinary people, living ordinary lives. The Manse had washed its hands of me, and I was content.

S

Luke had business to do in the town, so I made him put me down by the public library, where he promised to call for me in an hour or so. I wandered about the echoing, empty building; into the rather dreary reading-room; into the reference-room, where I idly scanned the *Oxford Dictionary* and received a quite unmerited glare from the young woman at the desk, and up the stone stairs to the museum, which depressed me so much that I dashed out again into the busy sunlight.

I had a sudden inspiration. I would go and visit Ada Morris. Her shop was only a penny tram-ride away, and I could be back at the library in plenty of time for Luke.

It was the first time I had travelled alone in the town and I felt highly venturesome, but by dint of using my tongue I eventually reached the shop, having purchased on the way a box of nougat, to which delicacy, I remembered, Ada had been extremely partial. Not until I was inside the dark, damp-smelling place did it occur to me that the holidays had not yet started, and Ada would probably be still at school.

A large, sleepy man, who could only be Ada's father, moved out of the shadows with an interrogatory lift of the head.

"I just wanted to speak to Ada," I said doubtfully.

He stuck his head round the door and yelled into the back premises.

"Ader! Yer wanted."

A clatter of crockery and a slow, heavy tread, and there she stood in the doorway, peering at me through her steel-rimmed spectacles.

"Goodness me! Is that you, Ruan Ashley?"

I felt suddenly shy. Ada was so different. She wasn't as old as David, but she might easily have been mistaken for a grown woman. Her face was haggard and her body thin to emaciation. Her hair was scraped back as of old, but secured now by side combs. She wore a print dress that had obviously belonged to someone older and bigger. It reached nearly to her ankles, and its ample folds were belted clumsily about her waist. She held a steaming dishcloth in her hand.

"It is Ruan, isn't it?"

"Yes," I said. "How are you, Ada? I brought you some nougat."

Her fat father seized the box from my hand.

"Nugget? Aye, our Ada's right partial to a bit of nugget, an't you, Ada? An' so's her old dad."

He made as if to unwrap the box, but Ada held out an authoritative hand.

"Give it here!"

He laughed easily and chucked the box at her. She caught it neatly.

"Here," he said suddenly, "if you gals is goin' to gab, you can mind t'shop while yer at it. Shan't be long."

He rolled out of the shop and I saw Ada's mouth tighten.

"And that's the last I shall see of him to-day," she commented grimly. Then, remembering her manners, she pushed forward a stool. "Take the weight off your legs. I'm right pleased to see you, Ruan, and thanks for the nougat. What's been happening to you all this while?"

I told her briefly, and she clucked and tutted but made no other comments.

"Why aren't you at school, Ada? Aren't you going to be a teacher, after all?"

"Aye, I am that!" she exclaimed fiercely. "Whatever they say, I'm going through with it. I went and got ill. They said I overworked, and Dad got round the doctor and they made me stay home. They don't want me to get on, Ruan. They're afraid I'll go away and leave 'em all to fettle for themselves. An' so I will!"—her eyes glowed behind the spectacles—"I'll not give up me whole life for them. They're a lazy, selfish lot. Ma spoilt 'em, and I've gone on with it, like a fool, till they can't lift a finger for themselves. But they'll have to learn. I won't stop in this place, selling cabbages and washing and scrubbing all my life. I won't! It's my life, an' I've a right to it. Men!" Ada's voice held bitter scorn. "Don't you ever get mixed up with men, Ruan. They'll take all you've got to give, and give nowt—nothing—back. I hate men! Don't you have nothing to do with them."

"But, Ada, if you're ill," I ventured.

She almost spat.

"I'll get well all right, if they'll let me alone. What *will* make me ill—what'll kill me outright—is keeping me here. But they shan't do it." She spoke solemnly, as if taking an oath. "They shan't do it, not even if I have to do *murder*!"

More to change the subject than anything, I asked about Phyllis Sharman, who was at the Central School with Ada.

"Sylvia would like to know how she's getting on, I'm sure."

Ada straightened her spectacles and sniffed.

"Then she could write and ask her, couldn't she? She's never sent a line to Phyllis since she left for that swanky school of hers, that I do know; never even troubled to answer the poor kid's letters. Phyllis has been rare put about over it." Her glance rested on me sardonically. "She's a sight too hard, is Sylvia. And you're too soft. If the two of you had been mixed up a bit, it'd have been all to the good, I reckon."

She gave me a red apple when I left, and I went back to the library and sat on the steps eating it, and reflecting that though I was quite fond of Ada she was an uncomfortable creature, with an uncanny knack of finding out your weakest spot. I sincerely hoped she would defeat her tiresome family and make a success of her life, but I feared very much that they would prove too much for her.

I need not have worried. The more obstacles that cropped up in Ada's path the greater grew her determination. She defeated her father and her fat brothers. She defeated the shop. She triumphed over her illness, her doctor, her examinations, her poverty, her appalling accent, and all her rivals in the scholastic race. She achieved a coveted professorship at a great university, a car, a fur coat, and a grim house in Manchester, to which none of her family was ever invited. They sponged on her from a respectful distance; not without success, for she was a kind creature at heart. I met her only once more, face to face, at a public dinner at which she was the guest of honour. She still wore steel-rimmed spectacles, and her hair was pulled back so tightly I marvelled that she could put her feet to the ground. She made a wonderful speech that was right above my head, and afterwards put me through a severe cross-examination as to my own attainments. The recital obviously disappointed her. She twitched at her dreadful evening gown, and read me a lecture on Concentration, and other dreary subjects. I found her quite terrifying.

§

Luke and I bowled rapidly out of the town, and my heart lightened with every hoof-beat. I never wanted to go there again. Even Bolton House seemed beautiful in my eyes, and the Farm was very heaven, to which I flew as soon as tea was over.

Rosie had waited for me and we had tea together in the cool drawing-room, in sociable silence.

I saw that Rosie was eating very little, but drinking cup after cup of the strong, sweet tea she liked. She began pacing up and down the room, staring first out of one window, then out of another; humming under her breath; fidgeting with the ornaments.

"Is anything the matter?" I yawned.

And then it all came out in one great, rushing spate of words, fed with tears and choked with laughter, and quite incomprehensible to me. But after a time she grew calmer and began to tell me in simpler words the thing she had done.

I suppose I must have been a disappointing audience. All my life money has meant very little to me, though the lack of it has often irritated and hampered me, and at that time it certainly meant nothing at all. The news that Rosie had disposed of the factory, lock, stock, and barrel, and had put nearly all the money in trust for David, seemed to me to have little dramatic value. The fact that Bolton House was to be made into a rest-home for factory workers left me cold. Even the startling news that I was to receive one hundred pounds a year, for the rest of my life, merely stunned me a little—though I was pleased to think that now Uncle Alaric would find me less of a burden.

What did please and excite me was the knowledge that, now Rosie had got rid of all her money, she would be able to marry Luke and live at the Farm happily ever after, and I thought her a very fortunate person indeed. Rosie seemed to read my thoughts.

"Aye, I've got shut on it all at last!" she exclaimed, with deep satisfaction. Her shoulders lifted as if a burden had dropped from them. "I nivver want to have owt to do with money again. Me mother and me, we nivver wanted it, and it brought us nowt but misery. I reckon me dad understands that right enough by now. I reckon he's glad he nivver made a will. We were allus talking about it, but he fair hated the thought of setting about it. And so I've got nothing—nothing at all," said Rosie, with a sort of ecstasy. Her eyes stared out over the moor to where the chimneys of the Farm just showed above a purple hillock. "Nothing at all!" she repeated; and her eyes were soft and bright.

"Rosie!" I suddenly shrieked. "David can be a doctor now!"

She smiled and nodded.

"Aye, so he can, luv."

But she was not thinking of David.

Rosie and Luke were married in September, when the moor was at its loveliest and proudest. Mr Lord married them, very quietly one morning, and nobody was there to see except David and me, and a very old man who came—ironically, it seemed to me—to give Rosie away.

When we came out of the church Rosie kissed us in a quiet, dreamy sort of way, and Luke shook hands with David and kissed my cheek with a bashful smile. His eyes were bluer than ever. And then they turned away and walked up the hill towards the Farm, as if there were nobody living in all the world besides themselves.

I made as if to follow them, but David caught at my hand and pulled me back.

"They don't want us, fathead," he said gruffly. "Come on, let's go up to the Ridge. I've got some grub."

Towards evening we went back to the House, where Cook and Ethel were still in residence. David went to his room to pack. My trunk had already gone. To-morrow we were to leave the House; David for Lowton and I for Cobbetts; and we should never come back here again.

I had never really loved the House, save as my gateway to the moor, but now I felt a pang of real regret. So much had happened to me in this place. It seemed impossible that I should never again lie in that over-stuffed bed under the pink eiderdown; never again wave good-bye to David from the pretentious gates; never again hear the jingle of Sally's harness as Luke brought her spanking up the gravel drive.

But the moor was still mine—and now its lovely gateway would be the Farm. Rosie had assured me of that, long ago. A warmth stole over my heart, and I stared out of the window to where the Farm chimneys peeped from behind the purple hillock. A plume of smoke lay across the calm evening sky. It looked like a beckoning finger.

"Come on, David!" I shouted, running down the stairs. I heard him thudding after me, and together we tore down the moor road, singing and laughing and leaping about, altogether happy for the first time that day.

The clank of a pail came from the barn, and the thin sound of milk squirting against a pail. A smell of hot scones drifted from the open doorway of the Farm, and Rosie's voice, singing a wordless song, mingled magically with the comforting smell. The sky was mauve and green behind the roof-top, pricked with pale stars. Sleepy hens crooned behind tarred doors.

It suddenly seemed as if all the happiness in the world had been drawn towards this quiet place, to lay hands of benediction upon it. And my heart and mind were filled with the knowledge and love of God, as they had not been filled for many months.

I think David felt it, too. But all he said was:

"Scones. Good."

Darling David.

Chapter Seven

§

Cobbetts was always at its loveliest in the autumn. As I stood with my little trunk where the station cab had dumped me in the courtyard, it seemed to me that the old house had waked for a brief spell from a dream of lost youth, and that its face still smiled with memories. Masses of gold and yellow and dark red chrysanthemums flowed over the garden unchecked. The ancient yellow walls glowed with stored suns of summer, half hidden by bronze-red climbing creeper. There was a jolly clatter of pails from the kitchen premises, where the maids were chaffing some tradesmen, and a sharp wind blew the chimney smoke about the bright air.

Old Blossom came shuffling and grumbling to let me in.

"Oh, so you're back, are you!" was his greeting.

I noticed that the paths had been swept and the windows polished, so I knew that Sylvia was at home. As I passed into the dark hall she came down the wide, shallow stairs, smiling and beautiful; so beautiful, indeed, that she quite took my breath away. All the light in that dim place seemed to be drawn into and to radiate forth again from her golden hair. She had been washing it, and it spread about her like a cloud of glory. She wore a long wrapper of angelic blue that gave her height and made her look far older than her years. Her long white hand rested lightly on the carved rail, and her feet, slender and highly arched, scarcely seemed to touch the oaken treads.

"Oh, darling!" she cried. "I'm so thankful to see you! I've been bored to death."

I hoped Uncle Alaric wasn't in his study, or he must have heard. But I couldn't find it in my heart to frown, she looked so lovely, and she was my own sister; all that was left to me of that remote past before my seventh birthday, when we had all been together in the Manse: Father and Mother, little Clem and grim, cross old Tanner, and Sylvia and me: that long-vanished past upon which, even now, I sometimes thought with regret, when we had just been ordinary children in an ordinary family.

"You look exactly like Mother, Sylvia!"

She smiled and tossed her hair about.

"Let's come into the garden," she said. "I've heaps and *heaps* to tell you!"

We sat in a sheltered corner, soaking in sun, and Sylvia chattered away nineteen to the dozen, while I played with the long, silky strands of her hair and gaped at the astonishing things that had happened to her. She had been staying in Scotland again, with her rich school friend, Monica Brent. There were dazzling accounts of dances and parties and of the new clothes Uncle Alaric had provided for these occasions ("without my having to ask him, my dear!"). There were tales of shooting-parties, at which she and Monica had joined the guns at lunch; of elaborate meals (menu cards, liveried servants, and all) for which they had been allowed to sit up; of motor drives and lawn tennis and jaunts into Edinburgh; of the glories of the shops in Princes Street, and the thrills of theatres. And there were other stories, too, even more astounding: whispered stories of secret meetings in moonlit gardens; of presents given and kisses taken; of people who were "absolutely mad" about her, and of how they one and all refused to believe she was only fourteen.

"What's happened to Monica's brother—the one you were going to marry and go to India with?" I asked timidly; for this new, worldly-wise Sylvia seemed alien to me. But Sylvia laughed easily, with a touch of scorn.

"Oh, he was there, too. But I'm not so keen on marrying him. I might, of course, in the end. But India's not all it's cracked up to be, according to Monica. She says the women in the clubs are awful cats; and there are snakes and fevers and native risings, and after a few years you get as yellow as a dried-up lemon and have things the matter with your liver. It doesn't sound worth it. Harold's all right, but he's not the only fish in the sea, by any means!" She giggled complacently, and I suddenly lost my awe and wanted to smack her. "There were lots of boys in and out of the house all the time; Monica's father and mother are lovely to her, and not a bit strict. She's going to Paris presently, the lucky thing, to a finishing school. Imagine going to Paris, Ruan! Oh, I'd give my *head* if I could go to Paris! ..."

We were silent while I tried to imagine Sylvia in Paris, and then, less successfully, to imagine myself in it. Whenever I had thought about Paris I had always been repelled by a vision of bright, loud streets filled with fashionable ladies leading white poodles tied with ridiculous blue bows; of enormous, intimidating shops and of "places of interest" which you had to visit, not because you wanted to, but because it was the thing to do. A hard, shining, supercilious place. In my vision, the city was cut in two by a broad, bright river, straight as a canal, which sharply divided the respectable from the disreputable. The Latin Quarter, vaguely heard of, meant dirt, drunken artists, and dark men in black cloaks with knives between their teeth. One side of that river attracted me as little as the other, and I had always felt I was better away from Paris. Nevertheless, the idea of Sylvia going there attracted me. It was so essentially the right setting for her.

"Don't tell Uncle Alaric if I tell you this," she continued impressively, "but Monica's mother wants to pay all my expenses for a year, if I'm allowed to go with Monica. She told me so herself. She said she didn't want Monica to go without a friend. Think of that!"

"Uncle Alaric would never allow it," I said coldly.

"I suppose not," was her glum reply.

"I wonder you can *bear* the very idea! It would put him under a *frightful* obligation to them. Mallinsons," I added passionately, "simply do not allow soap merchants to patronise them! Why, good heavens, Sylvia, Monica's grandfather was probably just a common shopkeeper selling soap behind a counter and calling at back doors for orders!"

"While our grandfather was lying under the dining-room table, dead drunk!" Sylvia retorted, with sudden venom. And I had to agree. Yet I felt, and I knew that she felt, too, that it was a far more gentlemanly thing to lie under a table, drunk, than to sell soap.

"I suppose I shall never be able to go," she said, sighing deeply. "There's no other possible way."

And then a thought struck me, so simple and yet so splendid that I was quite dizzy for a moment. When I could find speech I threw out casually:

"I wouldn't mind paying for you myself—just for one year."

"Ha ha!" Sylvia said drearily.

"I mean it, fathead."

"Don't be so silly, Ruan."

"I said I meant it, and I do mean it."

"You haven't got any money."

"Yes, I have, then! I've got a hundred pounds a year, for the rest of my life! Rosie's given it to me." My triumph was nearly choking me. It was very delicious to be able to patronise Sylvia for once in my life.

"Oh, Ruan—how *gorgeous* for you!" Her eyes shone with hope. "But I know Uncle Alaric would never let you."

"Then I shall get Rosie to talk him round. Uncle Alaric admires her tremendously."

"*Really!* Admires Rosie Day?" She was genuinely astonished. "But, Ruan, the Days are every bit as common as Monica's people. More so, if anything."

"Well, maybe. But Rosie doesn't pretend to be what she isn't, and Monica's people do," I explained, a trifle incoherently. "I tell you, when Rosie came to Cobbetts she looked *right* here, somehow. Anyway," I added, with a dignified gesture, "I'll think it over and decide what to do. Don't keep nagging at me about it, or perhaps I shall change my mind."

And that moment was a very sweet one!

Perhaps Sylvia thought she had talked enough about herself, for she began now to profess an interest in my affairs, asking questions about Rosie and the Farm and David, and listening to my replies with flattering interest.

"You know, Ruan, you really are almost pretty at times," she remarked reflectively. "You've changed a lot lately. You aren't nearly so dumpy, for one thing. If you'd only be more tidy, and do something about your hair—"

"Mother liked it this way," I said flatly.

"Oh, it was all right when you were a kid. But you can't go all your life looking like a floor-mop!"

It was news to me that I resembled a floor-mop. I felt a bit startled, and took the first opportunity of examining myself in a mirror. I suppose at that time I looked in a mirror roughly about three times a week; generally to find out if a torn hem or a hole in my stocking showed enough to matter. What little brushing I gave my hair could be done just as well hanging out of a window as standing by the dressing-table; and I liked myself so little in feminine attire that there was no point in prinking. But a floor-mop—dash it! ...

I looked myself over critically. Less dumpy, perhaps, but still squarish, broad in the shoulder, too long in the arm, stocky, and lacking in grace. My hair—well, it always had been like that and I was used to it. Still, it did need cutting dreadfully, and it might be a good thing to brush it every now and then. No harm in trying, anyway. I looked at my teeth. They were white and sound and very strong, but rather too large. My eyes were brown, like Mother's and Sylvia's, but the lashes, instead of curling, stood out straight, short and thick, and black as night. They made my eyes look startled and aware, not mysterious, like Sylvia's. My nose was nondescript and my complexion too apple-cheeked to be interesting, but at least I rarely had blemishes. On the whole, I was inclined to be satisfied with myself, and to reject the floor-mop theory. I made the resolve to wash my neck rather more frequently, and came away from the survey with much relief.

§

There was not the slightest doubt about Uncle Alaric's pleasure at my return, even though his greeting was nothing more demonstrative than an ironical bow and the remark: "Well, you have settled Yorkshire to your satisfaction, I trust?"

I grinned at him affectionately, but not without certain misgivings. Truth to tell, I was rather shocked by his appearance, which had altered alarmingly in my few months of absence. He was not a young man, but he had always looked younger than his years, in spite of grey hair and the lines on his thin face. But the man who sat at the dinner-table toying absently with his food was quite definitely old. His long, beautiful hands were ever so slightly tremulous. His eyes were cloudy and colourless. The skin stretched taut over the cheekbones was of a faint yellowish colour. It was quite obvious, even to me, that Uncle Alaric was a sick man. I felt some compunction about worrying him with our affairs; nevertheless, when dinner was over, I followed him into the library, thus breaking one of his strictest rules. He did not seem to mind, but stood in the window with his hands loosely clasped behind his back, staring out over the riot of colour into some world of his own. I stood beside him for a long time, silent, waiting until he should come back to earth; which presently he did with a short, exasperated sigh and a quick lift of the shoulders.

"At one time," he said quietly, "I imagined I should welcome the notion of dying. At another, I was indifferent to it. Now I find, to my extreme annoyance, that the world is beautiful, even desirable; that I resent the notion of being snuffed out like a candle. 'Rather bear those ills we have than fly to others that we know not of.' Illogical and unlike me, don't you think, Ruan? Or have I always been illogical and a coward, bolstered up with my own conceit? ... Well, don't answer that. I don't wish to lose all my illusions."

I wanted to cry out: "You aren't going to die!" But the earth had opened at my feet, and from its quaking depths fear rose about me like a cloud of mist. So I said nothing, but gulped down the horrible lump in my throat and thrust my hand into his. It closed on mine with a friendly pressure. He looked down at me with a quizzical smile.

"What is your idea of heaven, Ruan?"

When I had mastered my voice I replied:

"I don't know, Uncle Alaric. I've thought and thought and I never get any satisfaction. But I'm almost sure," I added, "that wherever it is, you and I will be together."

He was silent for a moment, and then he did what was for him a most surprising thing. He bent down and kissed me twice, with a warm friendliness.

"My dear child," he said gently, "you could not have imagined a nicer thing to say. ... And now," he went on, with a swift return to his usual manner, "why do you break my rules by following me in here?"

"I want Sylvia to go to Paris with Monica," I blurted out.

"So do I," he agreed.

"And I don't want Monica's people to pay for her."

"Certainly not."

"Rosie has given me a hundred pounds a year, for my own."

"As your legal guardian, my good child, I am aware of it."

"Well, then—" I faltered, suddenly afraid that I was going too far.

Uncle Alaric picked up an ivory paper-knife and stood tapping it gently on one thin hand. He did not seem to be angry, only thoughtful and a little amused.

"Don't you want to go to Paris yourself?"

"Oh, golly—no!" I cried, recoiling. And he laughed outright.

"A beautiful gesture on your part, Ruan. Why do you make it? Out of love for your sister, or in defence of Mallinson pride? Or are you just being a trifle smug?"

"I expect it's a bit of all three," I said honestly.

"And in any case, why should you suppose I cannot pay for Sylvia's education myself? I still have quite a number of valuable portraits I can sell, if necessary. For instance, this gentleman"—he pointed behind my head—"will pay for Paris very nicely, without troubling either you or Monica's upstart family."

I turned, and beheld to my horror the laughing face of my friend Giles.

"Oh, no, Uncle Alaric!" I cried. "Not Giles! You can't let him go out of the family. You *can't!*"

"Ruan, Ruan!" he exclaimed, half smiling, half impatient, "have all my lessons been in vain? Does the heathen in his blindness still bow down to wood and stone? ... I am expecting a man from London to-morrow, to look at Giles, and, I hope, to take him away immediately."

"Oh!" I muttered despairingly. And then I made my last throw.

"Why not sell him to *me*, Uncle Alaric? Then you'd get the money, and Sylvia could go to Paris, and Giles would be staying in the family just the same. Oh, please, do sell Giles to me. Please do. *Please!*"

Had I flung myself into his arms, in my passion of pleading, I should probably have lost the day; but I was inspired to fling myself against the portrait, arms outstretched in defence of my friend. And whether Uncle Alaric saw in my troubled face some fleeting likeness to the gay, debonair face above me, or whether he suddenly wearied of the whole business, I shall never know, but he suddenly nodded and said:

"Very well, Ruan; Giles is yours. He is a present from me to you. With my love," he added smiling, quite without mockery.

"Oh—please," I stammered, startled and very embarrassed.

"You see, Ruan, even if I wanted to, I couldn't use your money. Nobody can touch that—not even you—until you are twenty-one. The law is not-always an ass. But even if I could take it, I would not do so. I don't think I have ever made you a present, have I? Nothing of any value, anyway. I detest having to give people things just because they happen to be twelve or fifty, or because it is Christmas. I sent you the poems last June, not because it was your birthday, but because I suddenly wanted to give them to you. Spontaneous gifts are the only ones worth giving or taking. And I want to give Giles to you, so please don't argue about it. And believe me," he added, with an edge of sarcasm that bit into my smugness, "I can manage my own affairs, monetary and otherwise, without your guidance or help. That's all." And, ringing the bell, he ordered Blossom to have the portrait removed and hung in my room then and there.

On the following day I had the twofold pleasure of watching the disgruntled departure of the man from London, and of informing Sylvia that her Parisian education was fixed up. I said nothing about the portrait, for Sylvia simply wouldn't have understood; but I did have the honesty to admit that I was not allowed to pay for her myself. Whereupon Sylvia looked greatly relieved, and immediately became once more the elder sister.

It was not until many years later, when I refused an offer of six hundred and fifty pounds for the portrait of Giles Mallinson, that I understood just how big a sacrifice Uncle Alaric had made that day.

Chapter Eight

§

I think that winter was the loneliest I had ever known. Sylvia, of course, was back at Kettleby. Uncle Alaric was more silent than ever, and often too ill to do more than glance at the work I had prepared for him. Sometimes he stayed in bed all day, and then old Dr Greene would come to see him. The doctor was a small, cross-looking man, bald as a coot, and he always came downstairs muttering angrily to himself as he stuffed his stethoscope into his pocket. He always let himself out, for old Blossom was getting feebler and more negligent every day. Once I happened to be standing in the hall as he came grumbling down the oak stairs, and I opened the door for him.

"Thank'ee, thank'ee," he muttered. Then he gave me a searching glance.

"Have you got any influence with that lunatic up there?" he snapped. And while I hesitated, shocked at this description of my uncle, he hurried on: "Because if you have, get him out of here, or he'll go out in a box. You hear me? He'll go out in a box!"

"Where must he go?" I called out after his retreating figure.

"He knows!"

I closed the great door and stood silently in the hall. From the kitchens came the smell of cabbage and roasting meat. I suddenly recalled the same smells in the dirty little back streets around Cheddar Street Chapel, and I thought of my seventh birthday, when I had padded along with my hand in Father's, saying: "I will lift up mine eyes unto the hills, from whence cometh my help. …"

How long ago it all seemed!

Well, there were no hills to help me here. I went very slowly up the stairs and into Uncle Alaric's bedroom. I had never been in it before. It

- 224 -

was bare as a monk's cell. Just a bed, one chair, and a table on which books were neatly piled. The walls were distempered white, and the carpet was one small rug beside the bed. The only things of any beauty in that room were the long curtains of tapestry that hung at the windows. They were riddled with moth and dimmed by dust, but the colours still glowed with a faint echo of the beauty they must once have flaunted.

Uncle Alaric lay in the bed and watched me with a sardonic eye.

"Well, Ruan," he said, in a voice shockingly weak, "what has that lunatic down there been telling you?"

"You must go away at once, Uncle Alaric," I said earnestly. "You know where."

"Or else I shall go out in a box, I suppose?"

"Yes."

"Very well, Ruan, I'll go. See to things for me, will you?"

It was as simple as that.

My heart swelled with pride. See to things. Me! I was in charge here. I felt incredibly young and fantastically old. See to things—*me*! …

"I'll see to everything, Uncle Alaric, don't worry."

He closed his eyes and sighed, and I crept out of the room. Downstairs, I did a thing I had never done before, save at Uncle Alaric's request. I rang the bell for Blossom.

When he arrived, grumbling and panting, he fixed me with a baleful eye and growled: "Now then!"

"Please put dinner back an hour, Blossom," I managed. "I have to go out."

He was too staggered to retort, and I walked past him rather quickly, out into the cold, clean air. I went to the stable and saddled a most unwilling steed. I had ridden already that morning, and both he and John, who was taking a nap in the straw beside him, gave me to understand that this was just about the limit. It wasn't done.

"Come on, Fatty," I merely said callously. And to John: "You needn't come if you don't want to."

But he came, of course: yawning and stretching elaborately and pretending to limp a little, but determined to be in at whatever might be afoot.

I rode down to the doctor's house. He was still out on his round, but by many inquiries I eventually ran him to earth at Prescott's Farm, a mile away.

"What's to do now?" he said sharply. "Worse, is he?"

"I don't think so. He says he'll go, and I'm to manage everything."

He looked at me with grim amusement.

"Hark at that, now! And I've been raging at him and wheedling at him for six months and more!" His eyes disappeared in wrinkles, and he gave me a congratulatory slap on the knee, which greatly offended John's sense of propriety. "Call that damn dog off, will you! All right, I'll get the ambulance this afternoon. He'll need clean things, and his dressing-gown, and so on. Can you have him ready by two-thirty, think you?"

"Yes," I answered breathlessly—for the word ambulance had aroused horrible visions. "Is it—a hospital he's going to, then?"

"Yes, of course it is. God bless my soul—didn't you know?"

I suppose I must have looked queer, for his grim old face suddenly softened and he helped himself freely to snuff, afterwards making a great trumpeting into a brownish handkerchief.

"He'll be all right, my dear. But, hark now, is there nobody but you to take charge of that great house? What's that fat slut of a Maggie Blossom doing? Maybe there's some woman relative you can send for?"

"No, thank you," I replied, with dignity. "Uncle Alaric has asked me to take charge of everything, and I can manage perfectly well."

He nodded.

"I believe ye. Ye've got your head screwed on all right. Which is more than yer poor mother had, though she had ye whacked for looks, God bless her!"

I rode away home, wondering what part Mother had played in the life of the old doctor. His face had changed as he spoke of her, just as Mr Lord's face had changed, and his voice softened. And yet, both these men were old. Their lives had not touched Mother's life for many years. She could be nothing to either of them save a memory; a beautiful memory. Beauty. That was it. Beauty must be the strongest thing in the world, I thought. Even the memory of it could make a dry, snuffy old doctor blink, and a priest turn for a moment from his altar. It had taken Father by storm. It had completely changed the pattern of many people's lives: Tanner's, Captain Dalton's, Uncle Alaric's, Sylvia's, and mine. ... Would Sylvia's life be like that, too, I wondered. And for a moment I was glad that I was not beautiful; that this lovely, terrible power could never be mine.

But then, I thought, there would be nothing for anybody to remember me by when I was dead. In a confused, childish way, yet shot through with a curious adult insight that life had taught me, I pondered this subject. I was not beautiful. I had brains, but they mattered to nobody but myself. I was not particularly good. I had neither the instinct nor the courage to be outstandingly bad. I was nothing, and less than nothing.

In such dismal mood I rode into the courtyard of Cobbetts and unsaddled Bob. The postman, most suitably surnamed Packet, was crossing the yard as I came from the stables, and he gave me a letter. It was from David.

And suddenly beauty and wickedness, hope and sorrow, slid into their normal places again. I stuffed the letter into my breeches' pocket and went indoors whistling. Whatever I might or might not be, David would always remember me. David. ...

They took Uncle Alaric away, and life settled into a dull routine of eating and sleeping, riding and working, hoping for the best and fearing the worst. I was lonely, as I had never been lonely on the moor. Uncle Alaric had indicated a course of studies, and faithfully I carried out his suggestions, working from nine in the morning until one, when I dined in solitary and very slovenly state. I rode until dusk, Tom one day and Bob the next, with John always at my heels. After a meal which varied between bread-and-butter and milk, and "high tea" with tinned salmon, grocer's plum-cake and black, strong tea, according to Maggie's mood, I worked again, or sat on the hearthrug reading until my eyes popped and my legs would scarcely carry me up the dark staircase to bed.

I was not allowed to visit Uncle Alaric in hospital. He, himself, had given orders to that effect, and I did not dream of disobeying him. I wrote once or twice, but not often, since it was no use expecting replies, and nothing happened at Cobbetts worth reporting. From Dr Greene I learned that the operation had been successful, but that some time must elapse before they allowed Uncle Alaric home. He was having some sort of treatment. He never volunteered any information as to the illness, and I never asked for any.

I caught a very bad cold, and for a dreary week I stayed indoors, trailing miserably about the empty rooms, aching and sniffing, unable to work or settle to reading.

At the height of my misery, one dismal morning of rain and wind, the library door suddenly flung open, and Rosie came surging in, to envelop me in a vast, damp grip. I was never more pleased to see anyone in my life.

"Nay!" she cried indignantly, "the very idea, leaving you all alone in this great ruin of a house, with nobody to look after you but yon fat trollop an' her doddering old father! You pack your traps, luv, an' come back to t'Farm with me. Me and Luke'll take care of you. Why, you might have known that, wi'out telling!"

I knew that here I must walk far more delicately than Agag; like many north-country folk Rosie was mortally easy to offend, especially where any question of hospitality was involved, and I had no intention of leaving Cobbetts until Uncle Alaric was well again. The thought of the Farm was almost more than I could bear. The small rooms, snug in firelight; the high, bouncy beds with their thick eiderdowns and soft, soft pillows—relics of the Bolton House days—and warm, friendly kitchen; the hot scones and curling rashers of bacon, crisp and delicious; the immense fruit-cakes and jammy, satisfying puddings; Luke's kind blue eyes and sweet smile and Rosie's bustling efficiency—all these things were enough in themselves. But more than all—there was the moor. Now it would be lying asleep, dun and sere under sullen November skies, inimical to many, but never, never to me! Soon the snow would come; here, in these sheltered dales, a mere matter of an hour's Christmas-card prettiness, followed by days of slush and mud; but oh, how different on the moor! My heart quickened at the memory of mile upon mile of untrodden purity, white as angels' wings on the uplands, blue-shadowed in the hollows; of air like bright, sharp swords that you could almost see; of the breath-taking downward rush of sledge on polished track, eyes dazzled by sunlight, laughter frozen on the air as it left your lips; of the heart-warming friendliness of glowing cottage windows as you tramped homewards at dusk, feet squeaking and crunching in the snow; of the solemn beauty that awed you when you peeped under your bedroom blind at night; so still, so vast and pure in the light of the moon, that a lump came in your throat because so much loveliness was not to be borne.

"You see, Rosie, Uncle Alaric left me in charge," I began delicately.

Then followed an hour or more of argument, persuasion and wheedling on Rosie's part, and of polite evasion on my part, that might have gone on all night had not Maggie brought in the tea, which we both needed badly by then. I was amused to see that Maggie had spruced herself up for the confounding of Rosie, and that it had not the slightest effect on Rosie's opinion of her. Rosie sniffed loudly and turned her back on Maggie, and Maggie snorted and pounded round the table, clattering the crockery and making a hostile demonstration of the simple matter of laying tea for two. Still, it was a good tea, and Rosie and I felt mellower for it, and could spend the last hour of her visit in happy companionship.

"Is it nice being married to Luke, Rosie?"

Rosie laughed and said it was nice.

"Aren't you lonely when he's out all day?"

"Nay, I've nivver known what loneliness was since I left Bolton House, luv," she replied simply. And then her face went a deeper red, and she held my hand more tightly. "There'll be somebody else, besides Luke an' me, soon, please God," she added, her voice a little unsteady.

I did some mental arithmetic. And before I realised it I had blurted out: "About June, I suppose?"

She gave me a quick, startled glance.

"And what do you know about it, miss?"

"Oh, everything," I answered, surprised.

"Oh! And who told you?"

"David did. Ages ago."

"Nay!" Rosie gasped feebly. Had it been anyone but David she would have been thoroughly scandalised, but David could do no wrong in Rosie's eyes. And maybe even three months of living with Luke had torn down the few pitiful rags of social pretence that Bolton House had wrapped round her honest soul. There was no doubt about it, Rosie had changed for the better. Loving her as I always had, yet she had often been a figure of fun; a round peg in a square hole; a tree without roots. Since she had lived with Luke all that had changed. Her abundant figure was no longer lashed into the grim steel corset that Bolton House had demanded, and her carriage and complexion were the better for it. Her glance was softer and at the same time more assured. Her hands were roughened, but they lay quietly in her lap. Her speech had lost its few terrible refinements, no longer stumbling over recalcitrant aspirates and groping after elusive syntax. Rosic had found her niche in life. She had taken root and put forth strong branches swelling with promise of rich fulfilment.

I put my arms round her knees and laid my face in her comfortable lap.

"I do love you, Rosie. I do."

Then we both cried a little and then we laughed sheepishly and Rosie gave me a great tin of home-made toffee and some good advice about dealing with colds. When she had gone I sat on the hearthrug, my jaws clamped on the toffee, and thought about her, and about Luke and the baby they were going to have. I shut my eyes and saw the moor; and it stretched out its arms to me and murmured: "Don't worry. I shall always be here for you. ..."

Because of my loneliness, I looked forward to Christmas that year with an especial eagerness. Uncle Alaric would surely be home by then, and there would be Sylvia, with her strange, exciting stories of the world outside, and her own familiar, exciting personality. The servants would pull themselves together and wake the old house up; the dream-like quality of my days would dissolve, and life once more take on a definite pattern.

But alas for my hopes! Sylvia wrote that she had decided to go to Edinburgh. "If Uncle Alaric is home again he'll want to be quiet. And if there's only you and me, it'll be too deadly for words, won't it?" And at the end of the letter, a postscript, which must have cost her immense effort to write: "I might be able to wangle an invitation for you as well. Would you like that?"

Would I like it?

For a time I dallied with the idea, much as I imagine a mouse might consider pulling the whiskers of a sleeping cat. A bold notion, fraught with thrilling tremors and quaking fear. I saw myself, *soigné* in bright pink satin, queening it over an Edinburgh ballroom. Handsome young men fought for my favours and lowered in corners when they were refused. I galloped a blood mare over high brown moors; pursued, but never overtaken, by these same hapless gentlemen. I drifted elegantly in and out of the shops in Princes Street, drove in the famous motor-car, and was doted upon by Monica and her parents and a houseful of grovelling servants. I even saw myself, for one brief moment, snatching Sylvia's Sandhurst cadet from under her outraged nose.

But the cat stretched in his sleep, and the mouse whisked away into his little hole, grinning at the foolishness of dreams. Would I like it? Of course not. I should hate it, utterly and completely.

But even had I longed to go to Scotland nothing would have induced me to go. Sylvia and I were fond of each other, bound by memories of joy and sorrow, but our worlds lay far apart. Edinburgh was Sylvia's world. The moor was mine. I did not want them mixed up.

I was further dashed by a meeting in the village with Dr Greene, who pulled up his horse to ask me my plans for Christmas.

"Oh, I shall look after Uncle Alaric," I replied.

"That ye will not," the old man grunted, flourishing his unpleasant handkerchief. "He'll not be home yet awhile, m'dear. Best thing you can do is get away somewhere for a change. What about that place in Yorkshire you're so fond of—eh?"

"Oh, I've had several invitations," I threw out grandly, "but I've decided to stay at home. I like Christmas at home best. It's—such fun!" I blinked angrily at him, hoping I shouldn't cry.

"Ye do, do ye?" he mumbled, watching me with his shrewd old glance. "Ah, well, ye'll do as ye've a mind, no doubt. Your mother always did."

I turned towards home and went along the muddy lanes at a lagging pace. The air was muggy and unseasonable. A vague smell of rotting vegetation lay over the fields and a milky mist hung in the hollows. I felt enervated, uncomfortable, and submerged in self-pity.

Christmas at Cobbetts—alone! What on earth should I do with myself? If I went to the Farm the servants would be relieved, Rosie would be pleased, and I should be in the seventh heaven. Why not go, then? I didn't know why. I just knew that I must stay at Cobbetts until Uncle Alaric came home. I must stay and see to things for him.

Turning a sharp corner I suddenly stood motionless. There, in the middle of the lane, stood a magnificent fox, gleaming like a bronze statue in the pale sunlight. His brush swept the ground. One foot was lifted and his nose was up, sniffing the air. He stared at me insolently. From away in the distance I heard the faint sound of a horn, and saw a flash of pink on the horizon. They were a long way off. The fox had been very clever, and he knew it. His long tongue lolled out and slid round his muzzle, and I grinned back at him, congratulatory. Only a second he stood, poised and arrogant; then John came blundering up, and in an instant the fox had vanished. I wished him a good plump fowl for his dinner. He was a beautiful thing, and I was glad nobody would have their cheeks dabbled with his blood this time, at any rate.

John made a great fuss, blowing and snorting about the place where the fox had stood, every hair of his body quivering with importance. I laughed and left him to it. I felt cheered by the small incident, and went home humming a little tune.

Joy came with her peculiar sliding walk across the courtyard. She looked at me and giggled, rolling her fine eyes meaningly.

"There's a gentleman to see you," she whispered. "In the li'bry. You *are* a one!"

David! ... My heart leapt.

I began to run over the cobbles, bursting through the hall like a thunderbolt. It didn't occur to me to make myself more attractive. Sylvia would have nipped upstairs and done things to her hair. It mattered nothing to me that mine stood on end; that my sweater was torn and my breeches plastered with mud. David wouldn't care how dirty I was. ...

A tall figure rose from a chair as I burst into the library, and advanced, smiling nervously. My heart sank into my boots. It wasn't David. ... I hadn't the least idea who it was, but it evidently expected me to shake its hand and show some pleasure, so, as châtelaine of Cobbetts, I did my best.

"Well, Ruan—er—you've grown so tall, I feel I ought to say Miss Ashley!"

I stared at him blankly.

"I say—don't say you don't remember me!"

I cudgelled my brains. He was very tall, and rather heavily built. His dark hair was neat, shining with brilliantine, and his face was red, with a bluish tinge round the jaws. He was well dressed almost to the point of foppishness. For the life of me I couldn't place him.

Then suddenly I saw his gloves. They lay on the table; thick, expensive gloves of brown, shiny kid, plump from his hands; gloves that meant something in a man's life.

"Good lord!" I exploded, with a hoot of laughter. "You must be Stebbing!"

"That's right," he beamed.

"That fool of a Joy called you a gentleman!"

"Well—I hope I am," he said heavily.

"Oh, I don't mean *that*." How like him not to understand! Still, I was glad to see him. He had altered out of all recognition. He was only eighteen, but he looked twenty-five; large and solid, slow of speech and ponderous in all his movements. He had left school and was Going Into The Business. Something solemn and dry, dealing with imports and exports and travelling to and from India. "But I expect David has told you," he said weightily.

I hadn't heard from David for weeks, but I wasn't going to tell Stebbing that.

"David will miss you," I said politely; and was inspired to add; "and so will the football team."

He beamed and shuffled delightedly, and said, oh, no, he wasn't any good really—which I thought merely silly.

Rather hesitantly, I invited him to lunch, not being at all sure there would be any lunch, but rather proud of myself for not calling it dinner. I was relieved when he refused. They were expecting him back, he said: "they" being an aunt and uncle who lived in the neighbourhood, and with whom he was spending a few weeks before plunging into the world of business.

I told him about Uncle Alaric, and how I was in charge of Cobbetts, and he exclaimed "By Jove!" and "I say, what a rotten shame!" at intervals, and laboriously fitted on his gloves, which he instantly pulled off again in order to shake hands. Finally, he got himself out of the house and went away, having extracted a promise from me to ride with him the following afternoon.

It was a good thing he hadn't stayed to dinner, for all I had was a boiled egg and the remains of yesterday's bread-pudding, insufficiently heated up. Normally, I should have ignored this; but Stebbing's visit and his deference to me had restored my self-respect, and I actually tackled Maggie on the subject of food when she came to clear away.

"A nice thing if Mr Stebbing had stayed to lunch!" I pointed out.

"A good job he didn't," Maggie agreed, with a flat laugh.

"Well, please see that there *is* some food in the house in future," I said, in what I hoped was Sylvia's voice. "He will be coming here quite often, and I may ask him to stay at any moment."

"Hoity-toity!" Maggie grimaced. "Who's running this house, I should like to know?"

"Do you wish me to write to Mr Mallinson and ask him that question?" I asked coldly.

My knees were knocking together—but it worked. After that my meals were better served and noticeably more nutritious; and on the few occasions when Stebbing came to lunch or tea some ceremony was observed, with old Blossom waiting at table and the few remaining pieces of fine silver brought out to grace the ancient, much-darned damask. And Stebbing, I was glad to see, was impressed. He was awed by Cobbetts; by the ancient ceremony of the gates; by the dim, echoing rooms with their exquisite proportions, their dead, lovely tapestries, their few magnificent portraits of long-dead Mallinsons; by the wilderness of garden, where Fell wandered like an earth-bound ghost amidst the trailing smoke of his bonfires. The Mallinsons were old and the Stebbings were new. Mallinsons were County, Stebbings were City. Mallinsons were gone-to-seed, finished. Stebbings flourished fatly, marrying and giving in marriage, putting down sound port in sound cellars, entering names for public schools, giving handsome subscriptions to this and that, getting their feet dug into solid, respectable citizenship. They made no pretensions to good blood, but they had good hearts and good sense, neither grovelling nor underrating themselves; revering what was admirable in the Mallinsons, while soberly setting about the achievement of something better. The salt of the earth.

Chapter Nine

§

Harry Stebbing's Aunt Ella was a plump, white-skinned woman with a kind voice, who made me very welcome at The Hollies, never by an eyelash revealing that my torn and muddy riding-kit was hardly the thing for her nice, pink drawing-room, or that my manner of dealing with knives and forks was in any way unusual. I had once asked Uncle Alaric about this knife-and-fork business, and he had merely said, twinkling: "Use your fingers. Only the best people dare."

Mrs Joe Stebbing had no children of her own, and she was very fond of her nephew. "Dear Harry!" she said one day. "He's such a straight boy, so dependable and sincere. He'll make somebody a good husband one of these days."

We were alone, as it happened, taking tea by the fire in her frilly, feminine drawing-room. Her eyes rested on me, kind, speculative, faintly amused, and I could have no doubt as to the trend of her thoughts. Greatly embarrassed, I helped myself to more buttered tea-cake, and mumbled that I was sure of it.

"Have you ever thought of letting your hair grow, my dear?" she said, changing the subject abruptly.

I replied that I had always worn it that way, and she nodded.

"I think you would look very nice with long hair. It's so lovely and thick, and so full of life, isn't it? But if you like it short better, do you know what I should do? I should part it at the side, rather low down, and brush it vigorously across my head with the merest touch of brilliantine, and have the rest kept *very* short, like a man's." She gave me the kindest smile. "You don't mind my mentioning it?"

I didn't mind in the least. I submitted myself to another inspection that night, and decided that Mrs Joe was right about my hair, and the next day I rode into the nearest town and had it done at a good shop. I had a bit of trouble with the hairdresser, who seemed to think I ought to have some female with me—a mother or a governess. But I put on Sylvia's voice, and in the end he shrugged and gave a little bow from the hips, and began to clip away at the unruly mat. The result was astonishing. I looked a good two years older, and decidedly more attractive. In a day when fat sausage-curls and waist-length manes were all the rage, I was so far from the fashion that my very oddity took on a severe distinction of its own. I was so pleased that I drew upon the money Uncle Alaric had left me for emergencies and treated myself to two silk shirts and a short riding-jacket of brown tweed flecked with gold. All this I accomplished entirely on my own initiative: a thought which now fills me with pride and astonishment, having regard to the fact that I am the world's worst and most reluctant shopper. Joy was so impressed that she voluntarily cleaned my brown shoes and my riding-breeches, and the next time I visited The Hollies I was rewarded by Mrs Joe's soft voice exclaiming: "Why, Ruan! How *clever* of you!" Which pleased me a great deal more than if she had said how pretty or how smart I looked. She was a kind and tactful woman—and the two qualities are not by any means necessarily synonymous.

On the whole, Harry's Aunt Ella was the best possible thing that could have happened to me at just that time, when I was sadly in need of a woman. Better for me than dear old Rosie, for whom I could do no wrong. I was leading a most unnatural life for my age and, although I was happy enough, I was in grave danger of becoming introspective and precocious and sluttish. The sane, ordered life of The Hollies showed me my true image as in a mirror—with a most salutary effect.

I could talk to Mrs Joe, and she listened by the hour, her quiet, capable hands stitching away at some piece of embroidery, her glance resting on me from time to time with great kindness and understanding.

I told her all about Mother, and that terrible time when we were all caught in the dark tides that flowed about the Manse. I told her about Father and his strange, difficult life (for even then I could realise a little how difficult it had been) and his brave, solitary death. I told her about darling little Clem and poor, warped Tanner; about Hallelujah Johnson and Vera and Kitty and Ada Morris. I talked about Rosie and Luke, and about David, of whom she knew something already. I made her laugh by my descriptions of people at Cheddar Street Chapel (though she shook her head, too, when my humour became unkind), and she comforted my fears for Uncle Alaric.

Her comments were few, but those she did make were sensible and kind and to the point.

It was not until I was many years older that I came to know the true facts of my parents' marriage—that blazing glory and tragic failure—but I suppose I must unconsciously have conveyed something of the truth in my halting words, and her sympathy and sense supplied the rest. For it was she who made me understand that death in itself is not a terrible thing, nor even necessarily a sad thing, but more often the answer to a question; the lifting of a burden; a sudden light in a dark and tortuous passage.

She bade me forget the sadness of parting and remember only the gaiety of Mother's laughter, the beauty of Father's voice, the soft comfort of Clem's tufty head.

She took my small, mutilated soul in her capable hands, untied the knots and straightened out the tangles, washed the poison from my mind and let in the fresh air and healing sun. She took me shopping and made me a present of two frocks; one of dark-green velvet, made with a boyish little jacket and neat collar and cuffs of cream silk; the other of softest golden-brown taffeta with a feminine ruffle round the neck. It made a swishy sound when I moved. I did not mind accepting these things from Mrs Joe, for she made of it a great favour to herself, saying how often she had longed for a little daughter to dress in pretty things.

I do not doubt she would have done much more had she been able. She would have delighted in taking me from the lonely grandeur of Cobbetts to the comfortable sanity of her own home; in seeing me eat four hearty, well-cooked meals a day and keeping regular hours. I am sure she must have itched, many a time, to give me a thorough wash behind the ears and—probably even more often—a good smack bottom, which would doubtless have been to my benefit. But, lacking proper authority, there was nothing more she could do. For good or ill, Mallinsons went their own way, and neither fools nor angels interfered.

§

Stebbing's first capitulation to my charms had sprung from a mixture of measles and poetry—in that order. It had been fostered by David's ribaldry and the romantic view from his bedroom window. I had never given it the slightest encouragement, and it had died a natural death on the football field.

The second flowering was, perhaps, not so very different. Instead of measles, Stebbing was suffering from that heavy sense of age and responsibility that so often afflicts the very young. Life was a serious thing to Stebbing and the world a battlefield on which he was ready and eager to play his part, clad in the armour of staunch honesty, inherited caution, and brown kid gloves. Instead of the wild and lovely moor there was the ghostly grandeur of Cobbetts, with myself as the lonely heart of it; a sort of Mariana of the Moated Grange, before whom all the chivalry in Stebbing prostrated itself. Torn between his eagerness for the world and his reluctance to leave me, Stebbing fell.

"Only another day!" he said hollowly.

We were sitting before the library fire, making toast. It was a grey, streaming January afternoon. We had ridden that morning and my riding-kit was drying by the kitchen fire. I had put on the soft, frilly frock Mrs Joe had given me, and I was feeling pleased with my appearance, with the unaccustomed silkiness of each movement, and with life in general.

"Don't you want to go, then?" I asked idly.

Stebbing's face turned a darker red.

"No. Not now."

"Why ever not?"

"I … I don't want to leave you," he muttered.

Very slowly and deliberately I turned the toast. A warm, enjoyable sense of excitement filled me, flowing along my arms and legs, pricking up the back of my neck.

This was evidently It. The thing that had happened to Sylvia, and about which I had been scornful and impatient. I didn't feel scornful about Stebbing. I felt pleased and excited and not a little complacent.

"Here's another slice," I remarked casually.

He began clumsily to butter it and added it to the pile in the hearth.

"I … You. …" said Stebbing. He eased his collar and I spiked another piece of bread.

"You'll have a lovely time in London," I said cleverly. "You'll forget all about me in next to no time."

This piece of subtlety affected Stebbing almost to choking point.

"Don't say things like that, Ruan. I'll never forget you. I've always remembered that winter up on the moor."

"When we had measles together," I said, not so cleverly.

"When you used to come into my room and read poetry to me," he amended. "You read it so beautifully. 'So all night long the noise of battle rolled,' and *Maud*, and the one about the Eagle. I've never forgotten that one. I can still say it."

"Say it now."

Stebbing immediately took on the hue of a boiled lobster and pulled violently at his collar.

"Oh, I say, dash it! …"

I chanted it softly:

> "He clasps the crag with crooked hands;
> Close to the sun in lonely lands.
> Ring'd with the azure world, he stands.
> The wrinkled sea beneath him crawls;
> He watches from his mountain walls,
> And like a thunderbolt he falls!"

I had imagined I had outgrown Tennyson. But in an instant the old magic fell upon me, and I was alone with the Eagle in his crag; with the blue glare blinding my eyes and the sun beating fiercely on my head and the rock burning and blistering my clinging hands. I forgot Stebbing and the book-lined, fire-lit room and the rain falling heavily, persistently on the sodden lawns outside. Close to the sun, in lonely lands. ... And like a thunderbolt he falls. ... Not a word too much, not a line too little. With six strokes of the Master's brush a picture perfect in every detail, burning with light and colour, instinct with fate.

"Hey—look out!" Stebbing cried.

I leapt to my feet and tried stupidly to pull the blazing bread from the fork. Stebbing snatched it from me and threw it in the fire. I sucked my scorched fingers.

"Has it burned you, Ruan?" he cried, in a perfect agony of anxiety.

"No—nothing much."

"Let me look!"

He took my hand in his immense paws and held it awkwardly, gently.

"Ruan!" he exclaimed hoarsely. "You might have been hurt—badly. You might have set your frock on fire!"

"I'm all right," I muttered, feeling rather foolish, but by no means averse to the commotion I was causing.

"Ruan, if you had, I'd have—I'd—"

I don't know to what lengths Stebbing might not have committed himself; but at that moment old Blossom came in, carrying the silver teapot and sniffing suspiciously.

"Burn the house down, one of these days," he growled. Crossing the room with shambling steps, he drew the curtains, shutting out the sad dusk, and lit the singing gas. He clattered about the table ineffectually. John came running in, poked a cold nose into my hand and then into Stebbing's, and established himself in the middle of the hearthrug. Blossom went out, shutting the door behind him with a feebly vindictive slam. I began to pour out the tea. The great moment had passed. ...

We ate a hearty, unromantic meal, and afterwards Stebbing beat me three times at draughts, and I beat him at noughts and crosses, and we giggled childishly and happily together. Then Stebbing had to go, because of people coming to dinner, so I rang for Blossom and his key. Grumbling and shuffling he opened the great door and peered into the courtyard. The rain had died to a thin drizzle, and one or two stars made a feeble showing in the dark sky. It had turned bitterly cold and the old man was shivering and coughing, so I took the key from his hand and sent him back to the kitchen. In the hall cupboard I found a long coat of Uncle Alaric's and slipped it on. It reached my heels, flapping absurdly, but I clutched it round me and went to the gate with Stebbing.

I unlocked the gate and swung it slowly open.

"Good night, Stebbing."

He beat his gloved hands together, nervously.

"I say!—not Stebbing, please!"

"Well—good night, Harry."

"Good night, Ruan. ... You look so funny in that huge coat. Such a—a sweet little girl, Ruan."

"I'm not particularly little. It's you that's so big. I come up to here on you." I poked him in the chest with the key.

"That's my heart," he said huskily, and inaccurately. He put his arms round me and held me against it, and I could hear something bumping away under his heavy overcoat. It was bumping because of me, I reflected triumphantly. Surreptitiously I felt at my own heart, but it was disappointingly stolid.

I sensed rather than felt that I was about to be kissed, and I raised my face expectantly in the darkness.

On the whole it wasn't a great success; a blundering, amateurish affair that landed mainly in one eye, temporarily blinding me, with the rain off Stebbing's hat making an icy rivulet down my neck. But I was satisfied. I had been kissed. I had heard somebody's heart bump and bang under my ear, all because of me. I had been called "little" and "sweet." I was one of the initiate. ...

His boots went stumping away down the lane and I swung the heavy gate of Cobbetts and locked him out.

§

The following day was Stebbing's last, and we had arranged to ride as usual; but the sun rose on a world of solid ice. The courtyard was a death-trap and the lanes impossible for horses. Each window-pane was a fairy picture miraculously etched overnight. An unearthly silence lay over an iron-bound world.

Stebbing came to call for me and we decided to walk instead to Abbot's Leigh. It was a long tramp, but we could have a meal there and come back by train. It sounded a lovely programme and we set off in high spirits, slipping and sliding about the place until we developed "ice legs" and managed to maintain a sober, plodding progress. We left John at home, because the ice formed in hard balls on his pads, and made him unhappy.

Stebbing was all happed up in a heavy overcoat of navy-blue cloth, and was a little concerned that I wore only my usual outdoor garb of breeches and jerkin. He was horrified when I informed him I did not possess an overcoat, and for some time afterwards he walked silently, deep in thought. I was glad of his silence, for I had no wish to talk. It was one of those kind of days. The world itself was so silent that human laughter and chatter sounded thin and unreal and somehow presumptuous. The earth was beautiful in her sudden sleep. Trees stood motionless against a steel sky, each branch outlined in sparkling frost. Each blade of grass was a separate, exquisite gem. Each pond an enchanted sea. My breath was a floating, faery thing before my face.

If it were so lovely here, I thought wistfully, what must it be on the moor! And at once I fell to dreaming of the immense reaches of sky above the undulating lines of the hills; the beckoning smoke of the Farm chimneys; the smell of hot scones and the warm, comfortable sounds of milking-time. I suddenly felt very small and young; very tired of being the mistress of Cobbetts; of bothering about my hair and clothes and of being adored by Stebbing. I wanted to race along the moor road with David; to be called Tinribs and Fathead; to have my head clumped occasionally and my knees bound up and strange concoctions forced upon me when my stomach ached. I didn't want to be helped over stiles and guided across frozen ruts and worried about in case I was cold. David wouldn't have worried. He'd have seen that I was sensibly clad when we set out, and if, in spite of that, I had shivered, he'd have made me run.

I knew where I was with David. And it was always better than with anybody else.

David. … Where are you, David? What's happened to us? Why do you write so seldom? Are you really growing up, David, and away from me? Is it really happening at last? …

"Harry," I shouted, "let's run!"

We were on grass now, and it was hard and dry, crackling beneath our feet. It was sheer joy to run in that clear, cold silence. The air bit my nose and throat: it was like swallowing swords. My body felt light and vigorous. I could have run for ever. I heard Stebbing pounding after me, calling me to stop, that I should break my leg if I fell. I laughed scornfully and went on running, and presently I could not hear him any more. I ran until a stitch came in my side, and then I threw myself down on the frozen grass with eyes closed and arms dramatically outflung.

It was the sort of occasion on which I should have been soundly clumped by David. But Stebbing picked me up and reverently dusted me down, gently scolding and imploring me to say I was not hurt.

"You're so unexpected, Ruan. I never know where I am with you!"

I felt rather sorry for him then, and walked soberly beside him for the rest of the way, talking the pleasant commonplaces that Stebbing felt at home with, and being helpless when I saw that he wanted to help me, until we rounded the bend of the lane, and there above us, like a half-remembered dream, hung the frozen lace of the Abbey ruins.

"Well, it's awfully pretty, isn't it?" said Stebbing.

I swallowed hard, and agreed that it was awfully pretty. And we went down into the village.

There was a huge fire in the hotel and deep, comfortable chairs, and magazines. I had never in my life been in such a place before, but Stebbing seemed quite at home. He removed his greatcoat and his hat and gloves, and hitched his trouser knees in a grown-up fashion. A pale young waiter with a napkin over his arm presented Stebbing with a menu, and took an order for roast beef, baked potatoes, Yorkshire pudding and sprouts—and very good it sounded to me.

"Will you take anything to drink, sir?"

"I'll have a pint of bitter," said Stebbing.

"And the young lady?"

"I'll have a pint of bitter, too," I said sociably.

The waiter smiled, but Stebbing went very red in the face, and looked as if he would like to put his gloves on.

"I say, you can't have bitter, you know, Ruan."

"Why not?" I demanded, astonished.

"Well—you're not old enough for one thing."

"Of course I am!"

"Not for beer."

"*Beer!* ... Is *that* what bitter is?" If he had said hemlock I could not have been more shocked and incredulous. "But you only get *beer* in *public-houses!*"

"Well, this is a pub. All hotels are pubs—except the temperance ones."

The waiter placed water on the table and tactfully effaced himself. I think he was sorry for me; and well he might be, for I felt terrible. All the Nonconformist in me had risen up, flashing distress signals. I was in a *pub*, with a person who drank *beer!* With deadly clarity I saw again the pubs abounding in the mean streets around Cheddar Street Chapel. I smelt their peculiar, horrid, exciting smell. I saw the fat, blowsy women and the furtive men, and the dirty little children quarrelling about the doorsteps. I remembered how Sylvia and I had hurried past, shuddering. *Beer* in a *pub!* It was not only wicked—it was *common!*

Stebbing tugged at his collar.

"You and David always had beer when you went for picnics on the moor. You told me so."

"That was home-made beer. It was *quite* different, Stebbing. And it wasn't in a *pub*."

But when the food came it was so good, and I was so hungry, that by the time I had cleaned my plate my Nonconformist conscience was comfortably wedged down under beef and Yorkshire pudding, and I could watch Stebbing drinking his beer with no more than a faint sense of daring, rather pleasant than otherwise.

The waiter hovered again, and Stebbing said:

"Will you have a sweet, Ruan?"

"Yes, please. I didn't know you'd got any."

"What would you like?"

"Give me a chocolate walnut," I said hopefully.

Stebbing went red again, and the waiter grinned broadly.

"Will you have jam-roll or apple-tart?"

"Oh, you mean *pudding*! Why couldn't you say so! I'll have apple-tart. And plenty of cream," I added sternly, to show the waiter I was not as soft as he thought.

We ate the tart in silence, rather stiff with each other. But afterwards, basking over the great fire, with coffee in tiny dolls' cups and the Christmas Number of *Punch*, we forgot everything but the comfort of full stomachs and toasted limbs. I was nearly asleep, in fact, when Stebbing pulled out his watch and announced that it was time to go.

Stebbing put some money on the waiter's little tray, and the waiter said: "*Thank* you, sir!"—and helped him on with his coat. Stebbing put his gloves on, and took them off again, and pulled at his collar.

"Er—would you—er—like to wash, Ruan?"

I wondered if he had gone mad.

"Good lord, no!" I replied. "But I do want to go to the lavatory—badly!"

Stebbing flung a look of wild despair at the pale waiter, who bore up manfully and led me through a door and along a corridor and up some stairs to a door marked "Ladies," and shut me firmly inside it. I remembered, too late, that one did not mention lavatories to Stebbing. And once more I longed for David, who called a spade a spade, and no nonsense.

I resolved to be patient with Stebbing as it was his last day. But it seemed as if I could do nothing right; for in trying to find my way back to the dining-room I took a wrong turning and landed suddenly in a large, steamy kitchen. The young waiter was there, talking to a woman with an enormous bust, who was laughing immoderately.

"'Would you—ah—like to wash?' he says," said the waiter, in mincing tones. "And she says 'Not me!' she says, 'but I want'—"

Here the fat woman stuck her elbow violently in the waiter's ribs and he turned and saw me. Rolling his eyes up to heaven, he hurried out and with a solemn: "This way, if you please, miss," he returned me to Stebbing, bowed and vanished.

On the whole, I was glad when we were in the train, and I'm sure Stebbing was, too. He was still rather hot and bothered with my peculiar behaviour, but he was very kind, presenting me with an enormous box of chocolate-walnuts and opening and shutting windows with great efficiency and solicitude. Then from the depths of his greatcoat he produced a flat parcel, tied with coloured ribbon.

"A parting present," he said shyly. "It's a book of verses by a chap called Omar Khayyám. All about drinking the local brew in pubs. But maybe it was home-made, so I shouldn't worry." Which was, I suppose, about as near to a joke as he ever got in his life—poor Stebbing.

I was immensely pleased with the book, which was a suede-bound edition of FitzGerald's translation, with very beautiful illustrations in colour. It was all colour: pictures, letterpress, binding. I turned the thick pages eagerly, and the verses themselves, leaping from eye to brain, to heart, glowed with colour, shimmered with light. It was like holding a jewel in my hands. I shivered with happiness, and throwing my arms impetuously round Stebbing's neck I kissed him with heartfelt gratitude.

It was too much for Stebbing. Seizing me in a bear-like hug, he rained his clumsy kisses on my head, my cold, glowing cheeks, my rough, rather grimy hands.

"Oh, Ruan—darling!—I know I ought not to do this. You're only a child still—and I'm not much more myself—but I can't help it. You're so sweet, and I love you so much. You say the most awful things, and I can't understand you a bit, and sometimes I could sink into the ground—and it doesn't matter tuppence because it's you! ..."

"Don't!" I cried, struggling ineffectually.

"I must, Ruan, just this once. Because I'm going away to-morrow, and heaven knows when I shall see you again. They may even send me to India. I don't know. But please, Ruan, darling little Ruan, always remember that I'm working like blazes for you, all the time—will you?"

"Why for me?" I demanded, freeing myself at last, and recovering my precious book, which had slipped to the floor in the violence of Stebbing's passion.

"Why, so we can be married, if—if you'll have me, Ruan. Plenty of girls get married when they're about seventeen. I shall be twenty-two by then. It's not such an awfully long time. I've got to go through the mill first, you know, but in a few years' time, when I've got a working knowledge of the business, and had a bit of experience, they'll make me a junior partner and then. ... Oh, Ruan, we'll have such a glorious time together! I'll be so good to you. You shall have lots of clothes; you shall have a lovely warm overcoat then—a fur coat! And we'll travel about and see the world, and any books you want to buy you'll be able to. Oh! ..." And he went into a species of trance at the visions his own words had raised.

I felt pleasantly stimulated myself. To be the focal point of such adoration, such a surging, rich, eventful life as he looked forward to, made me regard Stebbing very kindly indeed. I liked the thought of crossing oceans. Strange cities with white domes blazing against a blue sky, and dark-eyed people clamouring in odorous bazaars. I liked the thought of having money to spend on books: books, books and yet more books. Horses and dogs. Maybe a motor-car. A fur coat. ... I wriggled my shoulders restlessly. The thought of all the hot, heavy coats that Stebbing would wrap me in brought me to earth again. I glanced at his rapt face less kindly. It was red and rather moist, and distinctly purple about the jowl. A kind, dogged, honest face that would be old and heavy long before its time. ...

I glanced down at my book and lovely words leapt at me:

> "There was a door to which I had no key.
> There was a veil past which I could not see. ..."

I caught my breath.

Life. Grown-up life. That mysterious business that still lay far ahead of me. I knew suddenly and quite definitely that Stebbing's key would never unlock that door for me, or his kid-gloved hands tear down that veil. Life was a lovely, a terrible thing; to be dreamed of, but not experienced; like the pink silk I would not cut and the circus I didn't want to see. ... The day I knew was so sweet, so sweet; why trouble about the morrow? ...

And as if old Omar himself answered me, my book opened of itself, and I read:

"Ah, take the cash in hand and waive the rest;
O, the brave music of a *distant* drum!"

❦

When we got out of the train I seized Stebbing's hand and shook it violently.

"Good-bye, Stebbing, I've got to hurry," I said. And then, remembering my manners: "Oh, and thank you for a lovely day and my book and—and everything! Good-bye."

"Here, I say, Ruan! I'm coming as far as the gate with you!" His voice began in a surprised stammer and ended in a roar; for I was away, running like the devil, out of the station, down the hill and in at the servants' entrance—for I would not wait for Blossom and his key.

What was I running from? From Stebbing? From Life? From myself? ... I did not know. And even now I do not know, so long a time it seems since I flew down that cobbled, hilly lane to sanctuary. So long a time— yet only yesterday!

❦

I burst into the library and shut the door behind me. Panting and dishevelled, clutching my book in grimy hands, I leaned against the door and gazed through the dancing firelight at Uncle Alaric, sitting in his usual chair, a book open on his knees and an empty tea-cup beside him— just as if he had never been away.

With great deliberation he placed a marker between the pages and closed the book. His glance flicked over me, from tousled head to snow-clogged boots, and his shrug was quite perceptible.

"Enter the Lady of Cobbetts."

"Oh, Uncle Alaric!" I breathed. I was so glad to see him I could have cried. I *was* crying! I wiped my face with the back of my hand.

"There were toast crumbs in most of my books," he remarked in a detached voice.

"Oh ... I'm so sorry."

"And John has been sleeping in my chair. The cushion is covered with hairs."

"I'll get them off."

"Apart from that," said Uncle Alaric, "you appear to have seen to things remarkably well. Thank you, Ruan."

I removed my wet boots and padded across the room to the fire's warmth. I squatted down on the hearth-rug, carefully keeping my wet eyes away from Uncle Alaric, who detested any show of emotion. I snapped my fingers at John, who was huffily pretending he hadn't noticed my entrance, and that he hadn't *wanted* to go walkies, anyway! He struggled with his dignity, but presently gave it up, and with a deep sigh came and laid his head on my lap and gave each of my hands a thorough wash.

Uncle Alaric touched my head with his long, delicate fingers, and I let it rest against his knee.

And thus, with life shut firmly out into the darkness, we sat together in peace. And presently I fell asleep.

Book Three

&

The Moor

Chapter One

§

Remembering. Remembering. ...

How strange a thing is memory!

Something happens; something horrific, beautiful, or poignantly sad; something that changes the whole course of life. And looking backwards to yesterday, and through a thousand yesterdays, the only things remembered clearly are the colour of somebody's tie, a wrong note played on a piano, the tuppence lost down the back of a sofa. ... The heart keeps the stone that splashed into the quiet pool; but the brain remembers only the shallow ripples that ran glinting across the surface—that will go on running for ever and ever, until they reach the ultimate shores of time. ...

And so, remembering, I see myself alone in the library at Cobbetts, curled up in the sunny window-seat, waiting for Sylvia to come home.

It was a perfect day of early June. The unmown lawns were lush and green. Lilac still lingered; the smell of it was sweet and heavy on the unstirred air. A great silence lay on the world. No clatter in the house, no movement in the garden. A lark sang somewhere in the blue, and the thin silver of his voice was silence articulate.

I was remembering David.

In the two years that had elapsed since Rosie's marriage I had seen David only once, and that was nearly a year ago now. He had spent a brief, busy week at the Farm after leaving school and before setting out on the year of travel Rosie had insisted upon. David had strenuously opposed the idea at first, but had gradually come round to Rosie's way of thinking, and in the end was wildly enthusiastic about it.

"After all, Ruan, it's my only chance of seeing the world. Once I've started medical school, I shall have to work like blazes, and I expect I shall go on working like blazes all my life, until I drop in my tracks. I shan't be one of those lukewarm blighters who retire as soon as they've made a bit of money, and just fool about with golf and bridge. I hope," he concluded rather grandly, "to die in harness."

I remember rolling on to my back and giggling unkindly.

"You're far more likely to be murdered by some infuriated patient!"

"I'd murder *you* if it wasn't so hot!"

That was the only really happy day we spent together that week. It had taken time to break down the barriers a whole year of being parted from each other had raised, and the last part of the week was such a rush of shopping and last-minute sewing and packing and re-packing. But for that one, perfect day barriers dissolved and time was not. Everything was as it had always been—almost. We raced over the moor and climbed the hills, regardless of heat. We lay on our backs, scorching our faces and arms, dozing and waking and giggling happily over old times. We ate hugely and walked a great number of miles, and talked of everything under the sun, and fell silent, just as we had always done—almost. But not quite.

There was something different. Something vague, intangible, probably unimportant, but *something*, surely.

I looked at David, lying beside me on the heather, half asleep. Rough brown hair; kind, deep-set eyes that crinkled at the corners when they laughed; undistinguished, freckled nose; sweet line of lips above stubborn chin; strong, flexible hands; immense length of legs in shabby grey trousers. ... This was David. My David, unchanged and unchanging; and I loved him.

"Know me next time you see me, Tinribs?" he murmured lazily; and his hand closed round mine, warm, firm, and reassuring.

No, the change was not in David. It was not in me. It was something that came between us every now and then; an irritating little ghost; a poltergeist I might have called it, had I ever heard of such a thing. It danced about between us, mocking and whispering malice. It got inside us, peeping at me through David's eyes and through my eyes at David. "Ask him why he hasn't bothered to see you for a whole year," it whispered to me, smirking. "Make him tell you where he spent last Christmas, and why he didn't go home for Easter, and why he's only here for one week now—especially as he's going abroad for another whole year." And it whispered: "It won't be the same when he comes back. It'll never be the same again."

And all the time, there was nothing there at all; nothing that mattered; and my heart knew it well, though it ached a little, too.

We went home through the village. Cracked Willy greeted us with mouthings and slobberings of joy. David shook hands with him and gave him a shilling, which he promptly put in his mouth.

"Now you've done it!" I muttered. But Willy's mother was not a whit dismayed.

"He'll none swally it!" she laughed, wrapping her steamy arms in a coarse apron. "Another one might, but not Our Willy. He's too much sense for that—an't you, Our Willy?"

"Hur! Hur!"

A ginger cat slunk out of the cottage. Willy shot it an evil glance, which it returned with interest, keeping well away from the shambling, iron-studded boots.

We inquired after Willy's brothers and sisters. Our May was in service at Bender's End. Our Fred was a baker's roundsman. Our John Henry and Our Albert were still at school and doing well, with jobs waiting for them as soon as they were fourteen.

"Aye!" said Willy's mother, sighing, "all on 'em's going. All on 'em but Our Willy. He's going to stay with his ma, an't you, Our Willy?"

"Hur!" grunted Willy, and hit her a vicious blow in the middle of her apron, temporarily winding her.

"It ain't one of 'is good days," she gasped apologetically. "You'd ought to hear him sometimes, it'd surprise you what that boy can say! Now then, Our Willy, be'ave, will you, an' say good-bye nicely!"

We paused at the blacksmith's and saw the bullet-headed boy working alone in the forge; more bullety than ever and twice as large. He shook hands with David and ducked at me, grinning sheepishly. No, he was no longer in the choir, as his voice had broken. Maybe he'd go back in a year or so. Yes, he'd left school and was working with his father, and a rare old slave-driver he was, an' all! We talked for a few moments, but he was so polite I lost interest in him. As we walked away up the hill I could not forbear to turn round and stick out my tongue at him, as far as it would go. And I had the satisfaction of seeing him roll his eyes inward in a super-squint. Unfortunately for him, his father entered the forge at that moment, and fetched him such a crack over the head as must surely have fixed that squint permanently.

"That's a woman all over!" remarked David. "Get a chap into trouble and then laugh at him. And after he's adored you all these years!"

"Don't be daft!" I shouted. "He's always pulled the most *frightful* faces at me!"

"It takes some chaps like that," he said thoughtfully.

I turned and gazed moodily down on the forge. A steady bang-clang-clang came from the dark, open doorway, and a shower of sparks flew upward.

We tidied up Karenhapuk Foljambe's grave, and then went to see Mr Lord, who gave us his China tea in fragile little cups and a great deal of advice to David about his coming travels.

"You don't know how fortunate you are, seeing Europe now," Mr Lord said. "Paris, Bruges, Rome, Florence, Algiers, Berlin, Vienna, the Fiords. ... You're a lucky fellow, David. Don't miss anything. See it all. Go everywhere. One day—who knows?—there may be nothing left to see."

"You mean there might be a sort of tremendous earthquake, or something?" I asked doubtfully.

"I mean war," he replied sadly.

"But surely, sir," David said, frowning, "not the whole of Europe! That sounds fantastic. Aren't we too civilised nowadays for war on such a tremendous scale?"

"It might be even worse—the whole world!" His eyes stared past us, as one seeing visions. "Not yet, not yet! Perhaps not in my lifetime. But almost certainly in yours. There are signs, and he who runs may read. ... But I'm casting a gloom over your bright faces and spoiling your day! Have some more tea, Ruan. Try one of these little cakes; my housekeeper is a dab hand at cakes. I eat far too many for my figure."

He came with us to the gate, his arm thrown about David's shoulder.

"When you come back we must have a great talk about your travels; compare notes, and see if the face of Europe has changed much since my time."

We walked back to the Farm in rather sober mood.

"There couldn't ever be a war like that, could there, David? Not the whole world at war! ... It's—it's like something Cracked Willy might dream about!"

"I shouldn't think so. The old boy's got some bee buzzing in his bonnet." He whistled tunelessly for a few steps. Then he added in his sane, comfortable way: "In any case, we can't do anything about it, Tinribs, so don't get into a flurry."

Remembering, remembering. ...

David going away from me for a year—a whole long year—and the weight of it heavy in my heart; and I remember a boy squinting, an idiot mumbling a bright shilling, and an old man's impossible dreams of Armageddon.

$$\mathcal{S}$$

We sat outside the Farm door that night, in a hot stillness that warned of storm. Luke had been weeding the flower border, but presently he gave it up and came to sit on the doorstep beside Rosie's chair. His great horny hands cupped the bowl of his pipe and the struck match lit his kind face in the deepening twilight. The heather was not yet in bloom, but all the air was heavy with the dear, familiar, quite indescribable smell of the moor. The kitchen lamp sent out a mild circle of radiance that touched Rosie's hair with flame. I saw Luke's eyes rest on it. He put up his hand and stroked it gently, and a look passed between them that made me turn my own eyes away. I remembered a hot noon in the orchard, when Rosie's hair had not been so neat, nor Luke's hands so gentle. There had been storm in the air then, too. I remembered the Scarlet Woman coming down the dark aisle of the church and my fists hammering at the iron-studded doors.

I moved closer to David.

A cuckoo flew silently across the sky and perched on a near-by tree.

"He'll be away soon, will yon," Luke said. "In July he make ready to fly."

"And no loss, the daft creature," Rosie replied.

"Nay, I don't know, I like t'cuckoo."

"You! You like everybody," she exclaimed shortly.

Rosie's temper was uncertain these days. She was recovering from a bad miscarriage. Her step was slower and her big shoulders held less gallantly. She had even flown out at me. I had arrived at the Farm with my hair grown to shoulder-length, and she had been loud in her praise and delight.

"Nay, Ruan luv, I'd no idea your hair was that lovely! Whatever was your mother thinking about to cut it! My word, it's thick! And such a shine on it! Nay, Luke, have you seen t'lass's hair? What do you think of her now? Doesn't she look different?"

My heart sank. Different! ... I scarcely knew why I had let my hair grow. I had a confused notion that it had something to do with David—with a David I had not seen for a year—but certainly it was not conscious coquetry. Not all Stebbing's impassioned stammerings had awakened that in me. With Uncle Alaric's return to Cobbetts I had thankfully abandoned all pretence of being grown-up, and had taken up my child's life again happily enough. Once again I was a little girl—torn jersey, dirty neck and all. And yet I suppose it was because I wanted to please David that I had let my hair grow. The heart of a child of thirteen is a strange, complex thing—and who am I that I should profess to understand it?

Rosie's assertion that I looked different caused me hours of anguished uncertainty. I gazed furtively in mirrors, shaking the dark cloud over my face, twisting it severely back. And in the end, twenty minutes before David's arrival, I hacked it all off with the kitchen scissors and promptly burst into tears.

Rosie came running to know what all the hullabaloo was about. When she saw what I had done her face reddened with vexation. "Nay!" she shouted, and banged my head against the wall.

But when David came he gripped my shorn locks in either hand and shook me gently from side to side, crinkling his eyes in their sweet smile.

"Good little Tinribs," he said, "just the same as ever. Nice little Tinribs!"

My darling David. How I loved him then!

§

We sat in the garden until it was very late. It seemed too hot and airless to attempt sleep and an oppression lay heavily on our spirits. I looked at the dark, distant hills, and for the first time they seemed inimical to me. They were black, surly giants who spat flame at each other, growling threats and giving sudden cracks of horrid laughter.

"I wish it'd come, and have done with it," Rosie said fretfully.

We went indoors at last, yawning and straggling up to bed. Hot though it was, I cowered under the bedclothes, listening to the thunder coming nearer and nearer. The night had to be faced, and I faced it trembling in mind and body. Ever since I had been shut in the dark church I had been terrified of storms beyond all reason. I patted the bed, and John leapt up to lie beside me, but it was too hot for him and he soon jumped down again, panting. I heard him flump down on to the linoleum.

For a few moments the thunder ceased altogether. Cautiously raising the bedclothes, I could hear a dry, stealthy wind rustling the heather, lifting the curtains, setting the climbing rose tap-tapping against the window. Perhaps, I thought hopefully, the storm was going round, as it sometimes did. I threw off the bedclothes and sat bolt upright. And in that moment the whole of creation crashed about my head; the storm leapt out from the ruined hills and was upon me.

"David!" I cried soundlessly.

I don't remember how I reached David's room, but suddenly there I was, and the door blessedly open. He was half out of bed, coming, as he has since told me, to my room. Without a word he got back and pulled me in beside him. I crouched close to his side in the hard curve of his arm. I smelt the sweet wholesomeness of his body and the new, crisp cotton of his pyjamas and the toothpaste he had been using and the bowl of stocks that stood on the walnut chest. The rain began to come down in torrents.

Thunder thumped and crashed and splintered close on the heels of the lightning. The room was lit with unearthly light and plunged into hellish blackness. I shut my eyes and pressed my forehead into David's shoulder.

And suddenly I found that I was no longer afraid. I was conscious of no feeling but that of overwhelming sleepiness. I opened my mind to it and relaxed my rigid body. The recurrent crashes gradually merged into an all-pervading noise that ringed the world with blackness; an impersonal, far-off, deep nothingness that weighed on my limbs, my eyelids, like a half-forgotten dream.

Vaguely I heard someone shutting windows, then coming nearer. Rosie's voice in the doorway.

"You didn't shut your window, David, there's a right pool on t'floor. Ee, what a storm!" She banged the window to. "Ruan'll be in a dither with this. I'll go see to her—"

I lay as still as death, but I heard her gasp.

"Well, I don't know!" exclaimed Rosie weakly.

"It's all right, Rosie, leave her," David said.

"Nay, but David—"

"Leave her." His voice was curt, unfamiliar. I had never heard David speak to Rosie like that before. I hung on to him and kept my eyes closed; and after a moment or two Rosie went away. I heard her voice and Luke's far off, mumble-mumbling. Then the sleep I had feigned became real and I remembered nothing more until I woke to a room filled with pale, washed sunlight and the scent of stocks. John lay asleep by the door. A bee bumbled about the window, heavy with importance. But David was not there.

❦

Rosie said nothing until David had been gone a day or two. Then, as we were shredding beans one morning, she said abruptly:

"You know, Ruan, you're growing up now."

"Oh, Rosie, no!"

"Well, but you are, luv, and you want to remember it."

"Why?"

"Well. ..." She looked at me perplexedly, hesitated a long time, said "well" again, and then gave it up. But as we finished the last of the beans she stood up, pressing a hand to her tired back, and threw me an oblique glance.

"Happen it's just as well you did cut your hair!" she remarked cryptically.

§

Remembering. Remembering. ...

How long ago it seemed, that night of storm up on the moor. How long we had been apart, David and I.

I sat curled up in the window-seat, waiting for Sylvia, alone. No clatter in the house, no movement in the garden. The lark had ceased her song. Alone.

It was not often that being alone made me feel lonely, but I was lonely that day. I longed for Sylvia to come. The telegram had been sent off two nights ago. If she had started at once she should be here now. Paris was not so far away. I wanted her. There was nobody else. Nobody at all. David was somewhere in Europe. Mrs Joe Stebbing was in the south of France. Harry Stebbing was in London and about to make his first trip to India. Rosie was ill. She had suffered another miscarriage and this time it had been serious. We knew now that there would never be any babies at the Farm.

And Uncle Alaric lay dead in his bare little room upstairs.

Alone! Nobody at all!

Gazing with shrinking distaste at my ugly black frock, I even began to wonder if I were there myself; if this sad stranger could really be I, Ruan Ashley, or if the whole thing were a dream which presently I should shake off, laughing with relief, as I had shaken off dreams before.

Maggie came into the room. Her eyes were red and swollen with crying. She carried a glass of hot milk on a heavy silver tray. The skin of the milk had slopped down the outside of the glass and the tray was tarnished.

"Drink this, dear," said Maggie, sniffing. "It'll pull you together."

She suddenly enraged me. I did not want her beastly milk and sloppy endearments. They were prompted neither by affection nor true pity, but by that ghoulish relish of death and all its horrid paraphernalia that she and her kind revelled in.

It was Maggie who had insisted on the black frock. In the first daze of bereavement I had allowed her to take me into the town, standing obediently while she and the shop assistant measured and fitted me, talking over my head with lugubrious sighs and hissings. It hadn't seemed to matter what they did with me; nothing mattered since Uncle Alaric was dead.

My dear Uncle Alaric, my good companion who had understood me and whom I had understood so well; who had taught me so much without seeming to teach; who had fed and sheltered me in my need; who had let me alone. ...

"I don't need pulling together," I said coldly, turning my back on the disgusting tray and Maggie's outraged expression.

"You're a hard piece if ever there was one!" she exclaimed violently. "If you can't feel no natural grief, you might at least pretend to, if only for decency's sake!"

She squeaked out, shutting the door as loudly as she dared in that quiet house of death—and immediately opened it again for a sullen postscript:

"Mr Nicholson's wanting to see you."

I curled up on the window-seat again.

Mr Nicholson could want. I wasn't feeling like Mr Nicholson at the moment. He was Uncle Alaric's lawyer, and from time to time had come to Cobbetts on business. I was perfectly aware that he was terrified of me. At our first meeting I had been a native in an African jungle and had stalked him through the gardens as he took the air after dinner, walking in his precise, nervous way. Fell had made me an assegai, which I had improved with a meat-skewer, and I prided myself on my prowess in killing. I had not quite killed Mr Nicholson: the assegai had gone through his hat, missing his skull by a fraction, and alienating for all time any tolerance he might have felt for me. On his next visit I hadn't improved matters by coming downstairs in my knickers and on a tin tray, as he was coming up, causing him to leap astride the stair rail in record time. The rail was liberally adorned with carved knobs—which I could never see was my fault in the least. Ever since then he had successfully avoided me. But all that was ages ago, and if he wanted to speak to me now, I decided, he could come and find me.

I pressed my hot face against the window. The trees spread their great arms to the sun. The grass was so intensely green, the flowers so bright, the sky so clear and vivid. ... Everything outside was vital, urgent with life. Everything indoors lost and dead.

My mind swept back over the last seven years, and I was appalled to think how much unhappiness I had lived through. Mother, Father, Clem, Tanner. Joshua Day and Mrs Abbey. They had all been parts of my life, and they had all gone. Each of them had caused me a special, separate grief; but I had never before experienced the dreadful gloom of a shrouded house; never been brought into direct contact with the solemn silence, the subdued whisperings, the furtive footsteps that attend the sorry business of civilised dying.

There had been a day nurse, Miss Pointer; an arch woman with a fearful smile and hard, icy hands, who had invariably referred to Uncle Alaric in the plural. "We are going to have a nice little nap now!" "We are ever so much better this morning, I'm sure!" "Aren't we the *teeniest* bit grumpy to-day?" ... How Uncle Alaric loathed her! And there had been a night nurse, Miss Begley, who was completely uninterested in anybody but Miss Begley and a person she described as "my Intended," who lived at Harrow, and who had to be written to every single night, or else he would "create something awful!"

There had been old Dr Greene stumping in and out, blowing his nose and grumbling. There had been the evening when Fell beckoned me out into the garden, saying he had something to show me up in the top orchard. I went with him obediently, for something told me they wanted me out of the way. Fell kept me searching for a nest he alleged to have seen but which had mysteriously disappeared. I joined half-heartedly in the pretence, realising that he meant to be kind, but in the end I blurted out:

"Are they bringing Uncle Alaric's coffin to-night?"

"Ar," Fell muttered, considerably taken aback.

"I hate it, Fell. It's—it's almost the worst part of dying, all this business."

He drew his hand slowly across his nose and spat.

"Ar. Yer right there, miss," he replied unexpectedly. "I don't 'old with it meself. They shan't never do that to me, I'll see to that. A damn great bonfire," said Fell dreamily, "that's the way to go. That's how it should be done. A damn great bonfire blazing up to the sky, an' nothin' left but a heap of white ash. That's the way it had ought to be done."

"The gipsies burn the caravan when the master dies," I told him.

And slowly we both turned to look at the ancient shape of Cobbetts, golden in the dying sun.

"Ar. That'd make a grand old flare, that would! Them old timbers, they'd go up like so much matchwood. That'd be seen fer miles around. Ar. It'd be a pity fer the old place to go. But if she had to go, I'd like to see her!"

How little we guessed, standing there in the quiet June evening, that thirty years or so later Fell would have his wish: that fire would fall from the angry skies, and old Cobbetts would lay her creaking bones upon it and give up her lovely, faded ghost. Thank God, I did not see it! But I know that Fell did. They wheeled him out to watch—an old, broken man in a broken bath-chair—and he watched until there was nothing left of Cobbetts but a heap of blackened stones and grey ash. "It meks a show," I can imagine him muttering. "Aye, it meks a show. ..."

Mr Nicholson came into the library with a letter in his hand. He stood as far away from me as possible and gave his irritating little cough, looking at me sideways, as if I might leap at him, inflicting bodily harm at any moment.

"Er—Miss Ruan—I have here a letter—"

"Yes?" I said listlessly.

"A letter addressed to you. Ah—it appears to have been written by your uncle, and it states upon the envelope that you are to receive it—ah—that is to say on the day previous to—er—the funeral. So—"

"Yes," I said.

He handed me the letter, and went away as rapidly as dignity permitted.

I held the letter in my hands for a long time; but at length I opened and read it:

My DEAR RUAN.—They tell me I have not much longer to live. I have examined this fact from all angles and I find myself quite undismayed by it. There comes a time when one has done with living; and beyond that point, life, not death, is sadness. Mr Nicholson will talk to you about the future. He will wrap it up in dry phrases and jaw-breaking syllables. The gist of it, briefly, is this. Until you are twenty-one (unless you marry before that) you will be in the care of Mrs Luke Abbey, and will live with her on your beloved moor. I have arranged matters so that you will have about one hundred pounds a year which, with the hundred you already have, makes you safe from starvation, at least. For your mental nourishment, all my books are at your disposal. In spite of the unorthodox nature of your schooling, I venture to believe that you are more highly educated than most persons of your age. Should you wish to go further, it must be by your own efforts.

Cobbetts goes to Sylvia. I am aware that she has little affection for the place, but she is the elder, and it is essentially her right setting, as the moor is yours. She will marry 'well' as they say, and do the old house credit. In the meantime she will make her home with the worthy soap manufacturer and his lady, who appear to cherish her as a daughter. They have made a very handsome offer to rent Cobbetts until Sylvia comes into possession. I have accepted this offer. If they strew the rooms with pink-silk cushions and bamboo what-nots— that is a small matter compared with the repairs to which they will certainly attend. Some people may think this division of property unfair; but you, my dear Ruan, will not be of these. I fully believe I am giving you the life that your heart most desires.

About this business of dying, Ruan. I know you will grieve for me and miss me, but do not let them get you down with their horrible mumbo-jumbo. Do not be daunted by the normal face of death. You are not frightened by an old coat—and that is all I shall leave behind me. A coffin is simply part of a beautiful tree, turned to a useful purpose. An undertaker is an ordinary fellow who takes his pint and is fond of his children and grows cabbages in his back-garden after a good day's work.

Do not, I beg of you, creep silently about the house draped in dismal trappings! Bang doors and whistle. Make the peculiar noise you call singing. Wear your old riding breeches and a comfortable jersey. I could wish you had some person of sensibility to see you through these days; but I am afraid you will have to face them alone. I hope this letter will make it easier for you.

In conclusion, do you remember a conversation we had some time ago, when I inquired as to your views on heaven? You said: 'Wherever it is, you and I will be together.'

That thought, my dear Ruan, has been much in my mind. And it warms my heart now as, for a time, I bid you good-bye.

Alaric Mallinson.

When I had read the letter I shed my first tears since he had died. But they were tears of release more than of sorrow. Afterwards, strengthened and comforted, I went to my room and took off the hideous black frock and pulled on my breeches and a heather-coloured jersey. I put the letter away with the portrait of Mother. Then I went back to the window-seat in the library.

He had said I should have to face things alone. Had he, I wondered, forgotten Sylvia, who must surely come soon?

No, Uncle Alaric had not forgotten Sylvia.

An hour later a long, expensive wire came from Monica's people, who were staying in Paris, stating that Sylvia was prostrated with grief and quite unable to travel. A letter would follow. ...

Maggie came in to fetch the tray. When she saw my attire her eyes bulged with horror.

"Think shame of yourself! ... It's a pity you're not more like your sister, poor sweet lamb; she's taken it to heart that much she can't do the journey. *She'd* wear her blacks, that I'll swear to!"

Yes, I thought, and I could swear to it, too. And very lovely she would look in them, with her face of wistful purity and her shining gold halo of hair. ...

No, Uncle Alaric had not forgotten Sylvia. He had remembered her even better than I.

Chapter Two

§

I was wakened by Maggie roughly shaking my shoulder. I sat up, dazed and blinking.

"What is it? What's the matter?"

Maggie looked at me sourly.

"What's the *matter*? ... Oh, *nothing's* the matter, of course, except that your uncle's being buried to-day—and you sleeping like a log, and making everything late! *That's* all that's the matter! Come on, now," she continued, her voice changing to a rough peremptoriness. "Get up at once and eat your breakfast and then get dressed. And put your blacks on, mind! Make *some* show of feeling, even if you've got none!"

Her heavy feet crossed the room and went clumping down the corridor. I looked at the breakfast-tray she had brought in so surprisingly. Why did I have to eat in bed because Uncle Alaric was dead? The bacon lay in a semi-solid puddle of grease. A poached egg with a watery eye sat beside it, and a thick hunk of brown bread reposed on the uncovered tin tray. The tea looked repulsive. It was dotted over with blobs of stale milk and some of it had slopped over into the saucer. A fly sat on the chipped rim, cleaning its back legs.

Uncle Alaric's funeral. ...

My heart sank deep into my stomach and then rose slowly into my throat and stuck there. I was alone. There was nobody; nobody at all. ... They were going to put Uncle Alaric into a coffin and carry him out and lay him deep down in the earth; in the black, cold, damp, lonely earth.

My fingers were shaking and I watched them curiously. Not only my fingers; my arms and shoulders; my knees; all of me was shaking. How curious that was! I felt queer all over, as if I had run for miles! I swung my legs over the edge of the bed and stood up. Was I going to be ill? Was I, perhaps, going to die, too, and be carried out and put in the damp, heavy earth? …

I poured water into the basin and washed myself very carefully, and brushed my hair until my scalp tingled. Then I put on my cleanest riding breeches and one of the white-silk shirts David had given me—short in the arm, now, but mercifully clean and fresh—and a Lowton tie, discarded by him long ago, and cherished by me.

I felt a little better now, but the thought of eating made me sick, so I went slowly downstairs into the great hall. And there I stood transfixed.

The hall was literally filled with flowers! Their colours flamed and glowed and shone in the faint light. The smell of them was so intense, so overpowering, that I sat weakly down on the lowest stair, drawing a difficult breath, looking blankly at the heaped masses of them, tortured with wire, twisted into wreaths and crosses and harps and other symbols of sympathy. Cards were attached to them, filled with writing in all shades of ink. Presently I stole forward and looked more closely at these. I recognised some of the names as being famous in the county, but many were strange to me.

Right in the front were two great circular wreaths of roses, one pink and white, the other yellow and white. On one a card was tied with broad pink-satin ribbon and bore the inscription: "To my darling Uncle, from his sorrowing niece, Sylvia." Yellow satin tied the other, which read: "To my darling Uncle, from his sorrowing niece, Ruan."

I stood rigid, staring at the atrocious things.

How dare they! How *dare* they do this thing without asking my permission! … Anger flowed through me, stiffening my trembling limbs, strengthening my will. I picked up the yellow wreath and went out into the sun-bathed garden. I carried it at arm's-length, loathing it.

Down by the shrubbery I came on Fell, who was standing idle, smoking a clay pipe. He wore a black suit, too short in the arms, too tight in the legs; a stiff, flat, turned-down collar, and a very small black bowler hat with a curly brim. He looked guilty when he saw me, and hastily stowed away his pipe.

"Fell," I said, "who ordered this wreath and wrote my name on it?"

"I reckon it'd be that lawyer chap," he replied, after some thought.

"I didn't tell him to, Fell!"

"Ar." He drew the back of his hand across his nose. "Well, you see, Miss Sylvia, she sent a telegram ordering the pink one, an' I reckon they thought it'd look a bit funny not to have one from you as well, see what I mean?"

"Who cares what it *looks* like!"

"Ar. Still, at times like these, you can't always do what you've a mind, see? Same with weddin's. Christenin's too, if it comes to that," he said gloomily. "You take my advice, you'll put that back with the others and think no more about it. It don't harm nobody."

"Uncle Alaric *hated* flowers at funerals!"

"Ar. Just the same fer that, if it was me, I'd put it back. Otherwise, there'll be an almighty fuss—an' that's what he'd hate even worse than the wreath."

I knew that Fell was right. If there was one thing Uncle Alaric detested above all others, it was any sort of fuss. So, although I still boiled with indignation, I let Fell take the monstrous thing from me and return it to its fellows in the hall.

"How long is it, before—?" I asked him, when he came back.

"Best part of a hour yet."

"I'll sit down here in the sun. I can't *stand* the smell of those flowers in the house! You sit down, too, Fell, and go on smoking your pipe."

Rather gingerly, because of the tightness of the trousers, he lowered himself beside me in the grass, and began to stuff the clay pipe with rank, black tobacco.

"So you ain't wearin' yer blacks?" he remarked diffidently.

"No, Fell. Uncle Alaric didn't want me to. I—I had a letter from him. He wrote it when he—when he knew he was going to die."

"Ar." He pushed at the tobacco with a stained fore-finger. "Have you told *them* that?" He jerked his head towards the house, and I understood him to refer to Mr Nicholson and Maggie.

"No," I said proudly. "Why should I tell them? It's my business!"

– 270 –

"So it is." Blowing out a noxious cloud of smoke, he ruminated awhile. Then he continued: "Just the same fer that, I should tell 'em. Then there won't be no fuss, see? … Maggie an' Blossom, they're rare put about, an' I can't see no good in makin' things worse, when it only wants a word. I wouldn't say it was *kind*, now, see what I mean?"

"They haven't been kind to *me*, Fell."

"Ar. They ain't always done right by you. Time an' again I've said it. But two wrongs," said Fell weightily, "don't make a right, see what I mean?"

I pondered this. And once again—and most reluctantly—I knew that he was right.

"Very well," I said meekly, "I'll explain to Maggie. After all, I shan't have to put up with her much longer."

"Nor her with you," Fell agreed.

I looked at him sharply; but he was gazing up into an oak-tree through the miniature bonfire in his clay pipe.

"What are you going to do, when—when everything's over, and the house is shut up?" I asked him.

"Fur's I can tell, it ain't goin' to be shut up, not fer long. That lawyer chap, he was telling us as how some folks from Edinburgh was comin' here, on an' off, along with Miss Sylvia, an' he reckoned as how we'd all be kep' on. Except Blossom, an' he's past it, an' has bin these five year. But what I says is, what will be, will be, an' them as lives longest will see most, see what I mean?"

I privately doubted if Fell and Maggie and poor, simple Joy Jolly would come within scraping distance of the soap manufacturer's standard of service, but I said nothing.

"An' if the new folks doesn't suit me," he went on, as if he had read my thoughts, "I'm not obliged to stay. I am not"—Fell concluded with dignity—"without means." With that, he consulted the fat silver watch again, and rose to his feet. "If I was you, I'd get back now, and have a word with Maggie. An' then, I should go up to yer room, *an' stay there*, till yer called, see what I mean?"

I did indeed see what he meant; for already the sound of slowly rumbling wheels came clearly on the quiet air, and old Blossom was peering at the gate. I ran like the wind across the courtyard, through the overpowering perfume of the hall into the servants' quarters.

Maggie was drinking something out of a little glass. She put it down quickly when she saw me, and her face darkened.

"What did I tell you?" she began.

"Maggie," I said quickly, "I ought to have told you before that Uncle Alaric asked me not to wear any black clothes. He wanted me to wear these things as usual."

"Didn't know what he was saying, poor Mr Al'ric, that's what I'd say!" Her voice had an aggrieved, almost a thwarted tone.

"Yes, he did. He was perfectly—perfectly all right—when—when—"

They were coming into the hall now! ... They were going up the stairs. Clump-clump, clump-clump, clump-clump. ...

"Oh—Maggie!" I whispered.

Suddenly she put her arms round me and held me tightly against the black curve of her breast.

"Now, now!" she said quietly. "Now, now!"

I clung to her for a moment.

"Maggie—I'm sorry if I've been beastly to you sometimes !"

She hugged me tighter.

"We're none of us perfect," she conceded gruffly.

And so we clung together while the slow feet trod their heavy measure about the silent house; united for one moment of living by the common fear of death. With my face pressed against the heaving crape of her bosom, I tried to think of Uncle Alaric's coffin as part of a tree; of the undertakers as ordinary fellows—but it was no use. I began to shake again from head to foot.

"Now, now!" said Maggie.

And presently she pushed me away and told me to be quick and get a hat, or everybody would be waiting for me. So I pulled myself together and put on a hat, and walked as steadily as my legs would take me out into the courtyard.

I had been told there would be two carriages: one for Mr Nicholson and Dr Greene and me, and one for the servants. But there were dozens of carriages! Carriages of all types: smart and shabby, open and closed, with a fair proportion of motor-cars amongst them. The long, black line of them stretched away up the road in a gleaming curve. They were all empty, save for the caped coachmen and the smart, liveried chauffeurs. It was amazing!

Old Dr Greene came across the courtyard and shook my hand.

"It's a grand day!" he said, helping himself to snuff.

"Where did all those carriages come from?" I asked. "There's nobody in them."

"There wouldn't be." He trumpeted into his handkerchief. "He'd shut everybody out of his life, ye see, years and years ago. Not that I blame him. He had to go his own gait. But he's a Mallinson, and the last of 'em, and the County remembers that, and quite right, too. Have ye had any breakfast?"

"Yes," I lied, wanting no fuss.

He looked at me doubtfully and trumpeted again.

"Well, keep your pecker up, my lass. It's nothing—all this!"

Mr Nicholson came fussing up, glancing at my breeches with extreme dislike.

"Have you—er—nothing more suitable to wear?" he snapped nervously.

"I am wearing what Uncle Alaric wished me to wear," I answered shortly.

"Quite right, too!" put in the doctor quickly. "She's well enough as she is." And he laid a kindly hand on my shoulder. "God bless my soul! You're getting to look like your mother!" I knew he only said it to comfort me, but I was grateful.

"Well, come along, come along!" Mr Nicholson muttered. "We're behind time as it is!"

Suddenly fear shot through every part of me.

I could not move!

I was rigid; my feet clamped to the cobbled yard; my arms and legs stiff and useless. I flashed an anguished glance at the old doctor, and his hand squeezed my shoulder encouragingly.

"It's all right, my lass. Take it easy! Take it easy!"

I could not move.

My heart began to thump and my head swam. What should I do! What should I *do*! ... I looked from one to the other, trying to explain that I could not move.

"Come along, now, if you please, Miss Ruan!"

Suddenly a figure swung in at the gates of the courtyard; a tall figure in correct morning coat and black tie, carrying a shining top hat in one hand. Brown hair, brushed to a decent smoothness, shone in the sun.

"David!" I cried weakly. For an instant I really thought my heart was going to burst.

And then I was running, running across the courtyard. I was flinging myself into David's arms. I was hearing his dear voice saying calmly and cheerfully: "Buck up, Tinribs!"—and his hand was swallowing mine in a comfortable grip.

"Oh, *David*!" ...

Mr Nicholson came fussing up, cross and suspicious.

"Good morning," said David pleasantly. "You are Mr Nicholson, I take it? I represent Miss Sylvia Ashley. I only landed last night. I do hope I have not delayed you."

And then he was shaking hands with Mr Nicholson and Dr Greene. And then we were all getting into the first carriage, and Blossom and Fell and Maggie and Joy were getting into the second one, and we were moving up the road to the village, with all the long fine of empty carriages moving slowly and respectfully behind us.

I did not look at David, nor speak to him. It was enough for me that a miracle had happened, and he was here. He talked over my head to the doctor and the lawyer; talked easily, yet with a deference for age that made them warm to him. I heard their voices going on and on over my head, but I did not listen to what they were saying. It was enough for me that David's hand was holding mine, safely, strongly.

A lark sang madly far above. The smell of the ripening grasses filled the air, and the sound of them, and the sheen of their heads as they bent before the wind.

"I am the Resurrection and the Life. …"

The lovely words were swept on the wind; blended with the lark's song and the rustling of trees and grasses and the contented crooning of farm-yard hens.

"He cometh up, and is cut down, like a flower; he fleeth as it were a shadow, and never continueth in one stay. …"

A milk-cart clattered past the churchyard: clop, clop, clop, clop, clop. The young milkman was whistling *Daisy, Daisy, give me your Answer, do!* But when he saw the long line of carriages he pulled his horse into a walk and took off his checked cap, and stopped whistling. One of the waiting horses tossed his jingling head and whinnied loudly.

"Earth to earth, ashes to ashes, dust to dust; in sure and certain hope of the Resurrection. …"

The wind tweaked the clergyman's surplice and set my tie flapping and billowed out the snowy sheets on the, washing line in the sexton's garden, so that they cracked like little guns.

The lark sang more loudly than ever; and away down the road the young milkman was whistling again.

So the last of the Mallinsons went on his last journey under the blue and blowing skies of June. And I stood with my hand in David's, to watch his passing. …

Chapter Three

After lunch I went into the library and Mr Nicholson talked for a long time. I did not listen, because Uncle Alaric had told me all I wished to know. As soon as I decently could I said good-bye—for he was leaving on an early train—and shook hands with him (which he did rather gingerly), and escaped into the garden with David.

We went into the shrubbery, to the place where my temple had once stood, and stretched ourselves out on the grass. David had taken off his black suit and wore flannels, and his hair was rough again. We did not talk much. There was too much to say; too much bottled up inside us; too much that needed explanation and understanding and effort. All that could come later. For the present, we were together again, and it was all that mattered.

Once I commented sleepily on the extreme smartness of his morning's attire, and he admitted with a grin that he rather fancied himself in the get-up.

"They're Stebbing's togs," he added. "I got back too late to buy any, so I routed the old boy out of bed and borrowed his. 'You won't need anything but a topee and a loin-cloth in India,' I said, 'so I might as well wear them out for you.' I must say he was very decent about it. I dossed down on a sofa in his room, and he got up early and cooked my breakfast while I shaved, and got me to St Pancras in time for the nine-fifteen. A very decent scout is old Stebbing. I'd like to see him in his topee and loin-cloth—and gloves, of course! By the way, he sent you his love."

"Oh," I muttered.

I was not feeling very well. Emotional strain and an empty stomach had brought me so low that I had gone to the other extreme and eaten too much at lunch.

"The coat fitted me all right, but the trousers were on the big side. You'd hardly credit it, but old Stebbing's running a corporation already! Can't you imagine him at fifty!"

"Let Stebbing alone!" I snapped.

David cocked an eye at me and hauled himself into a sitting position.

"What's up, Tinribs? You're all shades of green!"

"I want to be sick!" I gasped feebly.

"Well, why not?" he said calmly.

So I was sick, and felt the better for it. And David sat by me and held my forehead, which helped a little; and afterwards he got me upstairs and darkened the room and bathed my aching forehead, while I lay on the bed feeling shaky and weak, and loving him. Later, he performed some magic which resulted in Maggie's bringing me a tray—actually covered with a white cloth!—with tea, very hot and not too strong, and biscuits such as I had never before tasted at Cobbetts.

I must have slept then; but when I woke the sun was still shining behind the drawn curtains, and David was still there. He crinkled his eyes at me.

"Better, Tinribs?"

"Yes. ... Did you have a good time abroad, David?"

"Not so bad."

"It must have been wonderful; all those places you'd read about suddenly being *there*!"

"Pretty wonderful. But a year's too much, really, dodging about from one famous place to another. It's like eating a twelve-course dinner when you're not very hungry. I feel as if I never want to see another monument or picture-gallery in my life."

"Which country did you like best?"

"Oh, lord—ask me another! Well, on the whole, I think Austria. They've got some marvellous hospitals there. I made friends with a chap who was studying medicine and we had some great talks. ... I've brought you a present from each country I went to, Tinribs. They're all together in a special box."

"Oh, David—how lovely! When can I see them?"

"I should think they'll have arrived at the Farm by the time we get there. I'm taking you home to-morrow."

Home. Home with David.

"Does Rosie know?"

"I wired her while you were asleep."

"Oh. ... Will you pull the curtains back, David? No, I'll do it; I'm sick of lying here." I arranged the curtains and wandered about the room fidgeting with one thing and another. A slight constraint had fallen between us.

It should surely have been easy enough to say: "How did you happen to *know* about Uncle Alaric?" I longed to say it. I tried to say it, and failed.

The unspoken question lay between us like, a sheathed sword.

In the cool of the evening we rode together, David on Tom and I on Bob; and I bade farewell to the gentle slopes and green, curving lanes amongst which I had lived so peacefully. Afterwards, we groomed both the horses and fed them, and I kissed their soft, warm noses and gave them an extra handful of sugar.

"They'll get terribly fat again!" I sighed, as I shut the stable door. "I shall miss them awfully. David, do you suppose I can afford to buy a horse? I've got two hundred pounds a year. Oh, I forgot—I can't touch it until I'm twenty-one. Unless I get married before that!"

"I expect it can be wangled," he said easily.

We went upstairs and he helped me to pack my trunk. I had so few clothes that this was accomplished in a very short time. Then came the question of the books Uncle Alaric had bequeathed to me, and my rosewood desk, and the portrait of Giles.

"How many of these books do you want, Tinribs?" he asked, glancing round the library walls.

"All of them!" I replied promptly.

"Not possible, my girl! The Farm won't hold them."

"I've thought all that out. I'm going to ask Mr Lord to let me have one of the rooms at the Vicarage for a study. There are at least three rooms absolutely empty, so he'll probably be glad—especially as he can borrow the books whenever he wants to."

"Ha! You've got a nerve, young Tinribs! The next thing will be, you'll badger the poor old chap into coaching you."

"I shouldn't be surprised," I said serenely. "Uncle Alaric told me that any further education I wanted must be acquired by my own efforts."

"There are schools, woman!"

"Not for me. I'm not going to start fooling about with schools at my time of life."

David grinned affectionately at me.

"Still dodging the issue!" And then suddenly he wasn't grinning any more. "When are you going to face up to things, Ruan? You've got to live—really live—sooner or later. You can't dream the whole of your life away with old men and books."

"It's my life," I said stubbornly.

"Yes. Up to a point."

"Well, we haven't reached that point yet."

He looked at me absently—oh, how well my heart remembers it!—and I saw his eyes change; as the eyes of a sleeper suddenly awakened, and cloudy still with memories of night, will change to the clear knowledge of the coming day.

"No," he said, more to himself than me, "no, we haven't reached that point yet. ..."

$\mathcal{G}$

Very early the next morning I got up and dressed and made my own private farewells to Cobbetts. I went everywhere; into the Queen's Bedchamber and the haunted room and the low, dusty attics; into the dining-room and the library and all the dim, echoing, unfurnished places; into the untidy kitchen, loud with the snores of Blossom, whose bedroom opened off it. I went into Uncle Alaric's room, already stripped, bare, and impersonal. I dawdled along the dusty corridors and stood before the smiling faces of Rosemary and Cecilia. I went out into the gardens; wandered through the shrubbery, across the dew-soaked, knee-high grass to the top orchard. The sharp, white sunlight of early morning lay on everything. Shadows were long and unfamiliar. Birds were clamorous in tree-tops and hedges. A hidden cuckoo called and called again.

The old house lay yellow and tranquil behind its wrought-iron gates, dreaming of the past. It did not mind my going.

I did not mind, either. For me, when Uncle Alaric died, Cobbetts died, too.

A boy from the station fetched my trunk on a clattering truck and went whistling away up the hill with it. I put John on his lead and shook hands with Maggie and Blossom and Joy and Fell. I should have liked to give each of them a present to remember me by, but I had nothing to give. As I passed through the wrought-iron gates I heard them begin to swing-to behind me, and I heard the creak of old Blossom's key in the lock.

The gates would not need to be opened again for a long time.

$\mathcal{G}$

Luke met us with the trap. I don't know whether he was the more astonished at David or at me, for he declared we had both grown out of all recognition.

We anxiously inquired about Rosie, and he said she was on the mend, though very sad at the loss of this second baby. "There an't goin' to be no little 'uns for us, seem'ly," he said quietly, stroking Sally's ears with the whip. "Not as I'm fratchin' ovver it. It's Missus I'm thinkin' on. I reckon it'll tek time before she gets used to it. We'll have to mek it up to her someways, Ruan, you an' me." And he bent on me the blue, sweet glance that held all the kindness in the world.

I don't know how much I compensated Rosie for her childlessness. Doubtless I helped a little. I do know that she did all that any mother could have done for me, and did it most lovingly, with a personal pride no mother could have surpassed, and a wisdom and understanding beyond her experience.

But it was Luke who helped her more than anybody or anything. Luke, with his kind blue eyes and sweet smile; with his simple dependence on her strength and his strong support of her weakness; with his deep passion and his gentleness and his slow humour; his small, human failings and his almost superhuman patience. Luke had been Rosie's love. Now he became her whole life; her health and happiness; her reason for existence and her hope of heaven. ... I think their married life became happier, more serene, than any I have known. And still is, thank God!

She was up and dressed, sitting in the sun by her bedroom window, knitting a scarlet jersey for me. But when our first greetings were over she looked me up and down, and then held up the unfinished garment with laughing dismay.

"Nay!" she cried, "this'll never get over your shoulders, luv! My word, I didn't know anybody could grow that fast!" And she began at once to pull the knitting undone. "And as for you, David—you could knock me down with a feather, you could that! Ee! I've got that much to ask you both, I don't know where to begin!" She cried a little then, but she was smiling, too. "Tek no notice if I act a bit daft. It's nobbut because I'm that happy to have you both home."

A woman from the village had cooked the dinner, and Rosie was loud in her condemnation of it. Nothing was right for her. The potatoes were watery, the early peas tasteless, the chicken "boiled to a frazzle." "That settles it," Rosie exclaimed with spirit. "I'm comin' downstairs to-morrow! If I can't cook t'dinner meself, I've at least got strength to throw t'saucepan lids at her, if she spoils good food this way!"

I thought the dinner was delicious, but I stoutly upheld Rosie's view; and in the end we all agreed that, if she would take things very quietly for a time, she should be allowed to come downstairs and superintend matters. She would have done it in any case, as we well knew, but she liked the bit of fuss and argument and the little triumph.

After dinner we looked at the presents David had brought for us. The lids of the boxes were levered off, and the colours and perfumes, the stuffs and strange designs of many lands flung their glamour about the stolid, farm-house furniture. Fans from sunny Spain. Shawls of sheerest silk from Persia. Stout wooden sabots from Holland. Flasks of scent from France. Queer little wooden boxes, exquisitely carved, from Austria. Delicate, coloured glass from Bohemia. Sweets that melted in the mouth, and smelt as delicious as they tasted. A clock that played a different tune for each hour, and another that was attached to a miniature bandstand, complete with tiny soldiers who beat their drums with vigour to the beat of their leader's baton. Pipes of all sizes and patterns for Luke. A roll of sea-green silk for Rosie. A dressing-gown for me that flaunted all the colours of the rainbow. A praying-mat. A fine linen bedspread, intricately embroidered. An ivory horse.

"Nay!" was all Rosie could manage. And I could not say as much as that. I took my presents upstairs and laid them on my bed and hung over them, gloating. I could hardly tear myself away from them—even when David called to me to come for a walk.

We went to our hollow by the rowan-tree, up on Walker's Ridge. I plied him with eager questions about his travels. Had he seen a bull-fight? Was Holland as flat as we had always imagined it? Had he seen the Black Forest, and did the Tower of Pisa really lean that way? Was Persia mysterious, or just dirty? Wasn't it heavenly in a gondola by moonlight? …

He flapped his hands feebly and begged me to shut up. "To tell you the truth, Tinribs, I've got the whole jolly lot lumped together in my mind, and it'll take a bit of sorting out. I told you it was like a twelve-course dinner. Well, I'm still in the process of digesting it. In time, I suppose I shall appreciate the various flavours. I shall probably become a crashing bore with my reminiscences. 'Ah, my boy! When I was in Venice,' I shall say. Or 'Toledo' or 'Baden-Baden'—or wherever it is we're talking about. And when I'm a very old man I shall champ my toothless gums at you and chuckle horribly about the black-eyed piece in Brazil, and the saucy little baggage in Biarritz." He yawned, and stretched on the hot, wiry grass of the hollow. "You'll hear as much as you want to hear, I promise you, if you wait long enough. In the meantime, Old England for me—and in particular, Walker's Ridge on a hot June afternoon."

Almost immediately he fell asleep.

I sat watching him, hugging my knees. He looked beautiful, I thought. Clean and young and thin. Strong and helpless. Innocent and experienced. Open as the day, yet mysterious as night. ... David. My David. Mine.

"How did you happen to know about Uncle Alaric?" I thought.

The sheathed sword still lay between us. I wanted to be rid of it; but I knew it must first be drawn from its scabbard. I must see the sun glint on the narrow blade and feel the sharpness of its edge, even though it drew blood.

A kestrel hawk hung above us in the blue silence. I watched it for a long time, until it suddenly swooped downwards on some hapless innocent. "*And like a thunderbolt he falls.*" ... Poor Stebbing. Poor kind, clumsy heart! "You look so funny in that coat. Such a sweet little girl! ... I never know where I am with you. ... Would you—er—do you want to wash?" ... "Can't you imagine him at fifty!" I laughed silently and turned to look at David. And he was awake and looking at me.

"Don't you want to know how I happened to hear about your Uncle Alaric?" he said.

I nodded and waited.

"I went to Paris to see Sylvia."

The sword flashed from its scabbard and the keen blade shone in the sun. David sat up and began to pull at the wiry grass with his brown, sensitive fingers.

"It's a little difficult to make you understand about Sylvia and me."

"Don't, if you don't want to," I said quickly.

"I do want to. I meant to tell you ages ago, only—well, I didn't. You never asked any questions. Never seemed interested to know where I was, or why I didn't come home for the hols. ... Do you realise, Tinribs, that this is the first time we've been together for two years—except that week before I went abroad?"

"Yes, David."

"Didn't you care at *all*?" I could have laughed—or cried—at the honest indignation in his voice.

"Of course I cared."

"Well, why didn't you—well—*do* something about it? Kick up a fuss or something?"

"Would it have made any difference if I had?"

He chewed a piece of grass thoughtfully.

"No, you're right. It wouldn't have made any difference. ... You see, Tinribs, I don't know if you can understand what I mean, but—Sylvia was just something I had to get out of my system." He spat out the grass and chose another. "You remember that time I came to fetch you from Cobbetts—two years ago, or thereabouts? Well, it started then."

I remembered. She had worn white muslin, with a rose in her hair; and I hadn't wanted to kiss her good-bye.

"She—well, she knocked me endways. I only remembered her as a small kid. Pretty, but spoilt and rather soppy. And then she came out on the terrace in the sunlight, looking like—like—"

"I know how Sylvia looks."

"Yes. Well, I knew then that I'd got to get her out of my system. ... I wangled an invitation for Christmas from a chap who lives in Edinburgh. And again at Easter. The soap people gave me the run of their house. ... And then she went to Paris. So instead of starting my Grand Tour with Belgium, as I'd planned, I went straight to Paris after her. But it wasn't a success. She'd already got some other bloke in tow; one of Monica's brother's pals, complete with title, I believe. And anyway, I found I wasn't so keen on her, after all. So I left her to it, and went globe-trotting as per schedule."

After a long moment I said:

"But you went back."

"Yes. I called at Paris *en route* for home. Not because I particularly wanted to see Sylvia, but just to make sure I'd got her thoroughly out of my system. It was very important to be quite sure about that."

"I see. ... And had you?"

He nodded, beaming at me like a good child who has eaten his spinach,

"I kissed her, to make sure, and it might have been the cat I was kissing! If anything, I got more kick out of kissing Monica—and if you've ever seen Monica, you'll know what I mean!"

"Oh, David," I said weakly, "do you kiss every girl you meet, then?"

"Well, I haven't met so many yet," he replied cautiously.

I didn't know whether to laugh or cry with relief. It all seemed suddenly so small and unimportant. Where was now the bright sword that had leapt from its scabbard, bared for my blood! It was nothing but a child's toy, already bent and buckled; a foolish trifle out of a cracker, thrown aside and disregarded and trodden underfoot.

David stretched his long limbs and filled his lungs with the smell of the moor with deep satisfaction.

"We've got the rest of the summer here together Tinribs. And after that I'm going to start working for my degree. Life's pretty good, isn't it?"

Yes, life was good, that summer up on the moor. Good for Luke, for the Farm prospered exceedingly. The hay crop was exceptional. There was no sickness amongst the animals or blight in the kitchen garden, and the orchard groaned with fruit. Good for Rosie: once she took command again, her health returned in full measure, and she became once more the vigorous, good-tempered, laughing friend I had grown to love so well. Good for David and me. The days were hot with sun and clean with wind, and storms were very rare, and soon over.

Mr Lord was glad to give me one of his empty rooms for my study. I chose the smallest one. It looked out on to the lawn, facing south. A carpenter came from the village and fitted shelves round all the walls, and when my books arrived Mr Lord and David and I spent a happy, busy day arranging them. My rosewood desk was placed in the window, and the portrait of Giles hung, laughing and debonair, above the fireplace. A soft, many-coloured rug that David had brought home lay on the floor, and the clock with the drummer-boys stood upon the mantelpiece. Rosie gave me curtains and a comfortable chair, and Mr Lord himself contributed a round, low table and a pewter jug for flowers. I was enchanted with my room!

And so, much to David's amusement, was Mr Lord. Some of my books were very old, and far more valuable than I had realised. He wandered round the shelves, touching a rare edition here and there with loving fingers, and sighing with pleasure.

"If I can be of any assistance to you, Ruan, never hesitate to bring your questions to me. I am glad to know that youth will be learning under my roof again; I have missed this dear lad more than anyone realises. Of course, you are a good deal further advanced than he was at your age"—here the dear lad made a frightful face at me behind his back—"but I think I can still give you a tip here and there. Yes, yes, I think so."

"I wish you'd teach me as you did David," I blurted out. "I'd work like blazes, I promise you!"

His face lit up with pleasure.

"That would be delightful, my dear Ruan! Yes, yes, it is a splendid notion! I've been getting far too lazy. Now when shall we begin work?"

Yes, it was a good summer. I had been alone and sad, and now love and laughter and understanding surrounded me. I had been neglected, and now I was cared for. Doubts and questionings had darkened my heart that was filled to the brim with clear-shining. ...

David made me another present before he went away. A lovely little chestnut mare with a white star on her forehead and two white socks. He had gone off one morning by himself, without any explanation, leaving me rather disgruntled; and at tea-time he returned, leading the mare.

"Here you are, Tinribs. Like her?"

Did I like her! ... I put my arms round her neck, and she blew softly down mine; and right from the first we understood one another.

"Oh, David! ... Oh, David! ..."

He looked as pleased as Punch, but he only said in an off-hand way: "Oh, well, I had to do *something*, or you'd have had your nose in a book from now till Christmas! As it is, I expect I shall come back to find you with curvature of the spine, knock-knees, writer's cramp, and a frightful squint. All of which maladies," he added, with relish, "probably require the most painful treatments—if not major operations. Ah! ... I like the sound of those words. *Ma-jor op-er-ations!*" And he made sinister passes in the air with his thin, strong hands.

I called the mare Griselda. At first John was a little jealous of her, and she was inclined to pick up her white socks and dance sideways at John; and then he would go and lie down in the paddock by the old grey pony, long superannuated, and air his grievances to that placid friend. But, by degrees, he and my lovely Griselda came to a working agreement, which gradually ripened into affection, and the three of us were almost inseparable.

A lovely summer! Perhaps the loveliest I had ever known. And yet it had to end. Overnight, it seemed, the royal purple faded and the gold was dimmed. Winds had a bite to them, and mornings were white with frost. The swallows went away, and gulls came sailing and wheeling overland, screaming of wild weather. I wore my new scarlet jersey and was glad of it.

David's new suits came from the tailor's and the old ones came from the cleaner's, looking like new. His trunks were packed and sent off to London. He went into the town and had his hair cut very short and trim, and the dentist filled a tooth that had been worrying him. And on the last day we had a special tea, with piles of crumpets oozing golden butter, and Rosie's best strawberry jam, and a great cake covered with chocolate icing.

"Ee!" said Rosie, "I remember t'first time you went off to school, David. Me and Ruan had a good cry, hadn't we, luv?"

"And I cried in the train," David confessed, grinning. "Uncle Josh got behind *The Times* and pretended he hadn't seen me."

"Aye, yon were a great chap," Luke murmured. "Well, I reckon I'd best be getting trap ready."

David said:

"I'll meet you at the far turn of the road, Luke. Walk down with me, Ruan, will you? I must walk off that cake of Rosie's. It's lying very heavy on me stomach."

"Go on with you!" cried Rosie, slapping his head.

He said good-bye to her then, and we went out together, through the peaceful farmyard, down the little lane, and out into the moor road.

It seemed strange to be turning our backs to the moor and walking towards the town.

"It won't seem long till Christmas," David said. "I expect I shall have to swot quite a bit during the hols. Can I have a corner of your study? Then we can squint together, and slap each other to revive the circulation." He walked a few more steps, humming out of tune. Then he said abruptly, almost shyly: "It's jolly to know that you'll always be here when I come back, Tinribs. You will be here, won't you? Always?"

We had reached the turn of the road, and we stood watching for Luke.

"I shall be here, David—whether you come back or not."

He looked at me soberly.

"I shall always come back."

He took my short hair in both hands and shook me backwards and forwards, in the old way. It hurt horribly, and I loved him. "You do believe that, don't you, Tinribs? I mean—you *know* it, deep down inside you. You and me. ... I'd like to be quite sure that you do know it."

"I know it, David."

He let my hair go, and kissed me quickly, once. And then the trap came jingling up, and he climbed in, while Sally danced impatiently and Luke said "Whoa! Whoa, will you!"

"Good-bye, Tinribs!"

"Good-bye, David!"

He crinkled his eyes at me, and lifted the flap of his pocket; and a lump came into my throat, as I thought of my Little Man going to London with David.

Oh, David. My dear, dear David. How I loved him then! ...

§

I turned and ran through the cool evening air; ran like the wind, past the Farm and up on to the moor, where I could be sure of being alone.

It was calm that evening; calm and clear and very beautiful. The moor was settling down for her winter's sleep. The heather had faded and the gold was dimmed, but the bracken was high and tawny and the great hills held the sun in their arms. Far down in the valley I could hear the blacksmith's hammer. Cows were moving slowly homewards, lowing contentedly. The clock on Staving Church struck six.

I stood very still. So still that I could feel the heart of the moor beating beneath my feet: everlastingly patient with my foolishness: eternally kind. ...

David would come back. He would always come back. And with him, one day, life would come for me, hand in hand with David. The distant drum would beat louder and louder, nearer and nearer. And it would be no more terrifying than the beating of the moor's heart.

The smoke of the Farm chimney lay on the evening sky like a beckoning finger.

I began to go slowly homewards. And the peace of God, that passeth all understanding, filled my heart and mind. ...

§ § §

Afterword

§

Dorothy Evelyn Smith was relatively old for a first-time novelist when *O, The Brave Music* was published in 1943 – she was 50 – but she gets the reader straight into the mind of Ruan, a girl who is 7 at the outset of the novel.

The purpose of the Afterwords for the Women Writers series is to explore an aspect of contemporary life that is drawn on in the novel, particularly one that affected women of the time. That's less easy to do for a novel that is looking back about three decades in the past (though the novel is too wonderful to disallow it from the series on that count). It is technically written from the perspective of the 1940s, as occasional mentions make clear, but if *O, The Brave Music* has little to say directly about the decade it was published in, it is characterised by a nuanced nostalgia for time and place that wouldn't have been there if it had been published earlier in the century.

The title of the book refers obliquely to a distance in time – it quotes from Edward Fitzgerald's *Rubáiyát of Omar Khayyám*, an 1859 translation of verse attributed to the Persian astronomer Omar Khayyám (1048–1131). The full quote is given towards the end of the novel:

'Ah, take the cash in hand and waive the rest;
O, the brave music of a distant drum!'

In the novel, the 'distant drum' seems to work both ways in time – a young Ruan looking forward into her future, and the narrating, older

Ruan looking back. She merges nostalgia and anticipation together, as perhaps was inevitable for any author writing, as Smith was, during the Second World War. She described herself as writing 'on the end of the kitchen table with bombs falling around the house', and even wrote part of *O, The Brave Music* while confined to bed with an injured leg, though presumably this wasn't the direct result of those falling bombs. But there is no doubt that she wrote this novel from the midst of an ongoing war that was affecting everybody in the country, and it impacts the way the story is told.

Her writing career had started during the previous War, penning articles, poems and stories for magazines while her husband James was fighting abroad. She turned to a novel in the 1940s because many of these periodicals had stopped being produced due to shortages of both paper and staff. Novels published during the Second World War frequently looked back to what were perceived as simpler times, either in the interwar period or before the First World War. Other popular 1943 novels include *A Tree Grows in Brooklyn* by Betty Smith, set in the first two decades of the twentieth century, and Kate O'Brien's *The Last of Summer*, set in pre-war 1939. Smith's novel was compared to Betty Smith's in reviews, and she was joining a corner of the literary market that looked back – not suggesting that the previous world was free of sorrow or difficulty, but at least didn't include those bombs that were falling around the house. As a review in the *New York Times* said (for the American publication in 1951), '*O, The Brave Music* probably didn't seem any more fantastic or improbable to Mrs Smith than a buzz-bomb, and more fun to create'.

Indeed, Ruan's early childhood is depicted not as a time of unfettered joy but marked by sorrow. Particularly poignant is the curtailed storyline about Ruan's baby brother, Clem. It is never clear exactly what illness he has, but it's hard to forget the moments where Ruan realises that Clem may die, or when she sees her father's pre-emptive grief. As this passage puts it, her 'first, salt knowledge':

ᔆ ᔆ ᔆ

At the back of our house was a long, narrow strip of garden, very much overgrown with weeds, because Father did not care for gardening and had no money for professional help. But it was a garden, at least, and, the weather turning very hot and dry, I was allowed to wheel Clem up and down the weedy path, or sit on the rank lawn and play with him. I had always loved my baby brother dearly, and in those long, quiet June days my love became more articulate and, alas, more sharp of vision. I began to watch Clem more closely; to think and worry and make comparisons; but it was Annie Briggs who finally tore the scales from my eyes, and gave me my first, salt knowledge of the sorrowful thing love can be...

Like Ruan, Smith was the daughter of a Nonconformist minister living in the north, but *O, The Brave Music* isn't entirely autobiographical (though it was marketed as such when The Literary Guild chose it, upon publication in the US). The truth is somewhere between the two. Smith crafted the plot from her imagination but borrowed from her own life as necessary – whether her experiences as a minister's daughter, the rural Yorkshire setting or more incidental details. A rather lovely example of it working the other way, life imitating art, is the name 'Cobbetts': a few years after *O, The Brave Music* was published, Smith named her cottage Cobbetts after the 'square, solid house, in whose yellowed walls the forgotten suns of four centuries lay sleeping' that features in the second half of the novel. Though cottage and ramshackle mansion had little in common architecturally or geographically, perhaps she wanted to echo that sense of sanctuary that Ruan finds.

Like Ruan, Smith loved the moors – indeed, any reader of *O, The Brave Music* would be confident that the author shared the young heroine's passion for these wide-open, rugged spaces, and Smith returns to them in many of her other novels. Like the Brontës most famously before her, she sees them as a place of freedom and the forging of identity; unlike the

§ § §

Brontës, there is little sense of danger in the moors. They are a place where Ruan can instead escape from dangers and anxieties closer to home.

Though the moors have a timeless quality to them, and Ruan's childhood seems far away from any of the contemporary events happening in 1940s England, Smith does subtly compare the two periods. One motif that recurs throughout *O, The Brave Music* is clothing. The older Ruan, narrating, draws comparisons between outfits of the 1940s and her own experiences – comparisons that are not particularly nostalgic.

> I wore too many clothes for either comfort or hygiene. When I see the youngsters of to-day, in their brief, sensible garments, I sigh for that sturdy little figure in its petticoats and frills, its buttoned boots and woollen stockings and tight cotton gloves, its alpaca coat well and truly buttoned to the chin and its hard straw hat with the tight elastic.

Perhaps twenty-first-century readers won't think that garments from the 1940s are 'brief' or 'sensible', but they were certainly a world away from those of the pre-First World War era. The encumbrance of those clothes is something Smith, as the older Ruan, returns to frequently:

> The four-mile, uphill walk was deemed too much for our childish legs – which it probably was, hung about with clothing as we were.

One doesn't have to look too hard to see the links between being swathed in excess clothing and Ruan feeling trammelled by the restrictions and expectations of her upbringing. Similarly, she is shocked to see her mother in something as minimal and revealing as riding breeches – an indication of her character. Smith uses those yards of fabric and unnecessary layers as a metaphor for the lack of freedom, and makes the metaphor explicit a few pages later, as she morphs into a new form in the clothes that used to belong to her beloved David (and is, in fact, mistaken for a boy by a local vicar):

§ § §

Clothing was a problem at first. My frocks were too long and full, too 'fancy' for freedom, and they were reinforced by petticoats, starched and frilled. Rosie, wise beyond her generation, put me into a pair of grey shorts that David had grown out of, and bought me some blouses with short sleeves. My legs went bare. I wore sandals and no hat. The villagers clicked their tongues and said "Ee, well, I don't know!" – but that didn't worry me. Father would have been disgusted had he seen me; but he did not see me, so no harm was done.

Smith's family remember the author as preferring practicality to fashion in her own choices, and her grandson recalls her usually wearing identical outfits that only differed in colour. If the silhouette of the 1940s was more functional and slim-lined than earlier in the century, for women and children, this wasn't solely to do with emerging views on freedom. Rather, it was heavily influenced by the severe fabric shortages of the period. Clothes rationing was introduced on 1 June 1941, with everybody being given a number of coupons or points – initially 66 for an adult, with 11 coupons being needed for a dress, two for a pair of stockings, and so forth. As the War continued, the coupon allowance decreased, and, indeed, it was at its lowest after the War (24 coupons per adult per year) and clothes rationing lasted for several more years, ending on 15 March 1949. By the time *O, The Brave Music* was published, children were allotted 10 extra coupons, to allow for growing. None of this is mentioned in the narrative, where contemporary children's clothing is seen as a halcyon contrast to Ruan's childhood.

At the heart of the book is Ruan's steady and loyal adoration of David. Modern audiences may feel less comfortable than earlier readers with the romantic feelings between Ruan and two boys (later men) who are five years older than her. A friendship that is unusual when Ruan is 7 and David is 12 becomes something less appealing when both are six years older. Thankfully, nothing illicit happens. The theme of love throughout the novel is spread more widely than a simple romance;

S   S   S

as the novelist Erica Royde-Smith noted in her 1943 *Times Literary Supplement* review:

> *O, The Brave Music*, by Dorothy Evelyn Smith, is a refreshingly original love story, the story of a child's love for her beautiful faithless mother, for the Yorkshire moor on which her happiest hours were spent, for one bluff Yorkshire woman who had her greatest welfare at heart, for the uncle who was one of the few grown-ups to understand her, for the stately if ramshackle old home in which she lived with him for a time, and – like a golden thread on which these other loves were strung – her unfaltering devotion to the boy who was her childhood's dearest friend and in whose farewell at the end of the book lies the promise of all her love's fulfilment.

We can read this last element as the intense and enlivening friendship of kindred spirits that may develop into something more romantic whenever David does return and the five-year age gap is no longer significant:

> David would come back. He would always come back. And with him, one day, life would come for me, hand in hand with David. The distant drum would beat louder and louder, nearer and nearer. And it would be no more terrifying than the beating of the moor's heart.

Though the novel is written from the vantage of the 1940s, the narrative gives the reader no certainty about what eventually took place in the intervening years. That brave music remains a distant drum.

Simon Thomas

Series consultant **Simon Thomas** created the middlebrow blog Stuck in a Book in 2007. He is also the co-host of the popular podcast Tea or Books? Simon has a PhD from Oxford University in Interwar Literature.